D0017124

By the same author

The Virgin's Lover

The Queen's Fool

The Other Boleyn Girl

Meridon

The Favored Child

Wideacre

Earthly Joys

Philippa Gregory

A Touchstone Book
Published by Simon & Schuster
New York London Toronto Sydney

TOUCHSTONE
Rockefeller Center
1230 Avenue of the Americas
New York, NY 10020

This book is a work of fiction. Names, characters, places, and incidents either are products of the author's imagination or are used fictitiously. Any resemblance to actual events or locales or persons, living or dead, is entirely coincidental.

First Touchstone edition 2005
Originally published in Great Britain in 1998 by HarperCollins*Publishers*

TOUCHSTONE and colophon are registered trademarks of Simon & Schuster, Inc.

For information about special discounts for bulk purchases, please contact Simon & Schuster Special Sales:
1-800-456-6798 or business@simonandschuster.com

Manufactured in the United States of America

3 5 7 9 10 8 6 4 2

Library of Congress Cataloging-in-Publication data is available.
ISBN 0-7432-7252-8

Earthly Joys

April 1603

The daffodils would be fit for a king. The delicate wild daffodils, their thousand heads bobbing and swaying with the wind, light-petaled, light-stemmed, moving like a field of unripe barley before a summer breeze, scattered across the grass, thicker around the trunks of trees as if they were dewponds of gold. They looked like wildflowers; but they were not. Tradescant had planned them, planted them, nourished them. He looked at them and smiled—as if he were greeting friends.

Sir Robert Cecil strolled up, his uneven tread instantly recognizable in the crunch of the gravel. John turned and pulled off his hat.

"They look well," his lordship observed. "Yellow as Spanish gold."

John bowed. The two men were near each other in age—both in their thirties—but the courtier was bent under a humped back and his face was lined by a lifetime of caution at court, and with pain from his twisted body. He was a small man, little more than five feet tall—his enemies called him a dwarf behind his hunched back. In a beauty-conscious, fashion-mad court where appearance was everything and a man was judged by his looks and his performance on the hunting field or battlefield, Robert Cecil had started his life with an impossible disadvantage: crooked, tiny and struggling with pain. Beside him the gardener Tradescant, brown-faced and strong-backed, looked ten years younger. He waited in silence for his master to speak. It was not his place to prolong the conversation.

"Any early vegetables?" his lordship asked. "Asparagus? They say His Majesty loves asparagus."

"It's too early, my lord. Even a king new-come to his kingdom cannot hunt deer and eat fruit in the same month. They each have their season. I cannot force peaches for him in spring."

Sir Robert smiled. "You disappoint me, Tradescant, I had thought you could make strawberries grow in midwinter."

"With a hothouse, my lord, and a couple of fires, some lanterns and a lad to water and carry, perhaps I could give you Twelfth Night strawberries." He thought for a moment. "It's the light," he said to himself. "I think you would need sunlight to make them ripen. I don't know that candlelight or even lanterns would be enough."

Cecil watched him with amusement. Tradescant never failed in the respect he owed his master, but he readily forgot everything but his plants. As now, he could fall silent thinking of a gardening problem, wholly neglecting his lord who stood before him.

A man more conscious of his dignity would have dismissed a servant for less. But Robert Cecil treasured it. Alone of every man in his train, Sir Robert trusted his gardener to tell him the truth. Everyone else told him what they thought he wanted to hear. It was one of the disadvantages of high office and excessive wealth. The only information which was worth having was that given without fear or favor, but all the information a spymaster could buy was worthless. Only John Tradescant, half his mind always on his garden, was too busy to lie.

"I doubt it would be worth your effort," Sir Robert remarked. "There are seasons for most endeavors."

John suddenly grinned at him, hearing the parallel between his own work and his master's. "And your season has come," he said shrewdly. "Your fruiting."

They turned together and walked back to the great house, Tradescant a step behind the greatest man in the kingdom, respectfully attentive, but looking from side to side at every pace. There were things that wanted doing in the garden—but then there were always things that wanted doing in the garden. The avenue of pleached limes needed retying before their early summer growth thrust wands of twigs out of control, the kitchen garden needed digging over; and radishes, leeks and onions should be sown into the warming spring soil. The great watercourses which were the wonder of Theobalds Palace needed weeding and cleaning; but he strolled as if he had all the time in the world, one step behind his master, waiting in silence, in case his master wanted to talk.

"I did right," Sir Robert said half to himself, half to his gardener. "The old queen was dying and she had no heir with as strong a claim as he. Not one fit to rule, that is. She would not hear his name; you had to whisper King James of Scotland if she were anywhere in any of her palaces. But all the reports I had of him were of a man who could hold two kingdoms, and perhaps even weld them together. And he had sons and a daughter—there'd be no more fretting over heirs. And he's a good Christian, no taint of papistry. They breed strong Protestants in Scotland . . ."

He paused for a moment and gazed at his great palace set on the high terrace looking toward the River Thames. "I don't complain," he said fairly. "I've been well repaid for my work. And there's more to come." He smiled at his gardener. "I'm to be Baron Cecil of Essenden."

Tradescant beamed. "I'm glad for you."

Sir Robert nodded. "A rich reward for a hard task . . ." He hesitated. "Sometimes I felt disloyal. I wrote him letter after letter, teaching him the way of our country, preparing him to rule. And she never knew. She'd have had me beheaded if she had known! She'd have called it treason—toward the end she called it treason even to mention his name. But he had to be prepared . . ."

Sir Robert broke off, and John Tradescant watched him with silent sympathy. His master often strolled into the garden to find him. Sometimes they spoke of the grounds, the formal garden, the orchards, the park, of seasonal plantings, or new plans; sometimes Sir Robert spoke at length, indiscreetly, knowing that Tradescant could keep a secret, that he was a man without guile, with solid loyalty. Sir Robert had made Tradescant his own, as effectually as if the gardener had gone down on the loam and sworn an oath of fealty, on the day that he had trusted him with the garden of Theobalds Palace. It had been a massive task for a twenty-four-year-old but Sir Robert had taken the gamble that Tradescant could do it. He was a young man himself, desperate to inherit his father's position at court, desperate for older and more powerful men to recognize his merit and his skill. He took a risk with Tradescant and then the queen took a risk with him. Now, six years later, both of them had learned their craft—statesmanship and gardening—and Tradescant was Sir Robert's man through and through.

"She wanted him left ignorant," Sir Robert said. "She knew what would happen to her court if she named him as heir; they'd have all slipped away from her, slipped away up the Great North Road to Edinburgh, and she'd have died alone, knowing herself to be an old woman, an ugly old woman with no kin, no lovers, no friends. I owed it to her to keep them at her beck and call to the very end. But I owed it to him to teach him as best I could . . . even at a distance. It was to be his kingdom; he had to learn how to govern it, and there was no one but me to teach him."

"And he knows now?" John asked, going to the very heart of it.

Sir Robert was alert. "Why d'you ask? Is there gossip that he does not?"

John shook his head. "I've heard none," he said. "But he's not a lad who has sprung up from nowhere. He must have his own way of doing things. He's a man grown, and he has his own kingdom. I was wondering if he would take your teaching, especially now that he will have his pick of advice. And it matters . . ."

He broke off and his master waited for him to finish.

"When you have a lord or a king," John went on, choosing his words with caution, "you have to be sure that he knows what he's doing. Because he's going to be the one who decides what you do." He stopped, bent and whisked out the little yellow head of a groundsel plant. "Once you're his man, you're stuck with him," he said frankly. "He has to be a man of judgment, because if he gets it wrong then he is ruined; and you with him."

Cecil waited in case there was more but John looked shyly down into his face. "I beg your pardon," he said. "I did not mean to suggest that the king did not know what he has to do. I was thinking of us subjects."

Sir Robert waved away the apology with one gesture of his long-fingered hand. They strolled together up the great avenue through the large formal knot garden toward the front terrace of the palace. It was done in the old style, and John had changed nothing here since his arrival as gardener. It had been laid out by Sir Robert's father in the bleak elegance of the period. Sharply defined geometric patterns of box hedging enclosed different-colored gravels and stones. The beauty of the garden was best seen if you looked down on it, from the house. Then you could see that it was as complex and lovely as a series of neat diagrams of cropped hedging and stone. John had a private ambition to change the garden after the new fashion—to break up the regular square and rectangular beds and make all the separate beds one long whole, like an embroidered hem or scarf—a twisting pattern that went on and on, serpentined in and about itself. When his master was less absorbed with statecraft John was going to suggest melding the beds one into another.

Once he had persuaded Sir Robert to follow the new fashion for the knot garden he had an ambition to go yet further. He longed to take out the gravel from the enclosed shapes and plant the patterns with herbs, flowers and shrubs. He wanted to see the whole disciplined shape softened and changing every day with foliage and flowers which would bloom and wilt, grow freshly green, and then pale. He had a belief, as yet unexpressed, almost unformed, that there was something dead and hard about a garden of stone paths edged with box-enclosing beds of gravel. Tradescant had a picture in his mind's eye of plants spilling over the hedges, of the thick green of the box containing wildness, fertility, even color. It was an image that drew on the hedgerow and roadside of the wild country of England and brought that richness into the garden and imposed order upon it.

"I miss her," Sir Robert admitted.

John was recalled to his real duty—to be his master's man heart and soul, to love what he loved, to think what he thought, to follow him to death without question if need be. The image of the creamy tossing heads of gypsy lace and moon daisies encased by hawthorn hedging in its first haze of spring green vanished at once.

"She was a great queen," John volunteered.

Sir Robert's face lightened. "She was," he said. "Everything I learned about statecraft, I learned from her. There never was a more cunning player. And she named him at the very end. So she did her duty, in her own way."

"You named him," John said dryly. "I heard that it was you that read the proclamation which named him as king while the others were still hopping between him and the other heirs like fleas between sleeping dogs."

Cecil shot John his swift sly smile. "I have some small influence," he agreed. The two men reached the steps which led to the first terrace. Sir Robert leaned on John's sturdy shoulder and John braced himself to take the slight weight.

"He'll not go wrong while I have the guiding of him," Sir Robert said thoughtfully. "And neither I nor you will be the losers. It takes a good deal of skill to survive from one reign to the next, Tradescant."

John smiled. "Please God this king will see me out," he said. "I've seen a queen, the greatest queen that ever was; and now a new king. I don't expect to see more."

They reached the terrace and Sir Robert dropped his hand from John's shoulder and shrugged. "Oh! You're a young man still! You'll see King James and then his son Prince Henry on the throne! I don't doubt it!"

"Amen to their safe succession," John Tradescant replied loyally. "Whether I see it or not."

"You're a faithful man," Sir Robert remarked. "D'you never have any doubts, Tradescant?"

John looked quickly at his master to see if he was jesting, but Sir Robert was serious.

"I made my choice of master when I came to you," John said baldly. "I promised then that you would have no more faithful servant than me. And I promise my loyalty to the queen, and now to her heir, twice every Sunday in church before God. I'm not a man who questions these things. I take my oath and that's the end of it for me."

Sir Robert nodded, reassured as always by Tradescant's faith, as straight as an arrow to the target. "It's the old way," he said, half to himself. "A chain of master and man leading to the very head of the kingdom. A chain from the lowest beggar to the highest lord and the king above him and God above him. Keeps the country tied up tight."

"I like men in their places," Tradescant agreed. "It's like a garden. Things ordered in their right places, pruned into shape."

"No wild disorder? No tumbling vines?" Sir Robert asked with a smile.

"That's not a garden, that's outside," John said firmly. He looked down at the knot garden, the straight lines of the low clipped hedges, and behind them the sharply defined colored stones, each part of the pattern in its right place, each shape building up the design which could not even be seen clearly by the workers on the ground who weeded the gravel. To understand the symmetry of the garden you had to be gentry—looking down from the windows of the house.

"My job is to make order for the master's pleasure," Tradescant said.

Sir Robert touched his shoulder. "Mine too."

They walked together along the terrace to the next great flight of steps. "All ready for His Majesty?" Sir Robert asked, knowing what the answer would be.

"All prepared."

Tradescant waited to see if his master would speak more and then he bowed, and fell back, and watched Sir Robert limp onward, toward the grand house, to supervise the preparation for the visit of the Lord's Anointed, England's new, glorious king.

April 1603

They had news of the arrival long before the first outriders clattered in through the great gates. Half the country had turned out to see what sort of man the new king might be. The whole royal court moved with the king—the baggage trains behind his carriages carried everything from silver and gold cutlery to pictures for his walls. One hundred and fifty English noblemen had attached themselves at once to the new king, their hats banded with red and gold to demonstrate their loyalty. But traveling with him also was his own Scots court, drawn south by the promise of easy pickings from the fat English manors. Behind them came all the retainers—twenty for each lord—and behind them came their baggage and horses. It was a massive battalion of idlers on the move. In the center of the whole train came the king, riding his big black hunter and scarcely able to see the country he had come to claim as his own for the lords and gentry who milled about him.

Half of the commoners who had joined the progress as it moved along the dusty roads were turned back at the great palace gates by Sir Robert's retainers—a private army of his own—and the king rode down the great sweep of the tree-lined avenue to the house. When they reached the base court the followers broke away, looking for their own apartments and shouting for grooms to stable their horses. The king was greeted by Sir Robert's chief servant, the master of the house, who had a paper to read to welcome the king on coming to his kingdom, and then Sir Robert himself stepped forward and knelt before him.

"You can get up," the new king said gruffly, his accent extraordinary to those subjects who had only ever heard a monarch speak in the queen's ringing rounded tones.

Sir Robert rose, awkward on his lame leg, and led his king into the great hall of Theobalds. King James, prepared for English wealth and English style, nonetheless checked at the doorway and gasped. The walls and the ceilings were so massively carved with branches and flowers and leaves that the walls themselves looked like the boughs of a wood, and on the warm spring day even the wild birds were misled and came flying in and out of the huge open windows with their vast panes of expensive Venetian glass. It was a flight of fancy in stone, wood and precious metals and jewels, an excess of folly and grandeur in one splendid hall as big as a couple of barns.

"This is magnificent. What jewels in those planets! What workmanship in the wood!"

Sir Robert smiled, as modest as he could be, and bowed slightly; but not even his courtier skills were able to conceal his pride of ownership.

"And this wall!" the king exclaimed.

It was the wall which showed the Cecil family connections. Other older members of court, other greater families might sneer at the Cecils, who had come from a farm in Herefordshire only a few generations ago; but this wall was Sir Robert's answer. It was emblazoned with his family shield showing the motto "*Prudens Qui Patiens*"—a good choice for a family who had made their fortune in two generations by advising the monarch—and linked by swags and ropes of laurel and bay leaves to the coats of arms and branches of the family. The garlands showed the extent of the Cecil power and influence. This was a man who had a cousin or a niece in every noble bed in the land and, conversely, every noble family in the land had, at one time or another, sought the seal of Cecil approval. The rich swooping loops of carved and polished foliage which connected one shield to another were like a map of England's power from the fountainhead of the Cecil family, closest to the throne, to the most distant tributaries of petty northern lordships and baronetcies.

On the opposite wall was Cecil's great planetary clock, which showed the time of day in hours and minutes as it shone on Cecil's house. A great solid gold orb represented the sun, and then at one side was a moon hammered from pure silver, and the planets in their courses, all moving in their spheres. Each planet was made from silver or gold and encrusted with jewels, each kept perfect time, each demonstrated in its symmetry and beauty the natural order of the universe that put England at the center of the universe and mirrored the arrangement of the opposite wall that put Cecil at the center of England.

It was an extraordinary display even for a house of extraordinary displays.

The king looked from one wall to another, stunned by the richness. "I've seen nothing like this in my life before," he said.

"It was my father's great pride," Sir Robert said. At once he could have bitten off his tongue rather than mention his father to this man. William Cecil had been the queen's adviser when she had hesitated over the death of her cousin, Queen Mary of Scotland. It was Cecil's father who had put the death warrant on the table and told the queen that, kin or no, monarch or no, innocent or no, the lady must die, that he could not guarantee Queen Elizabeth's safety with her dangerously attractive rival alive. It was William Cecil who had responsibility for Mary's death and now his son welcomed the dead queen's son into his house.

"I must show you the royal apartments." Robert Cecil recovered rapidly. "And if there is anything you lack you must tell me, Your Majesty." He turned and waved to a man holding a heavy box. The man, whose cue should have come later, started forward and presented the jewel box on one knee.

The gleam from the diamonds completely obscured Cecil's small blunder. James beamed with desire. "I shall lack nothing," he declared. "Show me the royal rooms."

It seemed odd to Cecil, taking this stocky, none-too-clean man into the rooms which had belonged exclusively to the queen, and were always left empty when she was not there, filled only with the aura of royalty. When she was in residence, on her long and expensive visits, the place was scented with rosewater and orange blossom and the richest strewing herbs and pomanders. Even when she was absent there was a ghost of her perfume in the room which made any man coming into it pause in awe on the threshold. There was a tradition that her chair was placed in the center of the room like a throne, and like a throne it was vested with her authority. Everyone, from serving maid to Cecil, bowed to it on entering the room and on leaving, such was the power of England's queen even in her absence.

It seemed odd, against the grain of all things, and wrong in itself that the heir she had never seen, whose name she had hated, should cross her threshold and exclaim with greedy pleasure at her carved and gilded wooden bed where he would now lie, the rich curtains around it and the hangings on the walls. "This is a palace fit for a king indeed," James said, his chin wet as if he were salivating at the sight.

Sir Robert bowed. "I shall leave you to take your ease, Your Majesty."

Already the room was losing that slight scent of orange blossom. The new king smelled of horses and of stale sweat. "I shall dine at once," he said.

Sir Robert bowed low and withdrew.

John had the final ordering of the vegetables to the kitchen, checking the great baskets as they went from the cold house in the kitchen garden into the back door of the vegetable kitchens, and so he did not see the royal entourage arrive. The palace kitchens were in uproar. The meat cooks were sweating and as red as the great carcasses, and the pastry chefs were white with flour and nerves. The three huge kitchen fires were roaring and hot and the lads turning the spits were drunk with the small ale they were downing in great thirsty gulps. In the rooms where the meat was butchered for the spit the floor was wet with blood and the dogs of the two households were everywhere underfoot, lapping up blood and entrails.

The main kitchen was filled with servants running on one errand or another, and loud with shouted orders. John made sure that his barrows of winter greens and cabbage had gone to the right cook and made a hasty retreat.

"Oh, John!" one of the serving maids called after him and then blushed scarlet. "I mean, Mr. Tradescant!"

He turned at the sound of her voice.

"Will you be taking your dinner in the great hall?" she asked.

John hesitated. As Sir Robert's gardener he was undoubtedly one of his entourage, and could eat at the far end of the hall, watching the king dine in state. As one of the household staff he could eat in the second sitting for the servers and cooks, after the main dinner had been served. As Sir Robert Cecil's trusted envoy and the planner of his garden he could eat at a higher table, halfway up the hall: below the gentry of course, but well above the men at arms and the huntsmen. If Sir Robert wanted him nearby he might stand at his shoulder while his lord was served with his dinner.

"I'll not eat today," he declared, avoiding the choice which brought with it so many complexities. Men would watch where he sat and guess at his influence and intimacy with his master. John had long ago learned discretion from Sir Robert; he never flaunted his place. "But I'll go into the gallery to watch the king at his vittles."

"Shall I bring you a plate of the venison?" she asked. She stole a little glance at him from under her cap. She was a pretty girl, an orphan niece of one of the cooks. Tradescant recognized, with the weary familiarity of a man who has been confined to bachelorhood for too long, the stirring of a desire which must always be repressed.

"No," he said regretfully. "I'll come to the kitchen when the king is served."

"We could share a plate, and some bread, and a flagon of ale?" she offered. "When I've finished my work?"

John shook his head. The ale would be strong, and the meat would be good. There were a dozen places where a man and a maid might meet in the great house alone. And the gardens were John's own domain. Away from the formality of the knot gardens there were woodland walks and hidden places. There was the bathing house, all white marble and plashing water and luxury. There was a little mount with a summerhouse at the pinnacle, veiled with silk curtains. Every path led to an arbor planted with sweet-smelling flowers; around every corner there was a seat sheltered with trees and hidden from the paths. There were summer banqueting halls; there were the dozens of winter sheds where the tender plants were nursed. There was the orangery scented with citrus leaves, with a warm fire always burning. There were potting sheds, and tool stores. There were a thousand thousand places where John and the girl might go, if she were willing, and he were reckless.

The girl was only eighteen, in the prime of her beauty and her fertility. John was a cautious man. If he went with her and she took with child he would have to marry her, and he would lose forever his chance of a solid dowry and a hitch up the long small-runged ladder which his father had planned for him when he had betrothed him, two years ago, to the daughter of the vicar at Meopham in Kent. John had no intention of marrying before he had the money to support a wife, and no intention of breaking his solemn betrothal. Elizabeth Day would wait for him until her dowry and his savings would make their future secure. Not even John's wage as a gardener would be enough for a newly married couple to prosper in a country where land prices were rising and the price of bread was wholly dependent on fair weather; and if the wife proved fertile then they would be dragged down to poverty with a new baby every year. John had an utter determination to keep his place in the world and, if possible, to improve it.

"Catherine," he said. "You are too pretty for my peace of mind, I cannot go courting with you. And I dare not venture more . . ."

She hesitated. "We might venture together . . ."

He shook his head. "I have nothing but my wages, and you have no portion. We should do poorly, my little miss."

Someone shouted for her from the kitchen table. She glanced behind her, chose to ignore them and stepped closer to him.

"You're paid a vast sum!" she protested. "And Sir Robert trusts you. He gives you gold to buy his trees, and he is high in favor with the king. They say he is certain to take you to London to make his garden there . . ."

John hid his surprise. He had thought that she had been watching him and desiring him, as he, despite his caution, had been watching and wanting her. But this careful planning was not the voice of a besotted eighteen-year-old. "Who says this?" he asked, carefully keeping his voice neutral. "Your uncle?"

She nodded. "He says you are set fair to be a great man, although you are only a gardener. He says that gardens are the fashion and that Mr. Gerard and you are the very men. He says you could go as far as London. Perhaps even into the king's service!" She broke off, excited by the prospect.

John had disappointment like a sour taste in his mouth. "I might." He could not resist testing her liking for him. "Or I might prefer to stay in the country and try my hand at breeding flowers and trees. Would you come with me, to a little cottage, if I become a gardener in a small way, and husband a little plot?"

Involuntarily she stepped back. "Oh, no! I couldn't bear anything mean! But surely, Mr. Tradescant, that is not your wish?"

John shook his head. "I cannot say." He felt himself fumbling for a dignified retreat, conscious of the desire in his face, the heat in his blood and the contradictory, sobering awareness that she had seen him as an opportunity for her ambition, and never looked at him with desire at all. "I could not promise to take you to London. I could not promise to take you anywhere. I could not promise wealth or success."

She pouted her lower lip, like a child who has been disappointed. Tradescant put both his hands in the deep pockets of his coat so that he would not be able to put them around her yielding waist, and pull her to him for consolation and kisses.

"Then you may fetch your own dinner!" she cried shrilly and turned abruptly away from him. "And I'll find a handsome young man to dine with. A Scotsman with a place at court! There are many who would be glad to have me!"

"I don't doubt it," John said. "And I would too, but . . ." She did not wait to hear his excuses; she flounced around and was gone.

A serving man pushed past him with a huge platter of fine white bread; another ran behind with flagons of wine clutched four in each hand. John turned from the noise of the kitchen area and went toward the great hall.

The king was seated, drinking red wine at the enormous hearthside. He was already vastly, deeply drunk. He was still filthy from the day's hunting and the travel along the muddy roads and he had not washed. Indeed, they said that he never washed, but merely wiped his sore and blotchy hands gently on silk. The dirt beneath his fingernails had certainly been there since his triumphant arrival in England, and probably since childhood. Sitting beside him was a handsome young man dressed as richly as any prince but who was neither Prince Henry the older son and heir nor Prince Charles the younger brother. As John waited at the back of the hall and watched, the king pulled the youth toward him and kissed him behind his ear, leaving a dribble of red wine along the pleats of his white ruff.

There was a roar of laughter at some joke and the king plunged his hand into the favorite's lap and squeezed his padded codpiece. The man snatched up the hand and kissed it. There was high ribald laughter, from women as well as men, sharing the joke. No one paused for a moment at the sight of the King of England and Scotland with his dirty hand thrust into the lap of a man.

John watched them as if they were curiosities from another country. The women were painted white from their large horsehair wigs to their half-naked breasts, their eyebrows plucked and shaped so their eyes seemed unnaturally wide, their lips colored pink. Their gowns were cut low and square over their bulging breasts and their waists were nipped in tight by embroidered and jewel-encrusted stomachers. The colors of the silks and satins and velvet gowns glowed in the candlelight as if they were luminous.

The king was sprawled in his seat with half a dozen intimates around him, most of them already drunk. Behind them all the court drank flagon after flagon of rich wine, and flirted, and schemed and caroused, some inarticulate with drink, some incomprehensible with their broad Scots accents. One or two, with an eye to the English scrutiny, spoke quietly to each other in Scots.

There was to be a masque later representing Wisdom meeting Justice, and some of the court were already in their masquing clothes. Justice was dead drunk, slumped over the table, and one of the handmaidens of Wisdom was at the back of the hall, backed up against the wall, with one of the Scots nobles investigating the layers of her petticoats.

John, conscious of the great disadvantage of watching this scene stone-cold sober, took a cup from a passing servant and downed a great gulp of the very best wine. He thought briefly of the old queen's court, where there had been vanity and wealth indeed, but also the rigid discipline of the autocratic old woman who ruled that since she had denied herself pleasure, the rest of the court should be chaste. There had been parties everywhere she had gone, masques and balls and picnics, but all behavior that fell under the scrutiny of that fierce gaze had been strictly constrained. John realized that the long carnival-like journey from Scotland to England must have been a revelation to the English courtiers and what he was seeing was the consequence of a rapid recognition that anything was now permitted.

The king emerged from a slobbering kiss. "We must have more music!" he shouted.

In the gallery, the musicians who had been fighting to make themselves heard above the hubbub of the hall started another air.

"Dance!" the king exclaimed.

Half a dozen of the court formed two lines and started to

dance; the king pulled the young man down to sit between his knees and caressed the dark ringlets of his hair. He bent down and kissed him full on the mouth. "My lovely boy," he said.

John felt the wine in his veins and in his head but feared that no wine would be strong enough to persuade him that this scene was joyful, or this king was gracious. Such thoughts were treason, and John was too loyal to think treason. He turned around and left the hall.

July 1604

"What do we have that is the most impressive?" Sir Robert came upon John in the scented garden, a square internal court where John had grown jasmine, honeysuckle and roses against the walls to soften their grim grayness. John was balanced on the top of a ladder, pruning the honeysuckle which had just finished flowering.

John turned to look at his master and took in at once the new lines of strain on his face. The first year of the new king's reign had been no sinecure for his Secretary of State. Wealth and honor had been showered on Cecil and on his family and adherents; but wealth and honor had equally been poured on hundreds of others. The new king, born into a kingdom of bleak poverty, thought the coffers of England were bottomless. Only Cecil knew and appreciated that the wealth that Queen Elizabeth had hoarded so jealously was flowing out of the treasure room of the Tower quicker than he could hope to gather it back in.

"Impressive?" John asked. "An impressive flower?" His expression of complete bewilderment made his master suddenly laugh aloud.

"God's blood, John, I have not laughed for weeks. With this damned envoy from Spain at my heels all the time and the king slipping away to hunt at every moment and them always asking me, what will the king think? and I without an answer! Impressive. Yes. What do we grow that is impressive?"

John considered for a moment. "I never think of plants as impressive. D'you mean rare, my lord? Or beautiful?"

"Rare, strange, beautiful. It is for a gift. A gift which will make men stare. A gift which will make men wonder."

John nodded, slid down the ladder like a boy and turned from the garden at a brisk walk. At once he remembered who he was leading and slowed his pace.

"Don't humor me," his lord snapped from a few paces behind. "I can keep up."

"I was slowing to think, my lord," John said swiftly. "My trouble is that the main flowering season is over now we are in midsummer. If you had wanted something very grand a couple of months ago I could have given you some priceless tulips, or the great rose daffodils which were better this year than any other. But now . . ."

"Nothing?" the earl demanded, scandalized. "Acres of garden and nothing to show me?"

"Not nothing," Tradescant protested, stung. "I have some roses in their second bloom which are as good as anything in the kingdom."

"Show me."

Tradescant led the way to the mount. It was as high as two houses, and the lane which led the way to the top was broad enough for a pony and a carriage. At the summit was a banqueting hall with a little table and chairs. Sometimes it would amuse the three Cecil children to dine at the top of the hill and look down on all that they owned, but Robert Cecil only rarely came here. The climb was too steep for him and he did not like to be seen riding while his children walked.

The hedges of the lane which wound to the summit were planted with all the varieties of English roses that Tradescant could find in the neighboring counties: cream, peach, pink, white. Every year he grafted and regrafted new stock on to old stems to try to make a new color, a new shape or a new scent.

"They tell me this is sweet," he said, proffering a rose striped white and scarlet. "A Rosamund rose, but with a perfume."

His lord bent and sniffed. "How can you breed for scent when you cannot smell them yourself?" he asked.

John shrugged. "I ask people if they smell good or better than other roses. But it is hard to judge. They always tell me the scent in terms of another scent. And since I have never had a nose which could smell then it's no help to me. They say 'lemony' as if I would know what a lemon smells like. They say 'honey' and that is no help either, for I think of one as sour and one as sweet."

Robert Cecil nodded. He was not the man to pity a disability. "Well, it smells good to me," he said. "Could I have great boughs of it by August?"

John Tradescant hesitated. A less faithful servant would have said "yes" and then disappointed his master at the final moment. A better courtier would have guided him away to something else. John simply shook his head. "I thought you wanted it for today or tomorrow. I cannot give you roses in August, my lord. Nobody can."

Cecil turned away and started to limp back to the house. "Come with me," he said shortly over his sloped shoulder. Tradescant fell in beside him and Cecil leaned on his arm. Tradescant took the burden of that light weight and felt himself soften with pity for the man who had all the responsibility for running three, no, four kingdoms with the new addition of Scotland, and yet none of the real power.

"It's for the Spanish," Cecil told him in an undertone. "This gift that I need. What do people in the country think of the peace with Spain?"

"They mistrust it, I think," John said. "We have been at war with Spain for so long, and avoided defeat so narrowly. It's impossible to think of them as friends the very next day."

"I cannot let us stay at war in Europe. We will be ruined if we go on pouring men and gold into the United Provinces, into France. And Spain is no threat anymore. I must have a peace."

"As long as they don't come here," John said hesitantly. "No one cares what happens in Europe, my lord. Ordinary people care only for their own homes, for their own county. Half the people here at

Cheshunt or Waltham Cross care only that there are no Spaniards in Surrey."

"No Jesuits," Cecil said, naming the greatest fear.

John nodded. "God preserve us. We none of us want to see burnings in the marketplace again."

Cecil looked into the face of his gardener. "You're a good man," he said shortly. "I learn more from you in a walk from my mount to my orangery than I do from a nation full of spies."

The two men paused. The orangery at Theobalds was open at every doorway, the double white-painted doors allowing the warm summer sunshine to flood into the rooms. Tender saplings and whips of oranges, lemons and vines were still kept inside—Tradescant was a notoriously cautious man. But the mature fruit trees were out in the fine weather, housed in great barrels with carrying loops at four points so they could adorn the three central courts of Theobalds in the summer, and bring a touch of the exotic to this most English of palaces. Long before the first hint of frost Tradescant would have them carried back into the orangery and the fires lit in the grates to keep them safe through the English winter.

"I suppose oranges are not impressive," he said. "Not to Spaniards who live in orange groves."

Cecil was about to agree but he hesitated. "How many oranges could we muster?"

John thought of the three mature trees, one placed at the center of each court. "Would you strip the trees of all their fruit?" he asked.

Cecil nodded.

John swallowed at the thought of the sacrifice. "A barrel of fruit. By August, perhaps two barrels."

Cecil slapped him on the shoulder. "That's it!" he cried. "The whole point is that we show them that they have nothing which we need. We give them great boughs of oranges and that shows them that anything they have, we can have too. That we are not the supplicants in this business but the men of power. That we have all of England and orange orchards too."

"Boughs?" John asked, going to the central point. "You don't mean to pick the fruit?"

Cecil shook his head. "It is a gift for the king to give to the Spanish ambassador. It has to look wonderful. A barrel of oranges could have been bought on the quayside, but a great branch of a tree with the fruit on it—they will see that it has been fresh-cut by the quality of the leaves. It has to be boughs laden with fruit."

John, thinking of the savage hacking of his beautiful trees, suppressed an exclamation of pain. "Certainly, my lord," he said.

Cecil, understanding at once, hugged Tradescant around the shoulders and planted a hearty kiss on his cheek. "John, I have had men lay down their lives for me with an easier heart. Forgive me, but I need a grand gesture for the king. And your oranges are the sacrificial lamb."

John reluctantly chuckled. "I'll wait till I hear then, my lord. And I'll cut the fruit and send it up to London as soon as you order."

"Bring it yourself," Cecil directed him. "I want no mistake, and you of all men will guard it as if it were your firstborn son."

August 1604

John's oranges were the center of the feast to celebrate the peace. King James and Prince Henry held Bibles and swore before the nobles and the Spanish ambassadors that the Treaty of London would install a solemn and lasting peace. In a glorious ceremony de Velasco toasted the king from an agate cup set with diamonds and rubies and then presented him with the cup. Queen Anne at his side had a crystal goblet and three diamond pendants.

Then King James nodded to Cecil, and Cecil turned to where Tradescant was behind him and John Tradescant walked forward bearing in his arms, almost too great a weight to carry, a great spreading bough of oranges, their leaves glossy and green with drops of water like pearls still rolling on the central vein, their fruit round, scented like oil of sunshine, blazing with color, ripe and fleshy. The king touched the bough and at his gesture Tradescant laid it at the Spanish ambassador's feet as two of his lads laid another and then another in a heap of ripe wealth.

"Oranges, Your Majesty?" the man exclaimed.

James smiled and nodded. "In case you were feeling homesick," he said.

De Velasco threw a quick look back at his entourage. "I had no idea that you could grow oranges in England," he said enviously. "I thought it was too cold here, too damp."

Robert Cecil made a casual gesture. "Oh, no," he replied nonchalantly. "We can grow anything we desire."

A page came through the crowd, carrying a great pannier of fruit, and another followed him with a basket. In pride of place, nestling amid some aromatic southernwood leaves, was a large pale melon.

"Wait a minute," said John. "Let me see that."

The page was in Lord Wootton's livery. "Let me pass," he said urgently. "I am to present this to the king to give to the Spanish ambassador."

"Where's it from?" John hissed.

"From Lord Wootton's garden at Canterbury," the lad replied and pushed through.

"Lord Wootton's gardener can grow melons?" John asked. He turned to his neighbor, but no one but John cared one way or the other. "How does Lord Wootton grow melons at Canterbury?"

The question remained unanswered. In a nearby inn John sought out Lord Wootton's gardener, who merely laughed at him and said there was a trick to it but John would have to join Lord Wootton's service if he wanted to learn it.

"D'you plant them in the orangery?" John guessed. "D'you have an earth bed inside?"

The man laughed. "The great John Tradescant asking me for advice!" he mocked. "Come to Canterbury, Mr. Tradescant, and you shall learn my secrets."

John shook his head. "I'd rather serve the greatest lord in the greatest gardens in England," he said loftily.

"Not the greatest for long," the gardener warned him.

"Why? What d'you mean?"

The gardener drew a little closer. "There are those who are saying that he has signed his own letter of resignation from service," he said. "Now that Spain is at peace with England, who can doubt that the lords who stayed with the true faith through all the troubles will come back to court? They'll find their places at court again."

"Catholics at court?" John demanded. "With a king like ours? He'd never bear it."

The man shrugged. "King James is not the old queen. He likes differences of opinion. He likes to dispute with them. Queen Anne herself takes the Mass. My own lord takes the Mass when he is abroad and avoids the English church whenever he can. And if he is high in the king's favor, giving him melons and the like, then the tide is turning. And stout old defenders of the faith like your lord may find their time has gone."

John nodded, bought the man another ale, and left the tavern to find Cecil.

His master was in one of the courtyards at Whitehall, about to board his barge to take him upriver to Theobalds.

"Ah, John," he said. "Will you come home with me by water or travel back with the wagon?"

"I'll come with you, if I may, my lord," John said.

"Get your bag then, for we leave at once; I want to catch the tide."

John hurried to fetch his things and came back as the barge was preparing to cast off. The rowers stood at salute, their oars raised. The Cecil pennant flew at bow and stern. Robert Cecil was seated amidships, a canopy over his head and a rug at his side to ward off the evening chill. John leaped nimbly aboard and sat at the rear of the boat behind the golden chair.

The boatmaster cast off and the rowers started the regular beat, beat of their rowing, the oars splashing in the water and the boat pulling forward and then resting, pulling and then resting. It was a soporific, lulling movement, but John kept his eyes on his master.

He saw the head flecked with premature gray hair nod and then sink. The man was exhausted after months of painstaking negotiation and unending civility, mostly conducted in a foreign language. John drew a little closer and watched over his master's sleep as the sun went down before them and painted the sky gold and peach, and turned the river into a shining path which took them slowly and steadily back to their garden.

When the sky grew darker blue and the first stars came out, John reached for his lord and gathered the blanket around his crooked shoulders. The man, the greatest statesman in the land, probably the greatest in Europe, was as light as a girl. His head lolled to John's shoulder and rested there. John gathered his lord to him and guarded his rest as the boat went quietly on the inward-flowing tide all the way up the river.

Just before the Theobalds landing stage Cecil awoke. He smiled to find John's arms around him.

"A warm pillow you've been to me this evening," he said pleasantly.

"I did not want to disturb you," John replied. "You looked weary."

"Weary as a dog after a whipping," Cecil yawned. "But I can rest now for a few days. The Spanish are gone; the king will return to Royston for the hunting. We can prune our orange trees back into shape, eh John?"

"There's one thing, my lord," John said cautiously. "A thing that I heard and thought I should tell you."

Cecil was instantly awake, as if he had never dozed at all. "What thing?" he asked softly.

"It was Lord Wootton's man, he suggested that now there is peace with Spain the Roman Catholics will come back to court, that there will be new rivals for you at court, and in the king's favor. He knew that the queen has become a Roman Catholic. He knew she takes Mass. And he named his own lord as a man who worships in the old way when he can, when he is abroad, and avoids his own church when he can at home."

Cecil nodded slowly. "Anything else?"

John shook his head.

"Do they say I am in the pay of Spain? That I took a bribe to get the peace treaty through?"

John was deeply shocked. "Good God, my lord! No!"

Cecil looked pleased. "They don't know about that yet then."

He glanced at John's astounded face and chuckled. "Ah, John, my John, it is not treason to the king to take money from his enemies.

It is treason to the king to take money from his enemies and then do their bidding. I do the one; I don't do the other. And I shall buy much land with the Spanish gold and pay off my debts in England. So the Spanish will pay hardworking English men and women."

John looked scarcely comforted. Cecil squeezed his arm. "You must learn from me," he said. "There is no principle; there is only practice. Look to your practice and let other men worry about principles."

John nodded, hardly understanding.

"As to the return of the Catholic lords," Cecil said thoughtfully, "I don't fear them. If the Catholics will live at peace in England, under our laws, then I can be tolerant of some new faces in the king's council."

"Are they sworn to obey the Pope?"

Cecil shrugged. "I care nothing for what they think in private," he said. "It's what they do in public that concerns me. If they will leave good English men and women to follow their own consciences in peace and quiet, then they can worship in their own way." He paused. "It's the wild few I fear," he said softly. "The madmen who lack all judgment, who care nothing for agreements, who just want to act. They'd rather die in the faith than live in peace with their neighbors."

The boat nudged the landing stage and the rowers snapped their oars upright. A dozen lanterns were lit on the wooden pier and burned either side of the broad leafy path to the house to light the lord homeward. "If they attempt to disturb the peace of the land that I have struggled so hard to win . . . then they are dead men," Cecil said gently.

October 1605

The peace Cecil worked for did not come at once. A year later in mid-autumn John saw one of the house servants picking his way down the damp terrace steps to where he was working in the knot garden. Cecil had finally agreed that he should take out the gravel and replace it with plants. John was bedding in some strong cotton lavender which he thought would catch the frost and turn feathery white and beautiful in the winter, and convince his master that a garden could be rich with plants as well as cleanly perfect in shapes made with stones.

"The earl wants you," the servant said, emphasizing the new title, reflecting the pleasure the whole household felt. "The earl wants you in his private chamber."

John straightened up, sensing trouble. "I'll have to wash and change my clothes," he said, gesturing to his muddy hands and his rough breeches.

"He said, at once."

John went toward the house at a run, entered through the side door from the Royal Court, crossed the great hall, silent and warm in the afternoon quiet after the hubbub of the midday dinner, and then went through the small door behind the lord's throne which led to his private apartments.

A couple of pageboys and menservants were tidying the outer room, a couple of the lord's gentlemen gambling on cards at a small table. John went past them and tapped on the door. The sound of the Irish harp playing a lament abruptly stopped and a voice called: “Come in!”

John opened the door a crack and sidled into the room. His lordship was, unusually, alone, seated at his desk with his harp on his knee. John was instantly wary.

“I came at once; but I’m dirty,” he said.

He wanted Robert Cecil to glance up, but the man’s face was down, looking at the harp on his lap. John could not see him, nor read his expression.

“The man said it was urgent—”

The figure at the desk was still.

There was a silence.

“For God’s sake, my lord, tell me you are well and that all is well with you!” John finally burst out.

At last Cecil looked up and his face, normally scored with pain, was alive with mischief. His eyes were sparkling; his mouth, under his neat moustache, was smiling.

“I have a game to play, John. If you will take a hand for me.”

The relief to see his lord happy was so great that John assented at once, without thinking. “Of course.”

“Sit down.”

John pulled a little stool up to the dark wood desk and the two men went head to head, Robert Cecil speaking so softly that a man in the same room could not have heard them, let alone any of them waiting outside the door.

“I have a letter that I want delivered to Lord Monteagle,” he whispered. “Delivered to him and none other.”

John nodded and leaned back. “I can do that.”

Cecil reached across and pulled him closer again. “It’s more than a messenger boy I want,” he whispered. “The contents of the letter are enough to hang Monteagle, and to hang the messenger. You must not be seen delivering it, you must not be seen with it. Your own life depends on you getting it to him with no man seeing you.”

John’s eyes widened.

"Will you do it for me?"

There was a brief silence.

"Of course, my lord. I am your man."

"Don't you want to know what's in the letter?"

Superstitiously, John shook his head.

Cecil, mightily amused at the sight of his gardener stunned into silence, broke down and laughed aloud. "John, my John, what a poor conspirator you will make."

John nodded. "It is not my trade, my lord," he said with simple dignity. "You have others in your service better skilled. But if you want me to take a letter and deliver it unseen, then I will do that." He paused for a moment. "It will not undo Lord Monteagle? I would not be a Judas."

Cecil shrugged his shoulders. "The letter itself is nothing more than words on a page. It's not poison; it won't kill him. What he does with the letter is his own choice. His end will be determined by that choice."

John felt himself to be swimming in deep and dark waters. "I'll do what you wish," he muttered, clinging only to his faith in his lord and his own vow of loyalty.

Cecil leaned back and tossed a small note across the table. It was addressed to Lord Monteagle, but the hand was not Robert Cecil's nor that of any of his secretaries.

"Get it to him tonight," Robert Cecil said. "Without fail. There's a boat waiting for you at the jetty. Make sure you are not seen. Not in the streets, not at his house, and not, *not,* with the letter. If you are captured, destroy it. If you are questioned, deny it."

John nodded and rose to his feet.

"John—" his master called as he reached the door. John stopped and turned around. His lord sat behind his desk, his face, his whole stance alive with joy at plotting and trickery and the game of politics which he played so consummately. "I would trust no other man to do this for me," Cecil said.

John met his master's bright gaze and knew the pleasure of being the favorite. He bowed and went out.

* * *

He went first to the knot garden and gathered up his tools. The plants which were not yet bedded in he took back to his nursery plots and heeled them into the earth. Not even an act of high treason could make John Tradescant forget his plants. He glanced around the walled nursery garden. There was no one there. He rose to his feet and brushed the earth from his hands and then he went to the potting shed where he had left his winter cloak. He carried it over his arm, as if he were headed for the hall for a bite to eat, but turned instead toward the river.

There was a wherry boat waiting at the lord's private jetty but it was otherwise deserted.

"For London?" the man asked without much interest, "In a hurry?"

"Yes," John said shortly.

He stepped into the little boat and he thought the lurch it made at his weight was what caused the sudden pounding of his heart. He sat in the prow of the boat so the man might not have the chance to look in his face, and he wrapped himself warm in his cape and pulled down his hat over his face. He was sure that the sunlight along the river was pointing a rippling finger toward him so that every fisherman and riverside walker, peddler, and beggar took particular note of him as the boat went swiftly downstream.

The river flowed fast down to London, and the tide was on the ebb. They did the journey quicker than John had hoped and when the boat nudged against the Whitehall steps and John leaped ashore it was only dusk. He blamed his sense of sickness on the movement of the boat. He did not want to recognize his fear.

No one paid any attention to the workingman with his hat pulled down over his eyes and his cape up to his ears. There were hundreds, thousands of men like him, making their way across London for their suppers. John knew the way to Lord Monteagle's house and slipped from shadow to shadow, making little sound on the dirt and mud of the streets.

Lord Monteagle's house was lit by double burning torches in

the sconces outside. The front door stood wide open and his men, hangers-on, friends and beggars passed in and out without challenge. His lordship was dining at the top table at the head of the hall; there was a continual press of people all around him, friends of his household, servants, retainers and, toward the back of the hall, supplicants and common people who had come in for the amusement of watching the lord at his dinner. John hung back and surveyed the scene.

As he waited and watched, a man touched his shoulder and went to hurry past him. John recognized one of Lord Monteagle's servants, a man called Thomas, hurrying to dinner.

The note was in John's hand, the direction clear. "A moment," he said, and pressed it into the man's hand. "For your master. For the love of Mary."

He knew what a potent spell that name would weave. The man took it and glanced at him, but John was already turning away and diving into an alley out of sight. He took a moment and then peered cautiously out.

Thomas Ward had entered the big double doors and was making his way to the head of the table. John saw him lean to whisper in his master's ear and hand him the note. The job was done. John stepped out into the street again and strolled onward, careful not to hurry, resisting the temptation to run. He strolled as if he were a workingman on his way to an inn, hungry for his supper. As he turned the corner and there was no shout of alarm, and no running footsteps behind him, he allowed his pace to quicken—as fast as a man who knows that he should be home by a certain time. One more corner and John allowed himself to run, a gentle jogging run, as a man might do when he was late for an appointment and hoping to make up for the delay. He kept a sharp watch out among the dirt and cobblestones so that he did not slip and fall, and he kept a brisk pace until he was ten, fifteen minutes away from Lord Monteagle's, out of breath, but safe.

He took his dinner at an inn by the river and then found he was too weary to face the journey back to Theobalds. He headed instead for his lord's house near Whitehall, where Tradescant might always command a bed. He shared an attic room with two other men, saying that he had been sent to the docks for some rarity promised by an East India trader but which had proved to be nothing.

When all the clocks in London struck eight, John went down to the great hall and found his master, as if by magic, also resident in London, calmly seated to break his fast at the big chair at the head of the big table at the top of the hall. Robert Cecil raised an eyebrow at him, John returned the smallest nod, and master and man, at either end of the hall, fell on their bread and cheese and small ale and ate with relish.

Cecil summoned him with a crook of his long finger. "I have a small task for you today and then you can go back to Theobalds," he said.

John waited.

"There is a little room in Whitehall where some kindling is stored. I should like it damped down to prevent the danger of a fire."

John frowned, his eyes on his master's impish face. "My lord?"

"I've got a lad who will show you where to go," Cecil continued smoothly. "Take a couple of buckets and make sure the whole thing is soaked through. And come away without being observed, my John."

"If there is a danger of fire I should clear it all out," John offered. He had the sense of swimming in deep and dangerous water and knew that this was his master's preferred element.

"I'll clear it out when I know who laid the fire in the first place," Cecil said, very low. "Just damp it down for me now."

"Then I'll get back to my garden," Tradescant said.

Cecil grinned at the firmness of the statement. "Then your job is finished here; go and plant something. My work is coming into its flowering time."

It was only after November fifth that John learned that the whole Gunpowder Plot had been discovered by Lord Monteagle, who had received a letter warning him not to go near Parliament. He had, quite rightly, taken the letter to Secretary Robert Cecil, who, unable to understand its meaning, had laid the whole thing before the king. The king, quicker-witted than them all—how they praised him for the speed of his understanding!—had ordered the Houses of Parliament to be searched and found Guido Fawkes crouched amid kindling, and nearby, barrels of gunpowder. On the wave of anti-Catholic sentiment Cecil enforced laws to control papists, and mopped up the remaining opposition to the English Protestant succession. The handful of desperate, dangerous families were identified as one confession led to another, and as the young men who had staked everything on a barrel of wet gunpowder were captured, tortured and executed. The one bungled plot forced everyone from the king to the poorest beggar to turn against the Catholics in a great wave of revulsion. The one dreadful threat—to the king, to his wife, to the two little princes—was such that no monarch in Europe, Catholic or Protestant, would ever plot again with English Catholics. The Spanish and French kings were monarchs before they were Catholics. And as monarchs they would never tolerate regicide.

Even more importantly for Cecil, the horror at the thought of what might have happened if Monteagle had not proved faithful, if the king had not proved astute, persuaded Parliament to grant the king some extraordinary revenue for the year and pushed back for another twelve months the impending financial crisis.

"Thank you, John," Cecil said when he returned to Theobalds in early December. "I won't forget."

"I still don't understand," John said.

Cecil grinned at him, his schoolboyish conspiratorial grin. "Much better not to," he replied engagingly.

May 1607

After the king's first successful visit to Theobalds it was as if he could not keep away. Every summer brought the court hungry as locusts out of London and into the country, to stay at Theobalds and then to move on in a constant circle of all the wealthy houses. The courtiers braced themselves for the unimaginable expense of entertaining the king, and sighed with relief when he moved on. He might shower the host with honors or with favors, or with some of the new farmed-out taxes, so that a favorite might grow rich collecting a newly invented duty from some struggling industry; or the king might merely smile and pass on. Whether he paid for his board in privileges or took it with nothing more than a word of thanks, his courtiers had to provide him with the best of food, the best of drink, the best hunting they could manage and the best entertainment.

They had learned their skills with Queen Elizabeth; no one could teach them anything about lavish hospitality, extravagant gifts and outright sycophancy. But King James demanded all this and more. His favorites too must be honored, and his days filled with unending sport, hunting hunting hunting, until gamekeepers were at a premium and no man dared cut down a tree in a forest which the king knew and loved. His evenings must be filled with a parade of pretty men and pretty women. No one refused him. No one even thought to refuse him. Anything the new king wanted he had to have.

Even when he wanted Theobalds Palace itself.

"I shall have to give it to him." Sir Robert had left his palace as he often did to find Tradescant. The gardener was directing the garden lads at the entrance to the maze. A team of boys was being supplied with blunt knives and sent into the maze on their hands and knees to root up weeds in the gravel. A team of older men would go with them with little hatchets and knives to trim the yew hedging; they had already been lectured with passion and energy by John as to the care they must take to keep the top of the hedge even, and on no account, on pain of instant dismissal, were they to cut an unruly bough in such a way that it might leave a hole which would make a peephole from one path to another and spoil the game.

John took one look at his master's dark expression, abandoned the pruning gang and came to him.

"My lord?"

"He wants it. My house, and the gardens too. He wants it, and he's promised me Hatfield House in return. I'll have to give it to him, I suppose. I can't refuse the king, can I?"

John gave a little gasp of horror at the thought of losing Theobalds Palace. "The king wants this house? Our house?"

Robert Cecil gave an unhappy shrug, beckoned to Tradescant and leaned on his shoulder as they walked. "Aye, I knew that you would feel it almost as much as me. I came to tell you before I told anyone else. I don't know how I can bear to lose it. Built for me by my own father—the little islands and the rivers, and the fountains, and the bathing house . . . all this to be given away in exchange for that drab little place at Hatfield! A hard taskmaster, the new king, don't you think, Tradescant?"

John paused. "I don't doubt you will get a better price than you might have had from any other monarch," he said cautiously.

The earl's cunning courtier face crinkled into laughter. "Better than from the old queen, you mean? Good God! I should think so! There never was a woman like her for taking half your wealth and giving you nothing but a smile in return. King James has a freer hand for his favorites . . ." He broke off and turned back toward the house. "With all the favorites," he muttered. "Especially if they're Scots. Especially if they're handsome young men."

They walked side by side together, the earl leaning heavily on John's shoulder.

"Are you in pain?" John asked.

"I'm always in pain," his master snapped. "I don't think about it if I can help it."

John felt a sympathetic twinge in his own knees at the thought of his master's twisted bones. "Doesn't seem right," he said with gruff sympathy. "That with all the striving and worry you have to suffer pain as well."

"I don't look for justice," said England's foremost lawmaker. "Not in this world."

John nodded and kept his sympathy to himself. "When do we have to leave?"

"When I have made Hatfield ready for us. You'll come with me, won't you, John? You'll leave our maze and the fountain court and the great garden for me?"

"Your Grace . . . of course . . ."

The earl heard at once the hesitation in his voice. "The king would keep you on here if I told him you would stay and mind the gardens," he said a little coldly. "If you don't wish to come with me to Hatfield."

John turned and looked down into his master's wretched face. "Of course I come with you," he said tenderly. "Wherever you are sent. I would garden for you in Scotland, if I had to. I would garden for you in Virginia, if I had to. I am your man. Whether you rise or fall, I am your man."

The earl turned and gripped John's arms above the elbows in a brief half-embrace. "I know it," he said gruffly. "Forgive my ill humor. I am sick to my belly with the loss of my house."

"And the garden."

"Mmm."

"I have spent my life on this garden," John said thoughtfully. "I learned my trade here. There's not a corner of it that I don't know.

There's not a change that it makes from season to season that I cannot predict. And there are times, especially in early summer, like now, when I think it is perfect. That we have made it perfect here."

"An Eden," the earl agreed. "An Eden before the Fall. Is that what gardeners do all the time, John? Try to make Eden again?"

"Gardeners and earls and kings too," John said astutely. "We all want to make paradise on earth. But a gardener can try afresh every spring."

"Come and try at Hatfield," the earl urged him. "You shall be head gardener in a garden which shall be all your own; you will follow in no man's footsteps. You can make the garden at Hatfield, my John, not just maintain and amend, like here. You shall order the planting and buy the plants. You shall choose every one. And I will pay you more, and give you a cottage of your own. You need not live in hall." He looked at his gardener. "You could marry," he suggested. "Breed us little babes for Eden."

John nodded. "I will."

"You are betrothed, aren't you?"

"I have been promised these past six years, but my father made me swear on his deathbed never to marry until I could support a wife and family. But if I can have a cottage at Hatfield, I will marry."

The earl laughed shortly and slapped him on the back. "From great men do great favors flow like the water in my fountains," he said. "King James wants Theobalds for a royal palace and so Tradescant can marry. Go and tie the knot, Tradescant! I will pay you forty pounds a year."

He hesitated for a moment. "But you should marry for love, you know," he said. He swallowed down his grief, his continual grief for the wife he had married for love, who had taken him despite his hunched body and loved him for himself. He had given her two healthy children and one as crooked as himself, and it was the birth of that baby which had killed her. They had been together only eight years. "To have a wife you can love is a precious thing, John. You're not gentry, or noble; you don't have to make dynasties and fortunes; you can marry where your heart takes you."

John hesitated. "I'm not gentry, my lord, but my heart cannot take me to a maid without a portion." Irresistibly the thought of the kitchen maid from the first dinner for King James came into his head. "My father left me with a debt to a man which is cleared by this betrothal to his daughter, and she is a steady woman with a good dowry. I have been waiting until I could earn enough for us to marry, until I had savings which might take us through difficult years, savings to buy a house and a little garden for her to tend. I have plans, my lord—oh, never to leave your service, but I have plans to take my fortune upward."

The earl nodded. "Buy land," he advised.

"To farm?"

"To sell."

John blinked; it was unusual advice. Most men thought of buying land and keeping it; nothing was more secure than a smallholding.

The earl shook his head. "The way to make money, my John, is to move fast, even recklessly. You see an opportunity, you take it quickly; you move before other men have seen it too. *Then* when they see it, you pass it on to them and they crow at having spotted their chance, when you have already skimmed the cream of the profit. And move fast," he advised. "When you see an opening, when a place comes open, when you see a chance, when a master dies, take what you're owed and move on."

He glanced up into John's frowning face. "Practice," he reminded him. "Not principles. When Walsingham died, who was the best man to take his place? Who had the correspondence at his fingertips, who knew almost as much as Walsingham himself?"

"You, my lord," Tradescant stammered.

"And who had Walsingham's papers which told everything a man who wanted to be Secretary of State would need to know?"

John shrugged. "I don't know, my lord. They were stolen, and the thief never found."

"Me," Cecil admitted cheerfully. "The moment I knew he would not recover, I broke into his cabinet and took everything he had written and received over the previous two years. So when they were casting around for who could do the work there was no one but me. No one could read the papers and learn what needed doing, for the papers were missing. No one could know Walsingham's mind, nor what he had agreed, because the papers were missing. Only one man in England of the dozen who had worked for Walsingham was ready to take his place. And that was me."

"Theft?" John asked.

"That's principle," Cecil said swiftly. "I'm advising you to look to practice. Think what you want, my John, and make sure that you get it, for be very certain that no one will give it to you."

John could not help but glance up at the great palace of Theobalds, a place so grand that a king could envy it and insist on owning it, knowing that he could never build better.

"Aye," said the earl, following his gaze. "And if a more powerful man can do it, he will take it from you. He will be guided by practice and not principles too. Buy land and take risks is my advice. Steal if you need to and if you will not be detected. When your master dies—even if it is me—have your next place secure. And also—marry your woman with a dowry; she sounds the very one for a rising man like you. And bid her be careful with her housekeeping."

John Tradescant rode down the Kentish lanes to his old village of Meopham, where he had been expected every day for the last six years. The hedges were white with hawthorn and May blossoms, the air warm and sweet-scented. The rich green pastureland of Kent glowed lush where cattle were knee-deep in water meadows. These were prosperous times and rich fields. John rode in a daze of pleasure, the lushness of the fields and the greening of the trees and the hedges acting on him as strong wine might turn another man's head. In the hedgerows were the white floss of gypsy lace and the little white stars of meadowsweet. Through gaps in the hedge where trees had been coppiced was a sea of blue where bluebells had sprung up to carpet the floor of the forest. Ahead of him the road was drifted with the tiny petals of the hawthorn flower like spring snow, and at every verge the lemon-yellow flowers of primroses were stuffed into roots and nooks like nosegays in a belt. When the road wound through meadowlands, John could see the light yellow of cowslips nodding as the breeze ran across the grasses; they put a veil of gold over the green as a woman might toss a shawl of gold net over a green silk gown.

The oak trees were clench-fisted with flowers, the small delicate catkins which looked like lumpy little buds at the end of the tough contorted branches. The silver birches shivered with new pale leaves amid the dancing catkins, and the beeches on the uplands were wet with spring leaves, vibrant with growth.

John was not deliberately plant-collecting but his awareness of every small budding orchid, every flowering nettle, every thick clump of violets in purple, white, and even pale blue, was not something that he could ever ignore. By the time he had ridden into Kent his hatband and his pockets were stuffed with shoots and soft damp trailing roots, and he felt himself wealthier than his own lord because he had ridden for days through a treasure chest of color and freshness and life, and come home with his pockets stuffed with booty.

Meopham High Street wound up the little hill to the gray-stoned church set like a cherry on the top of a bun. To the right of it was the small farmhouse of the Day family, built near the church where Elizabeth's father had been vicar. There were fat hens in the yard, and the pleasing smell of roasted hops which always hung around the storeyards and the little oast house.

Elizabeth Day came out of the front door. "I thought I heard a horse," she said. She was dressed in sober gray and white, and had a plain cap on her head. "Mr. Tradescant, you are very welcome."

John dismounted and led his horse to a stall.

"William will take his tack off if you wish," she offered calmly.

It was a loaded question. "If I may, I'll stay the night," John said. "William can take his saddle and bridle and turn him out to graze."

She looked away to hide her pleasure. "I'll tell William," she said simply. "Will you take a glass of ale? Were the roads bad?"

She led the way into the house. The wainscoted parlor was dark and cool after the bright sunshine. She left him for a moment while she fetched a tankard from the brew house. John looked out of the tiny thickly leaded window at the orchard.

The pink and white blossoms of the apple trees were bobbing above the white and pink daisies starring the cropped grass of the orchard. The family had neither the time nor the inclination to make a good garden before the house, though Elizabeth had the care of the kitchen and herb garden in the walled area outside the back door. Six years ago, when John had visited and confirmed his engagement, he had planted a little square of lavender with a bush of rue at each corner in the area before the window; but this was a working farm and no one had the time to plan or weed an elaborate knot garden. He saw that the rue had gone straggly as if remembrance itself was wearing thin; but the lavender was looking well.

The door behind him opened and George Lance, her stepfather, came in.

"Good to see you, Tradescant," he said.

Elizabeth brought them two mugs of ale and went quietly out of the room.

"I'm come to ask for the marriage to take place," John announced abruptly. "I've delayed too long."

"You've not delayed too long for her," George said defensively. "She's a virgin still."

"Too long for me," John said. "I'm impatient to start a family. I've waited long enough."

"Still working for Sir Robert?"

John nodded. "He's an earl now."

"Still in favor?"

John nodded again. "Never better."

"Have you seen the new king?" George demanded. "Is he a great man? I had heard that he is a fine man—a huntsman and a man of God, an educated man and a father of fine children. Just what the kingdom needs!"

John thought for a moment of the slack-mouthed lecher and

the parade of pretty men who had come to Theobalds Palace a dozen times, the loud tempestuous Scots followers and the wanton drunken lechery of the new court.

"He is all kingly virtues, thank God," he said carefully. "And now the earl is secure in his place, and I in mine. There's a chance that the earl will have a new house, and I will have the ordering of the garden. I will be paid more, and I will be head gardener in a new garden to make all my own. At last I can offer Elizabeth a proper home."

"Your pay?" George asked directly.

"Forty pounds a year, and a cottage to live in."

"Well, she's been ready and waiting for six years," George said. "And she'll have what her father promised. A dowry of fifty pounds, and her clothes and some household goods. She'll be glad to go, I don't doubt. She and her mother don't always agree."

"They quarrel?"

"Oh, no! Nothing to disturb a man's quiet," George replied hastily. "She'll make an obedient wife, I don't doubt. But two grown women and only one kitchen to order . . ." He broke off. "It's sometimes hard to keep the peace. Shall you call the banns at the church here?"

John nodded. "And I'll take a cottage for us in the village. I shall be between Theobalds and my lord's new house for some time. Elizabeth will like to be near her family when I am away. I shall have to travel abroad to seek trees and plants, as soon as Hatfield is ready. I am to go to the Low Countries and buy their bulbs; I am to go to France and buy their trees. I am planning an orangery where the tender trees can be reared in winter."

"Yes, yes. Well, Elizabeth will want to know all about it."

John was reminded that his new kindred had little interest in gardening. "And I shall be paid a good wage," he repeated.

George hesitated for a moment, looking at his future son-in-law. "By God, you're a cool fish, Tradescant," he said critically. "Or have you been banging the ladies of the court all this time and only now thought of Elizabeth?"

John found himself flushing. "No. You misunderstand me. I have always been intending to come for Elizabeth. It was always agreed that when I had enough money to buy a house, and a little land, then we would marry; and not before. I was not able to offer her a house before now."

"Didn't you think you might chance it?" George asked curiously.

"And you and your wife?" John demanded, stung. "How much of a chance did you take?"

It was a shrewd blow. The whole of Kent knew that his wife had come to him with a farm and a handsome fortune from her husband, Elizabeth's father, and a widow's jointure from the husband before that. George nodded abruptly and went to the door.

"Elizabeth!" George shouted into the hall, and then turned back to John. "Shall you want to be on your own with her?"

John found himself suddenly embarrassed. "I think so . . . perhaps . . . or you could stay?"

"Speak for yourself, man," George said. "It'll hardly come as a surprise!"

They heard her quick footsteps coming across the wooden floor of the hall. George went to meet her.

"Never fear!" he whispered. "He has come for you at last. He has a good wage, and his future is secured. He's to buy a cottage here, in the village. He'll tell you himself. But you're to be a wife, Elizabeth."

The color rushed into her face and then drained away again. She nodded gravely, and stood for a moment in thought, her eyes downcast. She was saying a silent prayer of thanksgiving. There had been times in the long years of waiting that she had thought he had broken faith with her, and would not come. Then her head went up and she went with her quick steady steps to the parlor.

John was at the window again, looking at the apple trees. When she came in he turned. For a moment he saw not the grave Elizabeth in her sober Puritan dress, but little Cathy the serving maid in her mob cap with her gown cut low over her plump breasts, and her inviting smile. Then he put his hands out to Elizabeth, drew her to him and kissed her gently on the forehead.

"I can marry you," he said, as if it were the conclusion to a business arrangement which had been tediously delayed.

"Thank you," she said coolly. She wanted to tell him that she had been waiting for this moment ever since her father had come to her and folded her in his arms and said quietly: "I have got you the gardener, my dear. You will be John Tradescant's wife as soon as he has saved enough to marry." She wanted to tell him that in the nightmare summer when her little sister and then her father sickened of plague and then died, she had prayed every night for John Tradescant to come for her, like a hero in a romance, to take her away from the fear of sickness and from the depths of mourning. She wanted to tell him that she had waited and waited, while her mother put off her grief and gleefully remarried. That she waited while the newlyweds kissed before their fireside. That she waited though she thought he might never come, and that, with her father dead and a hard-hearted mother who used her labor and never paid her, there would be no one to hold John Tradescant to his binding promise to marry.

She waited, in the end, because she was in the habit of waiting, because there was no escape from waiting, because there was nothing else she could do. Elizabeth was twenty-seven years old, no longer a girl in her first looks. She had been waiting for John for six long years.

"I hope you are glad?" John retreated to his place at the window.

"Yes," she said carefully from her place at the door.

Three weeks later they were married at the parish church. They walked up the narrow path to the church door hand in hand; John could not stop himself noticing the yew trees, which were extraordinarily fine. One was growing like a castle with pretty pinnacle towers; the branches of the other fell like layers of cloth in a deep green dress. Elizabeth saw the direction of his gaze and smiled and patted his arm.

Her stepfather George Lance and Gertrude her mother were witnesses. Elizabeth wore a new gown of white, instead of her usual gray, and John wore a new suit of brown with white and crimson slashings in the sleeve. The sunlight through the stained-glass windows dappled the tiles on the floor with splashes of additional color. John stood tall and made his responses in a firm voice, and felt with pleasure Elizabeth's little hand resting lightly on his arm.

There were those waiting outside the flint-walled church to see the couple who complained that the bridegroom was dressed too fine for a workingman. They murmured that he was getting above his station and that the slashings in his sleeve were made of silk as if he thought himself to be a gentleman. But then the wedding ale at the back door of the farmhouse was strong and sweet, and the grumblings gave way to a roar of ribald jokes by mid-afternoon.

Gertrude had laid on a grand wedding dinner with three different sorts of cooked meats and half a dozen puddings. John found himself beside the vicar, the Reverend John Hoare, at the dinner table and took his compliments and accepted a toast and then tried to make stilted conversation.

"You serve a great lord," the vicar commented.

John warmed at once. "None greater."

The Reverend Hoare smiled at his loyalty. "And he has put you in charge of the gardens of his new palace?"

John nodded. "He has done me that honor."

"Will you have to live at Hatfield? Or shall you keep a house at Meopham?"

"I shall keep the house here," John said. "But I shall be much with my lord. My wife knows that his service must come first. Anyone who has the honor to serve a great man knows that his lord comes before everything."

The vicar assented. "The master comes before the man."

"I wonder if you can tell me one thing though, vicar?" John asked.

The vicar at once looked cautious. These were not the times for theological enquiry. Sensible men confined themselves to the catechism and the commandments and left questions to heretics and papists who would have to pay with their lives if they got their answer wrong. "What thing?" he asked.

"It puzzles me that God should have made so many things the same, and yet just a little different," Tradescant confided. "So many things He has made which are the same, but differ only in shape or in color. And I cannot understand why He should make the difference. Nor how Eden can have looked, crammed with such—" he sought the word for a moment "—such diversity."

"Surely every rose is the same," the vicar replied. "It differs only in color. And a daisy is a daisy wherever it grows."

John shook his head. "You wouldn't say that if you had looked as closely as I. To be sure they have their families, a rose is still a rose, but there are hundreds of different kinds of roses," he explained. "Every county has a different sport. They have different shapes of petals, they have different numbers of petals, they have different preferences as to light and shade. Some are scented, they tell me, and some are not. And sometimes I think I see them being made. Making themselves while I watch, almost."

"What d'you mean?"

"When they throw a sport, when from one main stem you can see another grow different, and if you take the different one you can breed another from it—God didn't make that, surely? I made it."

The vicar shook his head but John went on. "And daisies are not the same wherever they grow. I have seen a Kent daisy different from a Sussex daisy and a French daisy which was bigger and tipped with pink. I don't know how many daisies there are. A man would have to travel the whole world over with his eyes on his boots all the way to be sure. Why should such a thing be? Why should God make hundreds of the same thing?"

The vicar glanced around for rescue but nobody was looking his way. "God in His wisdom gave us a world filled with variety," he began.

He was relieved to see that Tradescant was not arguing. This was not a man who was quarrelsome in his cups. This was a man urgently in quest of a truth. The vicar had an odd sense of a man in search of his destiny. Tradescant was concentrating, passionately concentrating, with a deep line engraved between his brows as he listened to the vicar's answer. "It was God's great wisdom to give us many things of great beauty. We cannot question His choice to give us many things which are only a little different, one from another, if you tell me that is how they are."

Slowly John shook his head. "I don't mean to question my God," he said humbly. "Any more than I would question my lord. It just seems odd to me. And God did not make all things at once in Eden, and give them to us. I know that cannot be, though I read it in the Bible, because I see them changing from season to season."

The vicar nodded, quick to move on. "That is no more than a craftsman making a table, I suppose. It is using the skills which God has given you and the materials which He has provided to make something new."

John hesitated. "But if I made a new daisy, say, or a new tulip, and a man came along and saw it growing in a garden, he would think it was the work of God and praise Him. But he would be wrong. It would have been my work."

"Yours and God's," the vicar said smoothly. "For God made the parent tulip from which you made one of another color. Undoubtedly it is God's purpose to give us many things of beauty, many things which are rare and different and strange. And it is our duty to thank Him and praise Him for them."

John nodded at the mention of duty. "It would be a man's duty to gather the varieties?" he asked.

The vicar drank a little wedding ale. "It could be," he said judiciously. "Why would a man want to collect varieties?"

"To the glory of God," John said simply. "If it is God's purpose that we should know His greatness by the many varieties of plants that are in the world now, and that can be made, then it is to the glory of God to make sure that men know of His abundancy."

The vicar thought for a moment, fearful of heresy. "Yes," he said cautiously. "It must be God's will that we know of His abundancy, to help us to praise Him."

"So a man making a garden, a fine garden, is like a man making a church," John said earnestly. "Showing men the glory of God as a stonemason might carve the glory of God into his pillars and gargoyles."

The vicar smiled. "Is that what you want to do, Tradescant?" he asked, seeing his way at last to the heart of it. "Being a gardener and digging up weeds is not enough for you—it has to be something more?"

For a moment John might have disclaimed the idea, but the strong wedding ale was working on him and his pride in his work was powerful. "Yes," he admitted. "It is what I want to do. My Lord Cecil's gardens are to his glory, to be a setting to his fine house, to show the world that he is a great lord. But the gardens are also a glory to God. To show every visitor that God has made abundant life, life in such variety that a man could spend all his days finding it and collecting it and still not see it all."

"You have your life's task then!" the vicar said lightly, hoping to end the conversation. But John did not smile in return.

"I have indeed," he said seriously.

At the end of the dinner Gertrude rose from the table and the ladies followed her lead. The serving girls stayed behind with the poorer neighbors and drank themselves into a satisfying stupor. Elizabeth completed the last of the tasks in her old family home and waited for John in his turn to leave the dinner. At dusk he came away from the hall and the trestle tables and found her sitting at the kitchen table with the other women, waiting for him. He took his bride by the hand and they went down the hill a little way to their new cottage followed by a shouting, singing train of family and villagers.

In the cottage the women went upstairs first, and Elizabeth's cousins and half sisters helped her out of her new white dress and into a nightdress of fine lawn. They brushed her dark hair and combed it into a fat plait. They pinned her cap on her head, and sprayed her with a little water of roses behind each ear. Then they waited with her in the little low-ceilinged bedroom until the shouts and snatches of song from the stair told them that the bridegroom had been made ready too and was come to his bride.

The door burst open and John was half-flung into the room by the joyous enthusiasm of the wedding party. He turned on them at once and pushed them out over the threshold. The women around Elizabeth's bed made false little cries of alarm and excitement.

"We'll warm the bed! We'll kiss the bride!" the men shouted as John barred their way at the door.

"I'll warm your backsides!" he threatened and turned to the women. "Ladies?"

They fluttered like hens in a coop around Elizabeth, straightening her cap and kissing her cheek, but she brushed them off and they pattered to the door, ducking under John's arm as he held the door firmly. More than one woman shot a quick look at the gardener and the strength of his outstretched arm and thought that Elizabeth had done better than she could possibly have hoped for. John closed the door and shot the bolt on them all. The rowdiest hammered on the door in reply. "Let us in! We want to drink your healths! We want to see Elizabeth to bed!"

"Go away! We'll drink our own healths!" he shouted back. "And I shall bed my own wife!" He turned, laughing, from the door but the smile died from his face.

Elizabeth had risen from her bed and was kneeling at the foot, her head in her hands, praying.

Someone hammered on the door again. "What are you going to plant, Gardener John?" they shouted. "What seeds do you have in your sacks?"

John swore under his breath at their bawdy humor, and wondered that Elizabeth could stay so still and so quiet.

"Go away!" he shouted again. "Your sport is over! Go and get drunk and leave us in peace!"

With relief he heard the clatter of their feet going downstairs.

"We'll be back in the morning to see the sheets!" he heard a voice shout. "We expect stains, glorious red and white stains!"

"Roses and lilies!" shouted one wit. "Red roses and white lilies in John Tradescant's flower bed!" There was a great guffaw at this sally, and then the front door of the cottage banged, and they were in the streets.

"Dig deep, Gardener John!" came the shout from the darkness outside. "Plant well!"

John waited until he could hear the staggering footsteps go up the lane to the village's only ale house. Still Elizabeth kneeled at the foot of the bed, her eyes closed, her face serene.

Hesitantly John kneeled down beside her, closed his eyes and composed himself for prayer. He thought first of the king—not the man he saw and knew, but the man he thought of when he said the word "king"—a being halfway between earth and heaven, the fount of law, the source of justice, the father to his people. A man like the Lord Jesus, sent from God, directly from God, for the guidance and good ruling of his people. A man whose touch could heal, who could perform miracles, whose mantle covered the nation. "God save the king," Tradescant whispered devoutly.

Then he thought of his master, another man half-touched with divinity, a step lower than the king but so high in power that he must be, surely, especially favored by God, and was in any case John's lord, a role of unique potency. John thought of the word "lord" and had a sense of the holiness of it—Lord Jesus, Lord Cecil, both lords. But Cecil with his special trust in John, Cecil with his engaging child-size body and his cunning wise mind, was easy for John to bless in his prayers. John's lord, John's great love. Then his mind slipped at once to the old royal palace of Hatfield. Cecil would build a new house there, undoubtedly it would be a great house, and he would want a beautiful garden set around it. Perhaps an avenue . . . John had never planted an avenue. He lost the thread of his prayers altogether at the thought of the work of planting an avenue, and his great desire to see a double row of fine trees, limes, he thought longingly. They must be limes, there was nothing like lime for an avenue. "God give me the skill to do it," John whispered. "And grant me, in Your mercy, enough saplings."

Elizabeth was very close, kneeling beside him; he could feel the warmth of her body, he could hear the soft rhythm of her indrawn and exhaled breath. "God bless us both," John thought. "And let us live in friendship and kindliness together."

He did not expect more than friendship from Elizabeth, friendship and a lifelong partnership of indissoluble shared interest. Unbidden, the picture of Catherine with her dark eyes and low-cut bodice rose behind his eyelids. A man newly wedded to a girl like Catherine would not spend his bridal night on his knees praying.

John opened his eyes and got into bed. Still Elizabeth kneeled at the bedside, her head bowed, her lips moving. In sudden irritation, John leaned over and blew out his bedside candle. Darkness invaded the room. In the darkness and the quietness he felt, rather than saw, Elizabeth rise from her knees, pull her nightdress over her head, lift the sheets and slip in beside him, naked.

For a moment he was stunned at the frank sensuality of the gesture. That a woman could arise from prayer and strip herself naked confounded his simple division of women into good or bad, saintly or sexual. But she was his newly married wife and she had a right to lie beside him. John's desire rose at the glimpse of the moonlit body and he was sorry he had no light for the candle that he had blown out in a moment of temper and left himself in the dark.

They lay side by side on their backs.

"Like effigies on a tomb," John thought, awkwardly.

It was for him to make the first move, but anxiety locked him into place. After years of avoiding sin and living in mortal terror of sexual temptation which would lead to pregnancy and disgrace, John was unprepared for the free embrace of a willing partner.

His hand strayed toward her side of the bed and encountered the unmistakable solidity of her thigh. The skin was as smooth as the fruit of an apple, but yielding, like a ripe plum. Elizabeth said nothing. John stroked her thigh with the back of his hand like a man brushing the soft foliage of a scented plant. He rather feared she might be praying again.

Cautiously he moved his hand up her thigh to the round warm mound of her belly, the navel set in the flesh like a little duckpond in a hill. Up these new mysterious byways John's hand slowly went, one breast—and he heard her little indrawn breath as his hand moved across the soft rolling crest of her breast and took into its keeping the tender warm nipple which immediately hardened under his touch. He moved toward her, and heard that little gasp once more which was not quite alarm, and yet not quite welcoming. He raised himself up so that he was above her. In the moonlight he could see her face, her eyes resolutely shut, her mouth expressionless, as she had looked when she was praying. He bent his head and kissed her on the lips. She was warm and soft; but she lay completely still, as if she were asleep.

John stroked gently down her belly and beyond and found the downy softness of the hair between her legs. As he touched her she turned her head to one side, but still she did not open her eyes or stir. Gently he pressed his knee against her thigh and slowly, she opened her legs to him. Feeling like a king coming in to his kingdom, John moved across in the bed and lay between the legs of his wife, started to ease forward, started to know the power of his desire.

There was a sudden rush and a clatter of mud and stones against the window.

"God's wounds! What's that?" John exclaimed in alarm. "Fire?"

In one swift sinuous movement Elizabeth was out of bed, her gown clutched to her heavy swinging breasts, peering out of the window into the darkness of the village street.

"Are you done, John?" came a jovial beery yell. "Sowed your seeds, have you?"

"God's blood, I shall murder them!" John exclaimed, dashing his nightcap to the floor.

Slowly Elizabeth put her nightgown to one side and came back to bed beside him. At last she spoke to him, the first words she spoke in their bedroom, the first words she said naked before him: "Never take the Lord's name in vain, husband. It is His own commandment. I want our house to walk in His ways."

John flung himself back on the bed, deserted by desire, as soft as a gelding. "I shall sleep," he declared sulkily. "And then I shall avoid offending you." He humped all the bedclothes around him, turned his back on her and closed his eyes. "You can pray again if you like," he added spitefully.

Elizabeth, robbed of the blankets, lay in silence on the cool sheet, humiliatingly naked, her new nightgown spread across her breasts and belly. Only when she heard his breathing deepen and she was certain that he was asleep did she move close to his broad back and wind her arms around his sleeping body, pressing her cold nakedness against him. She wept a little before she finally fell asleep. But she did not wish her words unsaid.

June 1607

Next day, before Elizabeth had done more than stir the fire in the new grate and set the morning porridge on to heat, there was a knock on the door and a messenger from the earl.

"His Grace wants you in London," the man said shortly.

Elizabeth glanced at her new husband, half-expecting him to refuse, but John was already seated in his chair at the fireside pulling on his riding boots.

The man doffed his hat to her but looked beyond her to John. "At the docks," he said. "You're to meet him at Gravesend."

Another swift bow and he was gone. Cecil's servants were not encouraged to linger and gossip. The common belief was that Cecil had ears everywhere and an indiscreet servant would not last long.

Elizabeth took John's traveling cloak from the press where she had laid it in lavender. She had thought then that it was worth protecting it against moths for months of storage.

"When will you be back?" she asked quietly.

"I can't say," John replied briskly.

Elizabeth flinched at the coldness of his tone. "Am I to join you at Hatfield?" she asked. "Or come to Theobalds?"

He looked at her and saw the coat she was holding for him. "I thank you," he said courteously. "I'll send you word. I don't know what is happening, I don't know what he wants me for. These are dangerous times for him. I must go at once."

Elizabeth felt her village-based view of the world shudder under the weight of great events which would now impinge on her life. "I didn't think these were dangerous times. How are they dangerous?"

He glanced at her quickly, as if her ignorance surprised him. "All times are dangerous to men with great power," he explained. "My lord is the greatest in the land. Every day he faces one danger or another. If he sends for me I go without question and I make no plans other than his will."

Elizabeth nodded. There was no arguing with a man's duty to follow his lord.

"I'll wait till I hear from you then," she said.

John kissed her forehead in that passionless meaningless gesture which seemed to have started with their betrothal and hung over them still. Elizabeth curbed her impulse to turn up her face and kiss him on the lips. If he did not want to kiss her, if he did not want to lie with her, then it was not the part of a good wife to complain. She would have to wait. She would have to do her duty by him, as he did his by his lord.

"Thank you," John said, as if she had obliged him in some little courtesy, and went out to saddle his horse, mounted the animal and rode him from the back of the cottage to the village street. Elizabeth was at the doorway, her head high; none of the village gossips would know that her husband was leaving her as virginal as she had been on her wedding day.

John doffed his hat to her, conscious also of the dozens of watching windows. He did not lean down to kiss her, nor did he offer one word of assurance or comfort. Seated high on his horse he looked down on the pale face of the wife he was leaving without bedding and knew himself to be behaving badly, with his duty as an excuse as well as an obligation. "Farewell," he said shortly, and turned his horse and rode briskly out at a trot. The knowledge of his unkindness to a woman who, wedding night or no, mother-naked or clothed, had said no more than she had every right to say, and who, before that accursed interruption, had lain warm and pleasant to his touch, galled him all the way along the lanes going north to Gravesend.

He met his master at the quayside, at the docks of the East India Company, the air rich with the smell of cinnamon and spices and loud with the curses of the dockers.

A merchant welcomed them on board his ship at the gangplank. "Follow me," he said and led them between the sailmakers and the rope chandlers to the captain's cabin. "A glass of wine?" he offered.

The earl and his gardener nodded.

"I have some curious roots," he said when they had a glass each. "I bought them for their weight in gold because I knew that a man such as yourself, Your Grace, would pay much more for them."

"And what are they?" the earl asked.

The merchant opened a wooden box. "I have kept them dry and sweet, and hidden from the light as Mr. Tradescant advised me."

He held out a handful of woody twisted roots, brown, with a dusty earth still clinging to them. The earl took them gingerly and handed them to John.

"They are the roots of flowers of exceeding fineness," the merchant said rapidly, his eyes on Cecil's impartial face. "Roots of course, Your Grace, never look well. But in the hands of your gardener you could bring these on to flower in great profusion . . ."

"And what is the flower like?" John asked.

"Like a geranium," the merchant said. "And the leaves are sweet, like geranium leaves. But much finer, a quite extraordinary blossom."

Cecil raised an eyebrow at John. John made a small shrug of his shoulders. They looked like the roots of a geranium but with neither leaf nor flower no one could tell. They would have to be bought on trust. "Anything else?" Cecil asked.

"These." The merchant pulled a little hessian purse from the bottom of the box and opened it. Inside were fat green globes as large as a bantam's egg with hard little spines all over.

"A new chestnut," the merchant promised. Gently he prised

open one of the shells, and spilled, into John's cupped palm, a bold round handsome nut, dappled like a brown roan horse in light and dark brown, with a paler gray and brown circle at the top. John caressed the moist inside casing of the shell, turned the nut in the light to see the sheen on it. Bigger than a walnut, shinier than mahogany, it was a delightful nut, a great jewel of a nut, a brown warm pearl.

"Where did you get these?" John could not keep the quiver of excitement from his voice.

"Turkey," the merchant said. "And I saw the tree that gave this fruit."

"Can you eat them?" Cecil asked.

The man hesitated for that single half-moment which reveals a lie. "Surely," he said. "They are chestnuts, after all. And they are a powerful medicine. The man that sold them to me says they use them for curing broken-winded horses. They mend the lungs of horses, perhaps of men too."

"Is the leaf the same as our chestnut?" John asked.

"Bigger," the merchant replied. "And spreading. And the trees are massive round trees, better-shaped than ours, like a great ball on a stick. And when they are in flower they are covered all over with huge white cones of flowers, as big as both your hands. White blossoms and the tongues of the flowers are speckled with pink." He thought for a moment. The price would depend on his description. "Like apple blossom," he said at once. "White and pink together like apple blossom, but in a great shape like a cone."

John fought to keep the excitement from his voice. "Great trees? What height?"

The man waved his hand. "As big as a full-grown oak. Not tall like a fir but broad and tall, like a big oak tree."

"And the wood?" Cecil interrupted, thinking of the nation's insatiable demand for timber for shipbuilding.

"Fine wood," the merchant said quickly. Too quickly for truth, Cecil thought. "Though I did not see it myself, they tell me the wood is very fine."

"How many?" John asked, his eyes on the box, but he kept the chestnut in his hand. "How many do you have?"

"Only half a dozen," the merchant said seductively. "Just six. And that's the only six in the whole of the kingdom, the only six outside Turkey. The only six in Christendom. For you to own, Your Grace; for you to grow, Mr. Tradescant."

"Anything else?" Cecil asked nonchalantly.

"These seeds," the merchant said, and showed a little purse filled with hard black seeds. "Of rare flowers."

"What flowers?" John asked. The nut was warm and smooth and comforting in his hand. He thought he could almost feel the life enfolded inside it, like a new-laid egg.

"Rare beauties, like lilies," the merchant said.

Tradescant looked doubtful. Lilies grew from corms, not little seeds. He suddenly doubted the merchant, and his fingers closed tightly. At least the beauty and promise of the nut could not lie.

"How much?" Cecil asked. "For the roots, the seeds and the chestnuts?"

The merchant looked quickly from the gardener to the master, and read, correctly, the speechless desire in Tradescant's face. "Fifty pounds."

Cecil choked. "For a handful of wood?"

The merchant smiled and nodded at Tradescant. Cecil followed his gaze and was forced to laugh. John was turning the chestnut over and over in his hand, unaware of the two men. He looked besotted.

"It is a treasure beyond price to a gardener," the merchant said. "A new tree. A completely new tree, which blooms like a rose and stands as broad as an oak."

"Eight pounds now, and eight pounds if the tree grows," the earl said gruffly. "You may come to me next spring and if it has rooted I shall pay you the remainder. If it is a fine tree in five years with flowers like apple blossoms and broad as an oak I shall pay another eight then."

"Perhaps nine," the merchant said thoughtfully.

"No more than nine," the earl said, and got to his feet. "Nine now, and nine if it roots, and nine in five years if it is good."

"I shall take these to Theobalds at once," John said, emerging from his trance. He still had hold of the chestnut. The merchant put the roots and seeds back in the box and handed them to him.

"I thought you were newly wed?" Cecil commented.

"A wife can wait," John said firmly. "But I should like to see these well-planted and well-nursed. And the chestnut tree nuts should be in warm damp soil at once, unless—" He broke off and looked at the merchant. "Is it cold there, in winter?"

The man shrugged. "I have only been in the spring."

Cecil laughed shortly and led the way down the gangplank to the quayside.

John followed him, and then called back up to the ship as the thought struck him. "Do the leaves turn color in autumn? Or does it keep fresh and green all the year round?"

"How should I know?" the merchant called back. "I've never been there in autumn. Why does it matter to you? You'll see soon enough when it grows."

"So that I know when to plant, of course!" John shouted irritably. "If it grows all the year around then I can plant any time, best in the summer. But if it loses its leaves and its seeds in winter then it should be planted into cold ground!"

The merchant shrugged his shoulders and laughed. "I will ask when I go back! And if they do not take then I will get you some more! At double the price next time!"

Cecil had walked away limping on the cobbles. Tradescant ran to catch up with him.

"You really must learn a little cunning, Tradescant," Cecil complained. "If you are to travel and to buy for me you must learn to barter and hide your desire. Your face is as open as a book of receipts."

"I am sorry, my lord. But I couldn't be indifferent."

"They will cheat you from Flushing to Dresden."

"I will learn world-weariness," John promised. "I shall cultivate it. I shall be as weary as a Scotsman with a small bribe."

Cecil laughed shortly. "Do you come in my boat across the river? I'm going to Whitehall."

John looked down the quayside to where the earl's boat was gently rocking, the oars upright in salute, the bright colors of the liveried boatman reflected in the clean water of the Thames.

"I'll take a horse to Theobalds," he said. "And get these planted up at once."

"And then go back to your wife," Cecil called up to the quayside as he went down the steps to his waiting boat. "Take a few days to spend with her, Tradescant. You must dig your own garden too, you know."

At Meopham, Elizabeth was waiting for John again.

"Married only a day and left already," her mother said sharply. "I hope you did not do something to give him a distaste for you, Elizabeth?"

Elizabeth smoothed a loose strand of hair under her cap. "Of course not," she said levelly. "He was summoned by the earl himself; he could hardly send a message back and say he would not go!"

"And was the bedding properly done?" Gertrude asked in an undertone. "You will not hold him to the marriage if he can argue that the work was not undertaken or carried through."

"Of course. And he does not wish to withdraw from the marriage. He was summoned away to his lord. He sent me a message from London. I expect him back every day."

"The sheets were hardly marked at all," Gertrude pointed out.

Elizabeth flushed. She had resorted to strawberry jam on the bed linen. It was the tradition that the newlyweds' sheets be put to air over their windowsill so that the neighbors and the community might be assured that a marriage had been made and consummated and was now indissoluble. Not even people of the class of Elizabeth and John could escape public scrutiny.

"They were marked enough," Elizabeth said.

"Oh, well!" Gertrude sat back in the hard chair and looked around the little parlor. "He has left you comfortably, at least. As long as he provides for you I daresay you will not miss him, having been a spinster so long."

"He will provide for me, and he will return to me," Elizabeth replied calmly. "He had to go to Theobalds with some new plants for the earl. But I expect his return any day."

"You'd have done better to marry a farmer!" Gertrude gave a malicious little laugh. "Better a little mud on your parlor floor than a husband who leaves you the very morning after you are wed."

"Better to be married to a man high in the favor of the Earl Cecil himself than to be a woman who knows nothing beyond the hills of her home!" Elizabeth flared up.

"Do you mean me, you saucy miss!" Gertrude exclaimed, leaping to her feet. "For I shall not be insulted by you. Your stepfather shall hear of it! And he will make you sorry for your impertinence! I shall send him down here after he's had his dinner and he will tell you what we think of impertinent spinsters, married a night and abandoned the next day! You'll be lucky if your husband ever comes home at all! I shall see you at my back door wanting your own bed back, I don't doubt it!"

Elizabeth strode to the door and flung it open. "I am not a miss, saucy or otherwise," she declared. "And my stepfather has no rights over me anymore and neither do you. I do not have to listen to you, and I certainly don't have to obey him. My father would not have used me so!"

"Easy to say!" Gertrude retorted. "Since he is not here to contradict you!"

"He would not contradict me," Elizabeth rejoined. "He was like me. The faithful kind: we love and stay loyal. We don't flit from one to another like a drunk bee."

The reference to her mother's four marriages could not be borne. Gertrude flounced to the door. "Well, I thank you, Mrs. Tradescant!" she spat. "I shall go home to my husband at my fireside, and enjoy company and good cheer. We will drink and be merry. And I shall sleep in a warm bed with the man who loves me! And I daresay you wish you could say the same!"

Elizabeth waited until Gertrude was on her way and then she flung the door shut with a crack which sounded down the length of the street to mark her defiance. But when she was quite sure that Gertrude was gone, and not returning for a final retort, she dropped to her knees on the hearthrug, put her face on the empty seat of the master chair and cried for John.

August 1607

He did not come until late in the summer, nor did he send for her to go to Theobalds. He did not send her so much as a note to tell her that he was delayed—absorbed in the work of replanting and maintaining the most beautiful garden in England. First it was the newly designed knot gardens which took his attention. The continuous twist of hedging was much harder to keep cut than the old straight lines, and inside the box hedges the lavender had flourished too strongly. Now it needed cutting back so that it did not thrust wands of navy blue out of their place; but at least Cecil agreed that the softness of their shape and the spiky azure flowers had added beauty to the geometric precision of the garden and that Tradescant should plant other shrubs inside the hedging.

Then the bathing pools in the marble temple turned green in the hot weather, and he had them drained and scrubbed with salt and rinsed clean and refilled. Then the kitchen gardens started fruiting, first strawberries, then raspberries, gooseberries, peaches and apricots. It was not until the currants came into season that John took time from his work to borrow a horse and ride down the dusty lanes to his home in Kent.

He took two of the new chestnuts in his pocket, still shining from the polishing he continually gave them. Of the six in the merchant's box he had planted two in large pots and left them in a shady place in the garden, watering them gently every day from the dish placed underneath the pot to encourage their roots to grow down. Two he had kept in a net hung high out of the way of rats in his shed, planning that they should feel the heat of the summer on their glossy backs before he planted them in autumn, when the weeds died back and before the first frosts came, hoping to mimic the trees' natural time for growth. Two he carried in the safe darkness of his pocket, planning to plant them in spring in case they needed to be hidden from frost and to feel the warmth of a new season and the damp richness of the spring earth to make them flourish. He thought he should have left them in a stone box in the darkness and coldness of the floor of the marble bath house but he could not resist their smooth round shapes, tucked in his waistcoat. A dozen times a day his fingers found their way into the little pocket to caress them like a broody hen turning over two precious eggs.

He buttoned down the flaps with care when he mounted his horse.

"I shall stay some weeks with my wife," he said to the gardener's lad who held the horse. "You can send for me, if I am needed. Otherwise I shall come home at the end of September." He did not notice he had called Theobalds "home." "And have a care that you keep the gates shut," he reminded the boy, "and weed the grass every day. But do not touch the roses; I shall be back in time to see to them myself. You may take the heads off when they are finished flowering, and take the petals to the still room, but that is all."

It was a two-day journey to Meopham. John enjoyed traveling through the Surrey countryside where the hayfields were showing green again after the rain, and where the wheat stooks stood high in the field. Horsemen cantered past him, covering him in blinding clouds of dust; he sometimes rode alongside great wagons and could hitch his horse behind, taking a seat with the driver for a rest from the saddle and a sup of the driver's ale. There were many people walking the roads: artisans on the tramp looking for work, harvesting gangs at the end of their season, apple-pickers making their way to Kent like John, gypsies, a traveling fair, a wandering preacher ready to set up at any crossroads and preach a gospel which needed neither church nor bishops, peddlers waddling beneath the weight of their packs, goose girls driving their flocks to the London markets, beggars, paupers and sturdy vagrants forced away from parish to parish, bullocks being driven to Smithfield by swearing, anxious cattle drovers.

In the inn at night John ate at an "ordinary," the daily dinner with a set price which humble traveling men preferred, but he paid extra to sleep alone. He did not want to appear before Elizabeth scratching with another man's fleas.

At the long dining table in the inn's front room the talk was of the new king, who could not agree with Parliament although he had been in the kingdom only four years. The men dining at table were mostly on the side of the king. He had the charm of novelty and the glamour of royalty. So what if Parliament complained of the Scots nobles who hung around the court, and so what if the king was extravagant? The king of England could afford a little luxury, surely to God! And besides, the man had a family to support, a brace of princes and princesses; how else should he live but well? One man at the table had suffered at the hands of the Court of Wards and claimed that no man's fortune was safe from a king who would take orphans into his keeping and farm out their fortunes among his friends, but he gained little sympathy. The complaint was an old one, and the king was new and novelty was a pleasure.

John kept his head down over his mutton and kept his own counsel. When someone shouted for a toast to His Majesty, John rose to his feet as swiftly as any man. He was not disposed to gossip about the painted women and painted boys of court, and besides, no man who had worked for Robert Cecil would ever voice a dangerous political opinion in a public place.

"I care nothing if we have no parliament!" a man exclaimed. "What have they ever done for me? If King James, God bless him, can do without a parliament—why! then so can I!"

John thought of his master, who believed that a monarch could only rule by a combination of bluff and seduction to gain the consent of the people, and whose watchword was practice not principle, kept silent, touched the chestnuts in his waistcoat pocket for luck, took up his hat and went from the room to his solitary bed.

He arrived at Meopham at noon and nearly turned into the courtyard of the Days' family farmhouse, before he recalled that he should find Elizabeth in her new cottage—in their new cottage. He rode back down the mud track of the village street and then skirted around to the back of the little house where there was a lean-to shed and a patch of ground for his horse. He took off its saddle and bridle and turned the animal into the field. It raised its head and whinnied at the strangeness of the place and he saw Elizabeth's face at an upstairs window, looking out at the noise.

As he walked toward the little cottage's back gate he heard her running down the wooden stairs and then the back door burst open and she was racing toward him. As she suddenly recollected her dignity, she skidded to an abrupt halt. "Oh! Mr. Tradescant!" she said. "I should have killed a chicken if I had known you were coming today."

John stepped forward and took her hands and kissed her, formal as ever, on her forehead. "I did not know what time I should arrive," he said. "The roads were better than I thought they would be."

"Have you come from Theobalds?"

"I left the day before yesterday."

"And is everything well?"

"It is." He glanced down at her and saw that her usually pale face was rosy and smiling. "You look very well . . . wife."

She peeped up at him from under her severe white cap. "I am well," she said. "And very happy to see you. The days are rather long here."

"Why?" John asked. "I should have thought you would have much to do in a house of your own at last?"

"Because I am used to running a farmhouse," she said. "With care for the still room, and the laundry, and the mending, and the feeding of the family and all the farm workers, and the health of the staff, the herb garden and the kitchen garden too! Here all I have to look after is two bedrooms and a kitchen and parlor. I have not enough to do."

"Oh." John was genuinely surprised. "I had not thought."

"But I have started on a garden," she said shyly. "I thought you might like it."

She pointed to a level area of ground outside the back door. The ground was marked out with pegs and twines into a square shape containing the serpentine twists of a maze. "I was going to make it with chalk stones and flints in patterns of black and white," she said. "I don't think anything tender will thrive because of the chickens."

"You can't have chickens in a knot garden," John said decidedly.

She chuckled and John looked down and saw with surprise that rosy happy face again. "Well, we have to have chickens for their eggs and for your dinner," she said. "So you must think of a way that chickens can be kept out."

John laughed. "At Theobalds I am plagued with deer!" he said. "It seems very hard that in my own garden I shall still have pests to come and spoil my plants."

"Perhaps we could get another plot of land for the chickens," she suggested. "And fence this off so that you might grow whatever you wish."

John glanced down at the overworked light brown soil and the nearby midden. "It is hardly the ideal place," he said.

At once he saw the color and the happiness drain from her face. She looked weary. "Not after Theobalds Palace, I suppose."

"Elizabeth!" he exclaimed. "I did not mean . . ."

She turned away from him and was leading the way into the cottage.

He stepped after her and was about to take her hand but some stupid shyness checked the movement. "Elizabeth!" he said more gently.

She hesitated, but she did not turn. "I was afraid you were never coming back," she whispered. "I was afraid that you had married me to fulfil the agreement, and to get my dowry, and that you would never come back to me at all."

"Of course! Of course I would come back!" He was astounded at her. "I married you in good faith! Of course I would come back!"

She dipped her head down and then pulled up her apron to rub at her eyes. Still she did not turn around to him. "You did not write," she said softly. "And it has been two months."

Now it was he who turned away. He looked away from the house, over the little plot where his horse grazed, and toward the hill where the square-towered church pointed up at the sky. "I know," he said shortly. "I meant to . . ."

She raised her head but still she did not turn around. He thought they must look a pair of fools, back to back in their own yard instead of in each other's arms.

"Why did you not?" she asked softly.

He cleared his throat to hide his embarrassment. "I cannot write very fair," he said awkwardly. "That is to say, I cannot write at all. I can read a bit, I can reckon very swiftly, but I cannot write. And anyway . . . I should not know what to say."

She turned to him; but in his embarrassment, he did not see her. He was digging the heel of his riding boot into the corner of her little square of hen-scratched dust.

"What would you have said, if you had written?" she asked and her voice was very soft and tempting. It was a voice which a man would turn to and rest upon. John resisted the temptation to spin on his heel, snatch her up and bury his face in her neck.

"I would have said I was sorry," he confessed gruffly. "Sorry to have been ill-tempered on our wedding night, and sorry that I had to leave you that very morning. When I was angry with them for making a noise I had thought that we would have the next day in peace, and that anything troublesome could be mended then. I had thought to wake early in the morning and love you then. But then the message came and I went up to London and there was no way of telling you that I was sorry."

Hesitantly she stepped forward and put a hand on his shoulder.

"I am sorry too," she said simply. "I thought these things were easier for men. I thought that you were doing just exactly what you wished. I thought that you had not bedded me because . . ." her voice became choked and she ended in a thin whisper " . . . because you have an aversion to me, and that you went back to Theobalds to avoid me."

John spun around and snatched his wife to his heart. "I do not!" He felt her whole frame convulse with a deep sob. "I do not have an aversion!"

She was warm in his arms and her skin was soft. He kissed her face and her wet eyelids, and her smooth sweet neck and the dimples of her collarbone at the neck of her gown, and suddenly he felt desire sweep over him as easy and as natural as a spring rainstorm across a field of grass. He scooped her up and carried her into the house and kicked the door shut behind him, and he laid her down on the hearthrug before the little spinster's fire where she had sat, alone and lonely, for so many evenings, and loved her until it grew dark outside and only the firelight illuminated their enfolded bodies.

"I do *not* have an aversion to you," he said.

At suppertime they rose from the floor, chilled and uncomfortable. "I have some bread and cheese and a broth," Elizabeth said.

"Whatever you have in the larder will do for me," John replied. "I'll fetch some wood for the fire."

"I'll run up the road to my mother's house and borrow a jug of beef stock," she said, pulling her gray gown on over her head. She turned her back to him and offered him the ties on her white apron. "I'll only be a moment."

"Give them my good wishes," John said. "I'll call up and see them tomorrow."

"We could go up to the house for supper," she suggested. "They would be glad to see you tonight."

"I have other plans for tonight," John said with a meaning

smile. Elizabeth felt herself warm through with the intensity of her blush. "Oh." She recovered herself. "I'll get the beef stock then."

John nodded and listened to her quick step down the brick path and out into the main street. He stacked the fireplace with a liberal supply of logs and then went out through the backyard to the little field to see to his horse. When he came back Elizabeth was stirring a pot hung on a chain from the spit, and there was bread and new cheese on the table and two jugs of small ale.

"I brought my book," she said carefully. "I thought you might like us to look at it, together."

"What book?"

"My lesson book," she said. "My father taught me to read and write and I did my writing in this book. It has clean pages in it still. I thought, if you wished, I might teach you."

For a moment John was going to rebuff her; the idea of a wife teaching her husband anything was contrary to the laws of nature and of God; but she looked very sweet and very young. Her hair was tumbled and her cap was slightly askew. Lying on his cape on the floor of the little cottage she had been tender and ready to be pleased, and at the end, openly passionate. He found he did not feel much like supporting the laws of God and nature; instead he found that he was rather disposed to oblige her. Besides, it would be good to know how to read and write.

"D'you know how to write in French?" he asked. "And Latin words?"

"Yes," she said. "Do you want to learn French?"

"I can speak French, and a bit of Italian, and enough German to see that my lord is not cheated when I am buying plants for him from a sea captain. And I know some plant names in Latin. But I never learned to write any of it down."

Her face was illuminated with her smile. "I can teach you."

"All right," he said. "But you must tell no one."

Her gaze was open and honest. "Of course not. It shall be between the two of us, as everything else will be."

* * *

That night they made love again in the warmth and comfort of the big bed. Elizabeth, free from her fear that he did not love her, and discovering a sensuality which she had not imagined, clung to him and wrapped her arms and legs around him and sobbed for pleasure. Then they wrapped their blankets around their shoulders and sat side by side on the bed and looked out at the deep blue of the night sky and the sharp whiteness of the thousands of stars.

The village was all quiet; not one light showed. The road away from the village, north to Gravesend and London, was empty and silent, ghostly in the starlight. An owl hooted, quartering the fields on silent wings. John reached for his waistcoat folded on the chest at the foot of the bed.

"I have something I should like to give you," he said quietly. "I think it is perhaps the most valuable thing I own. Perhaps you will think it foolish; but if you would like it, I should like to give it to you."

His hand closed over one of the precious chestnuts. "If you do not like it I will keep it, by your leave," he said. "It is not really mine to give away; it is entrusted to me."

Elizabeth lay back on the pillow, her hair spread as brown and as glossy as his chestnut. "What is it?" she asked, smiling. "You sound like a child in the schoolyard."

"It is precious to me . . ."

"Then it is precious to me too, whatever it may be," she said.

He brought his clenched fist out of his waistcoat pocket and she put her hand out flat, waiting for him to open his fingers.

"There are only six of these in the country," he said. "Perhaps only six in the whole of Europe. I have five in my keeping and, if you like, you may have the sixth."

He dropped the heavy nut like a round smooth marble into her hand.

"What is it?"

"It is a chestnut."

"It is too big and too round!"

"A new chestnut. The man who sold it to me told me that it

grows into a great tree, like our chestnut tree, but it flowers like a rose, the color of apple blossom. And this great nut comes only one to a pod, not two nuts to a pod like ours, and the pod is not prickly like our chestnuts but waxy and green with a few sharp spines. He sold it to my lord for nine pounds down, and another eighteen pounds if it grows. And I shall give this one to you."

Elizabeth turned the nut over in her hand. It nestled heavily in her palm, its brown glossy color dark against her callused hand.

"Shall I plant it in the garden?"

John instantly flinched, thinking of the voracious chickens. "Put it in a pot, somewhere that you can easily watch it," he said. "In soil with some muck well stirred in. Water it from the base of the pot with a little water every day. Perhaps it will grow for you."

"Shall you not regret giving me this precious nut, if it fails for me?"

John closed her fingers around the nut. "It is yours," he said gently. "Do with it as you will. Perhaps you will be lucky. Perhaps together, now that we are married, we shall be lucky together."

John stayed a full month at Meopham with his wife, and when the time came for him to go back to Theobalds a number of innovations had been made. She had a pretty little miniature knot garden outside the back door, incongruously planted with leeks, beets, carrots and onions and fenced with rooted willow twigs woven into a dwarf living fence against the marauding chickens. He could both read and write a fair-enough script; the chestnut was in a pot on the windowsill showing a pale snout above the earth; and Elizabeth was expecting their child.

Summer 1608

"The boy should be called George, for his grandfather," Gertrude remarked. She was seated in the best chair in Elizabeth's parlor. The wooden crib stood beside the open window, and John, leaning against the windowsill, was rocking it gently with his foot and looking down into the sleeping face of the baby. He was a dark-skinned child, with black hair as thick as John's own. When he was awake his eyes were a deep periwinkle blue. John kept his foot nudging the crib, repressing the desire to lift his son to his face and smell again his haunting smell of spilled milk and sweet buttercream skin.

"George David, for his grandfather and godfather," Gertrude said. She glanced sideways at John. "Unless you wish to call him Robert and see if the earl can be persuaded to take an interest in him?"

John gazed out into the garden. The little vegetable knot garden was doing well and this spring he had added another square beside it, planted with herbs for strewing, for medicines and for cooking. There was now a withy hurdle penning Elizabeth's hens into the far end of the garden with wormwood planted around it to hide the fencing, to give them shade and to prevent fowl pest.

"Or we might call him James in a compliment to His Majesty," Gertrude went on. "Though it will do him little good, I suppose. We could call him Henry Charles for the two princes. But they say Prince Charles is a sickly boy. D'you ever see him at Theobalds, John?"

She glanced up to John, who had leaned out of the window and was thoughtfully weighing a flowerpot in his hand. Poking from the moist earth was a whippy slim stem crowned with a little hand of green leaves.

"Oh! that eternal pot! Every day Elizabeth sighs over it as if it were worth its weight in gold! I told her! No twig in the world is worth that sort of attention! But I was asking you—John—d'you ever see Prince Charles at Theobalds? I heard he was sickly?"

"He's not strong," John replied, putting the chestnut tree gently on the windowsill. "They say he is much better since he came from Scotland. But I rarely see him. The king does not keep his family by him. When he comes hunting, he comes with only his most intimate circle."

Gertrude leaned forward, avid for gossip. "And are they as bad as everyone says? I've heard that the king adores the Duke of Rochester, that he loads him with pearls, that the duke rules the king and the king rules the kingdom!"

"I wouldn't know," John said unhelpfully. "I'm just the gardener."

"But you must *see* them!"

John thought of the last visit of the king. He had come without his wife Anne, who now never traveled with him. She was completely replaced by his young men. John had seen him walking in the garden with his arm around the Duke of Rochester's waist. They had sat together in the arbor and the king had rested his head on the duke's shoulder, like a country girl mooning over a blacksmith. When they kissed, the court turned aside and pretended to be busy about its own concerns. No one pried, no one condemned. The young Duke of Rochester was the favorite of everyone who wanted to be the favorite of the king. A whole court was formed around his handsome lithe figure. A whole morality was lightly constructed around the king's love for him that permitted any sort of display, any sort of drunkenness.

At night the duke went openly to his bed in the king's room. The king was said to be afraid of assassination and it soothed him to sleep with a companion, but there were loud groans of pleasure from the inner chamber and the repetitive squeaking of the royal bed.

"They go out hunting; I weed the paths," John said unhelpfully.

"I hear the queen misses him and pines for him, and has become a papist for consolation . . ."

John shrugged.

"And what of the children, the royal princes and princesses?"

John looked deliberately vague. He was disinclined to gossip and in any case he had seen more than enough of the royal princes and princesses. Princess Mary was only a baby and not yet at court but Prince Henry, the heir and the darling of the whole court, was an arrogant boy whose charm could be blown away in a moment's rage. His sister, Elizabeth, had all the Tudor temper and all the Tudor hastiness, and poor little Prince Charles, the second surplus heir, the rickety-legged runt of the litter, ran behind his stronger, older, more attractive siblings all the day, breathless with his weak chest, stammering with his tied tongue, longing for them to turn and pay him attention.

They never did. They were courted beloved spoiled children, the first children of four kingdoms, and they had no time for him. John would see them boating on the lake or riding across the park and never looking back as poor little Charles struggled to keep up.

"I scarcely see Their Highnesses," he said.

"Oh, well!" Gertrude leaped to her feet in frustration. "Tell Elizabeth I called in to wish her well. I'm surprised she is not downstairs by now. Tell her that I said she should stir herself. And tell her that the baby should be called George David."

"No, I don't think so," John said in the same quiet tone of voice.

"What?"

"I will not tell her any of that. And you shall not tell her either."

"I beg your pardon?"

John smiled his easy smile. "Elizabeth shall stay in bed until she is well again," he said. "We were lucky not to lose her. It was a hard birth for her, and she was hurt inside. She shall rest as long as she wants. And we won't be calling the child George or Robert or James or Charles or Henry or David. He'll be John, after my grandfather, and after my father, and me."

Gertrude flounced toward the door. "It's very dull!" she exclaimed. "You should save your name for another child. The first child should be named in such a way as to encourage a sponsor!"

John's smile never wavered but his face was dark with regret. "There won't be another child," he said. "There will only ever be this one. So we will name him as we wish, and he will be John Tradescant, and I will teach him how to garden."

Gertrude paused. "Not another child?" she asked. "How can you say such a thing?"

He nodded. "I called the apothecary from Gravesend. He said that she could not manage another birth, so we shall only ever have this, our son."

Gertrude came back into the room and looked again into the cradle, shocked out of her normal irritability. "But John," she said softly. "To have to pin all your hopes on just one child! No one to bear your name but just the one! And everything to be lost if you lose him!"

John rubbed his face as if he would rub away his scowl of pain. He leaned over the cradle. The baby's sleeping fists were as tiny as rosebuds, his dark hair a little crown of fluff around his head. A tiny pulse like a vulnerable heartbeat at the center of his skull. John felt a deep passion of tenderness so powerful that his very bones seemed to melt inside him.

"It's as well I am used to growing rarities," he murmured. "I have not a dozen little seedlings to watch; I shall never have more than this one. I just have this one precious little bud. I shall nurse him up as if he was a new flower, a rarity."

January 1610

"It is done." Robert Cecil found Tradescant on his knees in the Theobalds knot garden. "I was looking for you. The king wants to call Theobalds his own this year. We are to leave."

John rose to his feet and rubbed the cold earth from his hands. "What are you doing?" the earl asked.

"Relaying the white stones," John said. "The frost disturbs them, throws up dirt and spoils the pattern."

"Leave it," he ordered peremptorily. "The king's gardeners can worry about it now. He wants it, he has pressed me for it, he hinted a hundred thousand different ways, and Rochester pushed him on every time he might have stopped. I've fended him off for three years but now I've given it to him, God damn it. And now he's happy, and Rochester is happy, and I have Hatfield."

Tradescant nodded, his eyes on his master's face. "You shall make me a splendid garden there," Robert Cecil said rapidly, as if he were almost afraid of John's calm silence. "You shall go abroad and buy me all sorts of rarities. How are the chestnuts coming along? We will take them with us. You shall take anything you want from the gardens here, take them with us and we shall start again at Hatfield . . ."

He broke off. Still John watched him, saying nothing.

The most powerful man in England, second only to the king himself, took two hasty steps away from his gardener and then turned back to face him. "John, I could weep like a babe," he confessed.

John slowly nodded. "So could I."

The earl held out his arms and John stepped into them and the two men, the one so slight and twisted, the other so broad and strong, wrapped each other in a deep firm hug. Then they broke apart, Cecil rubbing his eyes on the sleeve of his rich jacket while John cleared his throat with a harsh cough. John offered his arm and Cecil took help and leaned on his man. The two of them walked from the knot garden side by side.

"The bath house!" the earl said quietly. "I'll never manage anything like it at Hatfield."

"And the tulips I've just put in! And snowdrops, and lenten lilies!"

"You've planted bulbs?"

"Hundreds last autumn, for a show this spring."

"We'll dig them up and take them with us!"

John shook his head in silent disagreement but said nothing. They walked slowly toward the ornamental mount. A stream played beside the path on a bed of white marble pebbles. John hesitated. "Let's walk up," the earl said.

Slowly the two men followed the twisting path. John had pruned the rambling roses which bordered the path on either side and they lay flat and tidy like withy fencing. Cecil paused for breath, and to ease the pain of his lame leg, John put his arm around his master's waist and held him steady. "Go on," Cecil said and they walked slowly side by side round and round the little hill. There were a few foolishly early buds on the roses; John noticed the deep crimson of new shoots, red as wine. At the top of the hill there was a round lovers' seat, with a fountain plashing in the middle. Tradescant swung his cape down for his master to sit, and the earl nodded for John to sit beside him, as an equal.

The two men looked out across the palace gardens spread below them like a tapestry map. "Those woods!" the earl mourned. "The trees we have planted."

"The bluebells underneath them in springtime," John reminded him.

"The orchards, my peach-tree wall!"

"And the courts!" Tradescant nodded at the smooth grass laid out in every courtyard of the rambling palace. "There isn't grass like that anywhere else in the kingdom. Not a weed in it, and the mowing team trained to go to half an inch."

"I don't see any mud in the knot garden," Robert Cecil remarked, looking at the garden as it was meant to be viewed—from on high.

"There isn't any *now,*" John said with rare impatience. "Because I've been washing the stones in freezing water all morning."

"I shall be sorry to lose the hunting," the earl said.

"I shan't miss the deer eating my young shoots in spring."

The earl shook his head. "You know they say that this is the fairest garden in England? And the greatest palace? That there never was and never will be a palace and garden to match it?"

John nodded. "I know."

"I couldn't keep it," the earl said. "It's his revenge on my father for the execution of his mother, you know. He wanted to take my own father's house, his pride and his joy. What could I say? I hedged and twisted and turned and showed him other men's houses. It's my own fault. We built it too grand and too beautiful, my father and I. It was bound to draw out envy."

John shrugged. "It is all the king's," he said simply. "The whole country. And each of us is nothing more than his steward. If he wants anything, we have to give it."

The earl threw him a curious sideways glance. "You really believe that, don't you?"

John nodded, his face open and guileless. "He is the king under God. I would no more refuse him than I would skip my prayers."

"Please God he always has subjects as loyal as you."

"Amen."

"Leave washing the stones now and start preparing the plants for moving, and dig up those damned bulbs." The earl got to his feet with a grunt of discomfort. "My bones ache in this cold weather."

"I'll leave the bulbs," John replied.

The earl raised an eyebrow.

"You've given him the house and the grounds," John said. "I can be generous too. Let the king have these tulips in spring and I shall go myself to the Lowlands to buy you a fine crop for Hatfield, as we planned. We can make a new garden at Hatfield; we don't have to scrump from here."

"A lordly gesture from a gardener?" Cecil asked, smiling.

"I have my grander moments," John said.

Hatfield House in Hertfordshire had been the home and the prison of the young Elizabeth during the dangerous years of her half sister's rule, when she had been a studious girl with a deep fear of the executioner's axe. It had been Robert Cecil's father who had come to her in the garden to tell her that she was now queen.

"I'll keep the tree she was sitting under," Robert Cecil said to Tradescant as they surveyed the quagmire the workmen had made in the building of the huge new house. "But I'm damned if I'll do anything with that poky little hall. It can't have been impressive even when it was new-built. I'm not surprised the queen was in the garden. Nowhere else to sit."

"If you cut away all around it so that it stood on a hill instead of so low, you could make it into a banqueting hall for summer, or a masquing theater . . ."

The earl shook his head. "Leave it. An extra hall with its own kitchen and stables is always useful if someone important comes with a big entourage. Come and see the new house!"

He led the way up the garden, John following him slowly, looking everywhere with his quick perceptive glance. "Fine trees," he remarked.

"They can stay," the earl said. "Mountain Jennings does the park and a Frenchman has designed the garden. But you plant it."

John suppressed an instant, unworthy pang of envy. "I'd rather plant a garden than design it anyway."

"You know it comes to the same thing after the first summer,"

Cecil said. "The Frenchman goes back to Paris, and you have a free hand then. Anything you don't like, you can tell me it has died—I'm not likely to know."

John chuckled, "I can't see me lasting long in your employ if I kill off your plantings, my lord," he said.

The earl smiled. "Never mind the plants, what about the new house?"

It was a large stately house, not as big as Theobalds, which was built as a palace and had sprawled to become a village, but it was a grand beautiful house in the new style, fit to display the staggering wealth of the Cecils, fit to welcome the prodigal luxury of the Jacobean court, fit to take its place as a great display house of Europe.

"Surrounded by great courts on every side," the earl pointed. "A hundred rooms, separate kitchen and bake house altogether. I tell you, John, it has cost me nigh on thirty thousand pounds for the house alone, and I expect to spend as much again on the park and gardens."

John gulped. "You'll be ruined!" he said bluntly.

The earl shook his head. "The king is a generous master to those who serve him well," he said. "And even to those who serve him ill," he added.

"But sixty thousand pounds!"

The earl chuckled. "My money," he said grimly. "My show house, and in the end my grand funeral. What else should I do with it but spend it on what I love? And what a garden we will make, won't we, John? Do you want me to scrimp on the plantings?"

John felt his excitement rising. "Have you the plans?"

"Over here." The earl led the way to a little outhouse, his boots squelching in the mud. "As soon as the workmen have finished you can sow grass here, get the place clean."

"Yes, my lord," John said automatically, looking at the plans spread out on the table inside.

"There!" Cecil exclaimed.

John leaned over. The parkland was so immense that the grand house, drawn to scale, showed as nothing more than a little box in the center. He ran his eye over the gardens. All the courts were to be planted with different flowers, each with their own ornate knot garden in different patterns. There was to be a great walk of espaliered fruit trees, and a grand water feature of a river running along a terrace edged with seats and planted with tender fruit trees in tubs. The water for the terrace was to be fed from a gigantic fountain splashing from a copper statue standing on a great rock. Farther away from the house were to be wooded walks and orchards, a bowling green and a mountain large enough to ride a horse up a winding path to the top.

"Will this ease your homesickness for Theobalds?" Cecil asked jokingly.

"It will ease mine," John replied, looking at the magnitude of the plan and thinking, his imagination whirling, of how he would ever get the thousands of fruit trees, where he would buy the millions of plants. "Will it ease yours, my lord?"

The earl shrugged. "The service of a king is never easy, John. Don't forget that. No true servant of a king ever sleeps well at night. I shall miss my old house." He turned back to the plan. "But this will keep us busy into our old age, don't you think?"

"This will keep us busy forever!" John exclaimed. "Where am I to get a thousand golden carp for your water parterre?"

"Oh!" Cecil said negligently. "Ask around, John. You can find a hundred pairs, surely! And they will breed if they are well kept, I don't fear it!"

John chuckled reluctantly. "I know you don't fear it, my lord. That is to be my job."

Cecil beamed at him. "It is!" he said. "And they are reroofing a fine cottage for you here, and I shall pay you an increase. How much did I promise you?"

"Forty pounds a year, sir," John replied.

"Call it fifty then," the earl said genially. "Why not? I'm hardly going to notice it with the rest of these bills to pay."

Summer 1610

John decided that Elizabeth and Baby J should remain at Meopham while he was traveling in Europe to buy the earl's trees. Elizabeth protested that she wanted to live in the new cottage in Hertfordshire, but John was firm.

"If Baby J should be ill, or you yourself sick, then there is no one there who would care for you," he said in the last days of August, while he planned and packed his clothes for the journey.

"There's no one here in Meopham who would care for me," she said inaccurately.

"Your whole family is here, cousins, sisters, aunts and your mother."

"I can't see Gertrude wasting much time on my comfort!"

John nodded. "Maybe not. But she would do her duty by you. She would make sure that you had a fire and water and food. Whereas at Hatfield I know no one but the workmen. Not even the house staff are fully at work yet. The place is still half-built."

"They must be finished soon!"

John was incapable of explaining the scale of the project. "It looks as if they could build for a dozen years and never be done!" he said. "They have the roof on now, at least, and the walls complete. But all the inside fittings, the floors, the windows, there is all that to do. And the paneling is yet to come; there are hundreds of carpenters and woodcarvers on site! I tell you, Elizabeth, he is building a little town there, in the middle of a hundred meadows. And I must plant the meadows and turn them into a great garden!"

"Don't sound so overawed!" Elizabeth said affectionately. "You know you are as excited as a child!"

John smiled, acknowledging the truth. "But I fear for him," he confided. "It is a great task he has taken on. I can't see how he can bear the cost of it. And he is buying property in London too, and then selling it on. I fear he will overstretch himself and if he gets into debt—" He broke off. Not even to Elizabeth would he trust the details of Cecil's business arrangements, the bribes routinely taken, the Treasury money diverted, the men bankrupted by the king one day on charges of treason or offenses against the Crown whose estates were bought up by his first minister at knockdown prices the next.

"They say he is an engrosser," Elizabeth remarked. "Not a wood or a common is safe from his fences. He takes it all to himself."

"It is his own," John said stoutly. "He takes what is his by right. Only the king is above him, and God above him."

Elizabeth gave him a skeptical look but kept her thoughts to herself. She was too much like her father—a clergyman of stoutly independent Protestantism—to accept John's spiritual hierarchy which led from God in heaven down to the poorest pauper with each man in his place, and the king and the earl a small step down from the angels.

"I fear for myself too," John said. "He has given me a purse of gold and ordered me to buy and buy. I am afraid of being cheated, and I am afraid of shipping these plants so far. He wants a garden all at once, so I should buy plants as large and fruitful as I can get. But I am sure that little sturdy ones might travel better!"

"There's no one in the kingdom better able than you," Elizabeth said encouragingly. "And he knows it. I just wish I might come with you. Are you not afraid to go alone?"

John shook his head. "I've longed to travel ever since I was a boy," he said. "And my work for my lord has tempted me every time I go down to the docks and speak to the men who have sailed far overseas. The things they have seen! And they can bring back only the tiniest part of it. If I might go to India with them or even Turkey, just think what rarities I might bring home."

She watched him, frowning slightly. "You would not want to go so far, surely?"

John put his arm around her waist to reassure her, but could not bring himself to lie. "We are a nation of travelers," he said. "The finest of the lords, my lord's friends, are all men who seek their fortunes over the seas, who see the seas as their highway. My lord himself invests in every other voyage out of London. We are too great a nation with too many people to be kept to the one island."

Elizabeth was a woman from a village that counted the men who were lost to the sea, and tried to keep them on the land. "You don't think of leaving England?"

"Oh, no," John said. "But I don't fear to travel."

"I don't know how you can bear to leave us for so long!" she complained. "And Baby J will be so changed by the time you come back."

John nodded. "You must note down every new thing he says so that you can remember to tell me when I return," he said. "And let him plant those cuttings I brought for him. They are his lordship's favorite pinks, and they smell very sweet. They should grow well here. Let him dig the hole himself and set them in; I showed him how to do it this afternoon."

"I know." Elizabeth had watched from the window as her husband and her quick dark-eyed dark-haired son had kneeled side by side by the little plot of earth and dug together, John straining to understand the rapid babble of baby talk, Baby J looking up into his father's face and repeating the sound until between guesswork and faith they could understand each other.

"Dig!" Baby J insisted, thrusting a little trowel into the earth.

"Dig," his father agreed. "And now we put these little fellows into their beds."

"Dig!" Baby J insisted again.

"Not here!" John said warningly. "They need to rest quiet here so that they can grow and make pretty flowers for Mama!"

"Dig! J want dig!"

"Not dig!" John replied, descending rapidly to equal stubbornness.

"Dig!"

"No!"

"Dig!"

"No! Elizabeth! Come and take your son out of this! He is going to destroy these before they even know they've been transplanted!"

She had come from the house and swept Baby J up, and taken him down to the end of the garden to pet Daddy's horse.

"I don't know that he will make a gardener," she warned. "You should not count on it."

"He understands the importance of deep digging," John said firmly. "Everything else will follow."

August 1610

John set sail in September, and experienced a rough and frightening crossing after waiting for four dull days off Gravesend for a southerly wind. He landed in Flushing and hired a large flat-bottomed canal boat so that he could stop at every farm and enquire what they had to sell, all the way down the canal to Delft. To his relief the canal boatman spoke English even though his accent was as strong as any Cornishman's. The boat was drawn by an amiable sleepy horse which wandered along the tow path and grazed on the lush banks during John's frequent halts. He found farmers of flowers whose whole trade consisted of nothing but the famous tulips, and whose whole fortune rested on being able to produce and then reproduce the new colors of blooms. There were farms like John had never seen before. Row upon row of floppy-leaved stalks were tended by women wearing huge wooden clogs against the rich sandy soil, and big white hats against the sun, working their way down the rows with an implement like a wooden spoon, gently lifting the smooth round bulbs from the ground and laying them softly down, and the cart coming along behind to gather them all up.

John watched them. Each set of leaves which had grown from one bulb now had a cluster of three, perhaps even four, bulbs at the end of their white stems. Most of them even carried fat buds at the head where the petals had been and when the women spotted them, and they never missed one however long he watched, they cut them off and popped them in their apron pockets. Where one valuable bulb had been set in the ground and flowered there were now four, and maybe three dozen seeds as well. A man could quadruple his investment in one year for no more labor than keeping the field free of weeds and digging up his capital in the autumn.

"Profitable business," John remarked enviously under his breath, thinking of the price he paid for tulips in England.

At every canalside market town he had the boatman tie up and wait for him on board, sometimes for hours, sometimes for days, as he wandered around the market gardens and picked out a well-shaped tree, a sack of common bulbs, a purse full of seeds. Wherever he could, he bought in bulk, haunted by the thought of the rich green commonland and meadows around Hatfield waiting for forests and plantations and mazes and orchards. Wherever he could find someone who could speak English and had the appearance of an honorable man, he made a contract with him to send on more plants to England as they matured.

"A great planting scheme," one of the Dutch farmers commented.

John smiled but his forehead was creased with worry. "The greatest," he said.

Despite his rooted belief that Englishmen were the best of the world, and England undeniably the best country, John could not help but be impressed with the labor these people had put into their land. Each canal bank was maintained as smartly as each town doorstep. They took a pleasure and a pride in things being just so. And their rewards were towns which exuded wealth and a land which was interlaced with an efficient transport system that put the potholed roads of England to shame.

The dykes that held back the shifting sands and the high waves of the North Sea were a wonder to John, who had seen the feckless neglect of the marshes and waterlogged estuaries of the Fens and East Anglia. He had not thought it was possible to do anything with land soured by salt, but he saw the Dutch farmers had learned the way of it and were making use of land that an Englishman would call waste ground and abandon as hopeless. John thought of the harbors and inlets and boggy places all around the coast, even in land-hungry Kent and Essex, and how in England they were left to lie fallow, steeped in salt, whereas in Holland they were banked off from the sea and growing green.

He could not help but admire their labor and their skill, and he could not help but envy the Dutch prosperity. There was no hunger in the Holland Provinces, and basic fare was rich and good. They ate cheese on buttered bread, a double helping of richness and fat, and did not think twice about it. Their cows grazed knee-deep in lush wet pastureland and gave abundant milk. They were a people who saw themselves as divinely rewarded for their struggle against the papist Spanish, and John, idling down the narrow canals, looking left and right for plants and flowers tucked away in the moist grasses, had to agree that the Protestant God was a generous one to this, His favored people.

When they reached The Hague, Tradescant sent the loaded barge back with instructions to ship all the plants directly to England. He stood on the stone wharf and watched the swaying heads of trees glide slowly away. Some of the cherry trees were bearing fruit and he saw, with irritation, that once they were beyond hailing distance the bargee picked a handful and ate them, spitting the stones carelessly into the glassy water of the canal.

In Flanders he bought vines, and watched them pruned of their yellow leaves and thick black grapes in preparation for their journey. He ordered their roots to be wrapped in damp sacking and plunged into old wine casks for their voyage home. He sent a message ahead of them, in the careful script which Elizabeth had taught him, so that a gardener from Hatfield would meet them with a cart on the dockside, to take them back and heel them in the same day, without fail, making sure to water them religiously at dawn every day until Tradescant came home.

The Prince of Orange's gardener admitted Tradescant to the beautiful garden behind the palace of The Hague and showed him around. It was a garden in the grand European style, with large stone colonnades and broad sweeping walks. Tradescant spoke to him of his work at Theobalds, planting between the box hedges and replacing the colored stones of the knot garden with lavender. The gardener nodded with enthusiasm and showed Tradescant his version of the changing style in a little garden at the side of the palace where he had used tidily pruned lavender for the hedges themselves. They made a softer pattern and had more variation of color than the usual box hedge. They did not harbor insects and when a woman passed by, her skirts brushed against the leaves and released a cloud of perfume. When he left, Tradescant had a trayful of rooted cuttings and a letter of introduction to the great physic garden at Leiden.

He traveled overland to Rotterdam, uncomfortable on a big broad-backed horse, all the way seeking out English-speaking farmers who could tell him about the growing of their precious tulips. In the darkened cellars of ale houses, drinking a rich sweet beer which was new to John, called "thick beer," they swore that the new colors entered into the heart of the flowers by slicing into the very heart of the bulb.

"Does it not weaken them?" John asked.

The men shook their heads. "It helps them to split," one of them volunteered. He leaned forward and breathed a blast of raw onion into John's face. "To spawn. And then what do you have?"

John shook his head.

"Two, where you had one before! If they are of another color, and the color often enters at the split, then you have made a fortune a thousand times over. But if they are the same color but have doubled, then you have doubled your fortune at the least."

John nodded. "It is like a miracle," he said. "You cannot help but double your fortune every year."

The man sat back in his seat and beamed. "And it's more than double," he confirmed. "The prices are steadily rising. People are ready to pay more and more each year." He scratched his broad belly with quiet satisfaction. "I shall have a handsome house in Amsterdam before I retire," he predicted. "And all from my tulips."

"I shall buy from you," John promised.

"You have to come to the auction," the man said firmly. "I don't sell privately. You will have to bid against the others."

John hesitated. An auction in a foreign country in a language he did not understand was almost bound to drive up the price. One of the other growers leaned forward.

"You have to," he said simply. "The market for tulips is all agreed. It has to be done in the colleges, in the appointed way. You cannot buy without posting a bid. That way we all know how much is being made on each color."

"I just want to buy some flowers," John protested. "I don't want to post a bid in the colleges; I don't understand how it is done. I just want some flowers."

The first grower shook his head. "It may be just flowers to you, but it's trade to us. We are traders and we have formed a college and we buy and sell in each other's view. That way we know what prices are being charged; that way we can watch the prices rise. And not be left behind."

"Prices are rising so fast?" John asked.

The grower beamed and dipped his face into his great mug of ale. "No one knows how high it can go," he said. "No one knows. If I were you I would swallow my English pride and go to the college and post my bid and buy now. It will be dearer next season, and dearer the year after that."

John glanced around the ale house. The growers were all nodding, not with a salesman's desire for a deal but with the quiet confidence of men who are in an irresistibly rising market.

"I'll take a dozen sacks of plain reds and yellows," John decided. "Where is this college?"

The grower smiled. "Right here," he said. "We don't leave our dinner table for anything." He took a clean dinner plate, and scribbled a price on it and pushed the plate across to John. The man at John's elbow dug him in the ribs and whispered, "That's high. Knock off a dozen guilders at least."

John amended the price and pushed it back; the man rubbed

the number off and wrote his own total. John agreed and the plate was posted on a hook on the wall of the room. The grower extended a callused hand.

"That's all?" John queried, shaking it.

"That's all," the man said. "Business done in the open where everyone can see the posted price. Fairly done and well done, and no harm to either bidder or seller."

John nodded.

"A pleasure to do business with you, Mr. Tradescant," said the grower.

The tulips were delivered to John's inn the next day and he sent them off with a courier under strict orders that they were not to be out of his sight until he had put them into the Hatfield wagon at London dock. He also sent a letter to Meopham with his love and a kiss for Baby J, and news that he was going on to Paris.

It was as he sealed the letter and put it into the hands of the courier that John knew that he was a traveler indeed. He did not fear the strangeness of Europe; he had a deep intoxicating sense that he might hire a horse here and then exchange it for another, and then another, and then another, and ride all the way across Europe, through the heart of papist Spain and even on to Africa. He was an islander no more; he had become a traveler.

He watched the barge carrying his precious tulips slip away down the canal and turned back to the inn. The horse was waiting, saddled for him; he had paid his slate; his traveling pack was ready. John swung his thick cape around his shoulders, heaved himself into the saddle, and set the horse's head for the west gate.

"Where are you headed?" one of the tulip growers called to him, seeing a good customer departing.

"To Paris," John called back and nearly laughed at his own sense of excitement. "I'm to visit the gardens of the French king. And I am buying more plants. I need even more. I think I shall buy up half of Europe."

The man laughed and waved him on and John's horse, its metal shoes ringing on the cobblestones, stepped delicately out onto the highway.

The roads were good to the frontier and then they deteriorated into a mud track riddled with potholes. John kept a sharp lookout for great forests with a château set among the trees, and when he saw newly planted drives he turned off the road and went to find the French gardener to discover where he got his trees from. If he found a good supplier of rare trees, he placed an order with him to lift a hundred of them when the weather turned colder and they could be safely moved and sent on to Hatfield. For the great Earl Cecil himself.

As John drew nearer to Paris the woods became thinner except for the preserved forests for hunting, and then the road became lined with little farmhouses and market gardens to feed the insatiable appetite of the city. From his vantage point on horseback John overlooked garden and orchard walls and constantly surveyed what the French gardeners were growing. As a man from Kent he could afford to despise the quality of their apples, but he envied the size and ripeness of their plum trees and stopped half a dozen times to buy specimens of what looked like new varieties.

He entered Paris with an entourage following him like a traveling garden, two wagons loaded with swaying leaves, and he had to find an inn that was accustomed to great baggage trains where he could pack up his new purchases and send them on to England.

As soon as they were safely dispatched John called for a laundress to wash and starch his clothes, to clean the dust from his cape so that he might use his letter of introduction to the French king's own gardener, the famous Jean Robin.

Robin had heard of Tradescant and was desperate for news of the new great palace and gardens at Hatfield. Of course it would be in the French style, it was to be designed by a Frenchman, but what of the woods, what of the walks? And what did Tradescant think of the prices of tulips, were they rising or would they hold steady for another year? How high could the price of a bulb go anyway? Surely there must be a point where a man would pay no higher?

Tradescant and Jean Robin walked around the royal garden for a couple of hours and then retired for a grand dinner enhanced by several bottles of claret from the royal cellar. Jean Robin's son joined them for the meal, washing the mud from the garden off his hands before he sat down and bowed his head for a papist grace. Tradescant shifted uneasily in his seat while the ritual Latin was spoken, but when the young man broke bread he could not help but smile.

"I hope that my son too will follow me into my place," John said. "He's only a baby now, but I will bring him up to my work and—who knows?"

"A man who holds a craft should pass it on," Jean Robin said, speaking slowly for John's benefit. "But when it is a garden which takes so long to fruit, then you are planting for your son and his sons anyway. It is a fine thing to say to a boy, look out for this tree and when it is grown this high, I want it pruned like that. To know that the garden lives on, and your work and plans for it will live on, even after you are long dead."

"It is a poor man's posterity," John said thoughtfully.

"I should want no other than to leave a beautiful garden," Jean Robin declared. He smiled at his son. "And what an inheritance for a young man!"

When they parted, a week later, they had sworn eternal friendship in the brotherhood of gardeners, and Tradescant was loaded with trays of cuttings, purses of seeds and dozens of roots and saplings.

"And where d'you go now?" Robin demanded at a final farewell dinner.

John knew an instant temptation to say that he was going on to Spain, that he would ride slowly down the country ways and collect a plant from every roadside verge. "Home," he said, in his halting French. "Home and my wife."

Robin clapped him on the back. "And the new garden at Hatfield," he said, as if there was no doubt which was the most important.

* * *

John arrived back at Meopham in December to kiss Elizabeth and make his peace with Baby J, who was angry at being neglected. He had brought Baby J a little wooden soldier, carved by a Frenchman and dressed in the uniform of the king's personal guard. Baby J was talking clearly now and very firm in his opinions. He particularly disapproved of John's return to Elizabeth's bed.

"That's my place," he stated flatly, glaring at his father in the early hours of John's first day at home. John, who had planned to make love to Elizabeth when they woke, was rather taken aback by the unmistakable enmity in his son's little face.

"This is my bed," John said reasonably. "And my wife."

"She's my mother!" Baby J shouted and launched himself at his father.

John caught the little fists and tucked the writhing, angry body under his arm. "Hey day! What's this? I'm home now, Baby J, and this is my place."

Elizabeth smiled at the two of them. "He's been the man of the house for three months, John; you stayed away too long."

John bent his face down to his little son's wriggling body and smacked a kiss on his bare stomach. "He'll learn to love me again," he said. "I shall stay till Twelfth Night."

Elizabeth did not protest, she was learning that the lord's garden came before everything, but she swept out of bed in a way which made her feelings very plain. John let her go, his eyes on his son's bright little face.

"One time I shall take you with me," he promised. "It's not that I'm in your place here—you should be sharing my place with me." He nodded to the window which overlooked the village street but he meant the wider world, beyond the lanes to London, beyond even London. He meant Europe, he meant Africa, he meant the East.

Spring 1611

John stayed for little more than three weeks at Meopham, long enough to get under Elizabeth's feet in the little cottage and to make his peace with his son, before hiring another cart and driver and traveling down the mud-filled, almost impassable roads to Dorset, seeking more trees for sale: apple trees for the orchard, cherry, pear, quince, plum. Trees for the park: oak, rowan, birch, beech.

"Wherever will you get them all from?" Elizabeth wondered, bringing him his well-darned traveling cloak and packing a basket of food under the seat of the wagon.

"I shall buy them from the orchards," John said determinedly. "They sell apples by the dozen, why not trees?"

"And the wild trees for the earl's park?"

"I shall take them," John said recklessly. "From every forest I pass on my way. I shall be going through the New Forest; every sapling I see I shall stop and dig up."

"You will be hanged for certain!" Elizabeth exclaimed. "You will be hauled before the verderers' courts and hanged for damaging the royal chase."

"How else am I to find my lord's trees?" John demanded. "How else am I to do it?"

John traveled around England and brought back his swaying whispering carts filled with the bushy heads of trees. They came to know him on the West Road, and when children saw him coming into a town with his carts rumbling behind him they would run to the well to fetch a bucket to water Mr. Tradescant's trees.

The great house was nearly finished and the gardens were slowly shaping according to the master plan. There had only been one long delay when the workmen had run short of money, and even the great Cecil coffers had run dry. John had feared for his lord then, feared that the cost of the house and the cost of the garden had overstretched him, as everyone had warned that it would. John sensed, but did not know, that there were enemies on every side at court who might bow to and flatter the Secretary of State now, but at the least sign of weakness would pull him down like a pack of hounds upon an old stag. Just as the rumors got out that Cecil had overreached himself and would fail, there was more money delivered to the builders, and more money at the goldsmiths' in the little provincial towns for John to draw on to buy his trees.

"How did you manage it?" John asked Cecil. "Have you sold your soul, my lord?"

Cecil's smile was grim. "All but," he said. "I sold every other property I owned, and borrowed on the rest. But I had to have my house, John. And we had to have our garden."

John first labored on the acres which faced the house, especially the huge knot garden below the terrace where the earl had his private rooms. Each path leading from the house was precisely aligned to the windows of the private rooms so that Cecil, looking out, would always see a vista of straight lines, running outward to the distant horizon. Tradescant, breaking with tradition, planted different edging plants at each junction of the outward path so the color of the hedges melted and grew paler as the eye was drawn farther and farther from the house. At each crossroads was a little statue, an aid to meditation on the fleeting nature of life and the vanity of wishes.

"I might as well have put up a moneylender's sign," Cecil said dourly to John when they walked the new paths, and John grinned.

"You were warned, my lord," he said lovingly. "But you would have your own way."

"And are you telling me I was wrong?" Cecil asked with a dark upward gleam at the taller man.

Tradescant shook his head. "Not I! It was a great venture. And grandly carried out. And still much to do."

"You have given me a great gift," the earl said thoughtfully. They climbed the steps to the stone terrace, Cecil heaving his lame leg, refusing to take help, John beside him, his hands pushed deep into his pockets to prevent him reaching out and holding his master's arm. They gained the top of the terrace and Cecil gave John a quick glance which thanked him for his forbearance.

"Walk with me," he said.

The two men strolled side by side on the new paving stone, and looked down on the patterns of the twisting beds of the knot garden. "You have given me a great gift because every year it will grow more lovely. Most gifts are consumed in the first weeks, like young love. But you have given me a gift which will be here long after we are both gone."

John nodded. The sky above them was soft and gray; only in the west was there a line of rosy cloud where the sun had gone. An owl called in the wood and then they saw its pale shape drift across the new orchard in the distance where the land fell away down to the valley.

The earl smiled. "Sometimes I think the greatest thing that I ever did for England was to set you to work, my John. Nothing in my life gives me more joy."

Tradescant waited. Often these days, the earl was disinclined to talk and would walk in silence with his gardener through the slowly emerging shapes of the garden and park. His work was daily growing more arduous; the power of the favorites around the king was undiminished, the problems of the court profligacy greater than ever. The fashion for masques now dominated at court and every occasion was marked with a catastrophically expensive play: written, composed, designed and produced in one night, and completely forgotten the next. Every court favorite, the women as well as the men, had to have a costume blazing with jewels; every important role had to arrive in a chariot or depart with fireworks.

King James had inherited a fortune with the throne of England. The legendary meanness of the old queen had served the country extraordinarily well. Her father had left her a throne with two sources of revenue: the steady flow of money from the sale of places at court, favors and civic jobs, and the rare bounties voted in taxes by an agreeable Parliament. The balance was a delicate one. Tax the wealth of the industries too sharply and the merchants, traders and bankers would complain. Go cap in hand to Parliament too often and the country squires who sat there would buy control of royal policy. Only by scrimping on every expenditure, by borrowing, by insisting on constant gifts and by downright out-and-out corruption, had the Tudor King Henry and his daughter Elizabeth amassed a fortune for themselves, and a steady reliable prosperity for their kingdoms. The almighty theft of the Roman Catholic church possessions had started the process, but Tudor charm and Tudor guile had continued it.

King James was new to this process but he had Cecil and half a hundred others to advise him. The earl had thought that the new king, who had previously managed hand-to-mouth in cold castles in a poor kingdom, would show all of the family's legendary parsimony and have no experience of their love of show.

But it was a habit quickly learned. James, new-come to one of the richest thrones in Europe, could see no reason why he should not have everything he desired. The money from the royal treasury poured out in fountains over the new favorites, over the new luxurious court, for every beautiful woman, for every pretty man. Not even Cecil's constant struggle with the farming out of taxes, the sale of honors, the exploitation of orphans left in trust to the king, could keep the throne in profit; soon the king would have to call another parliament, and they would speak against him, and against the favorites at court, and the whole question of the king and the people would be thrown open, and who knew where such a debate might lead?

The earl limped forward. His arthritic hip pained him to walk, and it had grown worse in the last few months. John, without offering sympathy, moved a little closer and his master leaned on his shoulder.

"All I have ever done is juggle with the forces which drive us," the earl said. "All I ever have to do is to fend off consequences. He's running through the old queen's fortune as if there were no bottom to the well. And nothing to show for it. No roads, no Navy, no protection for shipping, no new colonies to mention . . . and not even a bit of show for the people."

It was growing darker; the cool early summer twilight hid the bare places of the garden, masked the awkward corners. The earl's favorite pinks, which John had planted in great ornamental urns on the terrace, scented the air as their cloaks brushed by. John bent to pick a spray and handed it to him.

"You brought the new king to his throne, and to his country," John observed. "You've served him well. And he came to his country without trouble. You've kept the country at peace."

The earl nodded. "I don't forget it. But that little chestnut tree of yours, John, that little tree in the pot, may bring more joy to more Englishmen than any of my schemes, in the long run."

"Most men's tastes are not political," John said apologetically. "I prefer the tree, myself."

The earl laughed. "I have something to show you. I think you may be surprised."

He turned and John followed him back toward the house. The wide double door stood open, two serving men at either side. The earl walked past them as if they were invisible; John nodded pleasantly to them.

The earl led John into the shady hall. The wood floor and paneling smelled sweet and new, there was sawdust still in the corners and the linenfold shapes on the paneling were sharp-cut and bright. The wood had not even had its first polish yet; it was still light and shining. Even in the twilight it gleamed as if it were bathed in sunshine.

At the foot of the stairs there was a great newel post, left swathed in a cloth by the woodcarver when he went home for the night. The earl took hold of the sheet and pulled it to one side.

"What d'you see?"

John stepped forward to look. The post was square and grand, a fitting size and solidity for the big hall, the ornaments carved on top with acanthus leaves and swags and ribbons. One face of the square pillar was ornate with half-finished carvings but the other was already complete. It showed a man, in the act of stepping down from the plinth, stepping out of the frame of the carving as if he would take his place in the outside world, as if he would take his work to the farthest corners of the world.

In one hand the figure had a long-handled rake, and in the other a grand fanciful flower springing from a huge pot, which was spilling over with fruit and seeds: a cornucopia of goodness. He was wearing comfortable baggy breeches and a stout overcoat, and on his head, at a rakish joyful angle, was his hat. With an awe-struck gasp John recognized himself, carved in wood on the earl's newel post.

"Good God! Is it me?" John asked in a whisper.

Robert Cecil's hand was gentle on his shoulder. "It's you," he said. "And a very good likeness, I think."

"Why have you put me on your stair post, my lord?" John asked. "Of all the things that you could have had carved?"

The earl smiled. "Of all my great choices: the Three Graces, or Zeus, or Apollo, or something from the Bible or the king himself? Yet I chose to have my gardener carved in the center post of my house."

John looked at the jaunty confidence of the set of the hat and the brandished rake. "I don't know what to say," he said simply. "It's too much for me. You have taken my breath away."

"Fame comes in many guises, Tradescant," Robert Cecil remarked. "But I think people will remember you when they sit beneath their chestnut trees and when your plants bloom in their gardens. And here you are, and here you will be, as long as my house stands, recorded forever, striding out with a plant in one hand, and your rake in the other."

Autumn 1611

Elizabeth and Baby J were at last to move to Hatfield House. Gertrude, suddenly seized with maternal tenderness, came to weep over their departure and to see them off, all their goods loaded into one wagon, and Elizabeth sitting beside John on the driver's seat with Baby J wedged between them.

"Where's the chestnut tree?" John asked.

"That tree!" Gertrude exclaimed, but she lacked her old spite.

"Safe in the back," Elizabeth said. "Beside the kitchen things."

John handed her the reins of the steady horse and went round to the back of the wagon to find the barrel with the tree. It was leaning at an angle against the rail. The movement could have rubbed the bark off the tender trunk. John compressed his lips over hard words. Elizabeth had much work to do: moving house, and a young child, active as a puppy under her feet all day. He should not blame her for being careless with something which had only meant much to her as a token of his love. She never cared for it as he did. It was unfair to expect that she should.

He unloaded a couple of stools and repacked the corner of the wagon so that the tree was fully supported. Then he came round to the driver's seat.

"Your baby safely settled?" Elizabeth asked sharply.

John nodded, not rising to the bait. "It's a precious rarity," he reminded her mildly. "Probably worth more than the whole cart of things put together. We would be fools if we broke it out of carelessness."

Gertrude shot a swift look at Elizabeth as if to bewail the stubbornness of men, then Elizabeth leaned out from the wagon and kissed her mother good-bye.

"Come and see us at Hatfield," Elizabeth said.

Gertrude stepped back as the wagon moved forward. She waved and saw Baby J wave back to her. For a moment she thought she might be able to cry, but though she screwed up her face and thought of the loss of her daughter and her grandson, no tears came.

"Safe journey!" she called, and saw Tradescant settle himself on the wagoner's hard bench seat as if he were ready to travel across half the world.

"Oh, yes," she said under her breath as the wagon drew away. "I see you, John Tradescant, with your heart leaping up at the very word 'journey.' She'd have done better to have married a good Kent farmer and be christened, married, and buried in her father's church. But that would never have done for you because you are Cecil's man through and through and you have all of his ambition—though it shows itself in funny ways with your rarities and your travels—and Meopham would never have been big enough or strange enough or rare enough for you."

A little handkerchief fluttered from the receding cart, and Gertrude whipped out her own and waved back.

"Still," she said philosophically. "He doesn't beat her, and there are a lot worse things a man can love better than his wife than a garden and a lord."

Elizabeth and John, unaware of this brutal and nearly accurate summary of their lives, found their spirits rising as they drew farther and farther away from Meopham.

"It seems odd to me to live anywhere else, but I shall grow accustomed," Elizabeth said. "And a bigger cottage and a better garden—"

"And the parkland all around instead of the lanes for J to play in," John reminded her. "And gardens the like of which no one in England has ever seen. Fountains and rivers!"

"We must take care he doesn't wander off and fall in," Elizabeth said. "He's very restless. I can't think how many times someone has brought him back to me and told me he was halfway to Sussex."

"He can stray all he likes in my lord's gardens," John said with satisfaction. "He'll come to no harm there."

"And we'll eat our dinner in hall or at our home as we wish?" Elizabeth asked.

"As we wish when the lord is away from home. But when he is at the palace he likes his men to dine in the hall. And I like to see him."

"Well enough when you had no one to cook your dinner at home," Elizabeth remarked. "But now I shall be there—"

John put a hand gently on hers. "If he looks down the hall to see me, I must be there," he reminded her. "It's not a question of a dinner cooked by you or a dinner cooked by the cooks. It's not even a question of whose company I would rather keep. It is just that if he looks down the hall for me, I must be there. You must know that by now, Elizabeth. You must know that now that we are going to live on his land, in a cottage owned by him and given to us free. You must know that he comes first."

For a moment he thought she would fly out at him and then there would be a quarrel and a sulk—for they were both terrible sulkers—which could easily last for the whole two days of the journey. But then he saw her recognize the simple truth of it.

"I know," she agreed. "But it is hard for me. The people I come from, my family, are freeholders on their own land. They dine where they please."

"Sometimes only on bread and bacon," John pointed out.

"Even so. It's their own bread and bacon and they fear no one's favor."

John nodded. "And if I had been content to be a farmer or perhaps a gardener on my own account in a small way with a little market garden for bulbs or flowers or fruit, then I should be a man like that too. But I wanted something more, Elizabeth. I wanted the chance to make the greatest garden in England. And he gave me that when I was a young man, so young that most masters would have made me work an apprenticeship under another man for another year or three before they even considered me. He trusted me, he took a risk with me. He gave me Theobalds when I was little more than a lad."

"And don't you see what you've paid for that?" she asked him. "You can't even choose where to eat your dinner. You can't choose where to live. Sometimes I think you can't even choose what to feel in your heart. It's his feelings that matter. Not your own."

"It's the way it is," he stated. "The way of the world."

She shook her head. "Not in Meopham. Not in my family. Not in the country. It's the way of the court where everyone has to have a great man's favor and protection to rise, where every great man has to have his followers to show his importance. But there are men and women all over the country who live according to their own lights and call no man master."

"You think that's a better life?"

"Of course," she said, but she could see that what seemed to her to be a freedom from an onerous duty was to him a loss, an emptiness which he could not have borne.

"I would have been a smaller man without my lord," he said. "And what you think of as freedom is a small price to pay for belonging heart and soul to a great man. It's the price I pay gladly."

"But I pay it too," she said quietly.

For a moment he glanced down at her as if something in her voice had made him feel tender for her, regretful, as if they should have been more to each other. She thought that he would put his arm around her and cuddle her against his side and drive one-handed like a lover and his lass on the way to the fair. "Yes, you pay too," he admitted, keeping both hands on the driving reins. "You knew you were marrying a man who had a duty already promised. I was Cecil's man before we were even betrothed, let alone married. You knew that, Elizabeth."

She nodded and kept her eyes on the unwinding road ahead of them. "I knew that," she agreed a little grimly. "I don't complain."

He left it at that, with her acquiescence, and trusted to the house that his lord had provided for them to persuade her, as he could not, that it was better to be the follower of a great man than a small man on your own account. He saw her face as he drew up outside the cottage and knew that there would be no complaints for a while about the earl.

It was not a cottage he had given them at all—not two cramped rooms on the ground floor and a rickety stair to a hayloft bedroom—but a proper house with a fence all around it and a path of handsome brick chippings leading up to the front door set flush in the middle with two windows, proper glazed windows with panes set diamond-wise in thick lead, on each side of it.

"Oh! oh!" Elizabeth slid down from the hard driving seat, lost for words.

A thick blond thatch sat weightily on the low roof. The beams in the walls were so new that they were still golden against the pale pink of the limewashed plaster.

"New built!" Elizabeth whispered. "New built for us?"

"For us and no other. Step inside," John invited her.

With J at her heels, looking around at everything with eyes as wide as a hunting owl, Elizabeth stepped over the threshold of her new home and found herself inside a stone-flagged hall with a fire already lit in the fireplace to welcome her. To the right was the kitchen, with a big stone sink and a broad fireplace. To the left was a small room she could use as she pleased: a still room, or a drawing room; and immediately before her was a genuine solid flight of stairs with well-made wooden treads and risers which led to two more rooms above. Each one of them was big enough for a full-size bed, never mind the cramped little bed and Baby J's truckle that they had brought with them on the wagon from Meopham.

"And a garden," John said exultantly.

"A garden!" Elizabeth laughed at the predictability of her man, but let him lead her back down the stairs and through the kitchen to the back door.

Cecil had bidden John take what he wanted from the saplings and plants of the palace gardens and make his own little Eden. John had created in the small walled plot a little orchard, a walk of trellised apple and plum trees, a pottager by the back door with herbs for cooking and salad vegetables, a bed of strawberries and a kitchen garden bed of beans and peas and onions and greens.

"It looks so—rooted!" Elizabeth found the word at last. "As if it had been here forever."

A brief gleam of pride crossed John's face. "That is what I have learned this year at least," he said. "I have learned how to make a garden new-made look as if it was there when Eden was planted. The trick of it is to put things too close, and bear the work of moving them before they get overcrowded. Also you have to take a risk of moving things which are really too big to be disturbed. Digging a wide trench around the roots. Those trees now—" He broke off. His wife was smiling at him but she was not listening. "I have found a way of moving trees so they don't wither," he finished. "But it's of little interest except to another gardener."

"It means that you have given me a beautiful garden which I will treasure," she said. She came into his arms and held him close. "And I thank you for it. I see now why the little patch at Meopham was not enough. I never thought of you making a cottage garden like you make grand gardens, my John, but you have given me a little beauty here."

He smiled at her pleasure and bent his head and kissed her. Her lips were still soft and warm and he thought with rising desire that tonight they would bed in a new room and tomorrow wake to look out on the great parkland of Hatfield, and their new life would begin.

"We'll see these trees grow strong," he said. "And we'll plant the chestnut sapling at the bottom of the garden and sit in its shade when we are old."

She nestled a little closer. "And we'll bide at home," she said firmly.

John rested his cheek against her warm cap. "When we're old," he promised, disarmingly.

The very next day the earl himself came down to visit the Tradescants in their new cottage. Elizabeth was flustered and overawed by the grandness of the pony carriage with one footman driving, and another hanging on the back. She came to the gate and curtseyed and stammered her thanks. But John opened the gate and went out to stand at the carriage door as to an intimate friend.

"Are you ill?" he asked Cecil quietly.

Cecil's face was yellow and the lines of pain were deeper than ever. "No worse than usual," he replied.

"Is it your bones?"

"My belly this time," he said. "I am sick as a dog, John. But I can't stop work yet. I have a plan to reform the king's finances despite himself. If I can get him to agree then I can sell the whole scheme to Parliament, and hand over to them the farming of benefits in return for a proper wage for the king."

John blinked. "You want the king to be paid by Parliament? To be its servant?"

Cecil nodded. "Better than this endless haggling, year after year, when they demand that he change his favorites and he demands more money. Anything is better than that. You have to be a king rich in charm to survive holding out an annual begging bowl, and this king is not as the old queen."

"Can you not rest and come back to it later?" John asked urgently.

The heavy-lidded eyes looked at him. "Setting up as apothecary, John?"

"Can you not rest?"

Cecil flinched as he stretched out his hand to his man, and John saw that even that small gesture cost him pain. He took the hand as gently as he would hold Baby J's while he slept. Unconsciously, he put his other hand on top of it and felt how cool were the fingers and how sluggish the pulse.

"Do I look so sick?"

John hesitated.

There was a gleam of a smile on Cecil's face. "Come, John," he said in a half-whisper. "You always prided yourself on telling me the truth; don't turn courtier now."

"You do look very very sick," John said, his voice very low.

"Sick to death?"

John snatched a quick glance at his master's heavy-lidded eyes and saw that he wanted a true answer to his question.

"I have no skills, my lord, but I would think so."

Cecil frowned slightly and John tightened his grip on the thin cold hand.

"I've so much more to do," the Secretary of State said.

"Look to yourself first," John urged him, and then heard himself whisper, "please, my lord. Look to yourself first."

Cecil leaned forward and laid his cheek against John's warm face. "Ah, John," he said softly. "I wish I had some of your strength."

"I wish to God I could give it to you," John whispered.

"Drive with me," the earl commanded. "Drive round with me and tell me what is planted and how it will be, even though neither of us will be here to see it. Tell me how it will be in a hundred years when we will both be dead and gone. Hale or sick, John, this garden will outlive us both."

Tradescant clambered into the carriage and sat beside his master, one arm along the back of the seat as if he would protect him from the jolting movement. Elizabeth, forgotten at the gate of her new house, watched them both go.

"You have made me a velvet setting for my jewel," Cecil said with quiet pleasure as the carriage moved slowly down the avenue of new-planted trees. "We have done well together, John, for a pair of youngsters learning our trades."

May 1612

Cecil was dying in the great curtained bed in the master chamber of his new fine house. Outside his door, the household staff pretended to go about their work in a hushed silence, hoping to hear the muttered colloquy of the doctors. Some wanted to send him to Bath to take the waters—his last chance of health. Some were for leaving him in his bed to rest. Sometimes, when his door opened, the servants could hear the harsh laboring of his breath and see him propped up on the rich embroidered pillows, the brightness of their spring colors a mockery of his yellowing skin.

John Tradescant, weeping like a woman, was deep digging in the vegetable garden, digging without much purpose, in a frenzy of activity as if his energy and effort could put heart in the earth, could put the heart back into his master.

At midday he abruptly left his vegetable bed and marched determinedly through the three courts on the west of the house, up the allée, past the mount where the paths were rimmed with yellow primroses, out into the woodland side of the garden. The ground was a sea of blue as if the whole wood was deep in flood. John kneeled and picked bluebells with steady concentration and did not stop until he had an armful. Then he went to the house, careless of the mud dropping off his boots, up the stairs where his likeness in wood still stepped blithely out of the newel post, up to the master bedroom. A housemaid stopped him at the door to the anteroom. He would not be allowed further in.

"Take these, and show them to him," he said.

She hesitated. Flowers in the house were for strewing on the floor, or for a posy to wear at the belt ot hatband. "What would he want with them?" she demanded. "What would a dying man want with bluebells?"

"He'd like to see them," John urged her. "I know he would. He likes bluebells."

"I'll have to give them to Thomas," she said. "I'm not allowed in, anyway."

"Then give them to Thomas," John pressed her. "What harm can it do? And I know it would please him."

She was stubborn. "I don't see why."

John gestured helplessly. "Because when a man is going into darkness it helps him to know that he leaves some light behind!" he exclaimed. "Because when a man is facing his own winter it is good to know that there will still be springs and summers. Because he is dying . . . and when he sees the bluebells he will know that I am still here, outside, and that I picked him some flowers. He will know that I am still here, just outside, digging in his garden. He will know that I am here, still digging for him."

The look she turned on him was pure incomprehension. "But Mr. Tradescant! Why should that help him?"

John grabbed her in his frustration and pushed her toward the anteroom. "A man would understand," he growled. "Women are too flighty. A man would understand that he will be comforted to know that I am still out there. That even when he is gone, his garden will still be there. That his mulberry tree will flower this year, that his chestnut saplings are growing straight, that the new velvet double anemone is thriving, that his bluebells are blowing under the trees of his woods. Go! And get those bluebells into his hands, or I shall have words to say to you!"

He thrust her with such force that she went at a little run to Thomas, who was standing outside the bedroom door, waiting for the orders from his master that never came.

"Mr. Tradescant wants these taken in to his lordship," she said, thrusting her armful of blossoms at him. Their slim whippy green stems oozed sap like the very juice of life. She wiped her hand on her apron. "He says they're important."

Thomas hesitated at the eccentric request.

"D'you know what he said? He said that women are too flighty to understand," she sniffed resentfully. "Impertinence!"

Thomas's sense of male importance was immediately stimulated. He took the flowers from her, turned at once to open the door and crept inside.

A doctor was at the foot of the bed, another at the window, and an old woman, part nurse, part layer-out, was at the fireside where a small fire of scented pine cones was crackling, pouring heat into the stuffy room.

Thomas came quietly forward. "Beg pardon," he said hoarsely. "But his lordship's gardener insisted he had these."

The doctor turned irritably. "What? What? Oh, nonsense! Nonsense!"

"Nothing but folly and superstition," said the doctor from the window. "And likely to spread noxious fumes."

Thomas stood his ground. "It was Mr. Tradescant, sir. His Grace's favorite. And he insisted, the maid said."

Cecil turned his head a little. The dispute was instantly silenced. Cecil crooked a finger at Thomas.

The doctor waved him forward. "Quick. He wants them. But it won't make a groat of difference."

Awkwardly, Thomas stepped up to the bed. The aquiline face of the most powerful man in England was etched in sandstone and grooved by pain. He turned his dark eyes sightlessly toward the manservant. Thomas thrust the bluebells into the slack hands. They spilled onto the rich coverlet of the bed, blotting out the scarlet embroidery and the gold thread with blue, blue, nothing but sky blue.

"From John Tradescant," Thomas said.

The light sweet scent of the bluebells poured like fresh water into the room, drowning the smell of fear and sickness. Their color shone like a blue flame in the dark chamber. The great lord looked down on the scattered flowers and inhaled their cold fresh perfume. They seemed to come from a world a hundred miles away from the overheated bedchamber, a clean spring world outside. He turned his head to the little window and his crumpled face stretched into a small smile. Though the casement was opened only the smallest crack, he could hear the thud of a spade into the flower bed beneath his window, loud as a faithful heartbeat, as John Tradescant and his master set about their different tasks: digging and dying.

October 1612

When they buried the earl, after dragging him to Bath for the cure and then back home again, there was still a place for John Tradescant at Hatfield House. But the heart had gone out of the garden for John. He kept looking around for Cecil, wanting to show him one of the grand new sights of the garden, expected to see him picking mulberries in summer and limping down the dark shade of the newly growing pleached allée. He kept wanting to consult him, he kept wanting to exchange that swift conspiratorial smile of triumph: that a plant had grown, that a rarity had taken root, that seeds had struck.

When he took a mug of small ale and a loaf of bread to his potting shed he kept expecting to see his lord there before him, lounging against the bench, be-ringed fingers dabbling in the soft sifted earth, taking a rest from letter writing, from plotting, from the sleight of hand of foreign policy, seeking John to share a bit of dinner together, a companion who needed no lies, no courting, seated on a barrel of bulbs to watch John transplanting seedlings.

"I am sorry, my lord," John said to the new earl, Cecil's son, finding his old master's title sluggish on his lips. "I cannot settle here without your father. I was in his service too long to make a change."

"You will miss the garden, I expect," the new Lord Cecil remarked. But he did not know, as his father had known, the intense joy of making a garden where before there had been nothing but meadow.

"I will," John said. Robert Cecil's favorite flowers, the pinks, were in full bloom. The chestnut saplings which they had bought as glossy nuts a full five years ago were leggy and strong and putting out green palmate leaves like beggars' hands. The cherry-tree walk was a maze of ordered blossom and the tulips were ablaze in the new flower beds.

"I can't garden here without him," he said simply to Elizabeth that night.

"Why not?" she asked. "It's the same garden."

"It's not." He shook his head. "It was his garden. I chose things that would delight his eyes. I thought of his tastes when I planned the walks. When I had something new and rare I considered where it would flourish, but also where would he be certain to see it? Every time I planted a seedling I had two thoughts—the angle of the sun shining on it, and my lord's gaze."

She frowned at the sound of blasphemy. "He was only a man."

"I know, and I loved him as a man. I loved him because he was a man and more mortal and frail than many others. He would lean on me when his back pained him—" Tradescant broke off. "I *liked* him leaning on me," he said, conscious that he could not explain the mixture of elation and pity that he felt all at once when the greatest man in England after the king would confide his pain and take help.

Elizabeth pressed her lips together on hasty words and kept her jealousy to herself. She put her hand on her husband's shoulder and reminded herself that the lord he had loved was dead and buried and a good wife should show some sympathy. "You sound as if you have lost a brother, not a lord."

He nodded. "A lord is like a brother, like a father, even like a wife. I think of his needs all the time, I guard his interests. And I cannot be happy here without him."

Elizabeth did not want to understand. "But you have me, and Baby J."

John gave her a sad little smile. "And I will never love another woman or another child more than I love the two of you . . . but a man's love for his lord is another thing. It comes from the head as well as the heart. Loving a woman keeps you at home; it is a private pleasure. Loving a great lord takes you into the wider world; it is a matter of pride."

"You make it sound as if we are not enough," she said resentfully.

He shook his head, despairing of ever making her understand. "No, no, Elizabeth. It doesn't matter. You are enough."

She was not convinced. "Will you seek another lord? Another master?"

The expression that passed swiftly across his face was deeper than mourning; it was desolation. "I will never see his like again."

That silenced her for a moment, as she saw the depth of his loss.

"But what about us?" she asked. "I don't want to lose this house, John, and J is happy here. We have put down roots here just as the plants in the garden have done. You said you would plant the chestnut here this spring and that we would sit under its branches when we are an old married couple."

He nodded. "I know. I'm forsworn. That's what I promised you. But I can't bear it here without him, Elizabeth. I have tried and I cannot. Can you release me from my promise that we should stay here, and let us make another home? Back in Kent?"

"Kent? What d'you mean? Where?"

"Lord Wootton wants a gardener at Canterbury and asked me if I would go. He has the secret of growing melons which I should be glad to learn; his gardener has always teased me that only Lord Wootton in all of England can grow melons."

Elizabeth tutted with irritation. "Forget the melons for a moment if you please. What about a house? What about your wages?"

"He'll pay me well," John said. "Sixty pounds where my lord paid me fifty. And we will have a house, the head gardener's house. J can go to the King's School in Canterbury. That'll be a fine thing for him."

"Canterbury," Elizabeth said thoughtfully. "I've never lived in a market town. There'd be much society."

"We could start there at once. He asked me on the death of my lord and I said I would tell him within the quarter."

"And will you not love Lord Wootton as you loved the earl?" Elizabeth asked, thinking it would be an advantage.

John shook his head. "There will never be another lord for me like that one."

"Let's go, then," she said with her typical sudden decisiveness. "And we can plant the chestnut sapling in Canterbury instead of Hatfield."

November 1612

John was working in Lord Wootton's garden, hands among cold clods of earth, when he heard the bell tolling. On and on it went, a funeral bell. Then he heard the rumble of cannon fire. He stood up, brushed the mud on his breeches, and reached for his coat where it was hooked over his spade.

"Something's happened," he said shortly to the garden lad who was working beside him.

"Shall I run into town and bring you the news?" the boy asked eagerly.

"No," John said firmly. "You shall stay and work here while I run into town and find out the news. And if you are not here when I get back it will be the worst for you."

"Yes, Mr. Tradescant," the boy said sulkily.

The bell was ever more insistent.

"What does it mean?"

"I'll find out," John said and strode out of the garden toward the cathedral.

People were gathered in gossiping circles all the way down the road but John went on until he reached the cathedral steps and saw a face he recognized—the headmaster of the school.

"Doctor Phillips," he exclaimed. "What are they ringing for?"

The man turned at the sound of his name and John saw, with a shock, that the man's face was wet with tears.

"Good God! What is it? It's not an invasion? Not Spain?"

"It's Prince Henry," the man said simply. "Our blessed prince. We have lost him."

For a moment John could not take in the words. "Prince Henry?"

"Dead."

John shook his head. "But he's so strong, he's always so well—"

"Dead of fever."

John's hand went to his forehead to cross himself, in the old superstitious forbidden sign. He caught his hand back and said instead, "Poor boy, God save us, poor boy."

"I forgot, you would have seen him often."

"Not often," John said, his habitual caution asserting itself.

"He was a blessed prince, was he not? Handsome and learned and godly?"

John thought of Prince Henry's handsome tyrannical disposition, of his casual cruelty to his dark little brother, of his easy love of his sister Elizabeth, of his royal confidence, some would say arrogance. "He was a boy born to rule," John said cleverly.

"God save Prince Charles," Doctor Phillips said stoutly.

John realized that the little eleven-year-old lame boy who ran after his brother and could never get nor keep his father's attention would now be the next king—if he lived.

"God save him indeed," he repeated.

"And if we lose him," Doctor Phillips said in an undertone, "then it's another woman on the throne, the Princess Elizabeth, and God knows what danger that would bring us now."

"God save him," John repeated. "God save Prince Charles."

"And what is he like?" Doctor Phillips asked. "Prince Charles? What sort of a king will he make?"

John thought of the tongue-tied boy who had to be taught to walk straight, who struggled so hard to keep up with the older two, who knew himself never to be beloved like them, never to be handsome like them. He wondered how a child who knew himself to be second best and a poor second at that would be when he was a man and was first in the land. Would he take the people's love and let it warm him, fill the emptiness in that ugly little boy's heart? Or would he be forever mistrustful, forever doubting, always wanting to seem braver, stronger, more handsome than he was?

"He'll be a fine king," he said, thinking that his master would not be there to teach this king, and how the boy would learn the Tudor guile and the Tudor charm with only his father to advise him and the court filled with men picked for their looks and their bawdiness and not for their skills. "God will guide him," Tradescant said hopefully, thinking that no one else would.

September 1616

The new cottage at Canterbury was little bigger than their first home at Meopham but Elizabeth did not complain, as the front door opened to a proper city street and the finishing of the house was elegant. They cooked and ate and lived in the large ground-floor room and Elizabeth and John slept in a curtained four-poster bed in the room next door. J, now a boy of eight years old, went up the shallow stairs to a pallet bed in the attic. During the day John went and gardened for Lord Wootton, and J went to Dame School where, for a penny a week, he was taught to read and write and to figure sums. They both came home for their dinner at four o'clock on the darkening autumn afternoons, John with a spade over his shoulder, J with his schoolbook clutched under his arm.

Elizabeth, slicing parsley for the soup one afternoon, heard three, not two, sets of boots stamping off mud in the porch of the little cottage and put her sacking apron off in the expectation of company. She opened the front door to John, to her son, and to a young man, brown-faced and smiling, with the unmistakable swagger and roll of a seafaring man.

"Captain Argall," Elizabeth said without pleasure.

"Mrs. Tradescant!" he exclaimed and swept into the house, kissing her heartily on one cheek and then the other. "The most beautiful rose in all of John's gardens! How are you?"

"Very well," Elizabeth said, disengaging herself and going back to the kitchen table.

"I have brought you a handsome ham," Sam Argall said, looking at the stewpot and sliced vegetables without much enthusiasm. J, his face a picture of moonstruck admiration, produced the leg of ham from behind his back and dumped it on the table. "And a taste of paradise too," Sam Argall went on, offering a flask of rum. "From the Sugar Islands, Mrs. Tradescant. A taste of sweetness and strength that will bring a taste of the tropics even here, to chilly Canterbury."

"I find the weather very mild for the time of the year," Elizabeth said stoutly. "Do sit down, Captain Argall. J will fetch you a glass of small ale if you would like one. We do not serve strong liquors in this house."

J rushed to do his mother's bidding while John and Sam sat at the table and watched Elizabeth slice the last pieces of parsley and toss them into the pot hanging over the fire.

There was a silence while they drank. Elizabeth busied herself with setting out the wooden bowls and a knife at each place, and a loaf of bread in the center of the table.

"Sam is to be master of a great venture," John began at last.

Elizabeth stirred the pot and prodded one of the floating parsnips to see if it was cooked.

"A great venture, and he has offered me a place," John said.

Elizabeth poured the broth into the three bowls, for the captain, for her husband, for her son, and stood behind them to wait on them. John saw that she would not sit and eat with them as she always did when it was just him and J at the dinner table. He read, correctly, her absolute opposition to Sam Argall and all the adventure and risk that he stood for, concealed behind chilly courtesy.

"Virginia!" Sam Argall exclaimed, blowing on his bowl. "Mrs. Tradescant, I have been entrusted with a great task. I am appointed Deputy Governor of Virginia and Admiral of the Virginia seas."

"Will you say grace, husband?" Elizabeth asked repressively.

John bowed his head over the bread and Sam, remembering Elizabeth's strictness in matters of religion, quickly closed his eyes. When he had finished John picked up his spoon and nodded to Sam.

"Amen," Sam said briskly. "I have come to ask John here to go venturing with me, Mrs. Tradescant. You shall be landowners, madam, you shall be squires. For every place you take on the ship with me you shall have a hundred acres of your own land. For the three of you that will be three hundred acres! Think of that! You, the mistress of three hundred acres of land!"

Elizabeth's face was as unmoved as if she were thinking of three yards. "This is three hundred acres of good farmland?"

"It's prime land," Argall said.

"Cleared and ploughed?"

There was a brief silence. "Mrs. Tradescant, I am offering you virgin land, a virgin land rich with woodland. Your land is standing with tall trees, wonderful rare bushes, fruiting vines. First you cut your own timber and then you build yourself a handsome house. A mansion, if you like. Built of your own timber!"

"A mansion from green wood?" Elizabeth asked. "Built by a man in his forties, a woman, and an eight-year-old boy? I should like to see it!"

He pushed his bowl away and cut a slice of the ham. Elizabeth, the very model of wifely obedience, poured the jug of small ale and stepped back, folding her hands on the front of her apron, her eyes cast down.

"What would we grow?" J asked.

Captain Argall smiled down at the bright face of the boy. "Anything you wish. The land is so rich, you could grow anything. But who knows? You might find gold and never trouble yourselves to plant anything ever again!"

"Gold?"

"I thought the first shipment of rocks was nothing more than fool's gold?" Elizabeth asked. "They tipped it out below the Tower and picked it over and found nothing but quartz. And there it stood for many a long day, a little monument to folly and greed."

"No gold yet. Not yet, Mrs. T," Captain Argall said. "But who can say what there might be deeper in the mountains? No one has gone farther than the shoreline and up the rivers a little way. What could be there? Gold? Diamonds? Rubies? And what need have we of these anyway while we can grow tobacco?"

"Why d'you dislike the idea so much, Elizabeth?" John asked her directly.

She looked from him to J's excited face and Captain Argall's determined good humor. "Because I have heard travelers' tales before, but I have heard nothing good of this plantation," she said. "There's Mistress Woods at Meopham who lost two brothers to Virginia in the starving time when half the settlement died of hunger. She told me that they were digging over the graveyards looking for meat, reduced to worse than savagery. There's Peter John who paid for his own passage home and kissed the ground at London docks, he was so glad to be alive. He said the forest was filled with Indians who could be kind or wicked as the mood took them, and only they knew whether they were your enemy or friend. There's your own friend, Captain John Smith, who swore that he would live the rest of his days there, and yet he was brought home a cripple—"

"John Smith would never say a word against Virginia!" Argall interrupted. "And he was hurt in an accident which could have happened anywhere. He could have been boating on the Thames."

"He was hurt in an accident but only after he had fought against Indians and been captured by them and been so close to death by execution that he near died of fear," Elizabeth maintained stoutly.

"The Indians are at peace now," Argall said. "And I have played my part in that. Princess Pocahontas is Mrs. Rebecca Rolfe now and all the Indians are coming into Christian schools and living in Christian homes. You're speaking of old fears. It was hard in the early years but it is all at peace now. Pocahontas is married to John Rolfe and other Indians and white men will marry. In a few years all the wars will be forgotten." He glanced down at J's attentive face, drinking in the stories. "You will have an Indian playmate to show you the paths through the woods," he promised. "Perhaps an Indian maid to be your sweetheart."

The boy blushed scarlet. "How did Princess Pocahontas come to marry Mr. Rolfe?" he asked.

Sam Argall laughed. "You know the story as well as me!" he exclaimed. "I captured her and held her hostage, and all the while she was weaving her spell and capturing John. So go to bed and dream of it, young J. Your mother and father and I will talk more of it later."

"I have to sleep too," John said. He and J lifted the board from the trestle legs of the table and stacked it to one side of the little room.

"I hope you will sleep well here?" Elizabeth asked, laying a straw mattress and an armful of bedding in the space.

"Like a babe in a cradle," Captain Argall assured her. He kissed her hand in his flirtatious way and ignored her lack of response. "Good night."

Elizabeth watched J go up the stairs to his little bed in the attic and then drew the curtains of the four-poster around her and John.

"I'd have thought you would have leaped at the chance of a fresh start in the new world," John remarked as he got into bed and pulled the covers up to his chin. "You who always want us to be freeholders. We would be freeholders in Virginia of land we could only dream of here. Three hundred acres!"

Elizabeth, pulling her nightgown over her head and only then dropping her skirt and shift, did not answer. John was too wise to demand a reply. He watched her kneel at the foot of the bed to say her prayers and closed his own eyes and muttered his thanks for blessings. Only when Elizabeth was in bed, tying the ties of her nightcap under her chin, did she say, suddenly, "And who is the governor of this new land?"

John was taken aback. "Sir George," he said. "Newly appointed. Sir George Yeardley."

"A courtier. Exactly," she said and blew out her candle with an emphatic puff. They lay for a moment in silence in the darkness, and then she spoke: "It's not a new land at all. It's the same land but in a different place. I won't go, John. It's just another form of service. We risk everything, we gamble our savings, our livelihood, and even our lives. We put ourselves in grave danger in a country—one of the few in the whole world where you could not earn a living doing your own trade; no one will want a gardener there, it's farmers they need—we put our son into a forest filled with unknown dangers, and we try to make a living from a land that no one has farmed before. And who makes the profits? The governor. The Virginia Company. And the king."

"It's their land," John said mildly. "Who else should make the profits?"

"If it's their land then they can take the risks," Elizabeth declared bluntly. "Not I."

Elizabeth's determined opposition to the Virginia venture could not prevent John investing money. While she watched, with her mouth in a hard ungenerous line, he counted over twenty-five gold sovereigns for two shares. Captain Argall promised that two men—poor men who could not find their own passage money—would be sent on John's account, and that the land granted to them on arrival in Virginia would be held in part for John.

"You'll be a squire of Virginia yet," Argall said to him, stowing the purse of gold beneath his coat with a swift glance at Elizabeth's stony face. "I shall pick you out a good piece of land, west of Jamestown, inland, upriver. I shall call it Argall Town."

He broke off as Elizabeth snorted quietly at his presumption.

"I beg your pardon?"

"Excuse me," Elizabeth said swiftly. "I sneezed."

"I shall call it Argall Town," Captain Argall repeated. "And there will always be a welcome there for you, John." He glanced down at J's adoring uplifted face. "And for you, J," he said. "Never forget that you are a landowner in the new world, in virgin earth. When you are weary of this old country you have your stake in the new. When you want to be away from here, there will be your headright in virgin land."

J nodded. "I won't forget, sir."

"And I shall take you to meet Princess Pocahontas," Argall promised. "She is visiting in England and she has a kindness for me. I shall introduce you to her."

J's eyes grew rounder and his mouth dropped into a perfect circle of astonishment.

"She would not want to be troubled with us," Elizabeth said quickly.

"Why not?" Captain Argall asked. "She would be delighted to make your acquaintance. Come up to London next week and I will introduce you. It is a promise." He turned to J. "I promise you, you shall meet her."

"Time for him to go to school," Elizabeth interrupted firmly. "I am surprised, husband, that you linger so long."

"I'll walk with you," Argall said, taking the hint. "And thank you for your hospitality, Mrs T. It's always a pleasure to be entertained by such a lady."

Elizabeth nodded, still unsmiling. "I wish you well in your ventures," she said. "I hope that you make a profit, especially as it is our money you are venturing."

Argall laughed without embarrassment. "Nothing ventured, nothing gained," he reminded her and took her hand in the way she disliked, and kissed it. Then he clapped John on the shoulder and the two men left the house with J bobbing behind, like an agitated duckling in the wake of two grand swans.

Argall was as good as his word and John took his son to London to see the Indian princess, traveling up on a wagon taking fruit to London market, staying overnight, and coming down the next day on the empty wagon.

Elizabeth tried not to encourage J's excitement, but she could not hide her own interest. "Was she black?" she asked.

"Not at all!" J exclaimed. "Just brown, a beautiful lady, and she had a little baby on her knee. But she didn't wear bear skins or anything, just ordinary clothes."

"J was bitterly disappointed," John said with a smile to his wife. "He expected something very savage and strange. All she is, is a pretty young woman with a little son. She calls herself Rebecca now and is baptized and married. You would pass her in the street and think nothing more but that she was a fine tall woman, a little tanned."

"She said that there are boys and girls of my age who live in the forest and hunt deer," J said. "And that they can fire a bow and spear a fish from four years old! And that they can make their own pots and sew their own clothes from deer hide, and—"

"She was making it up to amuse you," Elizabeth said firmly.

"She was not!"

"She truly wasn't," John said gently. "I believed every word she said and I should so like to go, Elizabeth. Not to settle there, but just to take a look at our land and see what the prospects are. Not as planters to be there forever, but just to take a little run over there and see what the land is like. It sounds very fine—"

"A little run?" Elizabeth demanded. "You speak of the ocean as if it were the cart track to your orchards. Lord Wootton could not spare you from his garden. I could not spare you now we are settled here. It is six weeks at sea on a huge sea. Why can you not stay in the same place, John? Why can you not be at peace?"

He had no reply for that, and she knew he would have no reply.

"I am sorry," he said at last. "I just long to see all there may be for me to see. And a new land would have new plants, don't you think? Things that I might never have seen before. But you are right. I have my garden here, and Lord Wootton's garden, and the house, and you and J. It is enough for me."

Summer 1618

Elizabeth had prevented John from uprooting the whole family and setting off for Virginia, but when he had an invitation to go venturing to Russia—of all places—and it came with the blessing of his master and a recommendation that he should go, there was little she could do to stop him. It was the king's business at the top of it, so no man in the country could refuse. The king wanted a new trade route to China and thought that Sir Dudley Digges might find one by making an agreement with the Russians. A loan of English gold coaxed from the coffers of the Muscovy and East India Companies was supposed to help.

Sir Dudley was a firm friend of Lord Wootton who wanted new plants for his garden. Sir Dudley said he needed a useful man and a seasoned traveler, not a gentleman who would be too proud to work, and not some dolt of a workingman who would be of no use in an emergency. Lord Wootton said he could have Tradescant, and Tradescant was as ready to leave as a bagged hare when the hounds are giving tongue.

All she could do was to help him pack his traveling bag, see that his traveling cloak was free of moth holes and tears and go down to the dockside at Gravesend with J—now a tall boy of ten years, and a King's Scholar at Canterbury—at her side to wave farewell.

"And beware of the cold!" Elizabeth cautioned again.

"It may be Russia, but it is midsummer," John replied. "Do you keep yourselves well, and J, mind your studies and care for your mother."

The dockers scurried about, pushing past Elizabeth and her son. With a moment's regret John saw that there were tears in her eyes. "I shall be back within three months," he called over the widening gulf of water. "Perhaps earlier. Elizabeth! *Please* don't fret!"

"Take care!" she called again but he could hardly hear her as the rowing barges took hold of the lines and the sailors cursed as they caught the ropes flung from the shore. Elizabeth and her son watched the boat move slowly downriver.

"I still don't understand why he has to go," J said, with the discontent of the schoolboy.

Elizabeth looked down at him. "Because he does his duty," she said, with her natural loyalty to her husband. "Lord Wootton ordered him to go. It is unknown country; your father might find all sorts of treasures."

"I think he just loves to travel," J said resentfully. "And he doesn't care that he leaves me behind."

Elizabeth put her arm around her son's unyielding shoulders. "When you are older you shall travel too. He will take you with him. Perhaps you will grow to be a great man like your father and be sent by lords on travels overseas."

Baby J—her baby no longer—disengaged himself from her arm. "I shall go on my own account," he said stiffly. "I shall not wait for someone to send me."

The ship was in midriver now; the sails which had been slack when sheltered in the dock flapped like sheets on washing day. Elizabeth gripped her son's arm.

"He is old to go venturing," she said anxiously. "So far, and into such regions. What if he is taken ill? What if they get lost?"

"Not he," J said with scorn. "But when I travel I shall go to the Americas. A boy at school has an uncle there and he has killed hundreds of savages and is planting a crop of tobacco. He says that a man who wants land can just cut it from the forests. And we have our land there. Father is going in the wrong direction; he should be going to our lands."

Elizabeth's eyes were still on the ship, which was picking up speed and moving smoothly downriver. "It's never been owning land for him," she said. "Never building a house or putting up a fence. It has always been discovering new things and making them grow. It has always been serving his lord."

J pulled at her arm. "Can we have some dinner before I have to go back?"

Elizabeth patted his hand absently. "When he's gone," she said. "I want to see the ship out of port."

J pulled away and went to the waterside. The river was sucking gently at the green stones. In the middle of the water, unseen by the boy, a beggar's corpse rolled and turned over. The harvest had failed again and there was starvation in the streets of London.

In a moment Elizabeth joined him. Her eyelids were red but her smile was cheerful.

"There!" she said. "And now your father gave me half a crown to buy you an enormous dinner before we take the wagon home."

John watched from the deck of the ship as his wife and son grew smaller and smaller, and then he could no longer pick them out at all. The sense of loss he felt as the land fell away was mingled with a leaping sense of freedom and excitement as the ship moved easily and faster and the waves grew greater. The voyage was to take them northward, hugging the coast of England, and then eastward, across the North Sea to the high ice-bound coast of Norway, and then onward to Russia.

Tradescant was as much on deck as any of the ship's watch, and it was he who first spotted a great fleet of Dutch fishing ships taking cod and summer herring just south of Newcastle.

They weighed anchor at Newcastle and Tradescant went ashore to buy provisions for the journey. "Take my purse," Sir Dudley offered. "And see if you can get some meat and some fish, John. My belly is as empty as a Jew's charity box. I've been sick every day since we left London."

John nodded and went ashore and marketed as carefully as Elizabeth might. He bought fresh salmon and fresh and salted meats, and by noising Sir Dudley's name and mission much around Newcastle he was able to lead the Lord Mayor himself on a visit to the ship. And the Lord Mayor brought a barrel of salted salmon as a timely present for his lordship. When the ship was provisioned again they set out to cross the North Sea but the wind veered to the northwest and started to rise before they were more than a day out of port, skimming the white tops off the gray waves which grew steeper and more frequent.

Sir Dudley Digges was sick as a dog from the moment the wind veered, and many of his companions stayed below too, groaning and vomiting and calling on the captain to return to shore before they died of seasickness. John, rocking easily to the movement of the boat, stood in the prow and watched the waves come rolling from the horizon and the ship rise up and then fall down, rise up and fall down, again and again. One night, when Sir Dudley's own manservant was ill, John sat at his bedside, and held his head as he vomited helplessly into the bowl.

"There," said John gently.

"Good God," Sir Dudley groaned. "I feel sick unto death. I have never felt worse in all my life."

"You'll survive," John said with rough kindliness. "It never lasts longer than a few days."

"Hold me," Sir Dudley commanded. "I could weep like a girl for misery."

Gently John raised the nobleman off the narrow bunk and let his head rest on John's shoulder. Sir Dudley turned his face to John's neck and drew in his warmth and strength. John tightened his grip and felt the racked body in his arms relax and slide into sleep. For an hour and more he knelt beside the bunk holding the man in his arms, trying to cushion him from the ceaseless rolling and crashing of the ship. Only when Sir Dudley was deeply, fast asleep, did John draw his numbed arm away and lay the man back down on his bed. For a moment he hesitated, looking down into that pale face, then he bent low and kissed him gently on the forehead, as if he were kissing Baby J and blessing his sleep, and then he went out.

As they drew farther north the wind wheeled around and became more steady but Sir Dudley could keep down no food. The little ship was halfway between Scotland and Norway when the captain came to Sir Dudley, who was wrapped in a thick cloak and seated on the deck for the air.

"We can go back or forward as you wish," the captain said. "I don't want your death on my conscience, my lord. You're no seafarer. Perhaps we'd best head for home."

Sir Dudley glanced at Tradescant, one arm slung casually around the bowsprit, looking out to sea.

"What d'you think, John?" he asked. His voice was still faint.

Tradescant glanced back and then drew closer.

"Shall we go back or press on?"

John hesitated. "You can hardly be sicker than you were," he said.

"That's what I fear!" the captain interrupted.

John smiled. "You must be seasoned now, my lord. And the weather is fair. I say we should press on."

"Tradescant says press on," Sir Dudley remarked to the captain.

"But what d'you say, my lord?" the captain asked. "It was you who was begging me to turn back at the height of the storm."

Sir Dudley laughed, a thin thread of sound. "Don't remind me! I say press on, too. Tradescant is right. We have our sea legs now, we might as well go forward as back."

The captain shook his head but went back to the wheel and held the ship's course.

Their luck was in. The weather turned surprisingly fair, the men became accustomed to the motion of the ship and even Sir Dudley came out of his cabin and strode about the deck, his pace rocking. They had been nearly three weeks at sea and slowly, the skies around them changed. It was like entering another world, where the laws of day and night had been destroyed. John could read a page of writing at midnight, and the sun never sank down but only rested on the horizon in a perpetual sunset which never led to dusk. A school of grampus whales came alongside and a flock of tiny birds rested in the rigging, exhausted by their long flight over the icy waters. John walked up and down the length of the ship all day and most of the bright night, feeling oddly unemployed with hours of daylight and nothing to grow.

Then a thick fog came rolling over the sea, and the daylight counted for nothing. The sun disappeared behind it and there was neither night nor day but a perpetual pale grayness. Sir Dudley took to his chamber again and summoned one man after another to play at dice with him. John found himself curiously lost in the half-light. He could sleep or wake as he wished, but he never knew when he woke whether it was day or night.

Despite Tradescant's watching, it was a sailor who first called "land ahoy!," spotting through the rolling fog the dark outline of the coast of the North Cape of Lapland.

Sir Dudley came up on deck, huddled in his thick cape. "What can you see, John?"

John pointed to the dark mass of land which was growing whiter as they grew closer. "More like a snowdrift than land," he said. "Bitterly cold."

The two Englishmen stood side by side as their ship drew closer to the strange land. A man-of-war detached itself from the shadow of some cliffs and sailed toward them.

"Trouble?" Sir Dudley asked quietly.

"I'll ask the captain," John said. "You go below, my lord. I'll bring you news the moment I have it. Get your pistols primed, just in case."

Sir Dudley nodded and went back to his cabin as John made his way the few steps to the captain's cabin and knocked on the door.

"What is it?"

"A man-of-war, coming this way, flying the Denmark flag."

The captain nodded, pulled on his cape, and came out of his tiny cabin. "They'll only want passes," he said. "Sir Dudley's name is permission enough for them."

He went briskly to the side of the boat, cupped his hands around his mouth and bellowed. "Ahoy there! This is Captain Gilbert, an English sea captain on a voyage of embassy, carrying Sir Dudley Digges and the Russian ambassador. What do you want with us?"

There was a silence. "Perhaps they don't speak English?" John suggested.

"Then they damned well should do so," Gilbert snapped. "Before trying to delay honest Englishmen going about their business."

"Ahoy, Captain Gilbert," the reply came slowly, muffled by the fog. "We require your passes and permits for sailing in our waters."

"Ahoy," Gilbert shouted irritably. "Our passes and permits are packed away for the voyage and besides, we need none. On board is Sir Dudley Digges and traveling with him is the Russian ambassador, homeward bound. You won't want to trouble the noblemen, I suppose?"

There was a longer silence as the Danish captain decided whether or not the troubling of the gentlemen was worth the possible embarrassment, and then decided it was not.

"You can pass freely," he bellowed back.

"Thank you for nothing," Gilbert muttered. "I thank you," he shouted. "Do you have any provision we can buy?"

"I'll send a boat over," came the reply, half-muffled by the fog.

Tradescant stepped swiftly down the companionway and tapped on the door to Sir Dudley's cabin.

"It's me, all's well," he said quickly.

"Shall I come out?"

"If you wish," John said and went back to the rail and watched with Captain Gilbert as a rowing boat, like a Dutch scuts, came out of the mist.

"Anything worth having?" Sir Dudley asked, from behind Tradescant.

The men waited. The little boat came alongside and threw up a rope. "What've you got?" Captain Gilbert shouted.

The two men on board simply shook their heads. They understood no English but they held up a basket of salted salmon. Sir Dudley groaned, "Not salmon again!," but he held up two silver shillings for them to see.

They shook their heads and held up a spread hand.

"They mean five," Tradescant remarked.

"They can add then, even if they can't speak a civilized language," the captain noted.

Sir Dudley reached into his purse and held out four silver shillings.

The men spoke briefly one to another and then nodded. Sir Dudley tossed the coins down into the boat and Tradescant caught the rope the sailors threw to him. He hauled in the basket of salmon and presented it to Sir Dudley.

"Oh, wonderful," Sir Dudley said ungratefully. "I know, let's have it with dry biscuit for a change."

Tradescant grinned.

The rest of the voyage they hugged the coastline and watched the landscape change from the steady unyielding white of snow to a russet dry brown, and then slowly to a green.

"Almost like England in a hard winter," Tradescant remarked to Captain Gilbert.

"Nothing like," Gilbert said crossly. "Because half the year it's under snow and half the year it's under fog."

Tradescant nodded and retreated to his vantage point at the bowsprit. Now there was more and more for him to see as the coastline unrolled before the rocking prow. On land John could see the people of the country, who startled him at first with their appearance of having no necks, but heads which grew directly from their shoulders.

"It can't be," he said stoutly to himself, and shaded his eyes from the sun to see better. As the people ran down to the beach, shouting and waving to the passing ship, and the ship drew a little closer to shore to avoid a midriver sandbank, John could see that they were wearing thick cloaks of skins over their heads and shoulders, giving them the illusion of a hooded misshapen head.

"God be praised," John said devoutly. "For a moment I thought we were among strange countries indeed, and that all the travelers' tales I had heard were coming true."

The people on the shore held up their bows and arrows and spread a deerskin for John to see. John waved back; the ship was too far out to make any bargaining a possibility, though he would dearly have loved to examine the bows and arrows.

The ship anchored at sunset, Captain Gilbert declaring that he was more afraid of sandbars in an unknown river than all the sailing he ever did across the North Sea.

"Can I have the boat take me on shore?" Tradescant asked.

The captain scowled. "Mr. Tradescant, surely you can see all you need from here?"

John smiled engagingly at him. "I need to gather plants and rarities for my Lord Wootton," he said. "I'll be back before dusk."

"Don't come to me with an arrow up your arse," the captain said coarsely.

John bowed and slipped away before he could change his mind.

A young sailor rowed him to the shore. "Can I wait by the boat?" he asked, his eyes round in his pale face. "They say there are terrible people on this shore. They call them the Sammoyets."

"Don't go without me," John said. "The captain is far more of a terror than the Sammoyets, I promise you. And he will kill you for sure if you maroon me here."

The lad managed a weak smile. "I'll wait," he promised. "Don't be too long."

John slung a satchel over his shoulder and took a little trowel. In the pockets of his breeches he carried a sharp knife for taking cuttings. He had decided against carrying a musket. He did not want the trouble of keeping the fuse alight, and he thought he was as likely to shoot his own foot off in a moment of abstraction as confront an enemy.

"You won't be too long, will you?" the lad asked again.

John patted his shoulder. "As soon as I have found something worth bringing home I will come straight back," he promised. "Ten minutes at the most."

He walked up from the shelving beach and at once plunged into the deep forest. Huge trees, a new fir tree that he had never seen before, interlaced their boughs above his head and made a twilight world which was shadowy green and sharply cold. Underfoot there were thick cushions, as big as bolsters, of fresh damp moss. John knelt before them, like a knight before the Holy Grail, and patted them with loving hands before he could bring himself to dig in his trowel and take a clump to stuff in his satchel.

There were shrubs he had never seen before, many in flower, white star-shaped flowers, and some tinged with pink. He walked on and came to a bush of whorts, with an unusual red flower. John brought out his little knife and took cuttings, wrapped them in more of the damp moss and laid them carefully in his satchel. A few steps more and he was in a clearing. Where the sunlight poured in there were bushes forming fruit like an English hedge mercury except that they were a brighter red and with three sharply shaped leaves at the head of the twig, and every leaf bearing a berry inside it. In the darker places, beneath the trees, John saw the gleaming blossom of hellebores, thickly growing and carpeting the forest floor.

There was an explosion of noise from the trees above his head and John instinctively ducked, fearing attack. It was half a dozen birds, a new species to John, big pheasant-sized birds in white with green bodies and slate-blue tails. John clasped his hands together in frustration, longing for a musket so he could have shot one for the skin, but they were gone with a clatter of wings and there was no one there for John to compare notes with, and wonder if he could possibly have seen aright.

He dug and snipped like a squirrel preparing for winter until, from the distance, he heard a faint voice calling his name and looked up, realizing that it was growing dark and that he had promised the lad that he would be little more than ten minutes—and that was more than an hour ago.

John trotted down the path back to the boat and the shivering lad.

"What is it?" he asked. "Cold or terror?"

"Neither!" the lad said stoutly, but as soon as he had the boat pushed off and rowed back to the ship he scampered up the ladder at the side and swore that he would never take Mr. Tradescant anywhere again, whatever the captain said.

He did not need to risk a charge of mutiny. The next day the captain waited for the fullness of the tide to save them from the dangers of being grounded on sandbanks, and the ship landed at Archangel. The ship's company were able to go ashore to eat the oat bread and cheese and drink the Russian beer. And the gentlemen traveling with Sir Dudley unloaded their goods and moved into houses on the quayside. The company were particularly scathing about the houses—which were wooden cabins—and about the bread, which was made in different shapes, some rolls no bigger than a single mouthful.

John waylaid the Russian ambassador and was given permission to hire a local boat and set sail around the islands in the river channel. He took a purse of gold with him and bought every rarity he could find for his lord's collection, and took cuttings and roots and seeds from every strange plant he saw. At every island John went ashore, his eyes on his boots and his little trowel in his hand. And at every place he came back to the boat with his satchel bulging with cuttings and plants which had never before been seen in England.

"You are a conquistador," Sir Dudley remarked when Tradescant arrived back at the Archangel quay and had his barrels of plants set in damp earth unloaded on the quayside. "This is a treasure for those who love to make a garden."

John, filthy and smelling strongly of fish, which was all he had eaten for many days, grinned and came stiffly up the quayside steps.

"What have you seen?" Sir Dudley asked. "I have spent all my time getting my goods unloaded and preparing for the journey to Moscow."

"It is mostly waste ground," Tradescant explained softly to him. "But when they clear a piece of land for farming, they are good farmers; they can lay their crops down into soil which is only just warm and get a harvest off it inside six weeks."

Sir Dudley nodded.

"But a poor country?" he suggested.

"Different," John judged. "Terrible ale, the worst taste I have ever had. But they have a drink called mead made with honey which is very good. They have no plane to work their wood, but what they can do with an axe and a knife is better than many an English carpenter. But the trees!" He broke off.

"Go on, then," Sir Dudley said with a smile. "Tell me about the trees."

"I have found four new sorts of fir trees that I have never seen before, the buds of the boughs growing so fresh and so bright that they are spotted like a dappled pony, the bright green against the dark."

Sir Dudley nodded.

"And a birch tree, a very big birch tree which they tell me they can tap for liquor and they make a drink from it. And they have a little tree for making hoops for barrels that they say is a cherry, but it was between the blossom and the fruit so I can't be sure. I can't believe there could be a cherry tree which could make hoops. But I have a cutting and a sapling which I will set to grow at home and see what it is. Its leaf is like a cherry. If you so much as bend a twig down to the ground it will grow where it is set, like a willow. That would be a wood worth growing in England, don't you think?"

Sir Dudley had lost his indulgent smile and was looking thoughtful. "Indeed. And it must be strong to survive this climate. It would grow in England, wouldn't it, John?"

Tradescant nodded. "And white, red and black currants, much bigger than our fruit, and roses—in one place I saw more than five acres of wild roses like a cinnamon rose. Hellebores, angelica, geranium, saxifrage, sorrel as tall as my son John at home—and a new sort of pink—" John broke off for a moment, thinking how pleased his lord would have been to hear that he had found a new sort of pink. "A new pink," he said quietly. "With very fair jagged leaves."

"These are treasures," Sir Dudley said.

"And there are plants which could yield medicines," Tradescant told him. "A fruit like an amber strawberry which prevents scurvy, and I was told of a tree which grows at the Volga River which they call God's tree. It sounds like fennel but they say it will cure many sicknesses. You might see it, my lord. You might take a cutting if you see it."

"Come with me, John," Sir Dudley replied. "Come and take your own cuttings. You've been here such a little time and found such novelties. Come with me to Moscow and you can collect your plants all the way."

For a moment he thought the man would say yes. John's face lit up at the prospect of the adventure and the thought of the riches he would see.

Then he shook his head and laughed at his own eagerness. "I'm like a girl running after a fair," he said. "I can think of nothing I would like more. But I have to go home. Lord Wootton expects me, and my wife and son."

"His lordship comes first?"

John was recalled to his duty. "My lord must come before everything. Even my own desires."

Sir Dudley dropped an arm carelessly around John's shoulders, and they strolled together to his waiting horses. "I am sorry for it," he said. "There's no man I would rather have beside me, all the way to China."

John nodded to hide his emotion. "I wish I could, my lord." He looked down the wagon train of the strong Tartar horses, tacked up with deep traveling saddles.

"All the way to China, you say?"

"Think what you would find—" Sir Dudley whispered temptingly.

John shook his head but his hand was on the stirrup leather. "I cannot," he said.

Sir Dudley smiled at him. "Then safe homeward journey," he said. "And if I find anything very rare or strange I will cut it and send it to you, and I will make a note of where I found it so that you can make the journey yourself one day. For you are a traveler, John, not a stay-at-home. I can see it in your eyes."

John grinned, shaking his head, and made himself release his grip on the stirrup, and made himself step back from Sir Dudley's horse. He forced himself to watch, and not run after, as the whole cavalcade of them turned from the quayside to set off on the track toward Moscow and the East.

"Godspeed," John called. "And good fortune at the court of the Russian king."

"God send you safe home," Sir Dudley replied. "And when I get home you can name me as your friend, Tradescant. I shall not forget your care of me when I was sick."

John watched them till the dust from the last of the train was gone, till the dust had blown across the gray sky, until the sound of the harness bells and the beat of the hooves was silent.

That night they rocked at anchor, and on the next tide they loaded the last of their goods and cast off with Tradescant's cuttings in boxes on the deck and his trees loosely lashed to the mast, and his heart in his seaboots.

Elizabeth was watering the chestnut tree in its great box on the morning that John returned. The earth in the rest of the garden was dry and parched. It had been a bad year for the harvest, wet in the early months and scorching in July. The wheat crop had failed and the barley was little better. There would be hunger in the cities and in the poorer villages the price of flour would rise beyond the pockets of the poor. But through sun or rain the little chestnut sapling had thrived. Elizabeth had made it a little shelter of thatched straw to keep off the strongest sun, and watered it without fail on the dry days.

"Now there's a pretty sight!" John said, coming up behind her.

Elizabeth jumped at the sound of his voice and turned to see him. "Praise God," she said steadily, and paused for a moment, her eyes closed, to give thanks.

John, impatient with her piety, pulled her close to him and held her tight.

"Are you safe?" she asked. "Was it a good voyage? Are you well?"

"Safe and well and with boxes full of treasures."

Elizabeth knew her husband too well to imagine that he was talking of Russian gold. "What did you find?"

"A Muscovy rose—bigger and sweeter than any I have seen before. A cherry tree with wood you can weave like a willow, which roots by bending its twigs into the ground, like a willow. Some new pinks with jagged leaves. I could have loaded the whole boat with white hellebores which grew so thick on one island that you could see nothing else, a new purple cranesbill, a great sorrel plant—" He broke off. "A cart is following me. And I bought some rarities too for Lord Wootton's collection: Russian boots and strange shoes for walking on the snow and rare stockings."

"And you are safe, and you were well?"

John sat down on the garden bench and drew Elizabeth onto his lap. "Safe as a summer garden, and I was well all the time, not even seasick. And now tell me your news," he said. "Is J well?"

"Praise the Lord, yes."

"And all your family? No plague in Kent?"

Elizabeth dipped her head in that familiar gesture which meant that she was swiftly praying. "None, thank God. Is there sickness in London?"

"I passed swiftly through to avoid the risk."

"And are you home now, John? Home for good?"

She saw his roguish smile but she did not respond to it. "John?" she repeated gravely.

"There is a ship which I will take passage on, but it does not go for a year or two," he assured her. "An expedition to the Mediterranean against the pirates, and I may have a place on a supply pinnace!"

She did not return his smile.

"Think of what I might find!" John said persuasively. "Think of what they grow in those hot places and what I might bring back. I should make my fortune for sure!"

Elizabeth folded her underlip.

"It will not be for a year or so," he said placatingly. "And it is all uncertain as yet."

"You will always travel whenever you can," Elizabeth replied bitterly. "A man your age should be staying home. I thought we would settle here, away from the courts of great lords; I thought you would be happy here."

"I am happy here, and it is not ever that I want to leave you . . ." John protested as she got up from his lap and went to one side, gently stroking the leaf of the chestnut. "But I have to obey, Elizabeth—if my lord says I am to go, I have to go. And I must seek plants if I have the chance of them. It is to the glory of God to show men the wealth He has given us, Elizabeth. And a trip to the Mediterranean could bring back great things. Flowers and trees, but also herbs. Maybe a cure for the plague? That would be godly work!"

She did not smile at his overt appeal to her piety. "It would be godly work to stay home and serve your lord at home," she said firmly. "And you are getting old, John. You should not be sailing out at your age. You are not a seaman, you are a gardener. You should be at home in your garden."

Gently he drew her back to him. "Don't be angry with me," he said softly. "I have only just got home. Smile for me, Lizzie, and see: I have brought you a present."

From deep in the pocket of his coat he brought a small pine cone. "A new tree," he said. "A beautiful fir tree. Will you nurse it up for me, Elizabeth? And keep it as well as you have kept our chestnut? I love you as much now as I did when I gave you the chestnut."

Elizabeth took it but her face remained grave. "John, you are nearing fifty years old," she said. "It is time for you to stay home."

He kissed the warm nape of her neck, slightly salt beneath his lips. Elizabeth sighed a little at the pleasure of his touch, and sat still. In the apple tree above their heads a wood pigeon cooed seductively.

"The next voyage shall be my last," he promised. "I will go to the Mediterranean on the *Mercury* and then I shall come home with orange trees and olive trees and all manner of spices and grow them quietly in my garden with you."

When J learned that his father was to go to the Mediterranean he insisted that he go too, but John refused. J went quite pale with anger. "I am old enough to come with you now," J insisted.

"I want you to continue at school," John said.

"What's the use of that!" J exclaimed passionately. "You never went to school!"

"And I felt the lack of it," John pointed out. "I want you to read and write in Latin as well as English. I want you to be brought up as a gentleman."

"I won't need that; I shall be a planter in Virginia. Captain Argall said that the last thing the new plantation needs is gentlemen. He said the plantation needs hardworking men, not scholars."

Elizabeth looked up at the mention of Argall's name and compressed her lips.

"He may be right," John said. "But I was counting on you to help me with my business, before you leave for Virginia."

J, who was in full flight, checked at that. "Help you?"

"All the plants these days are given new names, Latin names. When the King of France's gardeners, the Robins, write to me and send me cuttings, they send them with their Latin names. I was hoping you would learn to read and write Latin so you could help me."

"I shall work with you?"

"Of course," John said simply. "What else?"

J hesitated. "So you'll stay home and teach me?"

"I shall go on this trip to the Mediterranean," John stipulated. "Destroy Algiers, defeat the corsairs, collect all the Mediterranean plants and come home. And after that I shall stay home and we shall garden together."

J nodded, accepting the compromise. Elizabeth found that she had been gripping her hands tightly together under the cover of her apron, and released her grasp. "Tradescant and son," John said, pleased.

"Tradescant and son," J replied.

"Of Canterbury," Elizabeth added, and saw her husband smile.

Spring 1620

"They say that Algiers is a town which cannot be taken," Elizabeth said to John on the quayside, refusing to be optimistic even at this last moment.

"You are too doubting," John said mildly. "Algiers can be defeated; no town is invincible. And the pirates who use it as their base must be stopped. They cruise in the English Channel, even up the Thames. The king himself says that they must be taught a lesson."

"But why should it be you that goes?" she demanded.

"To go plant-hunting in the meantime," John replied mildly. "Captain Pett said he was shorthanded for officers and he would take me. I told him that I would want the ship's boat to call on shore wherever we could. It's a bargain on both sides."

"You won't take part in any battles?" Elizabeth pressed him.

"I shall do my duty," John said firmly. "I shall do whatever Captain Pett commands."

Elizabeth curbed her anger and put her arms around her husband's broadening middle. "You're not a young man anymore," she reminded him gently.

"For shame," John said. "When my wife is a girl still."

She smiled at that but he could not divert her. "I wanted you to stay home with us."

He shook his head and gently kissed the warm top of her white cap. "I know, my love, but I have to go when there is a chance for me like this one. Be generous and send me away with a smile."

She looked up at his face and he saw that she was closer to tears than to smiles. "I hate it when you go," she repeated passionately.

John kissed her on the mouth, on the forehead as he had first done when they were betrothed, and then again on the lips. "Forgive me," he said. "And give me your blessing. I have to go now."

"God bless you," she said reluctantly. "And bring you safe home to me."

"Amen," he replied, and before she could say more he had slipped out of her arms and run up the gangplank to the pinnace *Mercury.*

She did not wait to see his ship sail this time. She had good reason to hurry home. J would be back from school in the afternoon and she had planned to take a lift on the Canterbury wagon which went from Gravesend at midday. But in truth she did not wait because she was angry and resentful, and because she did not want to stand on the quayside like a lovelorn girl to wave her husband good-bye. She could not help but think that it was an infidelity to her and to his promise to stay home and dig his garden. She could not help but think the less of him that he could not resist the temptation of adventure.

John, looking down from the deck at the small indomitable figure walking stiff-backed away from the quayside, knew some of what was in her mind and could not help but admire her. He knew also that she would have been a happier wife coupled with another man, one who stayed at home and only heard travelers' tales in the village inn. And that he too would have been a happier man married to a woman who could wave good-bye and greet him home with a broad smile and not cling to him on leaving, nor greet him resentfully on his return. But it was not a love match between John and Elizabeth and it never had been. What love they had found, and what love they had made, had been a benefit which neither they, nor their fathers who had wisely made the match, could have predicted. It was a marriage which was primarily designed to resolve some debts. It was a marriage designed to place Elizabeth's dowry in the hands of a man who could make use of it, and place John's skills at the disposal of a woman who would know how to manage a house that should grow in size and splendor with every move. The old men had chosen well. John was richer every year with his wages and with his burgeoning trade in rare plants. Elizabeth managed the Canterbury house as she had managed the new house at Hatfield, as she had managed the cottage at Meopham—with confidence and honesty. She had managed the vicarage and farmhouse for Gertrude; she could cope with bigger houses than her marriage had yet brought her.

But their fathers never provided for temperament and desire and jealousy. And the marriage they made never had room for such emotions either. As John watched Elizabeth walk away from the quay and as the *Mercury* slipped its moorings and the barges took it in tow, he knew that she would have to come to terms with the disappointments of the marriage as well as its benefits. He knew that she would have to recognize that her husband was a venturer, an adventurer. And that when he came home she would have to know that he was a man who could not resist the chance of traveling overseas. And that when the chance came for him—he would always go.

John's Mediterranean voyage took him to Malaga, to join the rest of the English fleet in readiness for the assault on Algiers, and then they sailed in force to Majorca for revictualing. At both stops John begged for the use of the ship's boat and went ashore with his satchel and his little trowel; he came back with his satchel bulging.

"You look as if you have murdered a dozen infidels," Captain Pett said as Tradescant returned, mud-stained and smiling through the Mediterranean sunset.

"No deaths," John said. "But some plants which will make my name."

"What've you got?" the captain asked idly. He was not a gardener and only indulged John's enthusiasm for the undeniable benefit of having a steady and experienced man on board who might command a troop of men if needed.

"Look at this," John said, unpacking his muddy satchel on the holystoned deck. "A starry-headed trefoil, a sweet yellow rest harrow, and what d'you think this is?"

"No idea."

"A double-blossomed pomegranate tree," John said proudly, producing a foot-long sapling from his satchel. "I'll need a barrel of earth for this at once."

"Can it grow in England at all?" Captain Pett asked curiously.

Tradescant smiled at him. "Who knows?" he said, and the captain suddenly realized the joy that fired his temporary maverick officer. "Who can tell? We grow a cultivated sort in the orangeries. This is far more fragile and lovely. But I shall have to try it. And if I win, and we can grow wild pomegranates in England, then what a glory to God! For every man who walks in my garden can see things that until now he would have had to travel miles to find. And he can see that God has made things in such variety, in such glorious wealth, that there is no end to His joy in abundance. And no end to mine."

"Are you doing this for the glory of God?" Captain Pett asked, slightly bemused.

John thought for a moment. "To be honest with you," he said slowly, "I cling to the thought that it is for the glory of God. Because the other thought is heresy."

Captain Pett did not glance around, as he would have done on land. He was master of his own pinnace and speech was free. "Heresy? What d'you mean?"

"I mean that either God has made dozens, even hundreds, of things which are nearly the same, and that the richness of his variety is something which redounds to His holy name . . ."

"Or?"

"Or that this is madness. It is madness to think that God should make a dozen things almost the same but a little different. All a man of sense could think is that God did not make them. That the earth they feed on and the water they drink makes plants in different areas a little different, and that is the only reason that they are different. And if that is true, then I am denying that everything in the world was made first by my God in Eden, working like a gardener for six days and resting on the Sabbath. And if I am denying that, then I am a heretic damned."

Captain Pett paused for a moment, following the twisting path of Tradescant's logic, and then let out a crack of laughter and hammered Tradescant on the shoulder. "You are trapped," he exclaimed. "Because every variety that you discover must make you doubt that God could do all this in six days in Eden. And yet what you say you want to do is to show these things to the glory of God."

Tradescant recoiled slightly from the loud good humor of his captain. "Yes."

The captain laughed again. "I thank God I am a simple man," he said. "All I have to do is to sack Algiers and teach the Barbary pirates that they cannot hazard the lives of English sailors. Whereas you, Tradescant, have to spend your life hoping for one thing but continually finding evidence to the contrary."

A familiar stubborn look came across John's face. "I keep faith," he said stolidly. "Whether to my lord or to my king or to my God. I keep faith. And four sorts of smilax do not challenge my faith in God or king or lord."

Pett was optimistic about the ease of his task, compared with John's metaphysical worries. He was part of a well-victualed, well-commanded fleet with a clear plan. When they came to Algiers it was the task of the pinnaces to patrol the waterways to trap the pirates inside the harbor.

John and the other gentlemen recruited for the adventure were called into the captain's cabin on the day the whole of the English fleet was assembled and moored in readiness half a league off shore.

"We'll send in fireboats," Pett said. "Two. They are to set the moored shipping ablaze and that will destroy the corsairs' fleet. It'll also spread smoke across the harbor and under cover of the smoke we'll assault the walls of the harbor. That will be our task and that will be where you come in, gentlemen."

He had a map unrolled before him on the table. The English fleet was shown as a double line of converging white flags with the distinctive red cross. The corsair ships were shown as a black square.

"Which way is the prevailing wind?" Tradescant asked.

"Onshore," Pett replied. "It will blow the fireboats in, and then the smoke will go into their eyes."

"Do we have scaling ladders for the harbor walls?" someone asked.

The officers nodded, Tradescant among them.

"And you each of you know the men you are to lead and have checked their equipment?" Captain Pett confirmed.

Tradescant nodded and glanced around him, wondering if anyone else had a sense of sick dread in their stomachs, the fear of a man who had never seen a battle before.

"Then do your duty, gentlemen," the captain said simply. "For God and King James."

John wanted the attack to start at once, certain that his small core of courage would diminish if he had to wait a moment. He stood with his landing party at the side of the pinnace and watched the fireboats go in through the mouth of the harbor. The two little barges were loaded with explosives and tar and were rowed with a single oar by a volunteer. The rower's task was to get the little craft through the choppy water at the harbor mouth and then as close as he dared to the moored shipping, despite the rain of musket fire which came down from the trapped ships. He was to light the coil of pitch rope which served as a fuse, point the boat in the right direction and then plunge into the sea and swim as fast as he could back to the English ships while the fireboat, smoldering with its cargo of explosives, was supposed to float up against the enemy shipping.

"At least I wasn't ordered to do that," Tradescant whispered miserably to himself, watching the little boat head toward the harbor mouth and seeing a cannonball splash with horrid weight into the water beside it.

The boat bobbed in, the sailor's head just visible; they saw the flame of the fuse and his swift dive into the water, and then . . . nothing. The fuse had gone out and they heard the ironic cheers of the pirates as the fireboat bobbed uselessly against the wooden sides of their ships.

"A free gift of powder and explosives to our enemies," Captain Pett said savagely. "Stand down, everyone; there will be no attack until the tide is up tomorrow."

Tradescant spent a sleepless night, with the taste of fear like cold sweat on his lips, and in the morning showed a white face on deck at the head of his landing party. He checked them over. They all had muskets primed and ready, they all had brightly glowing fuses palmed confidently in their hands. One man had the scaling ladder and he was wearing a helmet Tradescant had managed to scrounge in Majorca. Tradescant nodded to his troop with affected confidence and was irritated to see, by the hidden smile one from another, that they saw and understood his pallor.

"Soon be over, sir," one of them said cheerfully. "And you're either dead or safe in minutes."

"Thank you," John said repressively, and went to the ship's rail to watch the fireboats go in.

They failed again, and the next day too. By day four Tradescant ate a hearty breakfast and was at the rail to watch the fireboats try once more and felt as nonchalant as his men. Boredom and disappointment had driven out fear and now he wanted the battle to be joined. What he could not tolerate was the waiting and the immense irritation when the winds dropped and the fireboats burned harmlessly in the middle of the bay and then exploded with a loud crack that made the pirates cheer.

It was dawn; the tide suited them high at dawn. The weather suited them at last, a gray mist on the water which would make the pirate muskets uncertain of their aim shooting into grayness, and a brisk onshore wind which should blow the fireboats inward to the harbor.

"But hardly a surprise attack," Tradescant grumbled, at the pinnace rail. The wind blowing steadily onshore lifted the brim of his hat.

"The principle is right," someone said behind him.

Tradescant thought of his old master's preference for sound practice over principle, but held his peace. They all watched together as the two barges were rowed to the harbor mouth. The sailors on board lit the fuses to the explosives, burning twists of rope dipped in pitch. No one could tell how long they would take to burn with any accuracy. It was a brave man who stayed on board a barge that would blow up at any moment to steer it closer and ever closer to enemy shipping.

The two sailors did well. "Jump!" Tradescant muttered under his breath as they went through the harbor mouth and drifted toward the ships, while the waiting English ships could see the sparks at the foot of the powder kegs. Then there were two dark shadows leaping and two splashes in the water, and then an almighty roar as the first barge went up in flames and drifted toward the trapped corsair ships.

But just as it should have collided with the wooden rowing ship there was a sudden lull.

"The wind!" Captain Pett yelled in anguish. "What the devil has happened to the wind?"

It was nothing, a lull before a storm, but it was enough to ruin the English plans. The fireboats exploded and burned as they should have done as two little torches afloat on the dark water of Algiers harbor, the corsair ships remained moored safe in its lee and the pirate crews came out on deck with toasting forks and made as if they were frying their bacon for breakfast on the English attack.

"What do we do now?" someone asked. "Stand down again?"

"Today we attack," Captain Pett said. "We follow orders."

John found his feet were strangely heavy in his boots. There was nothing for him to do until the *Mercury* was close enough either to shore or to a ship, and then he was to lead a boarding party.

"There will be no smoke," he said shortly. "No cover. And they are ready and waiting and confident."

"My orders are to attack whatever the success of the fireboats," Captain Pett declared.

He called for the sails to be crowded on and the *Mercury* moved slowly toward the mouth of the harbor. There was another pinnace before her, and one behind; all the English captains were staying within the letter of their orders though the chances of the attack succeeding with the wind down and the fireboats sputtering into darkness was remote. The Turkish guns, expertly manned from the high harbor walls, bombarded the incoming ships. "Like ducks on a moat," John said angrily.

The *Mercury* sailed in, obeying orders.

"Please God he does not put us ashore and expect us to scale the walls," Tradescant muttered into his neckerchief. He looked back at his men. They were waiting grim-faced for Tradescant to lead them; ahead of them were the high walls of the fort with the sharply etched windows where a dozen muskets waited for the English to come into range, clearly visible on the water which was brightening with the morning light and shielded neither by mist nor smoke.

Captain Pett sailed inward, obeying his orders to the letter, but with a man at his elbow with a telescope trained on the commander's ship, waiting for a signal. At last the flag reluctantly fluttered out.

"Retreat ordered," shouted the man with the telescope.

"Retreat!" Captain Pett bawled. At once the drum began to beat and the other English ships wheeled around and started forcing their way, against the prevailing wind, back out of the harbor mouth.

The rest of the fleet sent in barges and took the ships in tow. It was an ignominious end to an attack, but John caught a rope and made it fast, feeling as lighthearted as a lad. The desire for battle had been replaced completely with a profound longing for the safety and comfort of his home.

Elizabeth greeted John home with a touch of coolness. She had been painfully aware that he had left despite her wishes, and she had prayed every night that he would be spared so that he could come home and they could start again, start as friends and lovers again. But when he walked into the Canterbury cottage, not a scratch on him, his face tanned and smiling, and a small wagon of plants waiting outside in the lane, her most powerful feeling was deep irritation.

John sent the wagon on to Lord Wootton's garden with orders to see that the plants were unloaded and watered, and came into the house asking for a bath and that his linen be burned on the kitchen fire.

"It's lousy," he said. "It has driven me mad for days."

Elizabeth set water to heat, pulled out the big wooden washtub and set it on the stone flags of the floor. John stripped off his clothes and left them at a heap near the door.

"God be praised, I am glad to be home," he said and gave her a smile. She did not smile back at him, nor did she come into his arms and put her face against his warm bare chest. John did not hold out his arms. He was afraid he might smell and he knew his head and his beard harbored lice. But he would have been glad of a greeting which was passionate, or even affectionate. Elizabeth pouring hot water into the tub offered a dutiful welcome, not an exciting one.

"I am glad to see you safe home," she said calmly, and put on another pot of water to heat.

John tested the water with his foot and then stepped in. Elizabeth handed him the washball of herbs tied in cotton, and a bowl of sludgy soap.

"I was afraid you might be fired on, sailing past the Spanish coast," she said. "There were rumors that the fleet would go against Spain."

"I would have thought you would have been glad to see me put a cannonball into the heart of papistry," John observed, sitting in a bath of soapy water and sponging the salty grime of several months' voyage off his neck.

"Not if they fired back," she said. "And anyway, I thought your quarrel was with the infidels."

John splashed water into his face and puffed out like a grampus whale. "We had orders which could be read any way you wanted," he said. "It makes no sense to me. When I leave the garden for any length of time I say to the gardeners, take care of this, and when this flowers do this. I don't say to them, use your judgment, do as you wish. And that way, when I come home again, I know if they have done well or badly, and they know it too."

"But the king?" Elizabeth asked.

John lowered his voice. "The king gave them orders which told them to attack the infidel and release our poor captured countrymen, and gave them secret orders to attack Spain, and then orders which were to be open which told them to respect Spain as an ally."

Elizabeth shook her head. "This is dishonesty," she said flatly.

John smiled, as if at an old half-forgotten joke. "It's practice. But not principle."

"It's a sin."

John looked at her thoughtfully. "You're very sure what makes a sin and what does not, my wife. Are you setting up to be a preacher like your father?"

To his surprise she did not laugh and disclaim, as she would have done only a few years before. "I am studying my Bible more than I have done before," she told him. "There is a lecturer who teaches me and some other women on Wednesday nights. He's a man of much learning and wisdom too. And I find I am thinking of things with more care than when I was a girl full of folly."

John bent his knees awkwardly in the little wooden tub to get his shoulders under the suds. "I don't remember you as full of folly," he remarked. "I always thought you were a God-fearing serious woman."

Elizabeth nodded and again he saw the new gravity about her. "These are fearful times," she said. "The plague seems to get worse every summer and no one can tell where it strikes. There are rumors about a king and a court who don't walk in the way of the Lord. And a church which does not reproach them."

John straightened and rose up from his bath, water cascading all over the floor. Elizabeth handed him a linen sheet and he threw it around his shoulders. She was carefully looking away as if the sight of her husband's nakedness might lead her into sin. It was that turning away of her head which tripped John into irritation.

"We don't repeat gossip about the king in this household," he said flatly. And when Elizabeth was about to argue he held up his hand. "It's not a matter of piety or truth, Elizabeth. It's a lesson I learned from my lord. We don't gossip against the king. The price is too high if you're overheard. Whatever you are reading at your classes, you keep your mind on your Bible and off King James and his court, or you won't go again."

For a moment she looked as if she might argue. "Does this man preach against the authority of God vested in men over their wives?" he demanded.

She dropped her head. "Of course not."

John nodded, hiding his sense of immense smugness. "Good."

"You know that all I have ever wanted is for you to come home and stay home," Elizabeth said, dragging the big bath toward the back door where it could be tipped into the yard. "If you had been home I would have had no time to go to meetings."

John gave her a sharp look. "Don't lay it at my door," he said. "You can go where your conscience leads you as long as it does not take you into treason or into denying the authority of those set over you. *All* of those set over you. Me as your husband, my lord above me, the king above him, and God above him."

She flung open the door so a cool wind blew in around John's bare legs. "I would never deny God's authority," she said. "And I have not denied the authority of men. Mind you don't catch cold."

John turned abruptly and went to the bedroom to get dressed.

1622

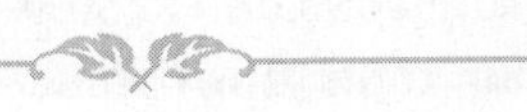

"Should we not transplant that chestnut?" J asked his father.

John was leaning on his spade, watching his coltish fourteen-year-old son at work. "It must be getting too big for that box," J said.

"I gave that to your mother the year we were married," John said reminiscently. "Sir Robert and I bought a dozen of them—no, half a dozen. Five I planted for him at Hatfield and one I gave to your mother. She kept it in a pot at Meopham, and then I moved it into the carrying box when we went to Hatfield, with you so little on the bench seat of the wagon that your feet didn't reach the board."

"Shouldn't we plant it out now?" J asked. "So it can put down great roots?"

"I suppose so," John said thoughtfully. "but we can leave it another year. I'm going to buy some land at the back of our house, make a bigger garden, so that we can see it spread out. The man who sold it to me said they grow as wide as an oak tree. There's no room for it in the cottage garden; it would overspread the house. And I'd be loath to plant it here."

J gazed around Lord Wootton's graceful garden, at the gray walls and the high tower of Canterbury Cathedral behind. "Why not? It would look well enough."

John shook his head. "Because it's your mother's," he said gently. "given from me to her the first time I loved her. She rarely comes in here; she'd never see it. It's her keepsake. We must buy her a bigger house with a bigger garden so she can sit underneath it and rock your babies on her knee."

J flushed with the quick embarrassment of a young man still too innocent for bawdy talk. "There won't be babies from me for a while," he said gruffly. "So don't count on it."

"You put your roots down first," John advised. "Like your mother's chestnut sapling. Shall we take a break for our dinner now?"

"I'll go on," J said. "I want to take a look at those Spanish onions of yours. They should be fit to taste soon."

"They'll be very sweet if they've grown as well as they do at their home," John said. "They eat them like fruit in Gibraltar. And take a look at the melon glasses when you're in the kitchen garden. They should be ripening. Bank up some straw around and under them to keep the slugs off."

J nodded and trudged off to the kitchen garden. John spread a napkin on the grass and opened his little knapsack. Elizabeth had given him a new-baked loaf, a slice of cheese and a flask of small ale. The crust was gray, the flour was poor this year, and the cheese was watery. Not even good money could buy good provisions. The country was feeling the pinch of bad finances and bad harvests. John made a small grimace and bit into his bread.

"John Tradescant?" John looked up but did not rise to his feet though the man standing above him was splendidly dressed in the livery of the Duke of Buckingham.

"Who wants him?"

"The Duke of Buckingham himself."

John put his loaf of gray bread to one side and stood up, brushing off crumbs.

"I am John Tradescant," he said. "What does His Grace want?"

"You're to go and see him," the man said abruptly. "You're summoned. He's at New Hall at Chelmsford. You're to go at once."

"My master is Lord Wootton . . ." John started.

The man laughed abruptly. "Your master can be Lord Jesus Christ for all that my master cares," he said softly.

John recoiled. "No need for blasphemy."

"Every need," the man insisted. "For you do not seem to understand who commands you. Above my master there is only the king. If my master wants something he has only to ask for it. And if he asks for it, he gets it. D'you understand?"

John thought of the painted youth at Theobalds who sat in King James's lap, and the jewels around the young man's neck and the purse at his waist.

"I understand well enough," he said dryly. "Though I've been away from court for some years."

"Then know this," the man said. "There is only one person in the world for King James, and that is my master—the beautiful duke." He stepped forward and lowered his voice. "The duke's friends can do anything they wish—poison, treachery, divorce! All this they have done and escaped scot-free! Had you not heard?"

John carefully shook his head. "Not a thing."

"Lord Rochester took the wife of another man, no less than the Earl of Essex's wife. They declared him impotent! How would you like that?"

"Not at all."

"Then Rochester and his new wife poisoned Sir Thomas Overbury, who would have betrayed them. She is a declared witch and poisoner. How d'you like that?"

"No better."

"Found guilty, imprisoned in the tower, and then what d'you think?"

John shook his head, maintaining his ignorance.

"Forgiven overnight!" the manservant said with satisfaction. "If you have the king's ear you can do no wrong."

"The king knows best," John said staunchly, thinking of his lost lord and his advice to be blind and deaf when other men are talking treason.

"And Rochester was as nothing to *my* lord." The man lowered his voice still further. "Rochester is the old favorite, but my lord is the new. Rochester may have had the king's ear, but my lord has all his parts. D'you understand me? He has all his parts!"

John kept his face very still; he did not smile at the bawdy humor.

"My master is supreme under the king," the man declared. "There is no one in England more beloved than my master, George Villiers. And he has decided that you are to serve him." The man looked down at John's plain dinner. "Chosen you from every other man in the kingdom!"

"I am honored. But I do not think I can be released from my work here."

The man flapped a letter in John's face. "Villiers's orders," he said. "And the king's seal. You're to do as you are told."

John resigned himself to the inevitable, and rolled up his half-eaten dinner in his napkin.

"And remember this," the man continued in the same boastful tone. "That what the duke thinks today, the king thinks tomorrow, and the prince thinks the next. When the king goes, the duke and the prince succeed. When you hitch your cart to the star of my master you have a long brilliant future."

John smiled. "I have worked for a great man before," he said gently. "And in great gardens."

"You have never worked for one like this," the servant declared. "You have never even seen a man such as this."

John thought that Elizabeth would dislike the move to His Grace's house at New Hall, Chelmsford, and he was right. She was passionately opposed to leaving Lord Wootton's service and going near to the hazardous glamour of the royal court. But the little family had no choice. J took his mother's worries to his father and gained no satisfaction. "Mother does not want to move house, and she doesn't want you to work for a great lord again," he said in his halting shy way. "Mother wants us to live quietly; she likes it here."

"Won't she speak to me herself?"

"She didn't ask me to tell you," J said, embarrassed. "I thought perhaps you didn't know. I was trying to help."

John dropped a gentle hand on his son's narrow shoulder. "I know what she fears, but I am no more free to choose where to live than your mother is free," he explained. "She is bound by God to follow me, and I am bound by God to go where I am commanded by my lord and by the king above him. And lord and king and therefore God say we must go to the Duke of Buckingham in Essex." He shrugged. "So we go."

"I don't believe that God wants us to go near to vanity and idleness," J protested.

John turned a stern gaze on him. "What God wants or does not want no man can say, only a priest or the king," he said firmly. "If the king tells the duke who tells my Lord Wootton that I am wanted in Essex, then that is enough for me; as if God had leaned down from heaven and told me himself." He paused. "And it should be enough for you too, J."

J, avoiding the challenge in his father's gaze, looked away. "Yes, sir," he said.

The little family had been expecting something impressive of New Hall. The duke had bought it as a palace near to London where he could entertain the king in a style befitting the royal favorite. It had been a summer palace for Henry VIII and had passed around the courtiers as a prize plum of patronage. Buckingham was said to have paid a fortune for it, and was now pulling the place apart to enrich it still further, under the direction of Inigo Jones, who was laying a great sweeping staircase of marble and noble stone gateways.

The Tradescants arrived, as the king himself would arrive on his frequent visits, up the great drive which turned in a full circle before the house. The house fronted the drive full-square, with great turrets on either side and a huge wooden doorway, wide and high enough for two coaches to be driven abreast into the inner courtyard. It was built of handsome stone, every inch carved and crenellated like marchpane on a cake, with three stories of bay windows bulging from the encrusted walls. At each corner stood great towers with bulbous cupolas and flags flying from the poles at the top. In the inner courtyard was a huge cobbled area, as big as a tilt-yard, with the great hall on the east side and a handsome oriel window looking out over the quadrangle. On the west side was the chapel for the house, and a bell tolling at the tower end.

Elizabeth looked askance at the stained glass in the huge chapel windows as the wagon halted in the yard. A maidservant came out with a tray of drinks for the travelers, and a groom from the stables emerged and said he would direct the wagon on to the Tradescants' own cottage.

"His Grace said that you should live in the great house if you please, but he thought you might prefer your own cottage so that you can nurse up plants in your own garden."

"Yes," Elizabeth said before John could reply. "We don't want to live in the hall."

John shot her a reproving look. "The duke is gracious," he said carefully. "I will need a garden under my eye. A cottage sounds a very good solution. Please show us the way."

He drained his mug of small ale, setting it back on the tray with a smile at the girl. J, still seated in the back, one arm around the precious chestnut tree, one hand on the tailgate of the wagon, did not even glance at the pretty serving maid but kept his eyes on his boots.

John sighed. He had not imagined the move would be easy but with Elizabeth suspecting papistry and luxury around every corner and with J sinking into the manners of a country bumpkin, he thought that returning to court life would be hard indeed, and that no master, however graceful or powerful, would make up for the differences in the little Tradescant family.

The cottage was some compensation. It had been built as a farmhouse and taken into the demesne of New Hall by the ever-widening wall and ambition of each successive owner. It was as good as Elizabeth's girlhood home at Meopham, a two-storied, four-bedroomed house with an orchard at the back and a stable yard with room for a dozen horses at the side.

Elizabeth might put up with the disruption of the move for the benefit of the house, John thought, and held that hope in his mind until they had unpacked their goods and penned up the cat so that she should not stray, when a liveried manservant from the house tapped on the open front door and ordered John to wait on His Grace in the garden.

John pulled on his jacket and followed the man back up the drive toward the house.

"He's in the yew-tree allée," the man said, gesturing to the right of the house. "He said you were to go and find him."

"How shall I know him?" John asked, hanging back.

The man looked at him with open surprise. "You'll recognize him the moment you see him. Without error."

"How?"

"Because he's the most beautiful man in the kingdom," the man said frankly. "Go toward the yew-tree allée and when you see a man as lovely as an angel, that's my lord Buckingham. You can't miss him, and when you've seen him, you'll never forget him."

John puffed a little at the courtier hyperbole and turned toward the colonnade of yew. He had time to note that the allée was overgrown and needed pruning at the head of the trees to make them thicken out at the bottom, before he stepped into the shade. He blinked against the sudden darkness of the thickly interleaved boughs. It was as dark as nighttime beneath the arching branches. The ground beneath his feet was soft with years of fallen brown yew needles. It was eerie and silent in the darkness; no birds sang in the still boughs of the trees, no sun shone into their shade. Then John's eyes adjusted to the dimness after the dazzle of the sun and he saw George Villiers, Duke of Buckingham.

At first he could see only a silhouette of a slim solitary man, of about thirty. He was dark-haired and dark-eyed, dressed like a prince, laden with diamonds. He had a bright mobile face above the wide lace-trimmed ruff with eyes that were smiling and wicked, and a mouth as changeable and as provocative as any pretty woman's. The pallor of his skin gleamed in the darkness as if he were lit from within, like a paper lantern, and his smile, when he saw John coming toward him, was as engaging as a child's, with the confidence and innocence of a child who has never known anything but love. He wore a doublet and cape of dark green, as green as the yew, and for a moment John, looking from trees to man, thought he was in the presence of a dryad—some wild beautiful spirit of the wood—and that some miracle had been granted him, to see a tree dancing toward him and smiling.

"Ah! my John Tradescant!" exclaimed Buckingham, and at that moment John suffered a strange falling feeling which made him think that he had taken the sun, riding all day on the open wagon. The man smiled at him as if he were a brother, as if he were a living angel come to give him tidings of great joy. John did not smile in greeting—years later he would remember that he had not felt any sense of meeting a new master but rather a grave sense of deep familiarity. He did not feel that they were well-met, new-met. He felt as if they had been together for all their lives and just accidentally parted until now. If he had spoken the words in his heart he would have said: "Oh, it is you—at last."

"Are you my John Tradescant?" the man asked.

John bowed low and when he looked up the sheer beauty of the young man made him catch his breath again. Even standing still, he was as graceful as a dancer.

"I am," John said simply. "You sent for me and I have come to serve you."

"Forgive me!" the duke said swiftly. "I don't doubt you were snatched away from your work. But I need you, Mr. Tradescant. I need you very badly."

John found he was smiling into the quick bright face of the young man. "I'll do what I can."

"It is here, at these gardens," the young duke said. He led the way down the allée, talking as he went, throwing a smile over his shoulder as John followed. "The house is a thing of rare beauty, King Henry's summer house. But the gardens have been sorely neglected. I love my gardens, Mr. Tradescant. I want you to make these rich and lovely with your rare trees and flowers. I have seen Hatfield and I envy you the planting of such a place! Can you work the same magic for me here?"

"Hatfield was many years in the making," John said slowly. "And the earl spent a fortune on buying in new plants."

"I shall spend a fortune!" the young man said carelessly. "Or rather, you shall spend my fortune for me. Will you do that for me, John Tradescant? Shall I earn a fortune and you spend it? Is that a fair agreement?"

Despite his sense of caution, John chuckled. "Very fair on me, my lord. But perhaps you had better take a care. A garden can gobble up wealth as it can gobble up manure."

"There's always plenty of both," Buckingham said quickly. "You just have to go to the right place."

John was tempted to laugh, but then thought better of it.

"So will you do it?" Buckingham paused at the end of the allée and looked back toward his house. It looked like a fairy-tale palace in the afternoon sunshine, a crenellated turreted palace set in the simple loveliness of the fertile green countryside of England. "Will you make me a fine garden here, and another at my other house in Rutland?"

John looked around. The ground was fine, the aspect of the house was open and facing south. The ground had been terraced in wide beautiful steps down the hillside; at the bottom was a marshy pond that he could do all sorts of things with: a lake with an island, or a fountain feature, or a man-made river for boating.

"I can make you a fine garden," he said slowly. "There will be no difficulty in growing what you will."

Buckingham slipped his hand in John's arm. "Dream with me," he urged him persuasively. "Walk with me and tell me what you would grow here."

John looked back at the long allée. "There's little that will grow under yew," he said. "But I have had some success with a plant that came from Turkey to France: lily of the valley. A small white flower, the daintiest thing you have ever seen. Like a snowdrop only smaller, a frilled bell, like a little model of a flower made in porcelain. It is scented, they tell me, as sweet as a rose, only sharp like lemons. A true lily scent. It will grow in great thick clumps and the white flowers are like stars against broad green leaves."

"What d'you mean, they tell you it is scented? Can't you smell them?" Buckingham asked.

"I have no nose for smell," John admitted. "It is a great disadvantage for a gardener. My son tells me when the earth smells sour or when we have some putrid rot. Without him I have to go by my eyes and touch."

Buckingham stopped and looked at his gardener. "What a tragedy," he said simply. "One of the greatest pleasures for me is the scent of flowers, what a tragedy that you cannot sense this! Oh! And so many other things! Good cheeses, and wine, and smell of a clean stable of straw! Oh! and perfume when it is warm on a woman's skin, or the smell of her sweat when she's hot! And tobacco smoke! Oh, John! What a loss!"

John smiled a little at his enthusiasm. "Having never known it I do not feel the lack," he said. "But I should like to smell a rose."

Buckingham shook his head. "*I* should like you to smell a rose, John. I feel for you."

They walked on a few steps more. "Now," Buckingham said. "What would you do here?"

The ground below them fell away to the marshy dip at the bottom of the field. As they watched, a herd of cows trudged through the mud and water, churning it up.

"Get rid of the cows," John said definitely.

Buckingham laughed. "I could have thought of that on my own! Do I need to hire you to tell me to mend the fences?"

"First get rid of the cows," John amended. "And then perhaps use that water to make a lake? Perhaps a water-lily lake? And at one side you would have a wet garden with plants that love moisture. Some reeds and rushes, irises and buttercups. And on the other a large fountain. At Hatfield we had a grand statue mounted on a boulder. That was handsome. Or perhaps some playful water feature? A fountain which throws an arc of water for boats to sail underneath? Or an arc of water thrown over the path? Or even from one side of the lake to another with a bridge passing beneath it."

Buckingham gleamed. "And one of those toys which sprinkle people when they approach!" he exclaimed. "And I should like a little mount as well, perhaps in the middle of the lake!"

"A grand mount," John suggested. "Planted thickly with a winding allée to the summit. Perhaps cherry trees, espaliered into a hedge to make them thick and shady. I have some wonderful new cherry trees. Or even apple trees and pears. They take time to establish but you have a pretty effect with blossom in spring, and at the end of summer it is very rich to walk under boughs heavy with fruit. We could thread them through with roses and eglantine, which would climb and hang their blooms down through the leaves. You could row out to your island and wander among roses and fruit."

"And where would you put the knot gardens?" Buckingham demanded. "Beyond the lake?"

John shook his head. "Near to the house," he said firmly. "But you could show me your favorite window-seat and I could plant a garden which leads the eyes outward, into the garden, a little maze for your eye to follow, in stone and with small pale-leafed plants, and herbs to aid your meditations."

"And an orchard with a covered walk all around it, and turf benches in every corner. I must have an orchard! Great fruiting trees which bow low to the ground. Where can we get quick-growing fruit trees?"

"We can buy saplings. But it will take time," John warned him.

"But I want it now," Buckingham insisted. "There must surely be trees which will grow swiftly, or trees we can buy full-grown? I want it at once!"

John shook his head. "You may command every man in England," he said gently. "But you cannot make a garden grow at once, my lord. You will have to learn patience."

A shadow crossed Buckingham's face, a dark flicker of frustration. "For God's sake!" he exclaimed. "This is as bad as the Spanish! Is everything I desire to go so slow that by the time it comes to me I am sick of waiting? Am I to grow old and tired before my desires can be met? Do I have to die before my plans come to fruit?"

John said nothing, only stood still, like a little oak tree, while the storm of Buckingham's temper blew itself out. Buckingham paused as he took the measure of John Tradescant, and he threw back his curly dark head and laughed.

"You will be my conscience, John!" he exclaimed. "You will be the keeper of my soul. You gardened for Cecil, didn't you? And they all say that when you wanted Cecil, you had to go out into the garden and find him; and half the time he would be sitting on a bench in his knot garden and talking to his man."

John nodded gravely.

"They say he was the greatest Secretary of State that the country has ever had, and that your gardens were his greatest solace and his joy."

Tradescant bowed and looked away, so that his new mercurial master should not see that he was moved.

"When I am tempted to overreach myself in my garden or in the great wild forests which are the courts of Europe, you can remind me that I cannot always have my own way. I cannot command a garden to grow," Buckingham said humbly. "You can remind me that even the great Cecil had to wait for what he wanted, whether it was a plant or policy."

John shook his head in quiet dissent. "I can only plant your garden, my lord," he said softly. "That's all I did for the earl. I can't do more than that."

For a moment he thought that Buckingham would argue, demand that there must be more. But then the young man smiled at him and dropped an arm around his shoulders and set them both walking back to the house. "Do that for me now, and when you trust me more, and know me better, you shall be my friend and adviser as you were Cecil's," he said. "You will make it grow for me, won't you, John? You will do your best for me, even if I am impatient and ignorant?"

Tradescant found that he was smiling back. "I can undertake to do that. And it will grow as fast as it is able. And it will be all that you want."

John started work that afternoon, walking to Chelmsford to find laborers to start the work of fencing the cows out, digging the lake and building the walls for the kitchen garden. He took a horse from the stables and rode a wide circle around the great estate to neighboring farms to see what trees they had in their orchards and what wooded copses he could buy and transplant at once.

Buckingham was careless about cost. "Just order it, John," he said. "And if they are tenants of mine just tell them to give you whatever you wish and they can take it off their rent at quarter day."

John bowed but made a point of visiting the steward of the household, at his desk in an imposing room at the very center of the grand house.

"His Grace has ordered me to buy trees and plants from his tenants, and command them to take the cost from their rent," Tradescant began.

The steward looked up from the household books, which were spread before him. "What?"

"He has ordered me to buy from the tenants," John began again.

"I heard you," the man said angrily. "But how am I to know what is bought or sold? And how am I to run this house if the rents are discounted before they are collected?"

John hesitated. "I was coming to you only to ask you how it should be done, if you have a list of tenants—"

"I have a list of tenants, I have a list of rents, I have a list of expenditure. What no one will tell me is how to make the one agree with the other."

John paused for a moment to take stock of the man. "I am new in this post," he said cautiously. "I don't seek to make your task any harder. I do need to buy his lordship trees and plants to stock his gardens and he ordered me to buy from his tenants and see that they deduct the cost from their rents."

The steward took in Tradescant's steadiness. "Aye," he said more quietly. "But the rents are already spent, signed away or promised. They are not free for deductions."

There was a brief silence. "What am I to do then?" John asked pleasantly. "Shall I return to his lordship and tell him it cannot be done?"

"Would you do that?" the man enquired.

John smiled. "Surely. What else could I do?"

"You don't fear taking bad news to a new master, the greatest master in the land?"

"I have worked for a great man before," John said. "And, good news or bad, I found the best way was to tell him simply what was amiss. If a man is fool enough to punish his messengers he'll never get his messages."

The steward cracked a laugh and held out his hand. "I am William Ward. And I am glad to meet you, Mr. Tradescant."

John took the handshake. "Have you been in his lordship's service for long?" he asked.

The steward nodded. "Yes."

"And are his affairs in a bad way?"

"He is the wealthiest man in the land," William Ward stated. "Newly married to an heiress and with the king's own fortune at his disposal."

"Then—?"

"And the most spendthrift. And the wildest. D'you know how he did his courting?"

John glanced at the closed door behind them and shook his head.

"He caught the lady's fancy—not surprising—"

John thought of that smile and the way the man threw back his head when he laughed. "Not surprising," he agreed.

"But when he went to her father, the man declined. Again, not surprising."

John thought of the rumors that Buckingham was the king's man in ways that a sensible man did not question. "I don't know," he said stoutly.

"Not surprising to those of us who have seen the king on his visits here," the steward said bluntly. "So what does my lord do?"

Tradescant shook his head. "I have been away, and in Canterbury, we don't hear gossip. I rarely listen to it, anyway."

The steward laughed shortly. "Well, hear this. Buckingham invites Lady Kate to his mother's house for dinner and when the dinner is ended they don't let her call for her carriage. They don't let her go home! Buckingham's mother herself keeps the girl overnight. So her reputation is ruined and her father is glad to get her wed at any price, takes the duke's offer and has to pay handsomely for the privilege of having his daughter dishonored into the bargain."

Tradescant's jaw dropped open. "He did this?"

William Ward nodded.

"To a lady?"

"Aye. Now you get some idea of what he can do and what he is allowed. And now you get some idea of his rashness."

Tradescant took a couple of swift steps and looked out of the window. Almost at once his sense of anxiety at this new post, at this madly impulsive young master, deserted him. He could see the site of what would be his kitchen garden, and he had it in mind to build a hollow wall, the first of its kind in England, and to heat the inside of it like a chimney. It might warm the fruit trees growing against the wall and make them come early into bud. He shook his head at the promising site and returned to the problem of his new master's wildness.

"And is his new wife unhappy?" he asked.

William Ward looked at him for one incredulous moment and then burst into laughter. "You've seen my lord. D'you think a new wife would be unhappy?"

John shrugged. "Who knows what a woman wants?"

"She wants rough wooing and passionate bedding and she has

had both from our lord. She wants to know that he loves her above everything else and there is no other woman in the land who can say that her husband risked everything to have her."

"And the king?" Tradescant asked, going to the key of all things.

Ward smiled. "The king keeps the two of them as lesser men keep lovebirds in a cage, for the pleasure of seeing their happiness. And in any case, when he wants Buckingham all to himself he has only to crook his finger and our lord goes. His wife knows that he must go, and she smiles and bids him farewell."

The steward fell silent. John looked out again at the parkland that stretched to the horizon. This was flat country; he thought the winds in winter would be cruel. "So," he said slowly. "I have a new lord who is a spendthrift, and wild, a breaker of hearts and no respecter of persons."

The steward nodded. "And any one of us would lay down our lives for him."

Surprised, John looked up. The steward was smiling.

"Yes," he said. "There isn't a man on the estate who wouldn't go hungry to keep him in his silks and satin. You'll see. Now go and buy your trees. Every time you agree a price, make sure that you note down the tenant's name and the price of his trees. And tell them that I—I and not they—will calculate the difference in the rents and discount the rents next quarter day. Bring me the list when you have done."

He paused for a moment. "Unless I have given you a disliking for your lord and you want to go back to Canterbury?" he asked. "He is as wild as I say, he is as spendthrift as I say and he is as wealthy as I say. He has more power at his fingertips than any man in the land, and that is probably including the king."

John had a strong sense of returning to his place at the very center of things, serving a lord who served his country, a man whose doings were the talk of every ale house in the land. "I'll keep my place here," he said. "There is much for me to do."

1623

John and J worked hard all the winter, planning the gardens and pegging out lines for the knot garden, for the terraces and for the turf benches in the lord's new orchards. Much of the work had to wait until the spring when the ground was soft enough for digging, but John had a small forest of trees waiting for the earth to warm so that they could be planted, each one labeled with its place, each with a plot reserved for it. For the workers who could neither read nor write, J had instituted a scheme of colored dots. They had to match the label on the tree marked with three red dots with the plot in the ground marked with three red dots. Or green or yellow. "This is code," John said admiringly to J.

"It's madness," J said bluntly. "Everyone should be taught to read at dame school. How else can they understand their Bible? How else do their work?"

"We're not all scholars like you," John said mildly.

J flushed in one of his sudden attacks of bashfulness. "I'm no scholar," he said gruffly. "I don't pretend to be one. I'm no better than any man. But I do think that all men should be taught to read and write so that they can read their Bible and think for themselves."

Work on the heated wall had already started to John's design. The plot was marked out and the foundations for the perimeter wall were already dug. The whole garden was to be walled with a double skin of deep red brick, and there were to be built three equally spaced fireplaces, one above the other, where the charcoal burners could be lit and the smoke drift sideways through the wall till every brick was warm to the touch. The beds of the garden were not to be edged with box in the usual way. John wanted to raise them after a fashion never seen before. He wanted little brick walls to edge them, and the beds were to be filled with sifted earth and rotted manure. He even instituted a pile of manure from the stables, which was to be left to molder and then turned over every month. "I don't want it all fresh and carrying the roots of weeds into my garden," he explained to J and to the other vegetable gardeners. "I want the earth in these beds to be free of weeds and free of stones. I want this garden to have soil so rich and so soft that I could lay a strawberry plant on it and leave it to set its own roots. D'you understand?"

They grumbled behind his back but to his face they nodded and pulled their caps. John's reputation as one of the greatest gardeners of the day had preceded him and it was an honor to work under him—raised beds, and stirred manure, hollow walls, or no.

The house was quiet after the festivities of Christmas; the duke had returned from the court in January and set up residence with Kate, his wife. His mother was to come later in the year. So Tradescant, rounding the stable yard in search of an errant weeding lad, was surprised to see an exceptionally fine horse, an Arab, being led from its stall into the yard, and the duke's hunter prancing around on the cobbles, all tacked up and ready to go.

"Whose horse is that?" John asked a groom and received nothing more than a wink for a reply.

"Dolt," John said shortly, picked up his hoe and went to pace out the orchard.

That afternoon, John was measuring the length of the new avenue which he planned to plant with lime trees leading from the Chelmsford road to the house when he heard hoofbeats on the drive, and there were the two horses with two strange men on their backs.

John stepped forward to challenge them. "Who are you? And what's your business here? That's my lord's horse."

"Let me pass, my John," said one of the men in a familiar voice. The stranger leaned down from the duke's horse and swept off his hat. Buckingham's dark eyes looked down at John, and John heard his irrepressible chuckle.

"Fooled you," Buckingham cried triumphantly. "Fooled you completely."

John stared at the face of his lord, absurdly concealed by a false beard and a muffler. "Your Grace—" He glanced across at the other horseman and recognized, with a sense of shock, the young prince he had last seen sniveling at the heels of his older brother. But now the young prince was the heir, Prince Charles. "Good God! Your Highness!"

"Will we pass, d'you think?" Buckingham demanded joyously. "I am John Smith and this is my brother Thomas. Will we pass, d'you think?"

"Oh, yes," John said. "But what are you about, my lord? Wenching?"

Buckingham laughed aloud at that. "The finest wench in the world," he whispered. "We're going to Spain, John, we're going to marry His Highness here to the infanta of Spain! What d'you think of that?"

For a moment John was too stunned to speak; then he grabbed the hunter's bridle above the bit. "Stay!" he cried. "You can't."

"You order me?" Buckingham enquired politely. "You had much better take your hand off my horse, Tradescant."

John flinched but did not let go. "Please, your Grace," he said. "Wait. Think on this. Why are you going disguised?"

"For the adventure!" Buckingham said merrily.

"Come on, Thomas!" the prince said. "Or are you John? Am I Thomas?"

"I beg of you," John said urgently. "You cannot go like this, my lord. You cannot take the prince like this."

The prince's horse pawed the ground. "Come on!" the prince said.

"Forgive me!" Tradescant looked over at him. "Your Highness

has perhaps not considered. You cannot ride into France as if it were East Anglia, Your Highness. What if they hold you? What if Spain refuses to let you leave?"

"Nonsense," Prince Charles said briefly. "Come on, Villiers."

Buckingham's horse moved forward and John was dragged along, not releasing his grip on the bridle. "Your Grace." He tried again. "Does the king know of this? What if he turns against you?"

Buckingham leaned low over the horse's neck so he could whisper to Tradescant. "Leave me go, my John. I am at work here. If I marry the prince to the infanta then I have done something which no man has ever done—make Spain our ally, make the greatest alliance in Europe and myself the greatest marriage broker who ever lived. But even if I fail, then the prince and I have ridden out like brothers and we will be brothers for the rest of our lives. Either way, my place is assured. Now let my bridle go. I have to leave."

"Have you food and money, a change of clothes?"

Buckingham laughed. "John, my John, next time you shall pack for me. But I must go now!"

His spur touched the hunter's side and it threw up its head and bounded forward. Prince Charles's horse leaped after, and there was a swirl of dust in John's face and the two of them were gone.

"Please God keep him safe, keep them safe," Tradescant said, looking after them. His new master and the prince he had known as a lonely incompetent little boy. "Please God, stop them at Dover."

Elizabeth saw at once that something had happened when John came home at dusk for his dinner and stared into his broth without eating. As soon as J had eaten she sent him from the room with a nod of her head, and then seated herself beside John on the settle which stood at the fireside, and put her hand on his. "What's the matter?"

He shook his head. "I cannot tell you." He glanced down into her worried face. "Nothing wrong with me, my dear. Nothing wrong with J, and nothing wrong with the garden. But I cannot tell you. It is a secret and not my secret. I cannot tell anybody."

"Then it's the duke," she said simply. "He's done something bad."

John's stricken look told her that her guess had struck home.

"What's he done?" she pressed.

He shook his head again. "Please God, it won't be too bad. Please God there will be a happy outcome."

"Is he at home?"

He shook his head.

"Gone to London? Gone to the king?"

"Gone to Spain," he whispered very low.

Elizabeth recoiled from him as if he had pinched her. "Spain?"

John gave her a swift unhappy glance and put his finger to his lips. "I cannot say more," he said firmly.

Elizabeth rose and went to the fire, bent and stirred the poker under the glowing logs. He saw her lips moving in a silent prayer. Elizabeth was a devout woman; a trip to Spain was like a trip to the underworld to her. Spain was the heart of Catholicism, the home of the anti-Christ against whom all good Protestants must struggle and fight from birth till death. Buckingham's choice of destination at once condemned him in her eyes. He must be a bad man if he chose to go to Spain.

John closed his eyes briefly. He could not imagine what condemnation would be released on his master if Elizabeth, and all the many hundreds, thousands, of devout men and women like Elizabeth, knew that he was planning to bring a Spanish princess home to be queen of England.

Elizabeth straightened up and hooked the poker onto the bracket at the side of the fire. "We should leave," she announced abruptly.

"What?" John opened his eyes again and blinked.

"We should leave now."

"What are you saying? We've only just gotten here."

She came back beside him, took his hand in hers and pressed it to her lips and then held it to her heart, like a pledge. He could feel her heartbeat, steady and reassuring, as her earnest face looked into his. "John, this duke is not a good man. I have spoken with the people of the house and half of them worship him and will hear nothing against him, and the other half say that he is a sinner of dreadful vices. There is no balance in this household. There is no steadiness. This is a whirlwind of worldly desires and we have strayed into the very heart of it."

John wanted to speak but she gently pressed his hand and he let her finish.

"I did not want to leave Canterbury but you prevailed and it was my duty to obey you," she said softly. "But please now, husband, hear this. We can go to any household in the world that you choose as long as we do not stay here. I will pack our goods and our clothes and go tomorrow, wherever you say, as long as we do not stay here. I will follow you overseas even, Virginia even, as long as we do not stay here."

John waited until she was silent; then he spoke cautiously, feeling his way. "I never thought to hear you speak so. Why do you dislike him so much? As a man? As my master?"

She shrugged and looked toward the fire, where the flames were leaping over the wood and casting a flickering light on her face. "I don't know him as a man, and it's too early to say how he will be as your master. All I have seen of him is worldly show. The diamonds in his hat, the horses in his coach. What man in England has ever had a coach before? No one but the old queen and King James, and now this man has one, with rare horses to go before it. All I have seen of him would make me suspect that he is not a true Christian. And all that I have heard of him, and all that I know of him, tells me that he is very deep in sin." She dropped her voice. "Have you not thought that he may even be in league with the devil himself?"

John tried to laugh but Elizabeth's sincerity was too much for him. "Oh, Elizabeth!"

"Where did he come from?"

"Not from hell! From Leicestershire!"

She frowned at the flippancy of his tone. "The son of a servant and a mere knight of the shires," she said. "Look at his rise, John. D'you think a man can get such fortune honestly?"

"He has enjoyed the favor of the king," John insisted. "He was a cup-bearer and then a groom of the bedchamber and the favorite of many great men. They helped him to the post of Master of the Horse and he has brought the king such horses as no prince ever had before. Of course he enjoys great favor; he has earned it. He brought the king an Arab horse, the only one in England. The finest horse that ever was seen in England."

She shook her head. "So they make him Lord High Admiral—for trading in a horse?"

"Elizabeth—" John said warningly.

"Bear with me," she said swiftly. "Hear me out, this once."

He nodded. "But I will not hear treason."

"I will speak nothing but the truth."

They looked at each other for a moment and she saw in the sliding away of his glance that he knew that the truth was treasonous. That you could speak the truth about Buckingham and the truth was that the king was mad for the man and unfit to rule through his madness. That Buckingham was higher than his ability, higher than any single man's ability could ever take him, because the king was mad to please him.

"What hold is it that he has over the king?" she asked, her voice very low.

"The king loves him," Tradescant said firmly. "And he is his faithful servant."

"He calls himself the king's dog," she said, naming the unthinkable.

"In play. The king calls him Steenie after St. Stephen—he admires his beauty, Elizabeth. Nothing wrong with that."

"He calls himself his dog and there are those who say that the king mounts him like a dog mounts a bitch."

"Silence!" Tradescant leaped to his feet and away from his wife. "That you should speak such words, Elizabeth! At your own hearthside! That you should listen to such things! Bawdy talk! Dirty tavern talk! And repeat them to me! What would your father say if he heard his daughter speaking of such things like a whore!"

She did not even flinch from her father's name. "I say what must be said, what must be clear between the two of us. And God knows that my heart is pure though my mouth is filled with filth."

"A pure heart and a dirty mouth?" Tradescant exclaimed.

"Better than a sweet mouth and dirty heart," she retorted. He checked; they were both thinking of Buckingham and the sweetness of his singing voice.

"Finish what you have to say," John said sullenly. "Finish this, Elizabeth."

"I say to you that his mother who was born a serving maid is now a countess, and is said by many to be a witch—"

John gasped, but she went on.

"A witch. And others say that she is a papist, a heretic, who would have been burned at the stake only a few years ago. I say to you that he is a man who has earned his place by sodomy under the king, and by pandering for the king, who won his wife by kidnap and by rape, who has seduced the king and seduced the prince. Who has been a sodomite with a man and with his son. For all I know he is leagued with the devil himself. Certain, he is deep, deep in sin. And I ask you, John, I beg you, John, to let us go now. To let us leave him now. He has gone to Spain, to the enemy of our country, so he is a traitor even to the king who sins with him. So let us go, John. Let you and me and J get away from here to somewhere where the air is not rank as sulphur with sin and debauchery."

There was a long silence.

"You are intemperate," John said weakly.

She shook her head. "Never mind about that. What's your answer?"

"I have been paid for the full quarter—"

"We can find a way to repay your wages if we leave now."

He paused for a moment, thinking of what she had said. Then slowly he rose and shook his head. He put his hand on the chimney breast, almost as if he needed to steady himself as he went against his wife's declared wish, and his own sense, his own deep and hidden sense, that she was right.

"We stay," he said. "I have given him my promise that I will make him a fine garden. I will not go back on my word. Even if all that you say were true, I would not go back on my word. All I will do for him is garden; there can be no sin in that for us. We stay, Elizabeth, until the garden is finished and then we will leave."

She stood beside him, looking up into his face, and John saw her face alter, as if he had failed some great test and she would never fully trust him again.

"I beg you," she said and her voice shook a little, "by everything that I hold sacred, which is everything that this new lord of yours denies, to turn aside from him and walk in the paths of righteousness."

John shrugged irritably at her scriptural tone. "It's not like that. I have agreed to make a garden for my lord and we will stay until I have completed it. When it is done we can leave, as I have said."

He went from the room and she heard him close their bedroom door and the floorboards creak as he undressed to get into their bed.

"It is like that for me," she said quietly to the dying fire, as if she were swearing a solemn oath. "You have turned aside from the paths of righteousness, husband, and I can walk by your side no more."

John waited for news of his master but there was silence for the first two, three days. Then news of the escapade of the young prince and the young duke began to leak out. They were incompetent conspirators and, indeed, such incompetent travelers that it was a wonder they were not stopped at Dover as John had hoped. But Villiers threw silver around their journey, and ordered the ships out of Dover harbor on his authority as Lord High Admiral, and soon the court and the old king heard that the boys had been entertained in Paris, ridden halfway across France and finally reached Madrid.

The king saw the whole business as a handsome piece of the knight errantry, like the court masques when the handsome hero wins the fairest lady and then they dance. But the rumor that came back to England, even to the King's Arms at Chelmsford where John had taken to drinking in the evening, alert for gossip, was that matters were more difficult. The weeks went by and the young men did not come home with a princess for a bride. Instead they sent demands for money and more money.

The king grew fretful, missing the duke, even missing his usually neglected son. The court was robbed of life when Villiers was not there to arrange amusements, the hunting, the masquing, the scandals. John, lingering in the steward's room, found the courage to ask him outright if he thought their master would hold his place if he did not come home soon, and saw his own worry reflected in William Ward's eyes.

"They will introduce the king to another man every day that our lord is away," Mr. Ward said quietly. "And the king does not like demands for money. He will hold it against our lord. He will resent it." He paused for a moment. "You knew the prince when he was a boy; is he faithful-hearted?"

John thought of the lame boy who stammered on his plea that his handsome brother should wait for him, and was always left behind. The sickly boy who was never anyone's favorite while his older brother was the heir. He nodded. "Once he gives his love he clings," he said simply. "If he loves our duke as he loved his brother, then he worships him."

William Ward nodded. "Then maybe our lord is playing a wiser game than we realize. He may be breaking the heart of the father but there will be another king when the father is gone."

John scowled at the thought of courtier's work which was not based on skill and turning of policy, but was grounded on courtship and heartbreak and jealousy; the skills of the bordello, not of the office.

"It must have been the same for Lord Cecil?" the steward asked.

John jerked back at the thought of it. "No! Nobody loved *him* for his looks," he said with a half-smile. "They needed him for his abilities. That was why no one could supplant him. That was why he was always safe."

"Whereas our lord—" The steward broke off.

"What's he doing in Madrid that takes so long?" John demanded.

"I hear that the Spanish are playing with him," the steward said very quietly. "And all the time the feeling against the Spanish is rising in the court, in Parliament and in the streets. He'd do better to come home without the Spanish princess. If he brings her home now he'll pay for it with his life. They'll tear him to pieces for arranging a heretical marriage."

"Can't you write and tell him?" John asked. "Warn him?"

William Ward shook his head. "I don't advise him," he said quickly. "He treads his own path. He said the Spanish marriage was a matter of principle."

"Principle?" John asked. And when the man nodded he turned and went from the room. "That's very bad," John said to himself.

Not until July, midsummer in Madrid, during the worst of the hot weather, was Prince Charles finally wearied of waiting, and Buckingham losing his nerve. At last the Spanish completed the marriage contract and Prince Charles put his name to it. He was allowed a brief visit to his bride to promise that she would be Queen of England after a proxy marriage, and that they would next meet as husband and wife at Dover. The King of Spain himself rode out of Madrid with the prince and duke to set them on their way, loaded them with presents and kissed Prince Charles farewell as a son-in-law.

"How do you think he will be received?" William Ward asked John. He had gone into the garden to seek John, who was opening the sluice gates and watching the flow of the river into the duke's new boating lake. It was a cool sheet of water just to the side of the house. John was planting yellow flag irises in the boggy corner where he had first told Buckingham to shut out the cows. "He must have some trickery up his sleeve. He must know that if he tries to bring a Spanish bride home they will tear him to pieces?"

John looked up from the water channel and wiped his hands on his old breeches. "He can't be such a fool," he said anxiously. "He cannot have gotten as far as he has and still be a fool. He must know that there is a balance between king and Parliament and church and people." He thought of Cecil; he could not help but think of Cecil in this, his successor's household. "He cannot hold the offices he has and be a fool," John said stoutly. "He must have some way to turn this all around."

John did his lord a favor with such faith. Buckingham had no master plan and no plan hidden behind it. He was not a Cecil, with a conspiracy for every eventuality. Everything in his life had come easily to him, and he had thought that this would come easily too. He had thought that he could seduce the Spanish as he had seduced everyone else. But the cold formal court of Spain proved hard-hearted even to England's heartbreaker, and his disappointment turned him against them. His letters from home from his mother and from his wife warned him that a Spanish bride would never be accepted and the man who tried to bring her to the English throne could meet with nothing but disaster. Buckingham turned like a weathercock; but Charles—who had learned early that love is always a matter of disappointment—clung to his picture of a desirable and unattainable woman. Indeed, the more unattainable she became, the more she mirrored Charles's vision of true love and desire.

It was Buckingham's task to lift the prince's view from a woman who might never love him, whom he could trail behind for the rest of his days, as he had trailed behind his brother, and encourage him to think that as a prince of England he might hope for a little more.

It was not easy. Buckingham reminded him of the concessions of the marriage contract—wild promises of religious tolerance and the children of the marriage to be brought up as papists. He questioned Spanish probity, wondering if the infanta could really be constrained into marrying a heretic, or if she would not, on her wedding day, make a dive for a nunnery and leave Charles looking like a fool. The steady drip, drip, of cynicism and doubt eroded the prince's confidence, which was, at the best of times, unsteady. By the time the two had ridden from Madrid to Santander to meet the English fleet, Buckingham and the prince were the best of friends, and Spain was their opponent. By the time they sailed into Portsmouth they were as close as brothers and Spain was not to be the new alliance, but was once again the deadliest enemy, and the marriage contract which they had worked for so fervently was a trap that they were determined to escape.

As they came into Portsmouth, through the cold sea mist of October, sailing in with the tide, uncertain of their welcome in the Protestant city in the staunchly Protestant country after trying for a marriage which would have brought the proud Tudor independence to an abrupt end, they saw a light blaze on the quayside; a bonfire had been lit. Then another, then another, in a string of light along the city walls. Then there was the boom of a cannon salute which echoed across the harbor, and then another, and the scream of loudly blown trumpets, and the sound of people cheering. Buckingham smiled to himself, slapped his prince on the back and went below to put the diamond studs in his hat.

"He did it, he brought the prince safe home," John said to Elizabeth when the news of the triumphant entry of the two young men into London reached New Hall. "There was dancing on the streets and roasted oxen at every corner. They are calling him a greater statesman than England has ever seen. They are calling him the savior of his country. Shall we go into Chelmsford tonight and see the merrymaking?"

He did not mean to crow but he heard the joy in his own voice. It was not that Buckingham had proved himself to be a statesman or a diplomat. But at least he was lucky, and in this new court, luck and beauty would do everything.

The face that Elizabeth turned to him was pinched and cold. "He took the prince into danger in the first place," she said unforgivingly. "Danger of his body and deadly danger to his mortal soul.

And the prince only escaped from marrying a disciple of the Devil by being forsworn. He gave his word of honor to a noble princess. He courted her and promised to marry her. But now he has broken his promise. I shan't go dancing because your lord took the prince into danger and then made him a jilt to bring him safe home. It was vanity and folly to go in the first place. I won't drink to his safe return."

John quietly put on his coat and hat and let himself out of the door. "I think I'll go then," he said mildly. "Don't wake for me."

1624

"He's home," J announced without enthusiasm.

John was standing on the mount he had created in the duke's new lake, checking the line of the winding path to the top. Below him, the men hired to plant the trees were digging and setting in apple, cherry, pear and plum alternately up the circling slope. Small stakes supported each tree against the constant easterly winds which were John's bugbear in this Essex garden. Bigger posts were set in the ground, tied tautly with twine, one to another, to guide the espaliered branches to reach out, one tree to another, so they would make unbroken lines of blossom in spring, and unbroken lines of fruit in autumn. J's task was to check that each tree was placed to its best advantage with the outstretched branches lying conveniently along the twine, and tied in so they could not stray and be wayward. John was following with a sharp knife to cut off any twigs which were growing out of the smooth line of the interlaced trees. It was one of John's most favorite tasks: a delicate marriage of wildness and artifice, an imposition of order upon unruliness which in the end looked as if it had grown ordered and well-ruled out of simple good nature. A garden as God might have left it, an Eden without disorder or weeds.

"God be praised!" John said, straightening up from his pruning. "Did he ask for me? Is he coming out into the garden?"

J shook his head. "He's sick," he said. "Very sick."

John felt his breath suddenly stop as if he too were ill. A sudden pulse of dread went through his body at the thought of his master's frailty. He suddenly remembered Cecil, dying in bluebell time. "Sick?" he asked. "Not the plague?"

J shrugged. "A great quarrel with the king, and he took to his bed."

"He is pretending to be ill?" John asked.

"I think not. The duchess is running all around their apartments and the kitchen is making possets. They want some herbs for medicine."

"Good God, why did you not tell me at once?" John ran down the path, slithering on the muddy track, and flung himself into the rowing boat moored at the delicate ornamental jetty. He grabbed at the oars and labored clumsily across the lake, splashing himself with water and cursing his own slowness. He got to the shore, beached the boat and ran through the shallows and up toward the house.

He went straightaway toward the great hall, his boots making wet prints on the floor. "Where is the apothecary? What does he need?"

The man gestured him toward the duke's private quarters, up the beautiful staircase which had cost him such a fortune. John went up the stairs at a run. The duke's apartments were in uproar, the doors wide open, the duke sprawled neglected on his bed, still in his riding boots. Dozens of men and women were running in and out with coals for his fire and fresh straw for the floor, warming pans, cooling drinks, someone opening the windows, someone closing the shutters. Amid it all was Kate, the young duchess, weeping helplessly in a chair, and half a dozen apothecaries quarreling over the bed.

"Quiet!" Tradescant shouted, too angry at the sight of such chaos for his usual politeness. He took a couple of footmen, spun them around and pushed them out of the room. He closed the door on them and then pointed to the maids who were sweeping the floor and the men who were stacking logs on the fire. "You! Out."

The room slowly emptied of complaining servants, and Tradescant turned his attention to the apothecaries. "Who's in charge here?" he asked.

The six men, all bitter rivals, burst into noisy argument. Kate, hunched in her chair, wailed like a child.

Tradescant opened the door. "Her Grace's ladies!" he shouted. They came at the run. "Take Her Grace to her own chamber," he said gently. "Now."

"I want to be here!" Kate cried.

Tradescant took her arm and half-lifted her from the room. "Let me see that he is comfortable and you can come when he is ready to receive you," he suggested.

She fought against him. "I want to be with my lord!"

"You wouldn't want him to see you weeping," John said softly. "With your nose all red, and your eyes puffed up so plain."

The appeal to her vanity struck her at once. She ran out of the room and John closed the door on her and rounded on the apothecaries. "Which of you is the oldest?" he demanded.

One man stepped forward. "I," he said, thinking that the prize was to be awarded to seniority.

"And which the youngest?"

A young man, barely thirty, stepped forward. "I am."

"The two of you get out," Tradescant ordered brutally. "The other four of you agree on a treatment in whispers, at once."

He opened the door and the two dismissed men hesitated, caught one fulminating look and stepped outside. "Wait there," Tradescant said. "If these can't agree you'll be employed in their place."

He shut the door on them and went back to the bed. The duke was as white as marble; he looked like a statue carved from ice. The only color about him was his dark eyelashes sweeping his cheeks and the blue shadows, the color of violets in springtime, under his eyes.

The eyelids fluttered and he looked up at John. "Splendidly done," he said softly, his throat hoarse. "I just want to sleep."

"Well enough," Tradescant said. "Now that I know." He pointed to the apothecaries. "You three—out of the room." He pointed to the other. "And you watch the duke's sleep and guard him from noise and interruption."

Buckingham made a little gesture with his thin hand. "Don't you leave me, John."

John bowed, and swept all the men from the room. "Consult among yourselves and make whatever he needs," he said firmly. "I shall watch his sleep."

"He needs cupping," one of them said.

"No cupping."

"Or leeches?"

John shook his head. "He's to sleep and not be tortured."

"What d'you know? You're nothing but a gardener."

John gave the apothecaries a hard unfriendly smile. "I wager I lose fewer plants than you do patients," he said accurately. "And I keep them well by letting them rest when they need rest, and feeding them when they are hungry. I don't cup them and leech them, I care for them. And that is what I shall do for my duke until he orders it otherwise."

Then he shut the door in their faces and stood at the foot of his master's bed, and waited for him to have his fill of sleep.

Tradescant could guard his master against the household. But when the king heard that the Favorite had been sick and near to death, he sent word that he would come at once, and the whole court with him.

Buckingham, still pale but only a little stronger, was sitting in the bay window which overlooked John's new knot garden, John standing at his side, when they brought the message from the king.

"I'm back in favor then," Buckingham said idly. "I thought I was finished for this reign."

"But you brought Prince Charles safe home," Tradescant protested. "What more did His Majesty want?"

Buckingham slid a sly sideways smile at his gardener and sniffed at the spray of snowdrops which Tradescant had brought him. "A little less rather than more," he said. "He envied me the triumphant entry into London. He thought I was setting up to be king myself. He thought I wanted Kit Villiers to marry the Elector Frederick's daughter and ally myself to the Stuarts." He laughed shortly. "As though I would put Kit over myself," he said scornfully. "And then he looks from me to the prince and back again and he fears my influence over the heir. And he's jealous as an old woman. He cannot bear to see us make merry when he is old and aching and longing for his bed. He cannot bear to think that we are merry without him when he has withdrawn. He has given me everything I ask and now he is jealous that I am wealthy and courted. Jealous that I am the richest man in the kingdom with the most beautiful house." He broke off and tossed his head.

"Though it is true that it is better not to flaunt your wealth," Tradescant remarked to the sky outside the bay window.

"What d'you mean?"

"I'm thinking that my old lord loved Theobalds Palace before anything else in the country and the king, *this* king, in very truth, saw it through his eyes, acknowledged its value and claimed it for himself. And here we've only just gotten the avenue planted."

Buckingham cracked a laugh. "John! My John! If he wants it, he'll have to have it! Avenue and all. Anything so long as I am back in his favor."

John nodded. "You think he will forgive you?"

The younger man lay back on the rich cushions heaped in the window-seat and turned his face to look out at the view. John noted, with affection, the perfect profile, white against red velvet.

"What d'you think, John? If I am very pale and very quiet and very submissive, and look—so—would you forgive me?"

John tried to stare at his master unmoved, but he found he was smiling as if his master were a tender wilful maid in the first years of her beauty, at the time when a girl can do anything and be forgiven by everyone. "I suppose so," he admitted ungraciously. "If I were a besotted old fool."

Buckingham grinned. "I suppose so too."

* * *

The duke waved farewell to the royal coach and the hundreds of courtiers and outriders, and watched them move slowly down the newly planted avenue. John Tradescant had done his best but the limes in the double-planted avenue were still only saplings. The duke watched the coach with the crown and the nodding feathers rumble from one thin leafy shade to another. When they grew, the trees would be a powerful symbol of the greatness of the house. And by then the prince would be on the throne, with Buckingham as his adviser, and the king, the jealous difficult bad-tempered old king, would be dead.

The king had wept and asked for forgiveness after a long bitter quarrel. He had tolerated Buckingham's marriage, indeed he loved Kate, and he was even amused by Buckingham's notorious affairs with every pretty woman at court, but he could not bear to feel that his son the prince had supplanted him in Buckingham's affections. Tearfully he accused them of conspiring against him and that Prince Charles—never the favored son—had stolen from his father his love, his only love.

He publicly called Prince Charles a changeling and wished that his brother, the handsome and godly Prince Henry, had never died. He publicly called Buckingham a heartbreaker and a false son to him. He called him a traitor and wept the easy tears of an old man, and swore that no one loved him.

It took all Buckingham's charm to talk the king into a more reasonable frame of mind, and all his patience to tolerate the moist kisses on his face and his mouth. It took all his ready humor and his genuine joy of life to seek to make the elderly king happy again, and the court happy with him. A sick man, newly up from his bed, Buckingham danced with Kate before the king, and sat at his side and listened to his rambling complaints about the Spanish alliance and the Spanish threat, and never showed so much as a flicker of weariness or sickness.

Buckingham waited until the royal carriage was out of sight before he put his hat back on his head and turned away toward the stone steps to the knot garden. Already it was as Tradescant had promised it would be. Each delicately shaped bed was filled with plants of a single uniform color, edged with dark green box and entwined in an unending pattern with another. Buckingham walked around them, feeling his anxiety melt away at the sight of the twisting patterns, at the perfection of the planting.

It was a joy he had not known before Tradescant had made this place for him. He had seen gardens as part of the furniture of a great house, something a great man must have. But Tradescant had made him see things with a plantsman's eye. Now he walked around and around the little twisting paths of the knot garden with a sense of renewed pleasure and a feeling of liberty. The little hedges destroyed the sense of perspective; when he looked across them from one end of the knot garden to the other they seemed as if they enclosed acres of land, one field after another. They were a little parable of wealth. They looked like great fields, great acres, and yet they were encompassed within a few hundred yards.

"A thing of beauty," Buckingham murmured softly to himself. "I should thank him for it. Thank him for making it for me, and then for training my eye to see it."

He walked down from the formal garden toward the lake. There were the lilies that Tradescant had promised him, and waving in the slight breeze were the golden buttercups and flag irises. A little pier jutted out into the water and the still reflection of the lake showed another pier reflected darkly beneath it. At the very end of it, looking down into the water, was John Tradescant himself, watching a boy drop baskets of osier roots into the deep mud.

When he heard Buckingham approach he pulled off his hat and nudged the boy with his foot. The boy dropped to his knees. Buckingham waved him away.

"Will you row me?" he asked Tradescant.

"Of course, my lord," John replied. He took in at once the dark shadows under the eyes, the pallor of Buckingham's skin. He looked like an angel carved in purest marble with sooty fingerprints on its face.

John pulled in the little boat by its dripping rope and held it steady while the duke climbed in and leaned back against the cushions.

"I am weary," he said shortly.

John cast off, sat down, and bent over the oars without speaking. He rowed his master first toward the island where the mount had been thrown up, just as they had first planned. He rowed slowly around it. Whitethorn and roses tumbled down to the water's edge and the blossoms nodded at themselves in the still water. A few ducks came quacking out of hiding but Buckingham did not stir at the noise.

"Do you remember Robert Cecil?" he asked idly. "In your thoughts, or in your prayers?"

"Yes," Tradescant said, surprised. "Daily."

"I met a man the other day who said that the first time he went to Theobalds Palace they could not find Sir Robert anywhere and in the end they found him in the potting shed with you, eating bread and cheese."

Tradescant gave a short laugh. "He used to like to watch me work."

"He was a great man, a great servant of state," Buckingham said. "No one ever thought the less of him because he served first one monarch and then her heir."

John nodded, leaned forward on his oars and rowed.

"But me . . ." Buckingham broke off. "What d'you hear, John? Men despise me, don't they? Because I came from nowhere and nothing and because I won my place at court because I was a pretty boy?"

He expected his servant to deny it.

"I'm afraid that's what they do say," John confirmed.

Buckingham sat bolt upright and the boat rocked. "You say so to my face?"

John nodded.

"No man in England has dared so much! I could have your tongue slit for impertinence!" Buckingham exclaimed.

John's oars did not break in their gentle rhythm. He smiled at his master, a slow affectionate smile. "You spoke of Sir Robert," he said. "I never lied to him either. If you ask me a question I will answer it, sir. I'm not impertinent, and I'm not a gossip. If you tell me a secret I will keep it to myself. If you ask me for news I will tell you."

"Did Sir Robert confide in you?" Buckingham asked curiously.

John nodded. "When you make a garden for a man you learn what sort of man he is," he explained. "You spend time together, you watch things grow and change together. We worked on Theobalds together and then we moved and made Hatfield together, Sir Robert and me, from nothing. And we talked, as men do, when they walk in a garden together."

"And what sort of man am I?" Buckingham asked. "You've worked for a king's adviser before now. You worked for Cecil and you work for me. What d'you think of me? What d'you think of me, compared with him?"

Tradescant leaned forward and pulled gently on the oars, and the boat slid smoothly through the water. "I think you are still very young," he said gently. "And impatient, as a young man is impatient. I think you are ambitious—and no one can tell how high you will rise or how long you will stay at the height of your power. I think that you may have won your place at court on your beauty but you have kept it by your wit. And since you are both beautiful and witty you will keep it still."

Buckingham laughed and leaned back on the cushions again. "Both beautiful and witty!" he exclaimed.

John looked at the tumbled dark hair and the long dark lashes sweeping the smooth cheeks. "Yes," he said simply. "You are my lord, and I never thought to find a lord that I could follow heart and soul ever again."

"Do you love me as you loved Lord Cecil?" Buckingham asked him, suddenly alert, with a sly searching look from under his eyelashes.

John, innocent in his heart, smiled at his master. "Yes."

"I shall keep you by me, as he kept you by him," Buckingham

said, planning their future. "And men will see that if you can love me, as you loved him, then I cannot be less than him. They will make the comparison and think of me as another Cecil."

"Maybe," Tradescant replied. "Or maybe they will think I am a man with a sense to garden in only the best gardens. It would be a man overproud of his sight to boast that he could see into men's hearts, my lord. You'd do better to follow your own counsel than wonder how it might look to others—in my view."

March 1625

John was working late. The duke had ordered a watercourse to flow from one terrace to another and it was his fancy that in each terrace there should be a different breed of fish, in descending orders of colors, so that the gold—the king of fish—should only swim in the topmost pool near the house. The garden around it was to be all gold too, and it was to face the royal rooms that King James used on his visits. Tradescant had sent out messages to every ship in the Royal Navy commanding them to bring him the seeds or roots of any yellow or gold flowers they saw anywhere in the world. The Duke of Buckingham ordered the highest admirals in the Navy to go ashore and look at flowers that John Tradescant might have his pick of yellow flower seeds.

It was a pretty idea and it would have been a delightful compliment to His Majesty, except Tradescant's goldfish were as elusive as swallows in winter. Whatever he did to the watercourse they slipped away downstream and mingled with the others: silver fish on one level, rainbow trout at the next, and dappled carp on the fourth level, who ate them.

Tradescant had tried nets, but they got tangled up and drowned themselves; he had tried building little dams of stones, but the water became sluggish and did not pitter-patter from one level to another as it should. Worse, when the water was still or slow it turned green and murky, and he could not see the fish at all.

His next idea was to build a little fence of small pieces of window glass through which the water could flow and the fish could not swim. It was a prodigally expensive solution—to use precious glass for such a fancy. Tradescant scowled and placed the small panes—each one carefully rounded at the corners so as not to cut the fish—in a line, with only a small gap for the water to flow between each. When he finished he stood up.

His feet ached with standing in the cold water, and his back was stiff with stooping. His fingers were numb with cold—it was still only March and there were frosts at night. He rubbed his hands briskly on the homespun of his breeches. His fingertips were blue. He could hardly see his work in the failing light but he could hear the musical splashing of the water flowing down to the next pool on the next terrace. As he watched a goldfish approached the fence of glass, nosed at it, and turned back and swam toward the center of the pond.

"Got you!" Tradescant grunted. "Got you, you little bastard."

He chuckled at himself and clapped his hat on his head, picked up his tools and set off for his shed to clean and hang them before he went home for his dinner. Then he stopped, listening: a horse, galloping at high speed, up the long spectacular winding drive and at full pelt to the front door of the house.

The messenger saw Tradescant. "Is His Grace at home?" he shouted.

John glanced toward the brightly lit windows of the house. "Yes," he said. "He should be dining soon."

"Take me to him!" the man ordered. He flung himself from his horse and dropped the reins, as if the high-bred animal hardly mattered.

John, wrenching his mind from yellow flowers, snatched at the reins and called for a groom. When one came running he handed him the horse and led the messenger into the house.

"Where's the duke?" he asked a serving man.

"At his prayers, in his library." The man nodded toward the door.

John tapped on the door and went in.

Buckingham was sprawled on his chair behind his grand desk listening to his chaplain reading prayers, playing idly with a gold chain, his dark eyes veiled. When he saw John his face lit up. "It's my wizard, John!" he called. "Come in, my John! Have you made the water flow backward up the hill for me?"

"There's a man here come in haste from the king," John said shortly, and pushed the messenger into the room.

"You're to go to Theobalds," the man blurted. "The king is sick with ague and asking for you. He says you're to come to him at once."

There was a sudden alertness about Buckingham, like the sudden freezing when a cat sees its prey, and then he moved.

"Get me a horse." Buckingham started from his desk. "John, get one too. Come with me. You know the way better than any. And a man to ride with us. How bad is he?" he threw over his shoulder to the messenger.

"They said more sorry than sick." The man trotted after him. "But commanding your presence. The prince is already there."

Buckingham ran up the stairs and looked down at John. His face was alight with kindled ambition. "Perhaps now!" he said, and turned into his room to change his clothes.

John sent orders for horses to be made ready and sent a man running to the kitchen for a knapsack of food and a flask of drink. He sent no message for Elizabeth. The urgency of the young duke, the call of the adventure and the sense of living in great times was too much for him to remember his domestic ties.

When the duke came clattering down the front steps, handsome in his riding boots and a long cape, John was mounted on one good horse, and holding another. The servant who was to ride with them was coming from the stable yard.

The duke glanced at John. "Thank you," he said, and meant it.

John grinned. The great fault of these large households was their slowness. Meat was always eaten half-cold, hunting expeditions had to be planned days ahead and always started hours after the time named. Nothing could be done on impulse, everything had to be prepared. John's ability to get a horse from the stables, groomed and ready to ride in minutes, was one of his greatest talents.

"Will you be all right to ride?" Buckingham asked, glancing at John's borrowed breeches and boots.

"I'll get you there," John said. "Never fear."

He led the way at a steady trot out of the courtyard, put the cold sliver of the rising moon on his right and rode due west to Waltham Cross.

They changed horses not once but twice in the twenty-four-hour journey, once knocking at the door of an inn until a reluctant landlord lent them his own horses when he caught sight of the gold which Tradescant carried. The second time when there were no horses to be hired, they simply stole a pair from the stable. John left a note to tell the owner in the morning that he had obliged the great duke and might call on him for repayment.

Buckingham laughed at Tradescant's enterprise. "By God, John, you are wasted in the gardens," he said. "You should be a general at least."

John smiled at the praise. "I said I would get you there, and I will," he said simply.

Buckingham nodded. "I'll not travel without you again."

It was near dawn when they came wearily up the drive to the sweep before the great door of Theobalds. The dark windows of the palace looked down on them. John glanced up to where the great breast of the bay window jutted outward like the poop deck on a sailing ship. He could see the light from many candles spilling out through the cracks of the shutters.

"They are awake in the king's chamber," he said. "Shall I go first?"

"Go and see," Buckingham commanded. "If the king is asleep I shall wash and rest myself. It may be a great day for me tomorrow."

John got stiffly down from his horse. His borrowed breeches were stuck to the skin of his thighs by sweat and blood from saddle sores. He scowled at the pain and went bowlegged into the house, up the stairs and to the royal rooms. A soldier extended his pike to bar the door.

"John Tradescant," growled John. "I've brought the duke. Let me pass."

The sentry stood to attention and John went into the room. There were half a dozen doctors and innumerable midwives and wise women, called in for their knowledge of herbs. There was a desperate gaiety about the room. There were courtiers, some dozing in corners, some playing cards and drinking. Everyone turned as John came in, travel-stained and weary.

"Is the king awake?" John asked. "I have brought the duke."

For a moment it seemed that no one knew. They were so absorbed in their own tasks of arguing about his health and waiting for his recovery that no one was actually caring for him. One doctor broke from the others and scuttled to the door of the bedroom and peeped in.

"Awake," he said. "And restless."

John nodded and went back down to the hall. Behind him he could hear the flurry of movement as the courtiers prepared themselves for the greatest courtier of all—George Villiers.

He was seated in a chair in the hall, a glass of mulled wine in his hand, a lad kneeling before him, brushing the mud off his boots.

"He's awake," John said shortly.

"I'll go up," Buckingham declared. "Many with him?"

"A score," John said. "No one of importance."

Buckingham went wearily up the stairs. "Make sure they make up a bed for me," he threw over his shoulder. "And get a bed for yourself in my chamber. I want to have you close, John; I may be busy these next days."

John poured himself a glass from the duke's own flagon and went to do as he had been told.

The household was starting to wake, although many had not slept at all. The word was that the king had been hunting and had fallen sick. At first it was a light fever and expected to pass, but it had taken hold, and the king was rambling. He feared for his life;

sometimes he dreamed he was back in Scotland with buckram wadding beneath all his clothes to ward off an assassin's knife; sometimes he called out for forgiveness from the enemies he had tried on a pretext and then hanged and drawn and quartered. Sometimes he dreamed of the witches that he thought had haunted his life, the innocent old women he had ordered drowned or strangled. Sometimes, and most pitifully of all, he called out to his mother, poor Mary of Scotland, and begged her forgiveness for letting her go to the executioner's block at Fotheringay without a word of comfort from him, though she sent letter after letter addressed to her beloved son and never forgot the baby he had been.

"But he will recover?" John asked one of the maids.

"It is only the ague," she said. "Why should he not recover?"

John nodded and went to the duke's bedroom. The cold March dawn was turning the sky from black to gray; the frost was white on the terraces. John leaned his elbows on the windowsill and watched the familiar landmarks of Theobalds, his first great garden, swim upward from the mist. In the distance he could see the woods, bare-branched now, and cold; and underneath them deep in the frozen earth would be the bulbs of the daffodils that he had planted for the king who was now old, and to please the master who was long dead.

He wondered what Cecil would have thought of his new master, if he would have despised or admired the duke. He wondered where Cecil was now; in a garden, he thought, the blessed last garden where flowers were always in bloom. John felt great tenderness for the master he had lost and this garden they had loved together.

Then the door behind him opened and Buckingham came into the room.

"Shut the window for the love of God, John!" he snapped. "It's freezing!"

John obeyed and waited.

"Get some sleep," the duke said. "And when you wake I want you to go to London, and fetch my mother."

"I could go now," John volunteered.

"Rest," the duke said. "Go as soon as you wake and are fit to ride. Take her this message, I shan't write it down." He crossed the room to John and spoke very low. "Tell her that the king is sick but not yet dying, and I need her help. Badly. D'you understand?"

John hesitated. "I understand the words, and I can repeat them. But I dare not think of your meaning."

Buckingham nodded. "John, my John," he said softly, "that is what I wish. Just remember the words and leave the rest to me." He met John's worried look with an open face. "I loved the king like my own father," he said persuasively. "I want him cared for with love and respect. That crowd in there will not leave him alone; they torture him with remedies, they bleed him, they turn him, they blister him, they sweat him, and chill him. I want my mother to come and nurse him gently. She's a woman of much experience. She will know how to ease his pain."

"I'll fetch her at once," John said.

"Rest now, but go as soon as you wake," the duke said and went quietly from the room.

John peeled the borrowed breeches off his sore buttocks, tumbled into the pallet bed and slept for six solid hours.

When he woke it was past noon. Someone had placed a jug and ewer on the dark wooden chest at the head of his bed, and he washed. In the chest was a change of clothes, and John slipped on a clean shirt and breeches. He did not trouble to shave. The duke's mother could take him as he was. He went quietly down the stairs and out to the stable yard.

"I need a good horse," he said to the chief groom. "The duke's business."

"He said you would be riding," the man replied. "There's a horse saddled and ready for you, and a lad to ride part of the way with you to bring back the horse when you need to change. In which direction are you going?"

"London," John said briefly.

"Then this horse will take you all the way. He's as strong as an ox." The groom took in John's stiff walk. "Though I imagine you'll not be galloping."

John grimaced and reached for the saddle to haul himself up.

"Where in London?" the groom asked.

"To the docks," John lied instantly. "The duke has some curious playthings come from the Indies which he thought might amuse the king and divert him in his illness. I am to fetch them."

"The king is better then?" the groom asked. "They said this morning he was on the mend, but I did not know. He has ordered his horses to move to Hampton Court so I thought he must be better."

"Better, yes," John said.

The groom released the reins and the horse took three steps back. With his bruised muscles aching, John leaned forward against the pain and sent his horse at the gentlest canter he could command, back down the road to London.

The countess was at her son's grand London house. John went to the stables first and ordered them to harness the carriage for her, and then went into the house. She was a powerful old woman, dark-eyed like her son, but completely lacking his charm. She had been a famous beauty when she was a girl, married for her looks and jumped from servitude into the gentry in one lucky leap. But her struggle for respect had left its mark, her face was always determined; in repose she looked bitter. John recited his message in a whisper, and she nodded in silence.

"Wait for me downstairs," she said shortly.

John went back down to the hall and sent a maidservant racing for some wine, bread and cheese. Within a few moments Lady Villiers was sweeping down the stairs, wrapped in a traveling cape, a pomander held to her nose against the infections of the London streets, a small box in her hand.

"You will ride in front to guide my driver."

"If you wish, my lady." John got stiffly to his feet.

She walked past him but as she got into the carriage she made a quick gesture with her hand. "Get up on the box; your horse can be tied behind."

"I can ride," John offered.

"You are half-crippled with saddle sores," she observed. "Sit where you will be comfortable. You are of no use to my son or to me if you are bleeding from a dozen bruises."

John climbed up to sit beside the driver. "Perceptive woman," he remarked.

The driver nodded and waited for the carriage door to shut. John saw that he was holding the reins awkwardly with each thumb between the first and second finger: the old sign against witchcraft.

The roads were bad, thick with mud from the winter. In the heart of London, beggars held out beseeching hands as the rich carriage went by them. Some of them were pocked with rosy scars where they had recovered from the plague. The driver kept to the line of the track at a steady pace, and left it to them to leap clear.

"Hard times," John remarked, thinking with gratitude to his lord of the little house at New Hall and his son and wife safely distant from these dangerous streets.

"Eight years of bad harvests and a king on the throne who has forgotten his duty," the driver said angrily. "What would you expect?"

"I don't expect to hear treason from the duke's own household," John said shortly. "And I won't hear it!"

"I'll say only this," the driver said. "There's a Christian prince and princess, his own daughter, driven from her throne by the armies of the Pope. There's a Spanish match that he would still make if he could. The Spanish ambassador is to return to him—by his own request! And year after year the country gets poorer while the court gets richer. You can't expect people to dance in the streets. The death cart goes past them too often."

John shook his head and looked away.

"There's those that think the land should be shared," the driver said under his breath. "There's those that think that no good will come to England while people starve every winter and others are sick of surfeit."

"It is as God wills," John insisted. "And I won't say more. To speak against the king is treason; to speak against the way things are and must be is heresy. If your mistress heard you, you'd be on the street yourself. And me too, for listening to you."

"You're a good servant," the man sneered. "For you even think in obedience to your lord."

John shot him a hard dark look. "I am a good servant," he repeated. "And proud of it. And of course I think in obedience to my lord. I think and live and pray in obedience to my lord. How else could it be? How else should it be?"

"There are other ways," the driver argued. "You could think and live and pray for yourself."

John shook his head. "I've given my allegiance," he said. "I don't withdraw it, and I don't pay three farthings to the penny. My lord is my master, heart and soul. And you'll forgive me saying, but you might be a happier man if you could say the same thing."

The driver shook his head and sulkily fell silent. John wrapped himself in his borrowed cloak and nodded off to sleep, only waking when they were driving toward Theobalds under the great double avenue of ash and elm, with the daffodils flooding around the trunks.

The carriage drew up outside the door and the duke himself came out to greet his mother.

"Thank you, John," he threw over his shoulder and drew her into the house and up to the king's chamber.

"Is the king better?" John asked a manservant as the countess's box was carried up the stairs.

"On the mend," the man said. "He took some soup this midday."

"Then I think I'll take a turn around the garden." John nodded toward the door and the enticing view. "If my lord wants me you will find me at the bath house, or on the mount. I have not been here for many years."

He stepped through the front door and toward the first of the beautiful knot gardens. They wanted weeding, he thought, and then smiled at himself. These were not his weeds anymore, they were the king's.

He saw Buckingham before dinner that night. "If you do not need me, I shall go home tomorrow," he said. "I did not warn my wife that I was going with you, and there is much to do in the garden at New Hall."

Buckingham nodded. "When you go through London you can see if my ship has come from the Indies," he said. "And supervise the unloading of the goods. They were ordered to bring me much ivory and silk. You can fetch them safely down to New Hall and see them installed in my rooms. I am making a collection of rare and precious things. Prince Charles has his toy soldiers, have you seen them? They fire cannon and you can draw them up in battle lines. They are very diverting. I should like some pretty things too."

"Am I to wait in London for the Indies goods to arrive?"

"If you will," Buckingham said sweetly. "If Mrs. Tradescant can spare you so long."

"She knows your service comes first," John said. "How does the king today? Still better?"

Buckingham looked grave. "He is worse," he said. "The ague has hold of him, and he is not a young man, and was never strong. He saw the prince privately today and put him in mind of his duties. He is preparing himself . . . I really think he is preparing himself. It is my duty to make sure he can be at peace, that he can rest."

"I heard he was getting better," John ventured cautiously.

"We give out the best reports we can, but the truth is that he is an old man who is ready to meet his death."

John bowed and left the room, and went down to the hall for his dinner.

The place was in uproar. Half a dozen of the physicians that John had first seen in the king's chamber were calling for their horses and their menservants. The courtiers were shouting for their carriages and for food to take on their journeys.

"What's this?" John asked.

"It's all the fault of your master," a woman replied shortly. "He has flung the physicians from the king's presence, and half the court too. He said they were troubling him too much with their noise and their playing, and he said the physicians were fools."

John grinned and stepped back to watch the confusion of their departure.

"He will regret it!" one doctor shouted to another. "I warned him myself, if His Majesty suffers and we are not at hand, he will regret this insult to us!"

"He is beyond counsel! I warned him but he pushed me from the room!"

"He snatched my very pipe out of my mouth and broke it!" one of the courtiers interrupted. "I know that the king hates smoke, but it is a sure prevention of infection, and how should His Majesty smell it in another room? I shall write to the duke and complain of my treatment. Twenty years I have been at court, and he pushed me out of the door as if I were his serf!"

"He has cleared the room of everyone but a nurse, his mother and himself," a man declared. "And he swears that the king shall have peace and quiet and no more meddling. As if a king should not be surrounded by his people all the time!"

John left them and strolled into dinner. Buckingham and his mother were at the high table; the place for the king was left respectfully empty. Prince Charles was seated next to the empty place, his head very close to the duke's.

"Aye, they'll have much to consider," a man said in an undertone and took his seat next to John.

John took some fine manchet bread and a large joint of pheasant from the plate in the center of the table. He snapped his fingers for a girl and she came to pour him wine.

"What's the countess doing here?" one man asked. "The king can't abide her."

"Caring for the king, apparently. The physicians have been sent away and she is to nurse him."

"An odd choice," another man said shortly. "Since he hates the sight of her."

"The king is on the mend," yet another man said, pulling out his stool. "The duke was right to send those fools away. His Majesty had the fever—why!—we've all had a fever. And if the countess knows a remedy which cured the duke, why should she not offer it to the king?"

The men glanced at John. "Was it you fetched her?" one asked.

John savored the taste of roast pheasant, the rich juices flowing in his mouth. "I can hardly remember," he said, muffled. "D'you know this is the first decent meal I've had in a day and a half? I was damming up a fishpond in Essex this time yesterday. And now here I am back at Theobalds. And very good fare to be had too."

One of the men shrugged and laughed shortly. "Aye," he said. "We'll get no secrets from you. We all know who is your master, and you serve him well, John Tradescant. I hope you never come to regret it!"

John looked up the hall to the top table where the duke was leaning forward to call to one of the officers. The candlelight made a reddish halo around his black curls; his face was as bright and delighted as a child's.

"No," John said with affection. "I'll never regret it."

John stayed late in the hall, drinking with the men at his table. At midnight he headed unsteadily to the duke's chamber.

"Where d'you sleep?" one of his drinking companions asked him.

"With my lord."

"Oh, yes," the man said pointedly. "I heard you were a favorite."

John wheeled around and stared at him, and the man held his gaze, half a question on his face which was an insult. John spoke a hasty word and was about to strike the man when a serving maid ran between the two of them, a basin in her hand, blinded with hurry.

"What's the matter?" John asked.

"It's the king!" she exclaimed. "His fever has risen, and his piss is blue as ink. He is as sick as a dog. He is asking for his physicians but he has only Lady Villiers to attend him."

"Asking for his physicians?" the man demanded. "Then the duke must send for them, to bring them back."

"He will do," John said uncertainly. "He is bound to do so."

He went to Buckingham's chamber, and found the duke seated by the window gazing at his own reflection in the darkened glass, as if it would answer a question.

"Shall I ride out and fetch the physicians?" John asked him quietly.

The duke shook his head.

"I heard the king was asking for them."

"He is well nursed," Buckingham said. "If anyone should ask you, John, you may tell them that he is well cared for. He needs rest; not a dozen men harrying him to death."

"I'll tell them," John said. "But they tell me that he is asking for his physicians and your mother is not a favorite."

The duke hesitated. "Anything else?"

"That's enough," John warned him. "More than enough."

"Go to sleep," the duke said gently. "I am going to bed myself in a minute."

John shucked off his breeches and shoes, lay down in his shirt and was asleep in moments.

There was a hammering on the bedroom door in the early hours of the morning. John started out of sleep, leaped from his bed and ran, not to the door, but to the duke's bed, to stand between him and whoever might be outside battering the door down. In that first moment, as he pulled back the bed curtains, he saw that the younger man was not asleep but was lying open-eyed, as if he were silently waiting, as if he had been wide awake and waiting all night.

"All's safe, Tradescant," he said. "You can open the door."

"My lord duke!" the shout came. "You must come at once!"

Buckingham rose from his bed and threw a cape around him. "What's to do?" he called.

"It's the king! It's the king!"

He nodded and swiftly went from the room. John, pulling on breeches and his waistcoat, ran behind him.

Buckingham went swiftly through the door to the antechamber but the guards barred John's way.

"I'm with my lord," John said.

"No one goes in but the prince and the Villiers: mother and son," the guard replied. "His orders."

John fell back and waited.

The door opened and Buckingham looked out. His face was pale and grave. "Oh, John. Good. Send someone you can trust to fetch His Grace the Bishop of Winchester. The king needs him."

John bowed and turned on his heel.

"And come back here," Buckingham ordered. "I have need of you."

"Of course," John said.

The court was subdued all day. The king was worse; there could be no doubt of it. But the countess was said to be confident. She was applying another plaster, the king was feverish; she was certain her cure would draw the heat from him.

In the evening a message came that the Bishop of Winchester was too ill to travel. "Get me another bishop," Buckingham said to John. "Any bloody bishop will do. Get me the nearest, get me the quickest. But get me a bishop!"

John ran down to the stables and sent three menservants riding out to different palaces, with three urgent summonses, and then went back to the gallery outside the king's rooms to wait for the duke.

He heard the long low groan of a man in much pain. The door opened and Lady Villiers came out. "What are you doing here?" she demanded sharply. "What are you listening for?"

"I am waiting for my lord," John said quietly. "As he bid me."

"Well, keep others off," she ordered. "The king is in pain; he does not want eavesdroppers."

"Is he getting better?" John asked. "Has his fever broken?"

She gave him an odd, sideways smile. "He is doing well," she said.

The fever did not break. The king lay sweating and calling for help for two more days. Buckingham said that John could go back to New Hall but he could not bear to go until he had seen the end. The court went everywhere on tiptoe; the flirting and gambling had ceased. Around the somber young prince was an aura of silence—everywhere he went people fell quiet and bowed their heads. The courtiers longed to recommend themselves to him; some of them had sided with his father against him, some of them had laughed at him when he had been a tongue-tied weakly younger son. Now he was the king-to-be, and only Buckingham had completely accomplished the great balancing act of being the greatest friend of the father and the greatest friend of the son.

Buckingham was everywhere. In the sickroom, watching at the king's bedside, walking with Prince Charles in the garden, moving among the men at court giving a word of reassurance here, a carefully judged snub there.

The Bishop of Lincoln arrived from his palace and was shown in to the king. The whisper came out of the sick chamber that the king, too ill to speak, had assented to the prayers by raising his eyes to heaven. He would die a true son of the English church.

That night John lay in Buckingham's chamber listening to the quiet breathing, and knew his master was affecting sleep but was wide awake. At midnight the duke got up from his bed, pulled on his clothes in the darkness and went softly out of the bedchamber. John lost all desire for sleep, sat up in his bed and waited.

He heard the sound of a woman's light footstep down the corridor and then her knock on the door. "Mr. Tradescant! The duke wants you!"

John got up, pulled on his breeches and hurried to the king's chamber. Buckingham was standing at the window embrasure, looking out over Tradescant's garden. When he turned from the night to face the room his face was alight with excitement.

"It is now!" he said shortly. "At last. Wake the bishop, and bring him quietly. And then wake the prince."

John went through the maze of wood-lined corridors, tapped on the bishop's door and forced his sleepy servant to wake His Grace. When the bishop came out of the room, robed in his vestments and holding King James's own Bible, John led him through the servants' hall, past sleeping men and dogs which growled softly as they went by. Only firelight illuminated their way and the moving silver moon which tracked their path through the great high windows.

The bishop went into the chamber. John turned and ran along the broad wood-paneled corridor to the prince's apartments.

He knocked on the door and whispered through the keyhole. "Your Highness! Wake up! The duke told me to fetch you."

The door was flung open and Charles came quickly out, wearing only his nightshirt. Without saying a word he ran down the corridor to the king's chamber and went in.

The palace was completely quiet. John waited outside the royal chamber, straining his ears to hear. There was the low dismal mutter of the last rites, and the prayers. Then there was a silence.

Slowly the door opened and the duke came out. He looked at Tradescant and nodded as if a difficult task had been well done.

"The king is dead," he said. "Long live His Majesty King Charles."

Charles was at his shoulder, looking stunned. His dark eyes fell unseeing upon Tradescant. "I did not know . . ." he said at once. "I did not know what they were doing. Before God, I had no idea that your mother . . ."

Buckingham dropped to one knee and John followed his example.

"God bless Your Majesty!" Buckingham said swiftly.

"Amen," Tradescant said.

Charles was silenced; whatever he might have said would never be spoken.

Spring 1625

Three hours later Prince Charles was proclaimed king at the gate of Theobalds Palace, and stepped into the royal coach to ride in state to London. Buckingham, the Master of Horse, did not follow tradition by taking the place of honor, heading the train that rode behind the royal coach. Buckingham walked into the royal coach a mere half-pace behind His Majesty and rode like a prince himself at the new king's side. Tradescant followed in the long train of the household, closing his ears to the general gasp of horror at his master's presumption.

They drew up at St. James's Palace in the afternoon and John waited for his orders. At first he could not find Buckingham's chamber and waited in the hall. The palace was in complete confusion. King James had been expected to stay hunting at Theobalds for many days, and go afterward to Hampton Court. In his absence his palace had closed down for cleaning and refurbishing. There was no food in the kitchens and no fire in the chambers. The few housekeeping staff who did not travel with the king had been spring cleaning and had swept up the strewing herbs from the floor, and taken down the curtains from the windows and the tapestries off the walls. Serving men and maids ran everywhere, trying to prepare the palace for the new king and his train and do in moments what usually took days to accomplish, delayed all the time by the storm of gossip that was running around the royal courts, explaining how the king had fallen sick, how the Villiers mother and son had nursed him and excluded all others and how the king had died under their care.

A feast had to be prepared and the comptroller of the royal household had to use all his cash and all of the new king's credit to buy in food, and set everyone in the kitchen—from the scullions laboring over the bellows to get the kitchen fires alight to the great master cooks—preparing and cooking food so that a king new-come to his kingdom might sit down to his dinner.

A great press of people invaded the palace to see the new king and the first man in the land: the Duke of Buckingham. The poorer people came just to see him, they liked to watch their betters eat, even when their own bellies were empty; and hundreds of others had complaints about taxes, about land ownership, about injustices, which they were eager to place before the new king. When King Charles and his duke came pushing through the hall Tradescant was forced to the back behind dozens of shouting demanding people. But even there, as he was fighting for a space in the crowd, his master looked over the bobbing heads and called to him.

"John! You still here? What did you stay for?"

"For your orders."

Men craned around to see who had taken the duke's attention and Tradescant fought his way forward.

"Oh—forgive me, John. I have been so busy. You can go to New Hall now. Call at the docks on the way and get my India goods. Then go home."

"Your Grace, you have no chamber prepared for you here," John said. "I asked, and there is none. Where shall you sleep? Shall I go to your London house and bid the lady, your mother, make ready for you? Or shall I wait and we will go to New Hall together?"

The duke looked across to where the young king was moving slowly through the crowd, his hand extended for people to kiss, acknowledging their bows with a small gesture of his head. When he saw Buckingham watching him he gave him a private, conspiratorial smile.

"Tonight I sleep in His Majesty's chamber," the duke remarked silkily. "He needs me at his side."

"But there is only one bed—" John started, then he bit back the words. Of course a truckle bed could be found. Or the two men could sleep in comfort in the big expanse of the royal bed. King James had never slept alone; why should his son do so if he wanted company?

"Of course, my lord," John said, careful to ensure that none of his thoughts appeared in his face. "I shall leave you, if you're well served."

Buckingham gave John his sweet satisfied smile. "Never better."

John bowed, and pushed his way to the back of the hall and out into the dusk. He wrapped his borrowed cloak around his shoulders and went outside to the stables. The horses were tired after the day's journey but he had no intention of riding hard. He chose a steady-looking beast and mounted.

"When are you back with us, Mr. Tradescant?" a groom asked.

John shook his head. "I'm going to my garden," he said.

"You look sick," the man remarked. "Not taken the king's ague, have you?"

John thought for a moment of the old king's long heartsickness for Buckingham, and the net of half-truths and deceptions which were the very heart of court life. "Maybe I have a touch of it," he said.

He turned the horse's head eastward, and rode down to the docks. There was only one cartload of goods waiting to be unloaded. He saw it packed on a wagon and ordered it to follow him down the lanes to New Hall, irritated all the way at the noise and the lumbering slowness of the cart in the muddy lanes. His hat pulled low over his eyes, his coat collar turned up against the light cold spring rain, John sat heavily in the saddle, and kept his thoughts on the seasonal tasks of planting and weeding. He did not want to think about the new king, about his great friend the duke, or the old king who had died, a healthy man aged only fifty-nine years, from a slight fever, under their nursing, after his doctors had been sent away. If evil had been done there were men whose duty it was to make accusations. It was not John's duty to accuse his master or his king, not even privately in his anxious conscience.

Besides, John was not a man who could live with a divided loyalty in his heart. If evil had been done Tradescant had to be blind to it, and deaf to it. He could not love and follow a master and set himself up as judge of that master. He had to give his love and his trust and follow blindly—as he had followed Cecil, as it had been possible to follow Cecil—a master who might bend all the rules but whom you could trust to act only for his country's gain.

John reached his home in the cool light of the early evening and found Elizabeth in the kitchen, preparing supper for J. "Forgive me," John said shortly, coming into the house and taking and kissing her hand. "I was called away in haste and I had no time to send you word. Afterward there were great deeds going on, and I was rushed."

She looked curiously at him but the usual warmth was missing. "J was told that you had gone with the duke to Theobalds at a moment's notice," she said. "So I knew you were on another errand for him."

Tradescant noted the slight emphasis she placed on "him" and found himself longing for a quarrel. "He's my master," he said abruptly. "Where else should I be?"

She shrugged slightly and turned back to the fire. The pot hanging over the flames was simmering with pieces of meat bobbing in a rich gravy. Elizabeth held it steady with one hand shielded by a cloth and stirred with a long spoon.

"I have said I am sorry for not sending you word," Tradescant insisted. "What more could I have done?"

"Nothing more," she said steadily. "Since you chose to ride with him and you went far away in the night."

"I did not choose . . ."

"You did not refuse—"

"He is my master . . ."

"I am sure I am aware of it!"

"You are jealous of him!" Tradescant exclaimed. "You think I am too devoted! You think that he treats me like a servant and takes me and uses me when he needs me and then sends me back to the garden when he has had his fill of my service!"

Elizabeth straightened up and one cheek was flushed on the side near the fire, but the other was pale and cold. "I did not say any of that," she pointed out. "Nor, as it happens, do I think it."

"You think he involves me in his plotting and his darker deeds," Tradescant persisted. "I know you suspect him."

She took up the hook and drew the hanging chain away from the flames of the fire, unhooked the pot and placed it carefully on the stone of the hearth. She worked with an absorbed quietness as if she would not let him disturb her tranquillity.

"You do!" Tradescant insisted. "You suspect him and you suspect me with him!"

Still in silence she fetched three bowls and one trencher. She sliced her home-baked loaf into three equal pieces, bowing her head for a moment over the breaking of the bread. Then she took the long-handled spoon and served broth and meat into each bowl and carried them to the table.

"I have seen things these days which he would trust to no other," John said urgently. "Things which I would tell no one, not even you. I have seen things which, if he were a lesser man, would give me grave pause. I have seen things which he trusts only to me. He trusts me. He trusts no one but me. And if—when he needs me no more—he sends me back to his garden, why, that is part of our understanding. I am at his side when he needs a man he can trust like no other. When he is in safe harbor, any man can serve him."

Elizabeth put out three knives and three spoons on the table, and pulled up her little stool and bowed her head. Then she waited for him to sit.

John threw himself on to the stool, unwashed and without saying his grace, and moodily stirred his broth.

"You are thinking that he is guilty," he said suddenly.

The face that she raised to him was completely serene and clear. "Husband, I am thinking nothing. I begged you once that we should leave this place, and when you would not, I took my sorrow to my God, in prayer. I have left it to Him. I am thinking nothing."

But John was burning to quarrel, or to confess. "That's a lie. You are thinking that I was present, that I was witness to acts which might ruin him, acts which are a dreadful crime, the worst crime in the world, and that he leads me on to love him so that I am ensnared in love, and then I am incriminated myself!"

She shook her head and spooned her broth.

Tradescant pushed his bowl away, unable to eat for the anger and the darkness on his conscience. "You are thinking that I have been an assistant to a murder!" he hissed. "To assassination. And that it is plaguing my conscience and making me sick with worry! You are thinking that I come home with guilt in my face! You are thinking I come home to you with a stain on my soul! And that even after all I have done for him, in closing my ears and my eyes to what I can see and hear, that even then he will not keep me by his side but vaults on my shoulders to go upward and upward and tonight he sleeps beside the new king and dismisses me with no more than a word!"

Elizabeth put her hands over her eyes, shielding her face from his anguish, incapable of disentangling the mortal sins at which her husband was hinting: murder, treason and forbidden desire.

"Stop it! Stop it!"

"How can I stop?" John yelled in terror for his mortal soul. "How can I go forward? How can I go back? How can I stop?"

There was a shocked silence. Elizabeth took her hands from her face and looked up at her husband.

"Leave him," she whispered.

"I cannot."

She rose from the table and went toward the fireplace. John watched her go, as if she might have the key for them to escape from this knot of sin. But when she turned back to him her face was stony.

"What are you thinking?" he whispered.

"All that I think is that I have given you the wrong spoon," she said with sudden clarity. She took off her apron, hung it on the hook and went out of the room.

"What d'you mean?" John shouted at her back as she went through the doorway.

"You need that one."

He recoiled as her meaning struck him.

She was pointing to the spoon she used for cooking, the long spoon.

The news that King James was dead and his son was to be crowned the first King Charles arrived at Chorley the next day. Elizabeth was told in the marketplace at her small stall selling herbs. She nodded and said nothing. Her neighbor asked her if her husband was home and if he had brought any news of the doings from London.

"He was very tired last night," Elizabeth said with her usual mixture of discretion and honesty. "He said hardly a word that made sense. I left him to sleep this morning. I expect he will tell me all the news from London when he wakes, and it will be old news by then."

"It's time for a change!" her neighbor said decisively. "I'm all for a new king. God bless King Charles, I say, and keep us safe from those damned Spaniards! And God bless the duke too! He knows what should be done, you can count on it!"

"God bless them both," Elizabeth said. "And guide them in better ways."

"And the king is to be married to a French bride!" the neighbor went on. "Why can he not marry a good English girl, brought up in our religion? Why does it have to be one of these papist princesses?"

Elizabeth shook her head. "I don't know," she said. "The ways of the world are strange indeed. You would think that with the whole of the country at their feet they would be content . . ." She paused for a moment and her neighbor waited, hoping against all likelihood for a juicy piece of gossip. "Vanity," Elizabeth concluded, unsatisfactorily. "It is all vanity."

She looked around the quiet market. "I shall go home," she said. "Perhaps John is awake now."

She packed her little pots of herbs into her basket, nodded to her neighbor and made her way through the muddy street to her own cottage.

John was seated at the table in the kitchen, a mug of small ale and a piece of bread untasted before him. When Elizabeth came in and hung her cape on the hook on the back of the door, he started up.

"I am sorry, Elizabeth," he said quickly. "I was tired and angry yesterday."

"I know," she said.

"I was troubled by what I had seen and heard."

She waited in case he would say more.

"The court life is a tempting one," he said awkwardly. "You think you are at the very center of the world, and it takes you further and further away from the things which really matter. What I love more than anything else is gardening, and you, and J—the last thing I should be doing is dawdling like a serving wench in the halls of great men."

She nodded.

"And then I think I am in the center of great events, and an actor on a great stage," he went on. "I think it will all go wrong if I am not there. I think I am indispensable." He broke off with a little laugh. "I am a fool, I know it. For look! He has come to the highest point of his power yet, and his first act was to send me home."

"Shall you go to the house?" Elizabeth asked. "Will you go to work today?"

John turned to the door. "No. I'll walk until I can live with myself. I feel . . ." He made a strange distressed gesture. "I feel all . . . racked . . . I can't say more. I feel as if I have pulled myself out of shape and I need to restore myself somehow."

Elizabeth took a small piece of linen and wrapped a piece of bread and cheese. "You walk," she advised. "Here is your dinner, and when you come home tonight I will have a good supper prepared for you. You look like a man who has been poisoned."

John recoiled as if she had slapped him. "Poisoned? What are you saying?"

Elizabeth's face was graver than ever. "I meant that you looked as if the court had not agreed with you, John. What else should I mean?"

He passed his hand quickly over his face as if he were wiping away a cold sweat. "It does not," he said. "It does not agree with me. For here I am as nervous as a deer when I should be quietly at peace and setting my seeds."

He took the bread and cheese from her. "I'll be home by dusk," he promised.

She drew him to her, took his worried face in her hands and drew his head down to her. She put a kiss on his brow, as if she were his mother blessing and absolving him. "You say a little prayer as you walk," she said. "And I shall pray for you while I set the house to rights."

John reached for his hat and opened the door. "What shall you pray for me, Lizzie?" he asked.

Elizabeth's look was calm and steady. "That you shall avoid temptation, husband. For I think you have chosen a way which is much among the snares of the world."

John worked through the spring with a dogged sullenness on the gardens of New Hall. The cherries which had always been his special pleasure blossomed well, and he watched the pink and white buds swell and then bloom, denying his own feeling that since their master did not see them their sweetness was wasted.

Buckingham did not come. The rumor was that London was dreadfully infested by plague, the dead lying in the streets of the poorer quarters and the plague cart coming by two and three times a day, healthy citizens shrinking back into doorways and locking themselves into their houses, every man who could afford it moving out to the country and then finding that villages on the road from the capital barred their doors to London trade. No one knew how the plague spread; perhaps it was by touch, perhaps it was in the air. People spoke of a plague wind as the season grew warmer and said that the soft warm breezes of spring blew the plague into your skin and set the buboes like eggs in your armpit and groin.

John longed to see Buckingham and to know that he was well. He could hardly believe that the court would linger in London while the hot weather came. The young king must be mad to expose himself to such danger, to expose his friends. But no one at New Hall could say when the court would move, no one could tell John if the court would come on a visit, or even if the duke might come home alone, tired of the squabbles and rivalry of the court and longing to be quietly in his own house, in his garden, among those who loved him.

John unpacked the India rarities and laid them out, as his fancy took him, in a small room. They looked well all together, he thought. There were some handsome skins and some silks, and he ordered the maids to sew them to strips of stout canvas which he could fix to the walls to make into hangings. He had a cabinet made to hold the jewels, fastened with an intricate gold lock with only one key, which he held for the duke. Still, the duke never came.

Then John had news. The king's delayed marriage to the French princess was to go ahead; the duke had already left for France.

"He's out of the country?" John asked the steward, in the safe privacy of the household office.

William Ward nodded.

"Who has he taken from his household?" John demanded.

"You know his way," Ward said. "He was up and gone within the day. He forgot half his great wardrobe. The moment the king said he was to go, he was gone. He took hardly a dozen servants for his own use."

"He did not ask for me?"

He shook his head. "Out of sight, out of mind, when you serve His Grace," he said.

John nodded and went back outside.

The plan for the fish had worked. The terrace was a delightful place in the April sunshine. The goldfish swam in their own pool on the top terrace and the banks around them were gleaming with kingcups and celandine, as gold as they. The stream overflowed and babbled down to the next level, where silver fish swam under the overhanging pale green stems of what would bloom into white carnations. The glass fence was quite invisible; the water rippled down just as John had planned. He sat in one of the arbors and watched the water play, knowing that it was only his own folly which made the sound mournful and made him feel that great events were taking place out of reach and out of sight.

There was much to do in the garden. The ships of the Navy still obeyed Buckingham's command that John should have the pick of rarities and new plants every time they returned from a voyage. Often a traveler would make his way to the garden at New Hall with something to sell: a plant, a seed, a nut, or some rare and curious gift. John bought many things and added them to the collection, keeping a careful account and submitting it to William Ward, who repaid him. The things accumulated in the cabinet, the India skins grew dirty and John ordered a woman to come into the rarities room to dust and clean. Still the duke did not come home.

Finally, in May a message came for Tradescant, scrawled in the duke's own hand and brought all the way from Paris. It read:

> *My best suit and shirts forgotten in the hurry. Do bring all the things I may need, and anything precious and rare which might amuse the little princess.*

"He sends for you?" the steward asked.

John read and reread the note and then laughed aloud, like a man who has been told that he shall be rescued. It was a laugh of relief. "He needs me. At last he needs me. I am to take his best suit and some curious playthings for the princess herself!" He stuffed the note in his pocket and headed for the rarities room, his step lighter, his whole being straighter, more determined, as if he were a young man commanded to set out on a quest, a chivalric quest.

"William, help me. Send for the housekeeper and get his things packed for me at once. He must have everything he might need. His best suit, but shirts as well, and I had better take a pair of his horses. Remember his riding clothes, and his hats. Everything he might want, I must take it all. His jewel box and his best diamonds. Nothing must be forgotten!"

The steward laughed at Tradescant's urgency. "And when is all this to be ready?"

"At once!" John exclaimed. "At once! He has sent for me, and he trusts me to forget nothing. I must leave tonight."

John scattered orders like plentiful seed up the stairs and down the stairs, in the stable and in the kitchen, until everyone in the household was running to pack whatever the duke might require in France.

Tradescant himself ran like a man half his age across the park to his cottage. Elizabeth was spinning, her wheel pushed alongside the window so that the sunshine fell on her hands. John hardly saw the beauty of the moving strands of wool in the sunshine and the quiet peace of his wife, humming a psalm as she worked.

"I'm off!" he cried. "He has sent for me at last!"

She rose to her feet, her face shocked, knowing at once who he meant. "The duke?"

"God be praised!"

She did not say, "Amen."

"I am to follow him to France, with his baggage," John said. "He wrote to me himself. He knows that no one else could get it done. No one else would take the care. He wrote to me by name."

She turned her face away for a moment, and then quietly put her spindle down. "You will need your traveling cape, and your riding breeches," she said and went to climb the little stair to their bedchamber.

"He wants me!" Tradescant repeated exultantly. "He sent for me! All the way from France!"

Elizabeth turned back to look at him and for a moment he could not understand her expression. She was looking at him with regret, with a strange inexplicable pity.

"This is what I have been waiting for!" he said. But at once the words sounded lame. "At last!"

"I know you have been waiting for him to whistle and for you to run," she said gently. "And I will pray that he does not lead you down dark pathways."

"He is leading me to the court of France!" John exclaimed. "To the heart of Paris itself to bring home the new Queen of England!"

"To a papist court and a papist queen," Elizabeth said steadily. "I will pray for your deliverance night and day, husband. Last time you went to court you came home sickened to your soul."

John swore under his breath and flung himself out of the cottage to wait on the road for his wife to pack his bag. So when they said farewell he did not take her in his arms but merely nodded his head to her. "I bid you farewell," he said. "I cannot say when I shall return."

"When he has finished with you," she said simply.

John flinched at the words. "I am his servant, as he is the king's," he said. "Duty to him is an honor as well as my task."

"Indeed, I hope his service always is an honor," she said. "And that he never asks anything of you that you should not perform."

John took her hand and kissed her lightly, coldly, on the forehead. "Of course not," he said irritably. The cart, packed with the duke's goods and drawn by two good horses, with his lordship's two best hunters tossing their heads at being tied on behind, clattered down the lane. John hailed it and swung up on the seat beside the driver. When he looked down on her he thought his wife seemed very small, but as indomitable as she had been the day of their engagement twenty-four years ago.

"God bless you," he said gruffly. "I shall come home as soon as I have done my duty."

She nodded, still grave. "J and I will be waiting for you," she said. The cart rolled forward; she turned and watched it go. "As we always are."

When J came in for his supper she sent him back out to the pump to wash his hands again. He came in wiping his palms on his smock, leaving muddy stains.

"Look at you!" Elizabeth exclaimed without heat.

"It's clean earth," he defended himself. "And I've never seen my father's hands without grimy calluses."

Elizabeth brought bread and meat broth to the table.

"Chicken broth again?" J asked without resentment.

"Mutton," she said. "Mrs. Giddings killed a sheep and sold me the lights and a leg. We'll have a roast tomorrow."

"Where's Father?"

She let him break bread and take a spoonful of soup before she answered. "Gone to France after my lord Buckingham."

He dropped his spoon back in his bowl. "Gone where?" he asked incredulously.

"I'd have thought you'd have heard."

He shook his head. "I was over at the far side of the estate all day, with the game birds. I heard nothing."

"The duke sent for him, wanted him to take some clothes, and some playthings for the French princess."

"And he went?"

She met his angry glare. "Of course, J my boy. Of course he went."

"He runs after the duke as if he were a dog!" J burst out.

Elizabeth shot a fierce look at him. "You remember your duty!" she hissed.

J dropped his gaze to the table, and fought for control. "I miss him," he said quietly. "When he is not there then people look to me to tell them what to do. Because I am his son they assume that I know things, and I don't know them. And the lads in the stable tease me when he is not there. They mock me behind my back and call me names. They say things about him and the duke which are not fit to be repeated."

"He won't be long," Elizabeth said without conviction.

"You cannot know that."

"I know he will come as soon as he can."

"You know he will come when the duke has finished with him, and not a moment sooner. Besides, he loves traveling; if he gets the chance he will be off around Europe again. Did he leave you with an address where we can reach him?"

"No."

"Or money?"

"No."

J sighed heavily and spooned broth. When his bowl was empty he took the last piece of bread and wiped it carefully around, mopping up the gravy. "So at the end of the month I shall have to go to the almoner for his wages and he will swear they will be paid to him in Paris, and we will have to make do on my money until he returns."

"We can manage," Elizabeth said. "I have some put by, and he will make it up when he gets back."

J knew how to bait his mother. "And he will be drinking and dining and living at a papist court. I doubt that there will be any church where he can say his prayers. He will come home crossing himself and needing a priest to pray for him."

She went white at that. "He will not," she said faintly.

"They say Buckingham himself is inclining that way," J went on. "His mother is turned papist, or witch, or something."

Elizabeth dropped her head and was silent for a moment. "Our Lord will keep him safe," she said. "And he is a godly man. He will come home safe, to his home, to his faith."

J tired of the sport of teasing his mother's piety. "When I am a man I shall call no man master," he asserted.

She smiled at him. "Then you will have to earn more money than your father has ever done! Every man has his better, every dog a master."

"I shall never follow a man as my father follows the duke," J said boldly. "Not the King of England himself. I shall work for my own good, I shall go on my own travels. I shall not be ordered to one place and then summoned away."

Elizabeth put out her hand in a rare gesture of tenderness and touched his cheek. "I hope you will live in a country where great men do not exercise their power in such a way," she said. It was the closest he had ever heard her come to any sort of radical thought. "I hope you will live in a country where great men remember their duty to the poor, and to their servants. But we do not live in such a world yet, my J. You have to choose a master and become his man and do his bidding. There is no one who does not serve another, whether you're the lowest ploughboy or the greatest squire. There is always another above you."

Instinctively he lowered his voice. "England will have to change," he said softly. "The lowest ploughboy is questioning if his master has a God-given right to rule over him. The lowest ploughboy has a soul which is as welcome in heaven as the greatest squire's. The Bible says that the first shall become last. That's not the promise that nothing can ever change."

"Hush," Elizabeth said. "Time enough to speak like that when things have changed, if they ever do."

"Things are changing now," J insisted. "This king will have to deal with the people of the country. He will have to listen to Parliament. He cannot cheat on honest, good men, as his father did. We are tired of paying for a court which shows us nothing but luxury and sin. We will not be allied to papists; we will not be brothers to heretics!"

She shook her head, but she did not stop him.

"At New Hall there is a man who knows another man who says that there should be a petition against the king that should tell him his duties. That he cannot levy taxes without calling a parliament. That he must listen to his advisers in Parliament. That the duke should not rule over everything and scrape all the wealth into his own pocket. That orphans and widows should have the protection of the Crown, so that a man can die in peace and know that his estate will be well managed and not farmed by the duke for his own good."

"Are there many that think this?" Her whisper was a thread of sound.

"He says so."

Her eyes were wide. "Does any say so in your father's hearing?"

J shook his head. "Father is known as the duke's man through and through. But there are many, even in the duke's own service, who know that the mood of the country is turning against the duke. They blame him for everything that goes wrong, from this hot weather to the plague."

"What will become of us if the duke should fall?" she asked.

J's young face was determined. "We would survive," he said. "Even if the country never wanted another duke, it would always need gardeners. I should always find work and there will always be a home for you with me. But what would become of my father? He's not just the duke's gardener—he is his vassal. If the duke falls then I think Father's heart will break."

May 1625

John met his master in Paris as he had been ordered. He waited for him in the black-and-white marble hall of the great house until the double doors swung open and the duke was framed in the bright Paris sunlight. He was wearing diamonds in his hat, on his finely embroidered doublet. His cape was hemmed with brilliants which John hoped very much were glass but feared were also diamonds. He sparkled in the spring sunshine like the new leaves on a silver birch tree.

"My John!" he exclaimed with delight. "And have you brought all my clothes? I am reduced to rags!"

John found he was beaming with delight at the sight of his master. "So I see, my lord. I was afraid that I would find you looking very poor and mean. I have brought everything and your coach and six horses is coming behind me."

Buckingham grasped him by the shoulder. "I knew you would do it for me," he said. "I would trust no other. How are things at New Hall?"

"Everything is well," John told him. "The garden is looking well, your water terrace is working and looks lovely. Your wife and mother are at New Hall and are both well."

"Oh yes, gardens," the duke said. "You must meet the gardeners to the French court; you will be impressed with what they do here. The queen will give me a note for you to introduce yourself to them." He bent toward John and spoke softly in his ear. "The queen would give me a good deal more too, if I asked for it, I think!"

John found he was smiling at the shameless vanity of the man. "I know the Robinses, but I shall be pleased to see them again. And you have been amusing yourself."

Buckingham kissed his fingertips like a Frenchman acknowledging beauty. "I have been in paradise," he said. "And you shall come with me and we shall see the palace gardens together. Come, John, I shall change my clothes and I shall take you around the city. It's very fair and very joyful, and the women are as easy as mares in heat. It's a perfect town for me!"

John chuckled unwillingly. "My wife would be most distressed. I will go and see the gardens but I cannot go visiting women."

Buckingham put his arm around Tradescant's shoulders and hugged him tight. "You shall be my conscience then," he said. "And keep me on the straight and narrow way."

It could not be done. The Archangel Gabriel with a flaming sword could not have kept the Duke of Buckingham on the straight and narrow way in Paris in 1625. The French court was besotted with the English, a new prince on the throne, a French princess as his chosen bride and the handsomest man in Europe at court to fetch her to her new home. Crowds of women gathered outside Buckingham's *hôtel* just to see him come and go, and to admire the astounding sight of his carriage and six, and the jewels and his clothes and his hat, the *"bonnet d'anglais"* which was copied by a hundred hatters as soon as they glimpsed it.

The queen herself blushed when he came near her, and watched him from behind her fan if he so much as spoke to another woman, and little Princess Henrietta Maria stammered when he was in the room and forgot what little English she knew. The whole of France was in love with him, the whole of Paris adored him. And Buckingham, smiling, laughing, fêted everywhere he went, passed through adoring crowds as if he were the king himself and not a mere ambassador: the bridegroom himself and not a proxy.

John was weary of Buckingham's ceaseless round of parties within days.

"Keep up, John," Buckingham threw over his shoulder. "We are going to a masked ball tonight."

"As you wish," John said.

Buckingham turned and laughed at John's stoical expression. "Have you no assignations? No dances promised?"

"I'm a married man," John said. "As you are, my lord." He paused for Buckingham's crack of laughter. "But I will attend you there and wait for you as long as you wish, my lord."

Buckingham rested his hand on Tradescant's shoulder. "No, I have a dozen men who can wait on me, and only one who loves me like a brother. I shan't waste your love and loyalty on watching me dancing. What would you like to do most?"

Tradescant thought. "I've seen some plants which would look very well at New Hall," he said cautiously. "If you could spare me, I shall visit the Robins's garden to order the plants and see them packed, and then they could come home with us when we leave."

Buckingham thought, his head on one side. "I think we can do better than that." He reached into the deep pocket of his coat and pulled out a purse. "D'you know what this is?"

"Money?"

"Better than that. A bribe. An enormous bribe, from Richelieu or his agents."

John looked at the purse as if it were a venomous snake. "Do you want me to return it?"

Buckingham threw back his head and laughed. "John! My John! No! I want you to spend it!"

"French money? What do they want for it?"

"My friendship, my advice to the king, my support of the little princess. Take it!"

Still John hesitated. "But what if you need to warn the king against them? What if things change?"

"Who's our worst enemy? Worst enemy of the faith? Greatest danger to the freedom of our Protestant brothers in Europe?"

"The Spanish," John said slowly.

"So we befriend the French to make an alliance against the Spanish," Buckingham said simply. "And if they want to give me a fortune for doing what I would be doing anyway—then they may!"

"But what if it all changes?" John asked. "What if the Spanish make an alliance with the French? Or the French turn against us?"

Buckingham tossed the purse in the air and caught it again. It fell as if it were indeed very heavy. "Then the money is spent and I have done my country the service of draining the coffers of our enemy. Here! Catch!" He threw the purse to John, and John caught it as a reflex action before he could stop himself.

"Take it to Amsterdam," Buckingham said, as skillfully tempting as a serpent in Eden. "Take it to Amsterdam, and buy tulips, my John."

He could have said nothing which would have worked more powerfully on Tradescant. Unaware of the action, John hefted the purse in his hand, guessing at the weight. "They are going at a terrible price," he said. "The market has gone mad for tulips. Everyone is buying, everyone is speculating in them. Men who have never left their money counters are buying the names of tulips on scraps of paper; they never even see the flower. I can't be sure how many bulbs I could get, even with this money."

"Go," Buckingham commanded. He flung himself into a chair and swung his long legs over the arm. He looked at Tradescant with his teasing smile. "You know you are longing for them, my John. Go and look at the tulip fields and buy as many as you want. There's that purse, and another to follow. Bring me a couple of bulbs back and we will put them in a pot, set ourselves up as burghers and grow rich."

"The Semper Augusta is scarlet and white," John said. "I've seen a painting of it. The color is most beautifully broken, and it has a most wonderful shape, the true tulip cup shape but with tiny points on each petal, so each petal stands a little proud from the others. And long curvy leaves . . ."

"In faith! This is love!" Buckingham mocked. "This is true love, John. I've never seen you so moved."

Tradescant smiled. "There's never been a more perfect flower. It's the best there is. There's nothing better. And there's never been one which cost more."

Buckingham pointed to the French bribe in Tradescant's hand. "Go and buy it," he said simply.

Tradescant packed that night and was ready to leave at dawn. He left a note for his master, promising that the gold would be safe in his keeping and that he would buy as many bulbs as could be gotten but, to his surprise, when he was about to mount his horse in the street outside the Buckingham *hôtel,* the duke himself came lounging out, pulling on a robe against the cold morning air, dressed only in his shirt and boots and breeches.

"My lord!" Tradescant dropped the reins of his horse and went toward him. "I had thought you would sleep till noon!"

"I woke and thought of you setting off on your own adventure and I chose to come down to bid you farewell," Buckingham said casually.

"I would have waited if I had known. I could have left later and you could have had your sleep."

Buckingham slapped John on the shoulder. "I know. It doesn't matter. I knew you were setting off early, and I woke and looked from my window and took a fancy to see you ride away."

John said nothing; there were no words to say to the greatest man in England who rose at dawn after a night's dancing to bid a servant farewell.

"Enjoy yourself," Buckingham urged. "Stay as long as you like, draw on my banker, buy anything which takes your fancy and bring it home to New Hall. I want tulips next season, my John. I want thousands of beautiful tulips."

"You shall have them," Tradescant said fervently. "I shall give you gardens of great beauty, my lord. Great beauty." He paused for a moment and cleared his throat. "And when am I to be home, my lord?"

Buckingham put his arm around John's shoulders and hugged him tightly. "When you are ready, my John. Go and spend some money, and enjoy yourself. I have never been happier; you be happy too. Go and joyfully spend some of my easily earned money and we will meet again at New Hall when you come home."

"I shall not fail you," John promised, thinking that if he were not an honest man he could disappear into Europe with the heavy purses of gold and never be seen again.

"I know. You never fail me," Buckingham said affectionately. "And that is why I want you to go and pleasure yourself with tulips. It is a reward for fidelity. If I cannot tempt you with easy French women and drink, then let me give you what is your greatest joy. Go and run riot in the bulbfields, my John. Lust after petals and slake your lust!"

He waved and turned inside the house. Tradescant waited, his hat in his hand, until the great double doors had closed behind his master, and then he mounted his horse, clicked encouragingly and turned its head eastward, out of Paris to the Low Countries and the tulip fields.

John found Amsterdam buzzing with infectious, continual excitement. All the taverns he had known where the tulip growers had met and sold tulips to one another were now expanded into double and treble the size and they opened for business in the morning in an atmosphere of teeth-gritting excitement. He looked in vain for the men he had known, the quiet steady gardeners who had told him how to cut the bulbs and plant them. They had been replaced by men with soft white hands who carried not bulbs but great books in which there were illustrations of tulips drawn with the beauty and care of fine portraits. The bidding for the bulbs was done on promisory notes; no money changed hands. John with his purses of French gold was an exception; he felt like a fool trying to pay men with money when everyone else was trading in credit.

And he felt even more of a fool when he tried to buy tulip bulbs to take away with him, when he wanted to exchange a sackful of gold—real money—for a sackful of bulbs—real bulbs. Everyone else was trading without ever holding a bulb in their hand. They bought and sold the promise of the tulip crop when it was lifted, or they bought and sold the name of a tulip. Some flowers were so rare that there were only ten or a dozen in the whole country. Such bulbs would never come to market, John was assured. He would have to buy the slip of paper with the name of the tulip written on the top of it, and have it attested at the Bourse. If he had any sense he would sell the slip of paper the very next day as the price jumped and leapfrogged. He should make his profit in the rising market and not hang around the dealers and ask them for real tulips to take home with him. The market was not for a bulb in a pot, it was for an idea of a tulip, the promise of a tulip. The market had gone light, the market had gone airy. It was the *windhandel* market.

"What's that?" John asked.

"A wind market," a man translated for him. "You are no longer buying the goods, you are buying the promise of the goods. And you are paying with a promise to pay. You don't actually have to give your gold and receive your tulip until—oh—next year. But if you have any sense by then you will have sold it at a profit and you will have made a fortune merely by letting the wind blow through your fingers."

"But I want tulips!" John exclaimed in frustration. "I don't want a piece of paper with a tulip name written on it to sell to someone else. I want a bulb that I can take home and grow."

The man shrugged, losing interest at once. "It's not how we do business," he said. "But if you go down the canal toward Rotterdam you will find men and women who will sell you bulbs that you can take away. They will call you a fool for paying money on the nail."

"I've been called a fool before," John said grimly. "I can bear it."

He was dining in a tavern at the end of this expedition, drinking deep of the thick ale which the Dutch loved and eating well of their rich food, when the door darkened and a well-loved voice shouted into the gloom. "Is my John in here?"

John choked on his ale and leaped to his feet, overturning his stool. "Your Grace?"

It was Buckingham, modestly dressed in a suit of smooth brown wool, chuckling like a madman at the sight of John's astounded face.

"Caught you," he said easily. "Drinking away my fortune."

"My lord! I never—"

He laughed again. "How have you done, my John? Are you rich in tulip notes?"

John shook his head. "I am rich in tulips, in real bulbs, my lord. The men in this town seem to have forgotten what they are buying and selling; they want only a piece of paper with a name written on it and the Bourse seal at the bottom. I had to go far inland to find growers who would sell me the real thing."

Buckingham came into the ale house and sat at John's table. "Finish your dinner; I have dined already," he remarked. "So where are they? These tulips?"

"They are packed away and ready to sail tonight," John said, reluctantly picking up a crust of bread smeared with creamy Dutch butter. "I was on my way home to New Hall with them."

"Can they sail alone?"

John thought quickly. "I'd send a man I could trust to go with them. It's too precious a cargo to leave to the captain. And I'd like someone to see them all the way to New Hall."

"Do it," the duke said idly.

John swallowed his question with his bread, rose from the table, bowed swiftly to the duke and went out of the tavern. He ran like a deer for his inn, engaged the landlord's son to go to England and to see the barrels of tulips safely delivered to New Hall, pressed money and a note of introduction to J into the young man's hand, and then ran back to the tavern as the duke was downing his second pint of ale.

"All done, Your Grace," he reported breathlessly.

"I thank you," the duke said.

There was a tantalizing silence. John stood before his master.

"Oh, you can sit down," the duke said. "And have an ale. You must be thirsty."

John slid into the seat opposite his master and watched him as the girl brought his drink. The duke was pale, a little tired from the festivities of the French court, but his dark eyes were sparkling. John felt a stir of his venturing spirit.

"Are you not attended, Your Grace?"

The duke shook his head. "I am traveling unknown."

John waited but his master volunteered nothing.

"Anywhere to stay?"

"I thought I'd bed with you."

"What if you had not found me?" John grimaced at the thought of the greatest man in England wandering around the Low Countries in search of his gardener.

"I knew I only had to wait somewhere near the tulip exchange and you would turn up," Buckingham said easily. "And besides, I do not crumple without a dozen servants to support me, you know, John. I can fend for myself."

"Of course," John agreed quickly. "I just wondered what you are doing here?"

"Oh, that," Buckingham said as if recalled to his mission. "Why, I have a job to do for my master and I thought you might help me."

"Of course," John said instantly.

"We'll drink a little more and then roister a little, and then in the morning we shall do some business," Buckingham suggested engagingly.

"Are we to go far?" John asked, thinking wildly of the ships which left for the Dutch Indies and for the spreading Dutch empire. "It may be that I should prepare while you make merry."

The duke shook his head. "My business is in town, with the gold and diamond merchants. But I want you with me. My amulet. I shall need all my luck tomorrow."

* * *

They slept in the same bed. When John woke in the morning the younger man had thrown an arm out in his sleep and John woke to a touch on his face like a caress. He lay still for a little while, under that casual blessing, and then slid out of bed and looked out of the little window down at the street below.

The cobbled quayside was crowded with sellers of bread and cheese and milk, up from the country by barge at dawn and spreading their stalls for all to see. Among them, and starting to lay out their wares, were the cobblers and sellers of household goods: brushes and soaps, kindling and brassware. Artists were setting up easels and offering to sketch portraits. Sailors up from the deep-water docks were moving among the crowd and offering rarities and foreign goods—silk shawls, flasks of rare drink, little toys. The low barges plied constantly up and down the canal; and ducks, in continual flurry away from the prows, quacked and complained. The sunlight glinted on the water of the canal and threw back the reflection of the market stalls and the dark shadows of the crisscrossing bridges.

Tradescant heard Buckingham stir in the bed behind him and turned at once.

"Good morning, my lord, is there anything I can get you?"

"You can get me a hundred thousand pounds in gold or I am a ruined man," Buckingham said, his face buried in the pillow. "That's what we're doing today, my John. We're going to pawn the Crown Jewels."

Cecil's long training stood John in good stead through that day. Buckingham was trying to raise the money to equip a mighty Protestant army to attack Spain and to free Charles's sister, Elizabeth of Bohemia, and her husband and restore them to their rightful throne. There was no money in the royal treasury. The English Parliament would vote no more to a king who had done so little to bring in the reforms they had demanded. It was left to Buckingham to raise the funds. And he had nothing to offer as security but the crowns of England, Scotland and Ireland and any related valuables that the moneylenders might require.

John stood with his back to the door, watching his master charming the powerful money men of Amsterdam. The scene looked like one of the new oil paintings that King Charles kept buying. The room was in half-darkness, windows shrouded with thick embroidered curtains. The table was lit only by a couple of candles behind an engraved shade which threw strange cabalistic patterns on the walls. There were three men on one side of the table and Buckingham on the other. One man was a solid burgher, a father of the city and a cautious man. To him Buckingham deferred with a charming youthful respect, and as the meeting went on John watched the big man slowly unbend, like a horse on the towpath bending its neck to be patted. Next to him was a Jewish financier, his eyes as dark as Buckingham's own, his hair as black and lustrous as the duke's. He wore a little cap on the back of his head and a long dark suit in plain material. The Low Countries was a place that prided itself on its tolerance; John thought that Buckingham would not have sat on equal terms with a Jew at any other table in Europe.

The duke was uneasy with the financier. He could not find the right tone to tempt him. The man was guarded, his long face giving away nothing. He spoke little and when he did, it was in French with an accent which John could not identify. He treated Buckingham with deference, but it seemed as if there was a secret inner judgment that he was keeping hidden. John was as superstitious and fearful of the Jews as any Englishman. He feared this man in particular.

The third man was from some strand of nobility who would have access to a vast fortune if these other two approved. He was slim and young and richly dressed, and he had no aptitude for the carefully written calculations of profit and interest on the small pieces of paper which the other two men were exchanging. He leaned back in his chair and gazed idly around him. Every now and then he and Buckingham would exchange a smile as if to agree that they two were men of the world and these vulgar details were beneath them.

"We have to consider the issue of the security of the jewels," the burgher said. "They will be lodged here."

Buckingham shook his head. "They cannot be taken from London," he said. "But you shall have your own man in London to guard them, if you wish. And a sealed letter from King Charles himself to acknowledge your right."

The burgher looked uneasy. "But if we should need to collect them?"

"If His Majesty cannot repay the loan?" Buckingham smiled. "Ah, forgive me, the king will repay. He will not fail. When Prince Frederick and Princess Elizabeth are back on their thrones then the wealth of Bohemia will repay all the debts incurred in the campaign to restore them."

"And if the campaign fails?" the Jew asked quietly.

Buckingham checked for a moment. "It will not," he replied.

There was a brief silence. The Jew waited for his answer.

"If it should fail then his Majesty will repay according to the schedule of repayments as you propose," Buckingham said smoothly. "We are speaking of the King of England, my lords. He is hardly likely to run off to the Americas."

The nobleman laughed at the joke and Buckingham shot him a swift smile. The Jew did not laugh.

"But how should we collect if, by some error, His Majesty were to default?" the burgher asked politely.

Buckingham shrugged as if such a thing were beyond the stretch of any imagination. "Oh. I can hardly think—well—we will follow the line of fairy tales. If the campaign fails and the Prince and Princess of Bohemia do not repay you themselves, and then if the King of England does not repay you then I, the Duke of Buckingham, will myself deliver to you the Crown Jewels of England. Will that satisfy you, gentlemen?"

John looked from one face to another. It satisfied the nobleman, who could not imagine that Buckingham could say one thing and do another. He was no obstacle. The burgher was wavering, half-convinced, half-fearful. The Jew was inscrutable. His dark serious face could not be read. He might be inwardly approving; he might have damned this project from the first moment. John could not tell.

"And you would put that in writing?"

"Signed in blood if you wish," Buckingham said carelessly, the glancing reference to the popular play a half-insult to all Jewish moneylenders. "I have promised my master the King of England that he shall have the funds to raise an army to restore his sister to her throne. It is a task which we should all do as good Protestants and good Christians. It is a task which most becomes me as His Majesty's most faithful servant."

The three men nodded.

"Shall I leave you to consult for a while?" Buckingham offered. "I must warn you, out of courtesy, that my time is a little limited. There are other gentlemen who would extend this loan to the king and think it an honor to so do. But I promised you I would see you first."

"Of course," the burgher said awkwardly. "And we thank you. Perhaps you would like a glass of wine?"

He drew back one of the thick hangings and showed a small door beyond. It opened into a walled courtyard. In a giant pot against the wall grew an apricot tree, at its feet the folded leaves of some tulips now past their prime. John saw at once that they had been Lack tulips, beautifully white and veined with scarlet. There were a couple of chairs and a table in the shade of the tree, and a flagon of wine with a small plate of biscuits.

"Please," the burgher said. "Enjoy this. And ring for anything further you need. We will delay you only a moment."

He bowed and went back into the room. Buckingham threw himself into the chair and watched John pour the wine and hand him a glass.

"What d'you think?" he asked quietly.

"It's possible," John said in the same undertone. "Do you have other men to borrow from?"

"No," Buckingham said. "D'you think they know that?"

"No," John said. "There is so much wealth flying around this city that they cannot be sure of it. The nobleman is in your pocket but I doubt the other two."

Buckingham nodded and sipped his wine. "That's good," he said with approval. "Alicante."

"What do we do if they say no?"

Buckingham tipped his beautiful face up to the sun and closed his eyes as if he did not have a care in the world. "Go home with the whole of the king's foreign policy in ruins," he said. "Tell the king that his sister is thrown out of her kingdom and insulted and that he can do nothing. Tell the king that unless he agrees with Parliament he will be a pauper on his own throne, and that his chief minister was a better Master of Horse than he is a diplomat."

"You got him the French princess," John observed.

Buckingham half-opened his eyes and John saw the glint of his look under the thick eyelashes. "Let's hope to God she pleases him. I don't guarantee it."

The door behind John opened and he whirled around. It was the Jew in the doorway, his head held low. "I am sorry, masters," he said quietly. "We cannot oblige you. The capital is more than we can afford without holding the security ourselves."

Buckingham jumped to his feet in one of his sudden rages, about to shout at the man. John threw himself forward and got both hands on his master's shoulders as if he were rearranging his cape.

"Steady," he whispered.

He felt the shoulders straighten under his grip. Buckingham lifted his head. "I am sorry you could not oblige me," he said. "I will tell the king of your reluctance and my disappointment."

The Jew's head bowed lower.

Buckingham turned on his heel and John dived before him to open the door so his smooth disdainful stride from the courtyard was not checked. They arrived out in the street by a side door and hesitated.

"What now?" Tradescant asked.

"We try another," Buckingham said. "And then another. And then we go and buy some bulbs, for I think that is all we're going to get out of this damned damned city."

Buckingham was right. John was back at New Hall by the end of May, preceded by wagonloads of plants, sacks of tulip bulbs and with six of the most precious bulbs—each costing a purse of gold—hidden deep inside his waistcoat.

His first act was to go to the rarities room of New Hall and to summon J to meet him there with six large porcelain pots and a basket of soil.

J came into the room and found the six bulbs laid out on a table. His father was, with infinite care, cutting slightly into the base of each bulb in the hope that it would encourage them to divide, and make new bulbs.

"What are they?" J asked reverently, holding a wicker basket of sieved warm weed-free earth, watching his father's meticulous care. "Are they the Semper Augustus?"

His father shook his head. "I had a king's ransom to spend and yet I could not afford it," he said. "No one bought the Semper. I was at the Bourse every day and the price was so high that no one would buy, and the merchant kept his nerve and would not drop the price. Next season he will offer them again at double the price, and all the year he will be praying that no one has grown a new tulip which supplants the Semper and leaves him with a pair of fine flowers which are out of fashion."

"Could that happen?" J was horrified.

John nodded. "It is not gardening, it is speculation," he said with distaste. "There are people dealing in tulips who have never so much as pulled a weed. And making fortunes from their work."

J extended a respectful finger and stroked the dry firm surface of the nearest bulb. "The skin is solid, and the shape is good. They are even lovely in the bulb, aren't they?" He bent and sniffed the firm warm skin.

"Is it clean?" John asked anxiously. "No hint of taint?"

J shook his head. "None. What sort is it?"

"This is the Duck tulip—yellow with crimson blush at the base of the petals." John pointed to the next bulb. "This is a Lack tulip, white and thin-petaled with thin red stripes through white, and this is a French bizarre tulip, very strong-stemmed and scarlet petals with a white border. Pray God they grow for us; I have spent nearly a thousand pounds on the six of them."

J's hand holding the trowel trembled. "A thousand pounds? A thousand? But Father—what if they rot?" he asked, his voice a whisper. "What if they grow blind and fail to flower at all?"

John smiled grimly. "Then we seek another line of work. But what if they grow and split into new bulbs, J? Then our master has doubled his wealth in one season."

"But we stay on the same wages," J observed.

John nodded and put the six pots in a cool cupboard in the corner of the room. "That is how it works," he said simply. "But there could be no objection to us taking a bulb for every two we grow for him. My master Cecil taught me that himself."

John was popular in the great dining room of New Hall on his return. He was able to tell a rapt audience of the prettiness of the little French princess: only fifteen and tiny, dark-haired and dark-eyed. He told them of her dancing and her singing, of her complete refusal to learn English. He told them that the news in London was that when the young King Charles met her at Dover Castle, he had covered her little face with kisses, laughed at her prepared speech, and spent the night in her bed.

The ladies wanted to know what she was wearing and John struggled through a description of her clothes. He assured them that the king and queen entered London by the river in a grand barge, both dressed in green, with the guns of the Tower roaring out a salute, and that was a vivid enough picture to be told and retold by a dozen hearthsides. He did not tell them that there had been a nasty quarrel between the king and his bride of only a day when she had wanted her French companions in the carriage from

Dover to London, and the king had insisted that she travel with Buckingham's wife and his mother.

The king had said that the French attendant was not of high enough station to ride with the Queen of England; and the young queen incautiously retorted that she knew well enough that the Buckinghams had been nobodies just ten years ago. She did not yet know enough to mind her sharp tongue; she had not yet learned of the extent of the duke's influence. As it was, she rode in her carriage with the duke's wife and the duke's mother for the long journey into her capital and it might be safely assumed that no promises of friendship were made on the drive.

"So did she look happy?" asked Mrs. Giddings, who worked in the New Hall laundry but had her own little farm and would kill another sheep for the Tradescants if John's story was good enough.

John thought of the fifteen-year-old girl and her un-English formality, her court which spoke only French, and her brace of confessors who spoke Latin grace over her dinner, and warned her not to eat meat even though her new husband had just carved her a slice, since she must observe a fast day.

"As happy as a maid can be," he said. "Laughing and chattering and singing."

"And the duke, does he like her?"

Only Elizabeth saw the swift shadow cross her husband's face. There had been a scandal in France, several scandals. Buckingham had told him the worst of it as they paced the deck of a little fishing boat, sailing from Rotterdam to Tilbury. The Queen of France had encouraged Buckingham further than a married woman, and one so carefully watched, should have done. He had climbed the wall into her private garden to meet her there. What took place Buckingham would not say, but everyone else in Europe was talking about it. The pair had been caught by her personal guard. Swords had been drawn and threats made. Some said that the queen had been assaulted by Buckingham; some said the queen had been seduced, and caught half-naked in his arms. The queen's ladies said that she had been elegantly flirting or—no such thing—

somewhere else all the time. There had been a whirlwind of rumor and innuendo and through it all Buckingham had sailed smiling, the handsomest man at court, the wickedest look, the most roguish smile, the irresistible charm. John had frowned when Buckingham had confessed to losing his heart to the Queen of France and thought that he should have stayed by his master and kept him from secret assignations with the most carefully guarded woman in Europe.

"What could have prevented it?" Buckingham sighed, but with a glint in his eye which always meant mischief. "It's love, John. I shall run away with her and take her from her dreary husband to live with her in Virginia."

John had shaken his head at his master. "What does her husband think?" he asked.

"Oh, he hates me," Buckingham said joyfully.

"And the Princess Henrietta Maria?"

"My sworn enemy now."

"She's your queen," John reminded him.

"She is only the wife of my dearest friend," Buckingham had replied. "And she'd better remember who he loves."

"So what does she think of him?" the questioner repeated. "What does the new queen think of our duke?"

"He is her greatest friend at court," John answered carefully. "The duke admires and respects her."

"Will he come home soon?" someone asked from the back of the crowd, packed into John's kitchen.

"Not for a while," John answered. "There are parties and masquings and balls at court to greet the new queen, and then there will be the coronation. We'll not see him here for a few weeks."

There was a general murmur of disappointment at that. New Hall was merrier when the duke was at home, and there was always the chance of a glimpse of the king.

"But you'll go to him," Elizabeth said, rightly reading her husband's contented serenity.

"I am to meet him in London. And then I have to go down to the New Forest, looking for trees. He wants a maze," Tradescant said with ill-hidden delight. "Where I am to get enough yew from I don't know."

John only ever told half the story to the curious, and he always emphasized the things that they should hear. He was ready to tell that the young King Charles had already dismissed dozens of his father's idle wastrel favorites, that the court now ran to a strict rhythm of prayer, work and exercise. The king seldom drank wine, and never to excess. He read all the papers set before him and signed each one personally with his own name. Sometimes his advisers would find small-handed notes written in the margin, and he would ask them later to ensure they were obeyed. He wanted to be a king with an eye to detail, to the meticulous observance both of ceremony and the minutiae of government.

John did not tell them that he had no eye to the grander picture; he was incapable of visualizing consequences on a long-term or big scale. He was faultlessly loyal to those he dearly loved, but quite incapable of keeping his word to those he did not. Everything to the new king was personal; and when a man or a nation displeased him, he could not bear to see them or think of them.

His sister Elizabeth of Bohemia, still in exile, still waiting for support from her brother, remained uppermost in his mind, and he ransacked his advisers for ideas, and his treasure chests for money to pay for an army to help her. John never mentioned to anyone, not even his wife, the long hours in the darkened rooms of the Dutch moneylenders, and the humiliation of finally seeing that no man in Europe had any faith in the partnership of the untried king and the extravagant duke.

It was not only the moneylenders who found the duke wanting. An itinerant preacher, his clothes ragged but his face shining with conviction, came to Chelmsford and set up to preach under the market cross.

"You surely won't go and hear him," John grumbled to Elizabeth as she laid his supper on the table and threw a shawl around her shoulders.

"I should like to go," she said.

"He's bound to preach heresy," John said. "You'd much better stay home."

"Come too," she invited him. "And if he speaks nonsense we can stop at the Bush on the way home and taste their ale."

"I've no time for hedgerow preachers," John said. "And every year there are more of them. I hear two sermons on a Sunday. I don't need to seek one on Tuesday as well."

She nodded, and slipped out of the door without arguing. She walked briskly down the street; a small crowd was at the center of the village, gathered around the preacher.

He was warning them of hellfire, and of the sins of the great. Elizabeth stepped back a little way into a doorway to listen. John was right; this was probably heresy, and it might well turn into treason too. But there was something powerful in how he moved his arguments slowly forward.

"Step by step we are going down the road to ruination," he said, so softly that his listeners craned forward and had the sense of being drawn into a conspiracy. "Today the plague walks the streets of London as freely as a favored guest. Not a home is safe against it, not a person can be sure he will escape. Not a family in the city but loses one or two. And it is not only London—every village across the land must be wary of strangers, and fearful of sickly people. It is coming, it is coming to all of us—and there is only one escape: repentance and turning to Our Lord."

There was a soft murmur of assent.

"Why is it come to us?" the preacher asked. "Why should it strike us down? Let us look at where it starts. It comes from London: the center of wealth, the center of the court. It comes in the time of a new king, when things should be new-made, not struggling against the old sickness of plague. It comes because the king is not new-made; he has his father's Favorite forever at his shoulder, he has his father's adviser forever ordering his ways. He is not a new king; he is the old king while he is ruled by the same man."

There was a movement of the crowd away from the preacher. He saw it at once. "Oh, yes," he continued swiftly. "He pays your wages, I know; you live in his cottages, you grow your vegetables on his ground, but look up from your dungheaps and your crooked chimneys and see what this man does in the greater world. He it was who took the prince into mortal danger in Spain. He it was who brought home a papist French queen. Every office in the land is his, or in his gift. Every great office has a Villiers sitting on the top of it, raking in wealth. When our king goes begging to the towns and to the corporations, why has he no money? Where has the wealth gone? Does the duke know—as he walks in his great house in his silk and diamonds—does the duke know where the money has gone?

"And if that were all it would be enough; but it is not all. There are more questions we should answer. Why can we win no battle neither by land nor by sea against the Spanish? Why do our soldiers come home and tell us they had nothing to eat? And no powder to fire their guns? Who is in charge of the army but the duke? When our sailors tell us that the ships are not fit to put to sea and the provisions are moldering before they are eaten—who is the High Admiral? The duke again!

"And when our brothers and sisters in faith at La Rochelle in France, Protestants like us, ask us for help against a papist army of France, do we send them our aid? Our own brothers, praying as we do, escaped as we have escaped from the curse of popery? Do we send them help? No! This great duke sends English ships and English sailors to help the forces of darkness, the army of Rome, the Navy of Richelieu! He sends good Protestant Englishmen for hire to the Devil, to the painted whore of Rome."

The man was sweating; he swayed back against the stonework and wiped his face. "Worst of all," he said very low, "there are those who wonder that in his last hours our King James, our good King James, was watched over only by Villiers and his mother. That the king seemed to be better, but they sent away his physicians and his surgeons and under their nursing he grew worse and died!"

There was an awestruck whisper at this scandal, which came so close to naming the greatest crime in the world: regicide. The preacher pulled back. "No wonder that the plague comes among us!" he exclaimed. "No wonder. For why should the Lord of Hosts smile down on us who are betrayed and betrayed and let the betrayal go on!"

Someone shouted from the back of the crowd and those around him laughed. The preacher replied at once to the challenge.

"You're right, I cannot speak like this to the duke himself! But others will speak for me. We have a parliament of men, good men, who know how the country feels. They will speak to the king and warn him that this duke is a false friend. They will advise him to turn from Villiers and to listen to the needs of the nation. And he will turn! He will turn! He will give justice to the people and food to the children, and land to the landless. For it is very clear in the Bible that every man shall have his own land to dig and grow, and every woman shall have her own place. This king will turn from his evil advisers and give us that. An acre for every man and a cottage for every woman, and freedom from want for every child."

There was a silence—this was an agricultural audience, and the thought of free land struck to the very heart of their deepest desire.

"Will the king do this for us?" a man asked.

"Once he is rid of false advisers he will certainly do it for us," the preacher answered.

"What, and break down his own park gates?"

"There is enough land. The commons and wastes of England are vast. There is more than enough land for us all, aye, and for all the city men too, and if we need more then we have only to look around. Why! The very gardens of New Hall would feed fifty families if they were brought under the spade! There is wealth in this country! There is enough for us all, if we can take the surfeit from the wicked men and give it to the children in need."

Elizabeth felt a gentle hand on her elbow. "Come away," John said softly in her ear. "This is not preaching, this is ranting: a sermon with more treason than writ."

Silently, she let him draw her away from the crowd and back up the lane to their home. "Did you hear it all?" she asked as they entered the house.

"I heard enough," John replied shortly.

J looked up at their entrance and then dropped his head and went on with his supper.

"He blamed the duke for everything," Elizabeth said.

John nodded. "Some do."

"He said that without his bad advice the king would give land away, and make no more wars."

John shook his head. "The king would live as a king whether or not my lord was at his shoulder," he said. "And no king gives away his land."

"But if he did . . ." Elizabeth persisted.

John pulled out his stool and sat beside J at the table. "It is a dream," he said. "Not reality. A dream to whisper to children. Think of a country where every man might have his own garden, where every man might grow enough for his own pot, and then grow fruits and flowers as well. This is not England, it is Eden. There would be no hunger and no want, and a man might draw his garden in the ground and plant it as he wished, and watch it grow."

There was a silence in the little room. John, who had been meaning to deride the preacher's vision, found himself tempted at the thought of a nation of gardens, of every park an orchard, every common a wheatfield, and no hunger or want.

"In Virginia they cut their land from the forest, however much land they want," J said. "It need not be a dream."

"There is no shortage of land here either," John said. "If it were shared equally among every man and woman. There are the commons and the wastelands and the forests . . . there is enough land for everyone."

"So the preacher was right," Elizabeth said. "It is the surfeit of the few which brings poverty to the rest. The rich men enclose the land and use it for parks and for wilderness. That is why there is not enough for poor people."

John's face closed at once. "That is treason," he said simply. "It is all the king's. He must do with it as he wishes. No one else can come along and ask for land as if it were free. It all belongs to the king."

"Except for the acres which belong to the duke," J remarked slyly.

"He holds it for the king, and the king holds it for God," Tradescant said, repeating the simple truth.

"Then we must pray that God wants to give land to the poor," J said, getting up from the table and pushing his bowl irritably to one side. "For they cannot survive another summer of plague and failed harvest without help, and neither the king nor the duke is likely to ease their pains."

Summer 1626

Tradescant had thought that complaints about the duke were in the mouths of ignorant men, boys like J, women like Elizabeth, and wayside preachers, whose opinions might disturb a man's peace but would not challenge him. But then the king called Parliament to Oxford, sitting outside London to escape the plague which made the streets of the city a charnel house. The king's debts forced him to deal with Parliament, though he suspected their loyalty and hated their self-importance.

Once they were in place they were not obliging. They refused to settle the massive bills of the court and instead the simple country squires confronted him with a long list of complaints against the duke and demanded that he be brought before a committee to be examined for his faults.

"I can't settle to anything, not knowing what is happening," John said to Elizabeth. He was working in their own garden at the little house at New Hall, planting peas in straight orderly rows. She saw that his fingers trembled slightly as he pressed each one into the earth. "They say they want him impeached! They say they want him tried for treason!"

"Do you want to go to him?" she asked, keeping her voice colorless.

John shook his head. "How can I? Without orders?"

"Won't he send for you?"

"If I can serve him, he will send for me. But there's no reason for him to think that I might serve him. He won't need a gardener at Oxford!"

"But he uses you for all sorts of work," Elizabeth said. "Dirty work," she thought to herself. "Private work," she said out loud.

John nodded. "If he sends for me I will go," he repeated. "But I may not go until he orders me."

She thought his head drooped a little at the thought of the duke in trouble or danger, and not thinking to get help from Tradescant. "I have to wait," John said.

One of the duke's servants brought the news from Oxford to New Hall. The steward saw John in the stable yard and sent down a message for him to come into the house, to the central household office.

"I knew you would want to know that the duke will not face his accusers!" William Ward beamed. "I knew you would have been worried."

John snatched off his hat and threw it in the air like a boy. "Thank God for it! Thank God!" he exclaimed. "I have been sick with worry these ten days. I thank God that they have seen sense. They threw out the charges, did they? Dismissed them? Who can stand against him, eh? Mr. Ward? Who could think wrong of him when they see him and hear him speak?"

Mr. Ward shook his head. "They did not dismiss the charges."

"How so? They must have done! You said . . ."

"I said he would not face his accusers . . ."

"So?"

"They had him impeached on eight counts," the steward said, his voice low and shocked. "They charged him with everything from the ruination of the Navy, to stealing from the king. They even accused him . . . they said he was implicated . . . they called him to account for the murder of King James."

John went pale. "Murder?"

The steward nodded, his face as horrified as John's. "They named it. They called it murder. And they named him as the regicide."

"My God," John said softly. "What did he answer?"

"He gave no answer. The king had his accusers arrested and dissolved the parliament. He sent the members back to their homes. He will not hear them."

For a moment John was relieved. "The king stands his friends, then. And his enemies are the king's enemies."

William Ward nodded. Then John saw the disadvantage. "And since the accusers were imprisoned, are the accusations withdrawn?"

Slowly, the steward shook his head. "No. That's the rub. His accusers are imprisoned without trial in the Tower, but they do not retract."

"Who are they? The damned liars. Who?"

"Sir Dudley Digges and Sir John Eliot."

Tradescant went white to his collar. "But Sir John is my lord's closest friend," he said quietly. "They have been like brothers together since they were children."

William Ward nodded.

"And I sailed to Russia with Sir Dudley; he's not a man for false accusations, he's a man of most careful honor! Why, I'd trust his judgment as I'd trust my own. We were shipmates on a long hazardous voyage and when he was sick I nursed him. I'd have gone with him overland to Moscow if I could have done. He's a fine man, a fair man. He'd not bear false witness against anyone. He would not do it."

The steward looked bleakly at him. "It is his word against the duke's."

"I would have wagered my life on his honesty," Tradescant said uncertainly.

The steward shook his head. "It was those two who spoke against our lord, and are imprisoned for it. And now the king has them in the Tower and they're not to be released."

"But what are the charges?"

"None. There are no charges—except that they spoke against the duke."

John took a swift stride to the window and looked out at the terraces below: the golden terrace with the goldfish, the silver beneath, and the dappled trout ponds at the lowest level.

"They are men you could trust with anything," he said softly. "If it was any other cause I would be with them."

The steward said nothing.

When Tradescant turned back his face was very grave. "This is a bad business. No one can call Sir Dudley a liar. But no one can say that my duke did—all these things that they say he did."

The steward looked at him closely. "You were there. At the king's death. You must have seen."

"I saw nothing," John answered swiftly. "I saw nothing but my lord watching and waking with his master. The prince was there; do they say he killed his own father? The Bishop of Lincoln was there. Do they say he did it too?"

"The Villiers mother was there," William Ward remarked. "And the doctors were dismissed."

John looked at him, baffled. "We have to trust him," he said stoutly, but it sounded more like an appeal. "He's our master. We are sworn to be his men. We have to trust him until we have absolute evidence that he has gone against the king or against the word of God itself. We can't give ourselves as his men and then take ourselves back again when his star is coming down. I am his man through good and bad times. I have eaten his bread."

William Ward nodded. "At least the duke is to come home for a few days. He writes me that he will stay and then go on to the New Forest for hunting with the king."

Tradescant nodded. "They're going hunting? But what about the parliament? The king only just called it."

"Dissolved," Mr. Ward said shortly. "It's only the king's second parliament and it's broken up with no agreement at all. No money voted, no policy decided. The king will rule with the duke alone, but without Parliament. But how is he to raise money to pay for anything? What will the country think of him?"

"What will they do?" Tradescant wondered. "How will they

manage? They are both such young men—and they have such enemies ranged against them abroad and . . ."

The steward shrugged slightly. "It is a dangerous road that they tread," he said. "God save them both."

That summer there was a meteor clearly seen for night after night, which burned very low and bright in the sky. You could see it most easily after sunset when the sky was still pearly before the stars shone out. It stood alone then, and its hair burned yellow with fire. Everyone knew that it was a sign, and most thought it was a warning. The plague had not eased, the new French queen was proving barren, and besides there were whispers that she could not tolerate the king. There had been fierce quarrels and shouting behind closed doors. The duke had been everywhere in the marriage, intervening, advising, even reprimanding Her Majesty. Now, it was said, she could not bear the sight of him, and she was never admitted to see her husband without the duke present.

The meteor was visible from New Hall, and in the village of Chorley they thought it was a sign of sins seeking the sinner out. The golden trail behind the meteor was said to be a certain sign of poison, poison somewhere in the land. John Tradescant, who had a hatred of superstition, snapped at J, and said that the meteor was a star fallen out of its place and that it meant nothing—it meant nothing to men of any sense. But he never saw it without crossing his fingers in his pocket, and whispering to himself: "God save the king! God save the duke!"

In July matters came to a head in the royal marriage. The king ordered the queen's French attendants out of his house and out of the country, and forcibly installed Buckingham's wife and sister in her household to take their place as the first ladies of the English court. John, watching the massive new fountains being installed at New Hall, found J by his side.

"Father, why can the king not live happily with his wife?" he asked him. "In the kitchen they are saying that he attacked her and that she screamed from the window for her priests and her ladies, and that the duke, our duke, threatened her that she could be beheaded for treason."

John took J firmly by the shoulder and marched him away from the workmen. "That's tittle tattle," he said sharply. "Women's gossip. D'you want to be an old beldame at the fireside?"

"I just want to understand," J said quickly. His father's face was dark with anger; he saw that he had gone too far.

"Understand what?"

J hesitated. "I want to know why you follow the duke above all else," he said in a sudden rush. "Why you leave me, and leave Mother, and sometimes we don't see you for months. I want to know what hold he has over you. What hold he has over the king?"

John was thoughtful for a moment; then he turned his son and walked beside him, his arm laid heavily on the young slim shoulders. "I love him as a master," he said. "Set above me by God to guide me and command me. I am his vassal, d'you see? He asked me to be his man and I consented. That means that I am bound to him till death, or until he releases me. I didn't go down on my knees and swear vassalship as I would have done in the old days but the thing is still the same. I am his man and he is my lord. That's the bond between us."

J nodded unwillingly.

"And I love him because of his beauty," John said simply. "Whether he's in white silk and showered with diamonds, or whether he's dressed in brown for hunting, he is as lithe as a willow and as lovely"—he looked around the garden—"as one of my chestnut trees in blossom. He's a rare rare thing, J. I have never seen his equal. He is as lovely as a woman and as brave as a knight in a story. He moves like a dancer and he rides like a devil, and he makes me laugh when we are together, and he grieves me every day we are apart. He is my lord. There is none like him."

"D'you love him more than us?" J asked, going to the heart of the question.

"I love him differently." John avoided the truth. "I love you and your mother as my own dear kin. I love my lord as I love the angels above him and my God above them."

"Do you never wonder," J asked spitefully from the depths of his hurt, "do you never wonder that your love might be misplaced? That your lord, just below the angels, might be what they call him in the marketplace? A false friend, a thief, a spy, a papist, a murderer . . . a sodomite?"

John whirled and smacked his son, a ringing blow which sent the youth sprawling, and then stood over him with his fists clenched, ready to hit him again should he come up fighting. "How dare you!"

J struggled backward, away from his furious father. "I . . ."

"How dare you insult the man whose bread you eat? Who has put food on our table? How dare you repeat the dirt of the streets in his very garden? I should whip you for this, John. You are a graceless, dirty boy. Your learning was wasted on you if it has taught you wicked thoughts."

J struggled to his feet and faced his father, his cheek blazing with John's handprint. "I want to think for myself!" he cried out. "I don't want a lord to follow, I don't want to have to shut my ears to the things that everyone is saying. I want to find my own way."

"You will find your own way to hell," John said bitterly. And he turned on his heel and left his son without another word.

Summer 1627

Buckingham, at New Hall for the summer, frightened back to Essex by the enmity of the parliament, found John in the fruit garden, tying back peach trees against the red brick wall. John turned when he heard the duke's quick step on the brick-chip path and Buckingham, seeing the leap of joy in Tradescant's face, put a hand on his shoulder. "I wish I was a hero to all the world as I am to you, John," he said.

"Is there trouble?"

Buckingham threw back his head and laughed his reckless gambler's laugh. John smiled in reply but felt a chill sense of unease. He had learned to be wary when his lord was in joyful mood. "There is always trouble," Buckingham said. "I snap my fingers at it. And what of you, John? What are you doing here?"

"I am trying a little experiment; I don't know if it will work. It is a fancy of mine to see if I can give the peach trees a little extra heat, where they grow, here in the garden."

"Will you set fire to their trunks?"

"I shall burn charcoal," Tradescant said seriously. "Here." He showed the duke the high wall and three small fireplaces placed one above the other. "The flues from the fireplaces run along the length of the wall and the hot smoke travels behind the bricks where the trees are tied. I am hoping it will keep the frost off them so that you can have early peaches and apricots. Weeks, perhaps even months, early. I think it must be something in the nature of the tree which makes it bear fruit; but then I am sure it is the heat of the sunshine which makes it ripen. The first year I scorched them and last year I was too cautious and the frost got them. But this year I think I may have done it right and you shall have sweet ripe fruit in June."

"I shall be eating no English peaches in June this year, and nor will you," the duke remarked.

Alerted, John turned away from his heated wall. "Not this year?"

"Unless you wish to eat peaches while I go to war!"

"You, my lord!"

Buckingham threw back his head and laughed once more. John thought for a moment that he might have crowed like a cock on the farmyard wall. "Listen to this, my John. We are to take on the French! Won't that be a game? While they trouble us in the Lowlands and threaten the fair Queen Elizabeth, driven off her rightful throne in Bohemia, we will sail around and attack their soft underbelly."

"In the Mediterranean?"

"La Rochelle," Buckingham said triumphantly. "We will sail in to a hero's welcome from the Protestants. They have been besieged by their own countrymen, martyrs for their faith, for long enough. Our arrival will turn the tables. I doubt we will need to fire a shot! And what a snap of fingers in the face of Richelieu!"

"But only last year you sent a fleet to fight for Richelieu, you were his ally against them—"

"Policy! Policy!" Buckingham dismissed the idea. "We should have supported our brothers in religion as soon as the siege was raised. The country was wild to go to war against the Catholics; I was wild for it. But with a French queen new-come to the English throne and the Spanish such a threat—what could I do? It's different now. It will be better now."

"The people may have longer memories," John warned. "They may remember that you hired our Navy out to Richelieu and English guns were trained on the Protestants at La Rochelle."

Buckingham shook his head and laughed. "What is wrong with you today, Tradescant? Don't you want to come with me?"

"You are never sailing yourself?"

Buckingham smiled his heart-stopping smile. "I? But of course! Who else is Lord High Admiral?"

"I didn't think . . ." John broke off. "Are you not needed at home, by the king? And your enemies in the country, will they not mass against you if you are gone on an expedition for months at a time? The gossip is loud against you, I've heard even here that they are making accusations—my lord, surely you cannot risk being away?"

"How better to silence them than with a victory? When I come home with a victory against France, a triumph against the papists and a new English port on the west coast of France, don't you think my enemies will disappear in a moment? They will be my dearest friends again. Sir John and Sir Dudley will love me like brothers again, come rushing out of the Tower to kiss my hand. Don't you see? It will turn everything around for me."

John put his hand on the richly slashed sleeve of his master's fine doublet. "But, my lord, if you fail?"

Buckingham did not throw him off, as he could have done; did not laugh, as John half-expected. Instead he put his white fingers on John's hand, and held his touch closer. "I must not fail," he said softly. "To tell you truth, John, I dare not fail."

John looked into his master's dark eyes. "Are you in so much jeopardy?"

"The worst. They will execute me for treason if they can."

The two men stood still for a moment, hands clasped, their heads close.

"Come with me?" Buckingham asked.

"Of course," John replied.

"You are going where?" Elizabeth demanded, icily furious.

"To France with the fleet," John said, keeping his head low over his dinner. J, at the other end of the table, watched his parents in silence.

"You are nearly sixty." Elizabeth's voice trembled with rage. "It is time you stayed home. The duke pays you as his gardener and the keeper of his rarities. Why can he not leave you to garden?"

John shook his head and cut himself a slice of ham. "This is sweet meat," he remarked. "One of our own?"

"Yes," she snapped. "Why does the duke want you?"

"He has asked me to go," John said in his most reasonable tone. "I can hardly ask him if he is sure, or what his reasons are. He has ordered me to go."

"You are at an age when men sit by their fireside and tell their grandchildren of their travels," she said. "Not going as a common soldier off to war."

He was stung. "I'm not a common soldier. I travel as a gentleman in his train. As his companion and adviser."

She slapped the table with her hand. "What can you advise him? You are a gardener."

He met her challenging eyes squarely. "I may be a gardener but I have traveled farther and faced worse danger than any other in his train," he said. "I was at the battle of Algiers, and the long voyage to Russia. I have traveled all over Europe. He needs all the wise heads he can muster. He has asked for me and I will go."

"You could refuse," she challenged him. "You could leave his service. There are many other places where you could work. We could go back to Canterbury; Lord Wootton would have you back. He says that no one can grow melons like you. We could go back to Hatfield and work for the Cecils again."

"I will not be forsworn. I will not leave his lordship."

"You took no oath," she pressed him. "You think of yourself as his man and he treats you like a vassal right enough, but these are new times, John. The way you served Lord Cecil with such love and devotion is the old way. Other men work for Villiers for nothing more than their wages and they move on as it suits them. You could serve him like that. You could tell him that it does not suit you to go to war with him, and seek another place."

He was genuinely shocked. "*I* tell him that it does not suit me to go to war when he is going? Tell him that it suits me to stay at home when he is fighting for my country in a foreign land? *I* to be a turncoat, having eaten his bread and lived in his house for five years? After he has paid me and trusted me, and employed my own son so he served his apprenticeship in one of the finest households in the land? *I* wait till now, till the worst moment of his life, to tell him that I was only here until it suited me to be elsewhere? This is not a matter of a wage, Elizabeth, it is a matter of faith. It is a matter of honor. It is a matter between my lord and me."

J made a little impatient gesture, and then sat still. John did not even glance at him.

"Then serve him where you are placed," Elizabeth said urgently. "Cleave to your master and do the work he employs you to do. Keep his cabinet of rarities, keep his gardens."

"I am placed at his side," John said simply. "Wherever he is, there I should be. Wherever that is."

She swallowed her pride as it rose up, a wife's pride, a jealous pride, stung by the devotion in his voice. She kept her temper with an effort. "I don't want you running into danger," she said quietly. "We have a good place here; I acknowledge our debt to the duke. You have a fine life here. Why d'you have to go away? And this time to make war against the French! You told me yourself what a court they have and what an army! What chance does the fleet have against them?"—"Especially commanded by the duke," she thought but did not say it.

"He thinks that we will sail into a heroes' welcome and sail home again," John said. "The Protestants of La Rochelle have been under siege by the French government troops for months. When we relieve the siege we will free the Huguenots and slap Richelieu's face."

"And why should you slap Richelieu's face?" she demanded. "He was an ally only months ago."

"Policy," John answered, concealing his ignorance.

She drew a breath as if she would draw in patience again. "And if it is not so easy? If the duke cannot slap Richelieu's face, just like that?"

"Then the duke will need me," John said simply. "If they have to build siege machines, or bridges, he will need me there."

"You are a gardener!" she exclaimed.

"Yes!" he cried, goaded at last. "But the rest of them are poets and musicians! The officers are young men from the court who have never ridden out for anything more arduous than a day's hunting, and the sergeants are drunkards and criminals. He needs at least one man in his train who can work with his hands and measure a length with his eye! Who in my lord's train will guard him? Who can he trust?"

She got up from her stool and snatched up the platters from the table. John saw her blink away angry tears and he softened at once. "Lizzie . . ." he said gently.

"Are we never to be at peace together?" she demanded. "You are a young man no longer, John; will you never stay home? We have our son, we have our home, you have your great garden and your rarities. Is this not enough for you that you have to go chasing off halfway round the world to fight the French, who were our allies and friends only last year?"

He got up and went over to her. His knees ached, and he was careful to walk steadily without a limp. He put his arm around her waist. He could feel the warmth and softness of her body beneath her gray gown. "Forgive me," he said. "I have to go. Give me your blessing. You will never make me sail without your blessing."

She turned her troubled face toward him. "I can bless you and I can pray for the Lord to watch over you," she said. "But I fear that you are sailing with bad company into a senseless fight. You will be badly commanded, badly ruled and poorly paid."

Tradescant flinched back from her. "This is not a blessing, this is ill-wishing!"

Elizabeth shook her head. "It is the truth, John, and everyone in the country but you knows it. Everyone but you thinks that your duke is leading this country into war to spite Richelieu and to tease the King of France whom he cuckolded already. Everyone but you thinks he is showing off before the king. Everyone but you thinks he is a wicked and dangerous man."

John was white. "I see you have been listening to the preachers and the gossips again," he said. "This poison is not of your cooking!"

"The preachers speak nothing but the truth," she said, confronting him at last. "They say that a new world is coming where men can share in the wealth of the country and that every man should have his share. They say that the king will see reason and give the country to his people when his adviser is thrown down. And they say that if the king will not turn against papist practices in his home, and ritual in his church, and poverty in his streets, then we should all go to make a new world of our own."

"Virginia!" John mocked scathingly. "That was an investment of mine in a promising business. It was not a dream of a new world."

"There is certainly no dreaming in this old world," she flashed back. "Innocent men in the Tower, poor men taxed into paupers. Plague in the streets every summer, starvation in the country, and the richest king in the world riding around in silk with his Favorite riding beside him on a horse from Arabia."

John put his hand under her chin and turned her face so that she was forced to meet his eyes. "This is treason," he said firmly. "And I will not have it spoken in my house. I have struck J for less. Mark me well, Elizabeth, I will put you aside if you speak against my lord. I will turn you out if you speak against the king. I have given my heart and soul to the duke and the king. I am their man."

For a moment she looked as if he had indeed struck her. "Say that again," she whispered.

He hesitated; he did not know if she was daring him to repeat it, or if she simply could not believe her ears. But either way he could not back down before a woman. The chain of command from God to man was clear; a wife's feelings could not disrupt the loyalty from man to lord to king to God. "I will put you aside if you speak against my lord," John said to his wife, as solemnly as he had spoken the marriage oath in church that long-ago day in Meopham. "I will turn you out if you speak against the king. I have given my heart and soul to the duke and the king. I am their man."

He turned on his heel and went out of the room. Elizabeth heard his heavy step going up the stairs to their bedroom and then the noise of the wooden chest opening as he took his traveling suit from where it was laid in lavender and rue. She put out her hand to the chimney breast to steady herself as her knees grew suddenly weak beneath her, and she sank down to the little three-legged stool at the fireside.

"I want to go with him," J suddenly said from his seat at the table.

Elizabeth did not look around. She had forgotten her son was there. "You're too young," she said absently.

"I'm nearly nineteen, I am a man grown. I could keep him safe."

She looked up at his bright hopeful face and his dark eyes, as dark as his father's. "I cannot bear to let you go," she said. "You stay home with me. This voyage is going to break hearts enough in this household and in others all over the country. I can't risk you as well." She saw the refusal in his face. "Ah, John, don't waste your time reproaching me or trying to convince me," she suddenly cried out bitterly. "He won't take you. He won't allow you to go. He will want to be with the duke alone."

"It is always the duke," J said resentfully.

She turned her face from her son to look into the fire. "I know," she said. "If I had been able to hide from that knowledge before, I would certainly know it now. Now that he has told me to my face and repeated it—that he is their man and not mine."

Elizabeth did not come to see the fleet sail from Stokes Bay near Portsmouth. It was too far from Essex, and besides she did not want to see her husband walking up the narrow gangplank to his master's ship, the *Triumph,* supervising the loading of his master's goods. On this warlike expedition Buckingham was taking a full-sized harp with a harpist, a couple of milk cows, a dozen laying hens, a massive box of books for reading in his leisure hours and an enormous coach with livery for his servants for his triumphant progress through La Rochelle.

Watching this fanciful equipment lumbering up the gangplank, John was rather relieved that Elizabeth was not with him. Six thousand foot soldiers slouched unwillingly aboard the fleet, a hundred cavalry. The king himself rode down to Portsmouth for a farewell dinner with his Lord High Admiral, and bade him farewell with a dozen kisses, wishing him Godspeed on his mission.

The mission itself remained uncertain. Firstly they were to harry French shipping as they sailed to La Rochelle, but, as it happened, though the July seas were calm and pleasant they saw no French shipping and could not complete their orders. Buckingham's court played cards for desperately high stakes and held a poetry competition as they sailed southward. There was a good deal of hard drinking and laughter.

The next part of the orders bade them to go to La Rochelle for the grateful welcome of the besieged townspeople. Even this apparently simple command could not be fulfilled. When the fleet hove to before the town and spread the pennants so that the town could see that the great duke himself had come to relieve the siege, the townspeople were neither grateful nor particularly welcoming. They were deep in complicated and subtle negotiations with Richelieu's agents for their rights to practice their religion, and to live freely among other Frenchmen. The arrival of Buckingham's fleet threw their diplomatic agreements into jeopardy.

"So we can go home with honor," John suggested. He was standing at the back of Buckingham's richly decorated cabin. Seated around the table were his advisers, French Protestant leaders among them.

"Never! We must show that we are serious," Soubise the Frenchman said. "We should take the Ile de Rhé at the harbor mouth and then they will see we are in earnest. It would give them the courage to declare against Richelieu, break off these negotiations and defy him."

"But our orders were to wait for them to declare," John said levelly. "Not stir up trouble. The townspeople must invite our help. And if they do not declare against Richelieu, we were ordered to sail to Bordeaux and escort the English wine fleet home. We need not fight for La Rochelle, if the townspeople do not invite us."

The Frenchman tried to catch Buckingham's eye. "My lord duke did not come all this way to fetch a wine fleet home," he laughed.

"Nor to find himself embroiled in a quarrel which no one wants," John said stoutly.

Buckingham lifted his head from admiring a large new diamond on his finger. "Are you homesick, John?" he asked coldly.

Tradescant flushed. "I am your man," he said steadily. "Nothing else. And I don't want to see you drawn into a battle for a small island opposite a small town on a small river in France."

"This is La Rochelle!" Soubise exclaimed. "Hardly a small town!"

"If they are not willing to fight for themselves," John persisted doggedly, "then why should we fight for them?"

"For glory?" Buckingham suggested, smiling across the room at John.

"You are glorious enough," John smiled back, indicating the new diamond, and a shining stone in Buckingham's thick plumed hat on the table before him.

The Frenchman swore softly underneath his breath. "Are we to go home as if we were defeated then?" he demanded. "Without firing a shot? That will please the king, that will silence Parliament! They will say that we were suborned, that we are the queen's men, papist men! They will say that this mission was a masque, a piece of theater. They will say we were players, not soldiers."

Buckingham rose from his seat and stretched, his dark curls brushing the gilded roof of his cabin. "Not them," he said softly. John watched warily. He knew the signs.

"They will mock us in the streets," Soubise lamented.

"Not them," Buckingham repeated.

"They will say it was a gesture to seduce the Queen of France," Soubise said, going as far as he dared. "That you were throwing down a glove to her husband and that you did not fulfil your challenge."

For a moment John thought that the man had gone too far. Buckingham stiffened at the mention of the queen's name. But then his smile returned. "Not them," he said. "And I will tell you why they will not mock. Because we *will* lay siege to the island, we *will* take the island, then we *will* take La Rochelle, and we will go home as conquering heroes."

The Frenchman gasped and then beamed as the cabin of men burst into applause. Buckingham gleamed at the praise. "Set to!" he shouted above the laughter and applause. "We will land tomorrow!"

It was a shambles but it did the job. Inexperienced sailors, press-ganged from ale houses up and down the south coast of England, fought to keep the landing boats steady in the currents that swirled around the boggy and uninviting beaches. Inexperienced soldiers press-ganged from the poorhouses and ale houses of England, Ireland, Wales and Scotland cringed from the waves and from the French soldiers, forewarned and splendidly armed, drawn up to greet them. All would have been lost but for the duke, conspicuous beneath his standard, dressed in glorious gold and crimson, who rowed up and down between the boats and urged the men on shore. Reckless of danger, laughing when the cannon from his ships roared over his head, he was a leader from a fable. He was indeed a champion fit to bed the most beautiful queen in Europe. When they saw him, still sporting his diamonds, with his golden sword on his hip, their spirits lifted. It was impossible that such a man, such a glamorous golden laughing man, could ever be defeated.

His clear voice could be heard above the noise of the waves, the thunderous bellow of the cannon and the yells of ill-trained officers. "Come on!" he shouted. "Come on! For God and the king! For the king! For me! And let's bugger the Catholics!"

They landed in a roar at his bawdiness, and the French, faced by an enemy suddenly renewed, powerful and even laughing, turned and fled. By the afternoon Buckingham stood on the beach of Rhé, his sword wet only with seawater, and knew himself to be triumphant.

John went inland with the scouts and saw the French cavalry driven back and back over brackish fields of rough grass where a hundred, a thousand, red poppies blew. "Like soldiers in red coats," John said. He shivered as if it were an omen and bent to pluck a couple of the drying seed heads.

"Still gardening, Mr. Tradescant?" one of the scouts asked.

"They are a fine color," he said. "A plentiful show."

"Red as blood," the scout said.

"Yes."

The English luck held. Within days Buckingham held the whole of the little island of Rhé and the French army was holed up in one tiny half-finished castle on the landward side: St. Martin. John was sent to spy out the lie of the land.

"Tell me what their fort is like, John. Give me an idea of the size and how strong it is," Buckingham commanded, as he strolled down the lines and came across Tradescant, digging a little nursery bed for any rare plants he might find during his stay. "Leave gardening, man, and tell me how their fort is placed."

John put his trowel to one side at once, and slipped his satchel on his back, ready to set out.

"I'm no engineer," he warned Buckingham.

"I know that," his lord replied. "But you're careful and you have a good eye, and you have been in a siege and under fire, which is more than can be said for any one of us. Go and have a look and when you come back, come to me privately and tell me what you think. I can't trust a word these Frenchmen speak. All they want is victory at whatever price, and that price would include me and they would still pay it gladly."

John nodded. He did not ask what, in that case, they were doing there, camped on a French beach on a small island off France. It was not his nature to complain of the obvious. He took up his blackthorn stick and set off, along the beach toward the other side of the island. Buckingham watched him go and noted the limp which favored John's aching arthritic knee.

He was back late in the evening, with a brace of cuttings and a rough sketch.

"Good God, what have you in your hat?" Buckingham demanded. He was seated before his tent, at a table of exquisite marquetry, looking young and careless with his white linen shirt undone at the throat and his hair tumbling in black curls about his shoulders.

John carefully took one of the plants by the leaf and held it up. "It's a new sort of gillyflower," he said. "I've never seen such leaves before." He held out the plant. "Do the leaves have a scent?"

Buckingham sniffed. "Nothing I can smell, John. And—forgive me—but you were sent out as a scout to bring us news of the French fortification, not to go plant-gathering."

"I sat among the plants while I drew a sketch of the fort," John said, with simple dignity. "A man can do two things at once."

Buckingham grinned at him. "A man such as you can do a dozen," he said sweetly. "Show me your plan, John."

John unfolded the paper and spread it on the little table before his master. "The fort is built like a star," he said. "And only half-finished on one side. Our trouble will be that the north side, on the strand, is facing La Rochelle over the sea and can be easily relieved by the French troops who are camped around the besieged city on the mainland. We hold the island, right enough; they will get no help from here. And the town of La Rochelle is holding out against the papist French army. But there are sally ports all along the base of the St. Martin's fort wall and they have boats moored ready. We will have to cut them off from the mainland before they can be reduced."

Buckingham looked at John's sketch. "What about a direct attack? Never mind starving them. An attack against the walls?"

John's mouth turned down. "I don't advise it," he said briefly. "The walls are new-built and high. The windows look very deep. You can't hammer your way in, and you will lose half your men trying to scale it."

"They have to be starved out?"

John nodded.

"So if we put our army all around them on the landward side, can you build me a barrier to span the seaward side to prevent them getting ships in and out?"

John thought for a moment. "I can try, my lord," he said. "But these are high seas. It's not like building a raft across the Isis, it's like building a raft across Portsmouth harbor. The waves come very high, and if there is a storm, anything we built would be smashed."

"Surely if we have enough wood, and chains . . ."

"If the summer weather remains calm it might hold," John said doubtfully. "But one night of high winds would smash it."

Buckingham got up swiftly and strode forward, looking down on the fort. "I tell you, John, I cannot stay here seated before a little fort, looking at it forever," he said, his voice so low that no one but Tradescant could hear him. "I am laying siege to them, and they are trapped inside the fort, right enough; but all I have to feed my men is what I brought in my ships. I need support as much as the fort. Their army and their suppliers are over a small channel of water, while my army and suppliers are many miles away. And their king is commanded by Richelieu, while my king . . ." He broke off, and then saw John's uneasy face.

"He will not forget me," he said firmly. "Even now he will be preparing a fleet to come after us and revictual and supply us. But you see that I am in a hurry. I cannot wait. The French in the citadel of St. Martin must starve and surrender at once. Otherwise we will beat them to it. We will starve and surrender even though we are supposed to be laying siege to them."

"I'll plan something," John promised.

There were no tents for the men nor for the poorer officers; no one in England had thought that the expedition would need tents. John laid his soldier's pack on the ground beside the other men, heeled in his new gillyflower in his little nursery bed, and then set about planning his blockade of St. Martin.

Within an hour or two he had his drawing of ships' timbers and a couple of spare masts chained together. The senior shipwright and John supervised the throwing of the wood in the water and watched the sailors leaning out from little boats and struggling to chain them together.

"Those were our spare masts and timbers to repair the ships," the shipwright observed dourly. "Better pray we don't lose a mast on the way home."

"We can't go home until the citadel falls," John reasoned. "First things first."

"And have you heard when they will come to relieve us?" the shipwright asked. "The lads were saying that a great fleet is coming behind us, now that the king knows that the duke has been successful, now they know that we are at war."

"It will come soon," John said, with more confidence than he felt. "My lord told me that the king had promised it."

John was right about the fragility of the timber barrier. The high wind blowing over their camp in the next week warned him of the storm that was coming. He crawled out of his makeshift shelter and looked out to sea. In the darkness he could see nothing. Then he felt a hand on his shoulder. It was Buckingham, sleepless too.

"Will your blockade hold?"

"Not if this wind keeps up," Tradescant replied. "I am sorry, my lord."

He could feel the warmth of Buckingham's breath as he leaned forward to be heard above the storm.

"Don't ask for pardon, John," he said. "You warned me of the danger and I told you of the need. But at first light tomorrow get out there and build me another barrier. I must have St. Martin cut off."

John's next attempt was to use the landing-craft ships, lashed together prow to stern across the channel before the St. Martin citadel. Two small camps of soldiers were set up at either side, to guard the barrier and to take the occasional pot shot at those citizens of St. Martin who were bold enough to peep over the half-finished walls. The building work on the fort had almost ceased, although the need to finish the citadel had never been greater.

"They're weary and hungry," Buckingham said with satisfaction. "We will outlast them."

Within a week of the new barrier being in place there were more high winds, and the stormy waters, pushing the landing craft in opposite directions, broke through. Some of the officers were openly contemptuous of Tradescant at the council of war.

"I am sorry," John said dourly. "But you are asking me to build a barrier in what is almost open sea. I can rebuild it. I shall bring the ships closer in to shore and run hawsers one from another. The men on board ship can keep watch, and if a hawser breaks we can replace it. But the weather is getting worse; I can think of nothing which will withstand the autumn storms."

Buckingham's face was grave. "The king's fleet will arrive this month," he said. "It will come without fail. His Majesty loves me and I have his solemn promise of a fleet in September. I have asked him to send more hawsers and timber as well as munitions, money and food. And three thousand more fighting men. As soon as it arrives we will take the castle and move on to La Rochelle itself. Once we're on the mainland all our troubles will be over."

There was a brief dispirited silence. Only John dared voice what they were all thinking. "If he is delayed . . . ," he began cautiously. "If the king cannot raise the money for the fleet . . ."

Buckingham's sharp gaze warned John to be silent; but he doggedly continued.

"I beg your pardon, my lord, but if His Majesty is delayed in sending succor then we will have to withdraw for this year," he said stoutly.

"You are afraid," one of the Frenchmen declared. He whispered something behind his hand about gardens and easy lives.

"I know that we are running short of food and munitions," John said steadily. "And the men are on half-pay. If there was anywhere for them to go they would have deserted already. We cannot make them fight if they are hungry. They cannot shoot their muskets if they have no powder." He looked at Buckingham, past the gentlemen who were openly laughing at him. "Forgive me, my lord. But I am much with the common soldiers and I know what they are thinking, and I know that they are going hungry."

Buckingham glanced at his table where a flagon of red wine gleamed beside a plate of biscuits. "Are we short of food?" he asked, surprised.

"We're not starving; but rations have been cut," John replied. "The Protestants are sending us all they can from La Rochelle—but it is not justice for us to eat their supplies. We came here to relieve *them,* not to devour their stores. And they themselves are surrounded by the papist French troops; they cannot go on supplying us forever."

"I will speak with the French commander," Buckingham said thoughtfully. "He is a gentleman. Perhaps we can make some sort of terms."

"We should starve them to death and drive them into the sea," Soubise said hastily. "We have raised the siege; we should smash them into nothing!"

"Next year," Tradescant said hastily. "When we come back with another fleet."

A package of letters for the English troops had gotten safely through. The king had written, Buckingham's wife Kate had written and his mother, the cunning old countess. None of them had sent money to buy food or pay the troops, and there was no news of the fleet being equipped and setting sail. The duke kept the bad news to himself but no one seeing the way he thrust the letter from the king inside his embroidered waistcoat could doubt that Charles had sent fond words but no news of an English fleet ploughing its way through stormy seas from Portsmouth to relieve his beloved friend.

The letter from the old countess was even more ominous. She urged her son to come home and reclaim his place at court. No man could risk being too far from one of the Stuarts; they had notoriously short memories. Buckingham himself had replaced Rochester, the previous Favorite, in the affections of King James, and now King Charles was coming under the sway of new advisers. William Laud, a new bishop, a common red-faced little man, was advising him at every turn. Buckingham must hurry home before he was forgotten.

Charles wrote to his dearest friend that he had no money but that he was raising funds by every means possible. He wrote that he was thinking of nothing but ways to get money to send a fleet. The old countess wrote to Buckingham in their private code that Charles had just bought the Duke of Mantua's entire collection of pictures for fifteen thousand pounds—enough to equip and send two fleets. He had been unable to resist them at such a bargain price, and now he was penniless again. The money for the fleet had been squandered twice over—Buckingham need not hope for support.

Buckingham tore up her letter and scattered the tiny pieces over the stern of the *Triumph.* "Oh, Charles," he sighed. "How can you love me as you do and yet betray me like this?"

The pieces blew in an eddy of wind, like flecks of snow. Superstitiously, Buckingham looked up at the September sky. There were thick clouds on the horizon; the fair weather was due to break. "He is a sweet man," he said to himself. "The sweetest man that ever lived, but the most faithless friend and king that could ever be."

He wrapped his cape around him a little closer. He knew that any time his name was mentioned at court, Charles would think of him with love. He knew that he would return to an open-hearted welcome. But he knew also that a collection of pictures like the Duke of Mantua's would be irresistible to a man who from boyhood had been able to have what he wanted at the instant he had wanted it. Charles would think that Buckingham, that the English fleet, that the full-scale war with France could wait while he amassed yet more money from the hard-pressed taxpayers of England. He would never understand that it was he who had to do without. He had no practice in self-denial. For all his sympathy and charm and sweetness, there was a core of pure selfishness in Charles that nothing could penetrate.

"I will have to win and return home or I will be left here to die," Buckingham said. The last pieces of his mother's letter blew, sank into water, and then slipped away. Buckingham watched them go down into the heaving greenness and realized that he was facing his own defeat and death, and that he had never thought before that his life and his charmed career could end in despair.

He looked up at the horizon at the dark layers of cloud. The wind was blowing the rain toward the *Triumph* and toward the string of English ships moored as a thin barrier between St. Martin and the sea of La Rochelle.

"I will win and return home," Buckingham vowed. "I was not born and raised so high to die in a cold sea off France. I was born for great things, for greater than this. I will see St. Martin razed to the ground and *then* I will go home and I shall have that fifteen thousand pounds poured into my hands for my pains; and I will forget I was ever here, in fear and in want."

He turned back to the waist of the ship and saw John Tradescant, standing a yard away, watching him.

"Confound you, John! You startled me. What the Devil are you doing?"

"Just watching you, my lord."

Buckingham laughed. "Did you fear an assassin's knife on my own ship?"

John shook his head. "I feared disappointment and despair," he said. "And sometimes a companion can guard you against them too."

Buckingham slid his hand around John's shoulders and pressed his face against the older man's thick-muscled neck. John smelled comfortingly of home, of homespun cloth, clean linen and earth. "Yes," Buckingham said shortly. "Stay by me, John."

Autumn 1627

That very afternoon a messenger came from the fort. Commander Torres was suing for peace, and for terms of surrender. Buckingham did not let the messenger, an officer, see his smile, but took the news as if it were a matter of indifference. "I daresay you are weary," he said politely, as one gentleman to another. He turned to his servant. "Bring him some wine and bread."

The man was not just weary but half-starved. He fell on the bread and devoured it in hungry bites. Buckingham watched him. The messenger's condition told him all he needed to know of the state of the soldiers within the fort.

Buckingham unfolded the letter the man brought and read it again, carefully, sniffing at the silver pomander he wore around his neck.

"Very well," he said casually.

One of his officers raised his eyebrows. Buckingham smiled. "Commander Torres asks for terms of surrender," he observed negligently, as if it did not much matter.

Taking his cue, the English officer nodded. "Indeed."

"I was told to take a reply," the messenger said. "The fort is yours, my lord."

Buckingham savored the moment. "I thank you. *Merci beaucoup.*"

"I'll call for a clerk," the English officer said. "I take it that we can dictate the terms?"

The messenger bowed.

Buckingham lifted his hand; the diamond winked. "No hurry," he said.

"I was told to take a reply," the messenger said. "The commander proposes the terms in the letter, our full and unconditional surrender. He said I could carry a verbal reply from you—yea or nay—and the business could be finished tonight."

Buckingham smiled. "I will write to your commander tomorrow, when I have considered what terms are agreeable to me."

"Can we not agree now, my lord?"

Buckingham shook his head. "I am going to my dinner now," he said provokingly. "I have a very good cook and he has a new way of doing beef in a thick red gravy. I shall think of you and Commander Torres while I dine, and I shall write tomorrow, after I have broken my fast."

At the mention of meat the man gulped. "I was ordered to take a reply, sir," he said miserably.

Buckingham smiled. "Tell Commander Torres I am going to my dinner and that he shall dine with me tomorrow. I will send him an invitation to a grand dinner, along with his terms of surrender."

The messenger would have argued but the French Protestant officers pushed him gently from the room. They heard his hesitant tread down the gangplank, and then one of the sentries giving him safe conduct back to the besieged fort.

"We'll let them sweat," Buckingham said cruelly. "They wanted to keep their weapons and safe conduct back to La Rochelle. They even wanted their cannon out of the fort. It was hardly a surrender at all. I want their weapons and their standards and then they can go. I have to have something to take home with me after all our trouble here. I want their cannon on my ships and their standards to show to the court. I need to lay the standards before the king. We need to have some gaudy props for the last act of this masque."

At dinner the officers drank deeply. John had a couple of glasses of the Rochelle wine but then he went out on deck. The ship was moving uneasily on its moorings as the wind freshened. The darkening sky was thick with clouds and the horizon where the sun had set was rimmed with a yellow line, like a fungus on a felled tree trunk. John wondered how the rest of the fleet, strung out across the bay, were faring in the wind.

He called to a sailor to bring him a boat.

The man reluctantly brought a little skiff to the foot of the ladder and John went down the side of the *Triumph.* The waves rose and fell under the keel of the little boat. John could see them, coming across the bay, frighteningly high from his low viewpoint in the water. The great swell of the Atlantic Ocean pushed them onward like an enemy to the little boats holding tightly to each other in a circle around the beleaguered fort.

"Take me round the point," he said, raising his voice above the wind. "I want to see the barricade."

The sailor leaned heavily on the oars and the skiff bobbed and fell as the big waves passed underneath. They rounded the point and John saw his barrier.

At first he thought it was holding. Squinting his eyes against the darkness he thought that the ships were still moored, nose to tail, and the unevenness of their rocking was the big waves passing through them, each one lifting and falling at a different moment. Then he saw that one had broken free.

"Damnation!" John yelled. "Get me on a ship! I have to raise the alarm."

The sailor headed for one of the moored ships and John scrambled up the ladder. His bad knee failed him and he had to grab like a monkey with his arms and haul himself up the side. At the top he turned and shouted down. "Get you back to the *Triumph.* Tell the admiral that the barrier is breached. Tell him I'm doing what I can."

The man nodded his agreement and set himself to row back to Buckingham's ship while John flung himself on the bell and sounded the alarm. The sailors scrambled out of the waist of the ship, clutching their dinner—nothing more than a thin slice of rye bread and a thinner slice of French bacon.

"Get me a light," John cried. "I need to signal to the ships to take that loose vessel up. The barrier is breached."

"I thought they had surrendered!" the captain shouted as one of the men ran for a lantern.

"They sent terms," John said. "His lordship is considering them."

The captain turned and roared for a light and ordered the gunners to their posts. The signaling officer came running up with flaring torches. "Tell them to take up that ship," John said.

The man ran forward and started signaling. John, looking past him, suddenly saw a gleam in the dark water, a reflection.

"What's that?"

"Where?"

"In the water, beside that ship."

One of the officers stared where John was pointing. "I can't see anything," he said.

"Hold a torch out!" John ordered.

They held a torch low over the water and saw the dark shadow of a French barge, rowed swiftly toward the gap in the barrier.

"To your places!" the captain yelled. John raced to the bell and rang it again. The gun crew opened the hatches and ran back the cannon for priming and loading; the soldiers poured out on deck. Someone lit and threw a flare toward the dark water below and in its briefly tumbling light John saw a string of barges rowing steadily and confidently from the papist camp around La Rochelle toward the fort of St. Martin.

From the other end of the barrier of English ships he heard the bells ringing for action stations. A single cannon started pounding in the darkness and then he felt the timbers under his feet shake at the explosion and recoil of the guns on his own ship. The loose ship which should have been lashed into the barrier was swinging wildly out of control, the crew swarming to get sails up, and to get her under way so that she could rejoin the line. But through the gap she had left the barges were pouring, heading straight for the citadel.

"A fire ship!" John gasped as he saw them launch the blazing raft toward the French barges from the English ships on the other side of the bay. One man stood at the back of the raft, courageously steering it straight toward the supply barges, the wind setting the flames in the bow leaping and crackling, reflected in the water until it looked as if the fires from hell were burning up from under the sea. The sailor stayed at his post until the last moment, until the heat beat him into the water, and the flames licked toward the kegs of powder. He dived off the back of the raft just as the charges on the fire ship exploded like celebration firecrackers. His head went deep under the water and for a moment John thought that the man was lost; then he came up, wet-headed like a seal, and swam to the nearest ship, clung to a rope and was hauled in.

The wind swung around; the unmanned fire ship, yawing wildly, blew before it, drifted away from the French barges and helpfully lit their way across the heaving glassy seas to the shore and the fort.

"Damnation!" Tradescant swore. "It's going to miss them."

Perilously the fire ship swung in a current and headed for the English line. The sailors scrambled to the side of the ship with buckets of water to try to douse the flames and poles to fend it off. By its brilliant flaring light the English gunners on the other ships could at last see their targets. The English guns pounded into life and John saw the French barges struck and men thrown into the water.

"Reload!" the gunners' officer yelled from below. The deck of the ship heaved and thudded under John's feet as the big guns fired and rolled back. Another direct hit, and another French vessel smashed amidships, men screaming as they were thrown into the rolling dark sea.

Squinting through the smoke, John could see that some of the barges were getting out of range, heading toward the citadel.

"Aim long!" he shouted. "Aim for the furthest barges!"

No one could hear him above the noise. Impotently, John saw the leading French barge run ashore below the castle on the tideline, the citadel's sally port gates flung open in welcome, and a line of defenders rapidly form to unload the barges and throw sacks of food and supplies of weapons into the fort. John counted perhaps a dozen barges safely unloaded before the light from the fire ship died and the English gunners could no longer see their target, and the battle was lost.

The citadel was reinforced and revictualed and there would be no visit from Commander Torres to dine with the duke and accept his terms of surrender tomorrow.

John did not attend the council of war. He was in disgrace. His barrier had failed and the fort, so near to surrender, was eating better than the besieging English soldiers. While Buckingham took advice from his officers John walked away from the fort, away from the fleet, deep into the island, watching his feet for rare plants, his face knitted up in a scowl. The same pressures would still be working on the duke as before, but the situation was worse than ever. The fort was revictualed, the weather was deteriorating and on one of the ships there were two cases of jail fever. The cold weather would bring sickness and agues, and the men were underfed. They had the choice of sleeping in the open under pitiful shelters of bent twigs and stretched cloth and risking ague and rheums, or inside the ships packed like herrings in a barrel, risking fevers from the close quarters.

John knew that they must withdraw before the winter storms, and feared that they were mad enough to stay. He turned in his walk and went back toward the fort. One of the French sentries on the castle walls saw him and shouted a cheerful yell of abuse. John hesitated; then the message became clear. The sentry hauled up a pike with a huge joint of meat on the tip, to demonstrate their new wealth.

"*Voulez-vous, Anglais?*" he yelled cheerfully. "*Avez vous faim?*"

John turned and trudged back to the ill-named *Triumph.*

Buckingham was certain what they should do. "We must attack," he said simply.

John gasped in horror and looked around the duke's cabin. No one else seemed in the least perturbed. They were nodding as if this were the obvious course.

"But my lord . . . ," John started.

Buckingham looked across at him.

"They are better fed than us, they have almost limitless cannon and powder, they are mending the defenses and we know that the citadel is strong."

Buckingham no longer laughed at John's fears. "I know all that," he said bitterly. "Tell me something that I have not thought of, John, or keep your peace."

"Have you thought of going home?" John asked.

"Yes," Buckingham said precisely. "And if I go now, with nothing to show for it, I can't even be sure that I will have a home to go to." He glanced around the cabin. "There are men still waiting to impeach me for treason," he said bluntly. "If I have to die I'd rather do it here leading an attack than on the block outside the Tower."

John fell silent. It was a measure of the duke's desperation that he spoke so frankly before them all.

"And if I return home in disgrace and am executed then the prospects for all of you are not golden," Buckingham pointed out. "I would not be in your shoes when you are asked what service you gave the king on the Ile de Rhé. I shall be dead, of course, so it will not trouble me. But you will all be hopelessly compromised."

There was a little uncomfortable movement among the men in the cabin.

"So are we all decided?" Buckingham asked with a wolfish grin. "Is it to be an attack?"

"Torres cannot stand against us!" Soubise exclaimed. "He was ready to surrender once; we know the measure of the man now. He's a coward. He won't fight to the last; if we frighten him enough he will surrender again."

Buckingham nodded to John as if there were no one else to convince. "That's true enough," he said. "We *do* know that he will surrender if he thinks a battle is lost. All we have to do is to convince him that the battle is lost."

He leaned forward and spread out some papers on the table. John saw that they were his sketch plans, drawn when they were new to the island and his new gillyflower was heeled into his little nursery bed. Now it was rooted and putting out new shoots, and the sketches were dirty in the margin from much use.

"We bring the ships as close as we can and pound the fort from the sea, then fall back," Buckingham said. "First one side then another, so as soon as they get our range we drop back. Then on the landward side of the fort we launch an attack. Scaling ladders to get the men to the tops of the walls. They must carry and throw down ropes. As the ships fall back from their attack they land the sailors and they support the soldiers in the attack on the walls. As soon as the soldiers are inside they open the sally ports and the rest of the sailors come off the ships and into the gate."

"Perfect!" Soubise exclaimed.

John was looking critically at the map. "How will the ships come forward and fall back?" he demanded. "What if the wind is in the wrong quarter?"

Buckingham thought for a moment. "Can we use the landing craft as barges?" he asked. "Take the ships in tow to help them around?"

A gentleman nodded. "The wind is bound to be right for either coming in or going out."

Buckingham looked to John. "What d'you think, Tradescant?"

"It might work," John said cautiously. "But we could only tow one or two ships in and out at a time. We couldn't do the big attack you described."

"One or two would do it," Buckingham said. "It's to keep their attention to the seaward side while we attack on land."

"We should do it on the turn of the tide," John proposed. "So the tide pulls the ships out of range, helps the barges to do their work."

Buckingham nodded. "Give the orders, John. You will know how it should be done."

"I shall make them practice first."

"Very well. But do it out of sight of the fort, and have them ready for dawn tomorrow, as near to dawn as the tides permit."

John bowed and went to leave the cabin. He hesitated at the door. "And the attack on the castle?" he asked.

"A textbook attack!" one of the officers enthused. "While they are looking out to sea we attack on land. Speed, stealth. May I have the command, sir?"

Buckingham smiled at his enthusiasm. "You may."

"What about the ladders?" John asked. "And the ropes?"

The officer turned on him impatiently. "You may leave all that to me!"

"I beg your pardon," John said politely. "But that's only a rough sketch I did. Someone needs to check the angle of the walls, any overhangs, the best places for the ladders. The ground beneath the walls."

The officer laughed. "I had no idea you were a soldier of experience, Mr. Tradescant!" He emphasized the "Mr." to remind John that he was among gentlemen on sufferance, he had no right to the title. Buckingham, leaning back in his chair, sniffed his pomander and watched John control his temper.

"I am a gardener, and a collector of my lord duke's rarities," John said tightly. "I've never pretended to be anything else. But I have seen action."

"Once," someone said softly at the back. "And hardly glorious."

John did not look around. "It is in my line of work to look at the little things, to see that they are not forgotten. All I am saying is that the height and the dimensions of the walls have to be known exactly."

"Thank you," the officer said with icy courtesy. "I am grateful for your advice."

John glanced at his duke. Buckingham gave a small jerk of his head to the door and John bowed and withdrew.

It was a small slight after three months of slights but it was the one conversation that John was to hear in his head, in his dreams, over and over again.

They could not make the attack when the duke wished; the tides were wrong and the moon was too bright. But two days after his final orders they launched the attack on the castle. John was on shore, watching the ships maneuver before the fort as he had planned they should. The scheme worked well. The French defenders took time to get their aim on each attacking ship, and as they got it in range, the ships dropped sail and the rowing barges and the ebbing tide pulled her out of range again. John watched for only a few minutes, to see that the ships were safe, and then turned to run to the landward side of the fort where the army was going in to attack.

The citadel was not taken unawares. They were fully armed and ready on the landward side, and they poured musket fire down the high walls onto the attacking English army. John pushed his way through the crowds of soldiers, sometimes surging forward, and then hanging back, until he was near his duke. Buckingham was at the very center of the line, dragging the men forward with him toward the musket fire.

Before him were the soldiers running with the scaling ladders. Buckingham was pushing them on, toward the deadly fire, toward the walls of the castle.

"Go on! Go on!" he was shouting. "For England! For God! For me!"

The men had suffered after three months on the island. Buckingham could not make them laugh anymore. They hesitated and went reluctantly forward. At every point in the line the officers were shouting and demanding that they advance. Only the musket fire—as dangerous for those who hung back as for those who ran forward—kept them moving.

"For the love of God get those ladders up!" Buckingham shouted. All down the line of the castle wall there were soldiers setting the feet of the scaling ladders into the rocks at the foot of the wall.

"Up! Up!" shouted Buckingham "Now! And get those damned gates open!"

Tradescant was flung back by a man falling against him as he took a musket ball. He turned to hold him; but at once a man on the other side went down too.

"Help me!" the man called.

"I'll come back!" John promised. "I have to . . ."

He broke off, abandoning both men, and plunged forward, trying to keep close to the duke. Buckingham was at the foot of a scaling ladder, urging men up it. For one dreadful moment Tradescant thought that his lord was going to climb the ladder himself.

"Villiers!" he shouted above the screams and the firing, and saw Buckingham turn his bare head to look for him.

John pushed his way through the crowd at the foot of the scaling ladder to get to his master's side and cling with all his weight on to his arm to prevent him going upward. Only then did he realize that something was wrong. Tradescant and Buckingham looked upward together. The men were climbing the ladder, head to heels all the way up, the new soldiers at the foot of the ladder pushing up and forcing the ones at the top onward and upward. But then they seemed to stick. No one was moving; the attack had paused. John stepped back a pace and looked up. The scaling ladders were too short. The men could not reach the top of the walls.

The picture of the ladders, crowded by men with nowhere to go, and their faces turned upward to where the musket balls were raining down on them, burned into Tradescant's vision.

"Retreat!" he yelled. "My lord! The day is lost! The ladders are too short. We have to go back!"

In the noise and the panic Buckingham did not hear him, did not understand him.

"We're lost!" Tradescant repeated. He fought his way back to Buckingham's side. "Look up!" he shouted. "Look up!"

Buckingham stepped out from the foot of the ladder and craned his neck to look upward. His face, bright with excitement and courage, suddenly drained of blood and lightness. John thought that his master aged ten years in that one upward glance.

"Retreat," he said shortly. He turned to his standard bearer.

"Sound the retreat," he ordered. "Sound it loud," and he turned on his heel.

John ploughed back, still flinching from the musket fire rattling from the citadel walls, to where the man had fallen. He was dead; there was nothing John could do for him except say a swift prayer as he ran, stumbling, like a coward, out of the range of the musket fire, and away from St. Martin's citadel—the fort where the walls were never measured and the scaling ladders were too short.

"I will fight him myself," Buckingham said at the council of war the next day. "I shall send a challenge."

John, weary and bruised, leaned against the doorway of the cabin and saw that his master was in despair, and making the grand gestures of a man in despair.

"He must accept!" Soubise exclaimed. "No gentleman could refuse."

Buckingham glanced across at John and saw the weary pity in his servant's face.

"Do you think he will accept, John?" he asked.

"Why should he?"

"Because he is a gentleman! A French gentleman!" Soubise exclaimed. "It is a matter of honor!"

John's shoulders slumped; he moved to take the weight off his aching knee. "Whatever you say," he said. "It can't do any harm. You would beat him with a sword, would you not, my lord?"

Buckingham nodded. "Oh, yes."

John shrugged.

"The scaling ladders were absurdly short," the officer burst out. "The wrong size had been loaded. They should have been checked as they were loaded. It was madness to think that they would be any use. You could not reach a thatched cottage roof with ladders that short. You would pick apples with ladders that short!"

There was an awkward silence.

"Send a challenge," Buckingham said to one of the officers. "He might be fool enough to take it."

* * *

As John had predicted, Commander Torres did not take up the challenge, but the following week the French tried to break out of their siege and capture the English camp. The alarm sounded in the night and the men stood to and fought like savages, pushing the French forces back to the citadel again. It was, in theory, a victory for the English besieging army, but there was little joy at dawn when they did a roll call for the wounded and dead and found that they had fought a long hard battle and were still no further forward.

The siege had held; but the cold weather was coming and it would be a better winter for those inside the fort with food, fuel and shelter than for those camping on marshy ground outside the walls. The duke had been promised that the reinforcing fleet was waiting in Portsmouth harbor under the command of the Earl of Holland, ready to sail any day. But there it stayed, and none of King Charles's protestations of love and constancy could relieve the English army on the island. The bad weather that kept the earl in harbor also made it impossible to sustain the siege in France. In October, another flotilla of French barges broke the English barricade and fresh French troops were successfully landed inside the fort. Buckingham decided to withdraw.

They had hoped that they might steal away at dawn, and that the citadel might not realize they were gone until it was too late. Following that plan, they did not disembark where they had arrived, on the beaches and dunes on the east of the island, but sent the ships northward to wait off the marshy waters around the Ile de Loix. The Ile de Loix was connected to the island by a tiny causeway, covered at high tide. Buckingham's plan was that the English army should slip across the causeway as the waters were rising and any French pursuit would be kept back by the swirling currents. Then the English could board the ships in good order and sail away.

Despite their safety behind the thick walls, the French sentries on duty were alert. As the little makeshift English tents were struck and the soldiers quietly formed into ranks, the French sentries watched and raised the alarm. As the ragged English army lined up in companies the gates of St. Martin opened and the French, well-fed, well-clothed, well-commanded, marched out. Buckingham's troops, nearly seven thousand of them, fell slowly back before the French force. They went in a textbook retreat, staying outside musket range, refusing to engage with the sporadic fire that the French troops offered.

"How does the tide?" Buckingham asked John quickly as he tried to keep the men maintaining a steady pace toward the causeway. The ground underfoot was marshy and wet and the men could not keep to a quick march. They floundered about and had to be ordered into single file on the narrow path. The sniping from the rear increased as the French soldiers gained on them.

"The tide's turning," John warned. "Let them run to the ships, my lord, or we'll not get them off the island before the tide rises."

"Run!" Buckingham shouted. "As fast as you can!" He sent his standard bearer ahead to show the men the way. One man stepped carelessly off the causeway and immediately sank to his waist in thick mud. He shouted to his friends for help and they, glancing anxiously toward the rear of the army where the French were coming closer, laid their pikes on the ground toward him and pulled him out.

"Go on! Go on!" John urged them. "Hurry!"

It was a race against three forces. One, the English, breaking ranks and running for their ships; two, the French coming behind them, as confident as poachers in a field of rabbits, pausing to fire and reload and then marching briskly on; three, the tide swirling in either side of the island, threatening to cut the narrow causeway in two, pushed on by the rising winds.

The men who had been ordered to lay timbers down over the mud flats to make a causeway to the ships had made the road too narrow, and there were no handholds. As the men pushed and shoved their way along the track, those at the very edge fell off and struggled in the marshy water, which grew deeper with every pulse of the tide. John stopped to haul a man back on the causeway. The man struggled, gripping tight to John's reaching hands until John felt his own feet slipping under him.

"Swim with your legs!" John shouted.

"Pull me!" the man begged.

A higher wave lifted him up and John landed him like a writhing frightened fish on the causeway. But the wave which had brought the lieutenant on shore was washing over the causeway, making the timbers slippery and wet. Men were stumbling and plunging off on either side, and the men at the rear, fleeing from the French, were tumbling over their comrades and falling over the edge.

John glanced back. The French were closer; the front ranks had cast aside their muskets and were stabbing out with their pikes. The only way the English army could be saved would be to turn and fight; but half of them had lost their weapons in the run through the marshes, and there were dozens swimming in the water and struggling in the mud. The currents swirling treacherously around were sucking them down, and they were screaming for help and then choking on the slurry of the marsh.

He looked around for the duke. He at least was safe on board, leaning out from the side of the *Triumph,* urging men on to the landing craft and up the nets to the ship.

"God bless you." The half-drowned man staggered to his feet and gripped Tradescant's arm, and then turned to see why Tradescant was staring in horror. The French were coming on, surefooted and closer than ever, stabbing and pushing men from the causeway into the marshes and the seas. The waves were coming in faster than a galloping horse across the flat sandbanks, rushing in and washing the exhausted English army off their narrow causeway, into the brackish stinking water, and under the sharp downward stabbing French pikes. The French were standing on the causeway and stabbing their long pikes into the waters, picking off the English soldiers like a boy needling fish in a barrel.

The lieutenant shook Tradescant by the arm. "Get to the ship!"

he shouted above the noise of the water and the screams of the men. "They're closer and closer! And we'll be cut off!"

John looked forward. It was true. The causeway was half underwater; he would be lucky, with his weak knee, to get to the other side. The lieutenant grabbed his arm. "Come on!"

The two men, clinging to each other for balance, pushed their way through the water to the other side, their feet unsteady on the wet wooden track. Every now and then a deeper wave threatened to wash them into the sea altogether. Once John lost his footing and only the other man's grip saved him. They tumbled together onto the marshy wetland on the other side and ran toward where the *Triumph*'s landing craft were plying from the boggy shore to the ship.

John flung himself on board one of the craft and looked back as the boat took him from shore. It was impossible to tell friend from enemy; they were alike mud-smeared, knee-deep in water, stabbing and clawing for their own safety as the high dirty waves rolled in. The landing craft crashed abruptly against the side of the *Triumph* and John reached up to grip the nets hung over the side of the ship. The pressure of the men behind him pushed him up, his weaker leg scrabbling for a foothold but his arms heaving him upward. He fell over the ship's side and lay on the deck, panting and sobbing, acutely aware of the blissful hardness of the holystoned wood of the deck under his cheek.

After a moment he pulled himself to his feet and went to where his lord was looking out to the island.

It was a massacre. Almost all the English soldiers behind John had been caught between the sea and the French. They had plunged off the causeway, or tried to escape by running through the treacherous marsh. The cries of the drowning men were like seagulls on a nesting site—loud, demanding, inhuman. Those bobbing in the water or trying to crawl back on to the causeway died quickly, under the French pikes. The French army, who were left dryshod on land before the causeway, had the leisure to reload and to fire easily and accurately into the marshes and the sea, where a few men were striking out for the ship. The front ranks, who had done deadly work off the submerged causeway, were falling back before the sea and stabbing at the bodies of Englishmen who were rolling and tumbling in the incoming waves.

The captain of the *Triumph* came to Buckingham as he stared, blank with horror, at his army drowning in blood and brine. "Shall we set sail?"

Buckingham did not hear him.

The captain turned to John. "Do we sail?"

John glanced around. He felt as if everything were underwater, as if he were underwater with the other Englishmen. He could hardly hear the captain speak, the man seemed to swim toward him and recede. He tightened his grip on the balustrade.

"Is another ship behind us to take off survivors?" he asked. His lips were numb and his voice was very faint.

"What survivors?" the captain demanded.

John looked again. His had been the last landing craft; the men left behind were rolling in the waves, drowned, or shot, or stabbed.

"Set sail," John said. "And get my lord away from here."

Not until the whole fleet was released from the grip of the treacherous mud and waves and was at sea did they count their losses and realize what the battle had cost them. Forty-nine English standards were missing, and four thousand English men and boys, unwillingly conscripted, were dead.

Buckingham kept to his cabin on the voyage home. It was said that he was sick, as so many of the men were sick. The whole of the *Triumph* was stinking with the smell of suppurating wounds, and loud with the groans of injured men. Buckingham's personal servant took jail fever and weakened and died, and then the Lord High Admiral was left completely alone.

John Tradescant went down to the galley, where one cook was stirring a saucepan of stock over the fire. "Where is everyone?"

"You should know," the man said sourly. "You were there as well as I. Drowned in the marshes, or skewered on a French pike."

"I meant, where are the other cooks, and the servers?"

"Sick," the man answered shortly.

"Put me up a tray for the Lord High Admiral," John said. "Where's his cupbearer?"

"Dead."

"And his server?"

"Jail fever."

The cook nodded and laid a tray with a bowl of the stock, some stale bread and a small glass of wine.

"Is that all?" John asked.

The man met his eyes. "If he wants more he had better revictual the ship. It's more than the rest of us will get. And most of his army is face down in the marshes eating mud and drinking brine."

John flinched from the bitterness in the man's face. "It wasn't all his fault," he said.

"Whose then?"

"He should have been reinforced; we should have sailed with better supplies."

"We had a six-horse carriage and a harp," the cook said spitefully. "What more did we need?"

John spoke gently. "Beware, my friend," he said. "You are very near to treason."

The man laughed mirthlessly. "If the Lord High Admiral has me executed before the mast there will be no dinner for those that can eat," he said. "And I would thank him for the release. I lost my brother in Isle of Rue, I am sailing home to tell his wife that she has no husband, and to tell my mother that she has only one son. The Lord High Admiral can spare me that and I would thank him."

"What did you call it?" John asked suddenly.

"What?"

"The island."

The cook shrugged. "It's what they all call it now. Not the Isle of Rhé; the Isle of Rue, because we rue the day we ever sailed with him, and he should rue the day he commanded us. And like the herb rue his service has a poisonous and bitter taste that you don't forget."

John took up the tray and went to Buckingham's cabin without another word.

He was lying on his bunk on his back, one arm across his eyes, his pomander swinging from his fingers. He did not turn his head when Tradescant came in.

"I told you I want nothing," he said.

"Matthew is sick," John said steadily. "And I have brought you some broth."

Buckingham did not even turn his head to look at him. "John, I want nothing, I said."

John came a little closer and set the tray on a table by the bed. "You must eat something," he urged, as gentle as a nurse with a child. "See? I have brought you a little wine."

"If I drank a barrel I would not be drunk enough to forget."

"I know," John said steadily.

"Where are my officers?"

"Resting," John said. He did not say the truth, that more than half of them were dead and the rest sick.

"And how are my men?"

"Low-spirited."

"Do they blame me?"

"Of course not!" John lied. "It is the fortune of war, my lord. Everyone knows a battle can go either way. If we had been reinforced . . ."

Buckingham raised himself on an elbow. "Yes," he said with sudden vivacity. "I keep doing that too. I keep saying: if we had been reinforced, or if the wind had not gotten up that night in September, or if I had accepted Torres's terms of surrender the night that I had them, or if the Rochellois had fought for us . . . if the ladders had been longer or the causeway wider . . . I go back and back and back to the summer, trying to see where it went wrong. Where I went wrong."

"You didn't go wrong," John said gently. He sat, unbidden, on the edge of Buckingham's bed and passed him the glass of wine. "You did the best you could, every day you did your best. Remember that first landing when you were rowed up and down through the landing craft and the French turned and fled?"

Buckingham smiled, as an old man will smile at a childhood memory. "Yes. That was a day!"

"And when we pushed them back and back and back into the citadel?"

"Yes."

John passed him the bowl of soup and the spoon. Buckingham's hand trembled so much that he could not lift it to his mouth. John took it and spooned it for him. Buckingham opened his mouth like an obedient child, John was reminded of J as a baby tucked into his arm, seated on his lap, feeding from a bowl of gruel.

"You will be glad to see your wife again," he said. "At least we have come safe home."

"Kate would be glad to see me," Buckingham said. "Even if I had been defeated twenty times over."

Almost all the soup had gone. John broke up the dried bread into pieces, squashed them into the dregs and then spooned them into his master's mouth. Some color had come into the duke's face but his eyes were still dark-ringed and languid.

"I wish we could go on sailing and never get home at all," he said slowly. "I don't want to get home."

John thought of the little fire in the galley and the shortage of food, of the smell of the injured men and the continual splash of bodies over the side in one makeshift funeral after another.

"We will make port in November, and you will be with your children for Christmas."

Buckingham turned his face to the wall. "There will be many children without fathers this Christmas," he said. "They will be cursing my name in cold beds up and down the land."

John put the tray to one side and put his hand on the younger man's shoulder. "These are the pains of high office," he said steadily. "And you have enjoyed the pleasures."

Buckingham hesitated, and then nodded. "Yes, I have. You are right to remind me. I have had great wealth showered on me and mine."

There was a little silence. "And you?" Buckingham asked. "Will your wife and son welcome you with open arms?"

"She was angry when I left," John said. "But I will be forgiven. She likes me to be home, working in your garden. She has never liked me traveling."

"And you have brought a plant back with you?" Buckingham asked sleepily, like a child being entertained at bedtime.

"Two," John said. "One is a sort of gillyflower and the other a wormwood, I think. And I have the seeds of a very scarlet poppy which may take for me."

Buckingham nodded. "It's odd to think of the island without us, just as it was when we arrived," he said. "D'you remember those great fields of scarlet poppies?"

John closed his eyes briefly, remembering the bobbing heads of papery red flowers which made a haze of scarlet over the land. "Yes. A bright brave flower, like hopeful troops."

"Don't go," Buckingham said. "Stay with me."

John went to sit in the chair but Buckingham, without looking, put out his hand and pulled John down to the pillow beside him. John lay on his back, put his hands behind his head and watched the gilded ceiling rise and fall as the *Triumph* made her way through the waves.

"I am cold in my heart," Buckingham said softly. "Icy. Is my heart broken, d'you think, John?"

Without thinking what he was doing, John reached out and gathered Buckingham so that the dark tumbled head rested on his shoulder. "No," he said gently. "It will mend."

Buckingham turned in his embrace and put his arms around him. "Sleep with me tonight," he said. "I have been as lonely as a king."

John moved a little closer and Buckingham settled himself for sleep. "I'll stay," John said softly. "Whatever you want."

The horn lantern swung on its hook, throwing gentle shadows

across the gilded ceiling as the boat heaved and dropped in gentle waters. There was no sound from the deck above them. The night watch was quiet, in mourning. John had a sudden strange fancy that they had all died on the Isle of Rue and that this was some afterlife, on Charon's boat, and that he would travel forever, his arms around his master, carried by a dark tide into nothingness.

Sometime after midnight John stirred, thought for a moment he was at home and Elizabeth was in his arms, and then remembered where he was.

Buckingham slowly opened his eyes. "Oh, John," he sighed. "I did not think I would ever sleep again."

"Shall I go now?" Tradescant asked.

Buckingham smiled and closed his eyes again. "Stay," he said. His face, gilded by the lamplight, was almost too beautiful to bear. The clear perfect profile and the sleepy languorous eyes, the warm mouth and the new sorrowful line between the arched brows. John put a hand out and touched it, as if a caress might melt that mark away. Buckingham took the hand and pressed it to his cheek, and then drew John down to the pillows. Gently, Buckingham raised himself up above him and slid warm hands underneath John's shirt, untied the laces on his breeches. John lay, beyond thought, beyond awareness, unmoving beneath the touch of Buckingham's hands.

Buckingham stroked him, sensually, smoothly, from throat to waist and then laid his cold, stone-cold face against John's warm chest. His hand caressed John's cock, stroked it with smooth confidence. John felt desire, unbidden, unexpected, rise up in him like the misplaced desire of a dream.

The lantern dipped and bobbed and John moved at Buckingham's bidding, turned as he commanded, lay face down in the bed and parted his legs. The pain when it came to him was sharp like a pain of deep agonizing desire, a pain that he welcomed, that he wanted to wash through him. And then it changed and became a deep pleasure and a terror to him, a feeling of submission and penetration and leaping desire and deep satisfaction. John thought he understood the passionate grief and lust of a woman when she can take a man inside her, and by submitting to him become his mistress. When he groaned it was not only with pain but with a deep inner joy and a sense of resolution that he had never felt before, as if at last, after a lifetime, he understood that love is the death of the self, that his love for Villiers took them both into darkness and mystery, away from self.

When Buckingham rolled off him and lay still, John did not move, transfixed by a profound pleasure that felt almost holy. He felt that he had drawn near to something very like the love of God, which can shake a man to his very core, which comes like a flame in the night and burns a man into something new so that the world is never the same for him again.

Buckingham slept but John lay awake, holding his joy.

In the morning they were easy with each other, as old friends, as brothers-in-arms, as companions. Buckingham had thrown off some of his melancholy; he went to visit his injured officers and checked the stores with the ship's purveyor, he said his prayers with the priest. In the companionway a weary-looking man asked to speak with him and Buckingham gave him his charming smile.

"My captain was killed before me, drowned off the causeway in the retreat," the man said.

"I am sorry for it," Buckingham replied. "We have all lost friends."

"I am a lieutenant; I was due for promotion. Am I captain now?"

Buckingham's face lost its color and its smile. He turned away in disgust. "Dead men's shoes."

"But am I? I have a wife and a child, and I need the wages and the pension if I fall . . ."

"Don't trouble me with this," Buckingham said with sudden anger. "What am I? Some beggar to be hounded about?"

"You're the Lord High Admiral," the man said reasonably. "And I am seeking you to confirm my promotion."

"Damn you to hell!" Buckingham shouted. "There are four thousand good men dead. Shall you have all their pay too?" He flung himself away.

"That's not just," the man persisted doggedly.

John looked at him more carefully. "You are the man who held me on the causeway!" he exclaimed.

"Lieutenant Felton. Should be captain. You pulled me out of the sea. Thank you."

"I'm John Tradescant."

The man looked at him more closely. "The duke's man?"

John felt a swift pulse of pride that he was the duke's man in every sense. The duke's man to his very core.

"Tell him I should be a captain. He owes it to me."

"He's much troubled now," John said. "I will tell him later."

"I have served him faithfully; I have faced shot and illness in his service. Am I not to be rewarded?"

"I'll put it to him later," John said. "What's your name?"

"Lieutenant Felton," the man repeated. "I am not a greedy man. I just want justice for myself and for us all."

"I'll ask him when he's calm again," John said.

"I wish that I could refuse to do my duty when my temper is against it," Felton said, looking after the admiral.

John had set some sailors to spinning for mackerel and that night he was able to serve Buckingham with a plate of fish. When he set the tray down, Buckingham said idly, "Don't go."

John waited by the door as Buckingham ate in silence. The ship seemed very quiet. Buckingham finished his dinner and then stood up from his table.

"Fetch me some hot water," he commanded.

Tradescant took the tray back to the galley and came back with a pitcher of heated seawater. "I am sorry, it's salt," he said.

"No matter," Buckingham replied. He stripped off his linen shirt, and his breeches. Tradescant held a towel for him and watched while Buckingham washed himself, and ran wet fingers through his dark hair. He stood to let John pat a sheet around him and then he lay, still naked, on the rich scarlet counterpane of his bed. John could not look away; the duke was as beautiful as a statue in the gardens at New Hall.

"Do you want to sleep here tonight again?" his lordship asked.

"If you wish, my lord," John said, keeping the hope from his face.

"I asked what *you* wished," Buckingham said.

John hesitated. "You are my master. It must be for you to say."

"I say that I want to know your thoughts. Do you wish to sleep here with me, as we did last night? Or go back to your own bed? You're free to do either, John. I don't coerce you."

John raised his eyes to the duke's dark smile. He felt as if his face was burning. "I want you," he said. "I want to be with you."

The duke sighed, almost as if he were relieved of a fear. "As my lover?"

John nodded, feeling the depth of sin and desire as if they were one.

"Take the jug and ewer away and come back," the duke commanded. "I want to feel a man's love tonight."

The next morning they sighted Cornwall and then it was just another night before they arrived in Portsmouth. John expected to be dismissed, but when the priest had left after evening prayers Buckingham crooked his finger and John locked the door behind everyone else and spent the night with the duke. They were learning each other's bodies, apprentices in desire. Buckingham's skin was smooth and soft but the muscles in his body were hard from his horseriding and his running. John was ashamed of the gray in the hairs of his chest and his callused hands, but the weight of his strong body on Buckingham made the younger man groan with delight. They kissed, lips lingering, pressing, exploring, drinking from each other's mouths. They struggled against each other like wrestlers fighting, like animals mating, testing the hardness of muscle against muscle in a lovemaking which gave no quarter and showed no sentimentality but which had at its core a wild savage tenderness, until Buckingham said breathlessly, "I can't wait! I want it too much!" and lunged toward John and they tumbled together into the darker world of pain and desire until pain and desire were one and the darkness was complete.

November 1627

They woke at dawn with the sound of the sailors making ready for port. There was little time for words and, in any case, what was between them went deeper than speech. John believed that they were bonded together in a way that nothing could break—the love of a man for his brother-in-arms, the strong powerful love of a vassal for his lord, and now the passionate devotion of lovers who have found all the pleasure of the world in each other's bodies. Buckingham lay back in bed as John swiftly dressed, and smiled. John felt his desires—now insatiable it seemed—rise again at that seductive mischievous smile.

"Where will we lie tonight?" he asked.

"I don't know what reception will meet me," Buckingham said, his smile fading. "We'll have to find the court. Chances are that Charles will be at Whitehall this season. I may have to work hard to keep my place."

"Whatever place you win I am yours," John said simply.

Buckingham gleamed at him. "I know," he said quietly. "I shall need you by me."

"And after Whitehall?"

"Home for the New Year," Buckingham decided. He shot John a rueful smile. "To our loving wives."

John hesitated. "I could send Elizabeth to Kent," he offered. Elizabeth and his long years of marriage seemed part of another life; nothing could interfere with this new way of being, with this new love, with this sudden arrival of passion. "My wife has family in Kent. She could visit them. I could be alone at New Hall with you."

Buckingham smiled. "No need. We will always be traveling, you and I, John. I will always need you at my side. People will talk, but people always talk. You will serve me in my chamber again as you have done on this voyage. Nothing will part us."

John kneeled on the bed and reached for Buckingham. The two men embraced; Buckingham's curly hair tickled John's cheek, his neck. He slipped his hand down into the warmth of his lord's body and felt the hardness of his desire rising to greet his touch.

"You want me," John whispered.

"Very much."

John straightened up. "I had feared that this was not going to last," he confided. "That this was part of the madness of these days. The defeat and the grief. I had feared that when we came into port I would be forgotten."

Buckingham shook his head.

"I could not bear to be without you, not now." John felt strange, speaking of his feelings after years of self-imposed silence. He felt strangely freed, as if at last he could lay claim to a strange land inside his own head, an inner Virginia.

"You will not be without me," the lord said easily. He threw back the covers and John felt his breath catch at the sight of the perfect body. The shoulders broad, the legs long, the thatch of dark hair and the rising penis, the smooth white skin of his belly and chest and the tumble of dark curls.

John laughed at himself. "I am as besotted as a girl! I am breathless at the very sight of you."

Buckingham smiled and then pulled on his linen shirt. "My John," he said. "Love no one but me."

"I swear it."

"I mean it." Buckingham paused. "I won't have a rival. Not wife nor child nor another man, not even your gardens."

John shook his head. "Of course there is no one but you," he said. "You were my master before, but after this you have me heart and soul."

Buckingham pulled on his scarlet hose and red breeches slashed with gold. He turned his back absentmindedly and John tied the scarlet leather laces for him, relishing the intimacy, the casual touch.

"You are my talisman," Buckingham said, speaking half to himself. "You were Cecil's man and now you are mine. He died without failure or dishonor and so must I. And today I shall know if the king forgives me for failing him."

"You didn't fail," John said. "You did all he set you to do. Others failed, and the Navy failed to supply you. But you were faultless in courage and honor."

Buckingham leaned back against him, feeling John's warm solid body behind him, and briefly closed his eyes. John put his arms around the younger man's body, relishing the hardness of his chest and the contrasting softness of his curly hair.

"I need you for words like that," Buckingham whispered. "No one else can tell me such things and make me believe them. I need your faith in me, John, especially when I have no faith in myself."

"I never saw you show a moment's fear," John said earnestly. "I never saw you hesitate or fail. You were the Lord High Admiral for every minute. No man could say less. No man did more."

Buckingham straightened up and John saw the set of his shoulders and the lift of his chin. "I shall hold those words to me," he said. "Whatever else befalls me today. I shall know that you were there, you witnessed everything, and you say this. You have been here with me and I have your love. You are a man whose judgment is trusted, and you are *my* man—what did you say?—heart and soul."

"Till death."

"Swear it." Buckingham turned and held John's shoulders with sudden passionate intensity. He took John's face roughly in his cupped hands. "Swear that you are mine till death."

John did not hesitate. "I swear on all that I hold sacred that I am your man, and none other's. I will follow you and serve you till death," he promised. It was a mighty oath but John did not feel the weight of it. Instead he had a great sense of joy at being committed, at last, to another person without restraint, as if all the years with Elizabeth had been only a circling of another, a moving toward intimacy which could never be truly found. Elizabeth's femininity, her faith, her every difference from John, had meant that he could never reach her. Always between them were the dividing fissures of opinion, of taste, of style.

But Buckingham had been in John's heart, had penetrated deep inside him. There was nothing which could part them now. It was not a love between a man and a woman which always founders on difference, which always struggles with difference. It was a passion between men who start as equals and fight their way through to mutual desire and mutual satisfaction as equals.

The tension left Buckingham's shoulders. "I needed to hear that," he said thoughtfully. "It is like a chain of command; the old king needed me and called me his dog, took me like a dog too. Now I need you, and you shall be my dog."

The noises on deck grew more urgent, they could hear the sailors shouting to the barges for tow ropes, and then came the gentle bump as the ship dropped her sails and was taken in tow.

"Fetch hot water," Buckingham said. "I must shave."

John nodded and did the work of a cabin boy with a heady sense of delight. He stood beside Buckingham while he shaved his smooth skin of the dark stubble, held a linen sheet for him while he washed, and then handed him his clean shirt and his waistcoat and surcoat. Buckingham dressed in silence; his hand when he reached for his perfume bottle was shaking. He sprayed his hair with perfume, set his plumed hat, winking with diamonds, on his head and smiled at himself in the mirror: a hollow smile, a fearful smile.

"I shall go on deck," he said. "No one shall say that I was afraid to show my face."

"I will be with you," John promised.

They went through the door together. "Don't leave me," Buckingham whispered as they went up the companionway. "Whatever happens, stay at my shoulder this day. Wherever I go."

Tradescant realized that his master was fearing worse than humiliation; he was fearing arrest. Better-loved men than he had died in the Tower for failed expeditions. They had both seen Sir Walter Raleigh taken to the Tower for less.

"I shall not leave you," John assured him. "Wherever they take you they will take me too. I shall always be with you."

Buckingham paused on the narrow companionway. "To the foot of the gallows?" he demanded.

"To the noose or the axe," John said, as bleak as his master. "I have sworn I am yours, heart and soul, till death."

Buckingham dropped his hand heavily on John's shoulder and for a moment the two men stood, face to face, their eyes locked. Then with one accord they moved together and kissed. It was a passionate kiss, like a couple of fierce animals biting, no tenderness, no gentleness in it. It was a kiss no woman could give. It was a kiss between men, men who have been through a battle where there was death on either side of them and who are finding, in each other's passion, the strength to face death again.

"Stay by me," Buckingham whispered, and went up the companionway to the deck.

A cold morning wind was blowing. The beaches of Southsea were spread before them and the green of the town common behind them. The narrow entrance to Portsmouth harbor was ahead, the gray sea walls lined with people, their faces white dots of anxiety. The flags flying over the fort flapped against their poles. Tradescant could not make out if the royal standard was there, or if Buckingham's flag had been raised in his honor. The sun was not yet up and there was a ragged cold sea mist blowing in with them, as if the ghosts of the men who would not be coming home were drifting in with them across the gray waters.

There was no gun salute, there was no band playing music, there was no applause. The *Triumph,* ill-named, undermanned and defeated, edged into the quayside, as if the ship itself felt shame.

John stood beside Buckingham by the steersman. Buckingham was dressed defiantly in red and gold, like a victorious leader, but when the people on the quayside saw him they let out a deep groan. Buckingham's bright smile never wavered but he glanced slightly over his shoulder as if to assure himself that John was there.

They ran the gangplank ashore and Buckingham, with a generous gesture of his hand, indicated that the men should go before him. It was a fine gesture but it would have been better if the two of them had gone first, and gotten quickly on horses, and ridden away. For there was another deep groan and then a horrified silence from the dockers and the sailors' and soldiers' families waiting on shore, as the walking wounded struggled up the companionways from below.

Their faces were blanched white with sickness except where the sun had burned them brick red, their clothes were torn and tattered, their boots worn thin. They were half-starved, their legs and arms pocked with ulcers. There were only a few men brought out on stretchers, very few, and that was because the sick and injured had died in the low-lying marshes, or bled in agony on the voyage home.

As the men came ashore they were claimed by their families. Some stayed to watch the unloading, but most turned for home, wives sobbing over the wrecks of their husbands, mothers grieving over sons, children staring upward, uncomprehending, into the newly aged face, into the head laid open with a livid new scar, or a weeping wound, a man they could not recognize as their father.

The crowd hardly diminished at all, and that was when John realized how many men they had left behind in the marshes of the Ile de Rhé, since more than half of the families waiting to welcome their men home were still waiting. The men would not come, they would never come. They had been left on a small island in a small river before a small French town, as he had warned. As many as four thousand families had lost a father.

If Buckingham had such thoughts he did not show them. He stood very still and straight beside the wheel of his ship, balancing his weight lightly on the balls of his feet like a dancer, his hand on his hips, his head up. When someone from the quayside shouted abuse at him, he turned and looked for them, as if he did not fear to meet their gaze, his smile as ready as ever.

"He has not sent a herald for me," he said softly so that only Tradescant could hear. "Not soldiers to arrest me; but equally, not a herald to greet me. Am I to be ignored? Simply forgotten?"

"Hold fast," Tradescant replied. "We are early. It's only the poor people who have been sleeping at the quayside and around the city who will have known when we were sighted. The king himself could arrive at any moment."

Someone shouted a curse from the quayside and Buckingham turned his bright smile toward them as if it were a hurrah.

"He could," he agreed levelly. "He could."

"There! Look! cried John. "A coach, my lord! They have sent a coach for you!"

Buckingham turned quickly and squinted down the quayside into the bright autumn sunshine. For a heart-stopping moment they could not see the livery of the coach. It could have been a royal warrant to arrest him. But then Buckingham's laugh rang out.

"By God, it is the royal coach! I am to be met with honor!"

It was unmistakable. Buckingham himself had introduced the fashion for six-horse carriages into England and only he and the king used them. Two postillions in royal livery jogged on the two leading pairs of horses, the coachman sat in scarlet and gold on the box, a footman beside him, and two liveried footmen clung to the rear. The horses had plumes of scarlet in their bridles; their hooves rang on the cobbles. The king's flags were on the four corners of the coach. The royal herald was inside.

Buckingham ran like a boy to the head of the gangplank to see this bright guarantee of his continuing wealth and power trotting toward him. Behind it came another coach with a crest on the door, and another. Behind that came another coach, and a marching band playing whistles and drums. Two heralds carried Buckingham's flag. The coach stopped at the gangplank and they let down the steps for the royal herald. Behind him from the second coach came Kate, Buckingham's wife, and his redoubtable mother the papist countess.

Buckingham strode to the head of the gangplank to greet them, his head tilted, his smile quizzical. John followed, a pace behind him. The herald marched up the gangplank and dropped to his knee.

"My lord duke, you are welcome home," the man said. "The king sends you greetings and bids you to come to him at once. The court is at Whitehall. And he bids me give you this."

He produced a purse. Buckingham, with a slight smile, opened it. A bracelet heavy with enormous diamonds spilled out into his cupped hands. "This is a pretty gift," he said equably.

"I have private messages for you, from His Majesty," the herald added. "And he bids you use his coach for your journey to him."

Buckingham nodded as if he had never expected anything less. The herald got to his feet and stood to one side. Buckingham stepped down the gangplank to where his wife was waiting beside his coach. John bowed to the herald and followed his master. Kate Villiers was in her husband's arms, her little hands clutching his broad shoulders.

"You are ill?" Kate whispered passionately. "You look so pale!"

He shook his head and spoke over her head to his mother. "Things are indeed prosperous?"

She nodded in grim triumph. "He is waiting for you in London, desperate to see you. We have orders to bring the Favorite straight to him."

"I am the Favorite still?"

Her hard face was bright with triumph. "He says that no one shall call it a defeat. He says that you could have lost the men and the ships and the standards a hundred times over as long as you are safe. He says he cares nothing for four thousand lives as long as the most precious one comes safe home."

Buckingham laughed aloud. "I am safe then?"

"We are all safe," his mother said. "Come to the city. Captain

Mason has put his house at your disposal. There is a barber waiting for you, the tailor has a new suit of clothes and the king has sent you gloves and a cape."

Tradescant drew a little closer to his lord. There was a press of fashionable people pouring out of the coaches and gathering all around him. Someone had pressed a glass in Buckingham's hand and they were drinking to his safe return. The women's necks and shoulders were bare to the cold morning air; they were painted as for a masque at court. The men were teetering on high heels, laughing and pressing close to Buckingham. Someone elbowed John in the side and he was pushed to the edge of the crowd. A party was starting, here on the quayside, beside the tattered bulk of the *Triumph* despite the resentful stares of the poor people, drowning out the sobbing of women whose husbands would never come home.

"Tell us all about it!" someone cried. "Tell us about the landing! They say that the French cavalry just vanished!"

Buckingham laughed and disclaimed, his beautiful wife pressed close to his side, his arm around her waist. "I am grieved to my heart that we came home without accomplishing what we intended," he said modestly.

There were immediate cries of disagreement. "But you were ill-supplied! And what could any commander do with such men? They are fools, every one of them!"

John looked away. There was one woman clinging to the handrail of the gangplank, looking up at the deck of the empty ship. He went toward her, his place at the fringe of the crowd instantly taken by a pretty woman, her face bright with desire.

"What is it, mistress?"

She turned a face to him which was hollowed by long hunger, and sightless with grief. "My husband . . . I am waiting for my husband. Will he come on another ship?"

"What was his name?"

"Thomas Blackson. He's a ploughman, but they took him for a soldier. He'd never held a gun before."

John remembered Thomas Blackson because the man had offered to keep his plants watered while John was on a mission for his master. He was a big man, as patient and hard-working as the oxen he had driven. John had last seen him before the citadel of St. Martin. He had been ordered up a ladder to attack the defenders at the top of the wall. He had gone obediently up the ladder, which was five feet short of the top. The French had leaned over the wall and shot downward at a ridiculously easy target: the big man at the top of the ladder, stalled, just five feet below them.

"I am sorry, mistress, he is dead."

Her white face went whiter still. "He can't be," she said. "I am expecting his baby. I promised him a son."

"I am sorry," John repeated.

"Perhaps he will come on another ship."

John shook his head. "No."

"He would not leave me," she said, trying to persuade him. "He would never leave me. He would not have gone in the first place but they pressed him and took him against his will. They promised me that the duke was sailing with them, and that the duke would care for his men."

John felt a deep weariness spread through him. "I saw him fall," he said. "He died a hero. But he died, mistress."

She moved away from him as if his news made him distasteful, as if she would refuse to listen to such a liar. "I shall wait," she said. "He'll come in on another ship. He won't fail me. Not my Thomas. He was never late for a single meeting, not through our courtship. He's never even late home for his dinner. He won't fail me now."

John glanced back. The court party were getting into their coaches. There was a breakfast laid at Captain Mason's house and fine wines and food waiting. Someone hurled an empty bottle into the sea. John turned from the woman and hurried to Buckingham's side as he stepped into his coach.

"My lord?"

"Oh! John."

"Where is Captain Mason's house?"

Kate laid hold of her husband's coat and pulled him into the coach.

"Up from the cathedral," Buckingham said. "But you needn't come, Tradescant. You can go home."

"I thought I would be with you . . ."

Buckingham smiled his merry smile. "See how well I am greeted!" He dropped into his seat, his arm around his wife. "I don't need your service, John. You can go home to New Hall."

"My lord, I . . ." John broke off. The old countess looked sharply at him; he was afraid of her black stare. "You said I should stay with you this day," he reminded his master.

Buckingham laughed again. "Yes, but thank God I don't need your care. The king is my friend, my wife is at my side, my mother guards the interests of my family. Go home, John! I shall see you at New Hall when I come."

He nodded to the footman and the man shut the door.

"But when shall I see you?" John called as the carriage started to move. The footman jostled past him and swung up on the back of the carriage. John wished that he too might at least ride at the back of the carriage, or run behind, or lie like a dog on the floor at their feet. "When shall I see you again?"

"When I come!" Buckingham cried. He waved his hand as John dropped back from the window. "I thank you for your care of me, John. I won't forget it."

The lead horse slipped on the cobbles and the carriage checked for a moment. John seized his chance and sprang to the window again. "But I thought I was to stay with you! At your shoulder! . . . As you said . . . my lord . . . as you said!"

Buckingham's wife was pressed to his side, her fine silk gown crushed in his hold. She peeped up at her husband in a laughing complaint at John's persistence.

"I have given you leave," Buckingham said firmly. "Don't be importunate, John. Go to New Hall. Don't offend me by asking for more."

Tradescant skidded to a halt on the cobbles and stood watching the coach rock away down the quayside. The other coaches followed behind the royal coach like some great promenade. Tradescant had to step back to make room for them; and then they were all gone, the trotting horses, the laughing courtiers, the brightness of the liveries, of the courtiers' clothes, and the dock was left to grayness and mourning once more.

Tradescant stood until the last of them was gone. He could hardly believe the words he had heard his master use to him. When he had been pleading for a place at his side, Buckingham had answered him as if he had been begging for money. Buckingham had slipped, like some beautiful bird, from John's keeping to another's. And John might as well whistle to a free bird to come back to its cage as ask the duke to come back to him. John was held and bound by an obsessional desire, by a passionate love and by a sacred oath. He had sworn to love his lord until death. But only now did he realize that Buckingham had sworn nothing.

Tradescant went slowly up the gangplank, to his cabin. Someone had stolen his walking boots and his warm cape on the voyage when he had been too seldom there. He would have to replace them in Portsmouth, where such things were overpriced. He pulled out his pack and started to put his things together. The movement of the ship, rocking at anchor in the harbor, felt half-dead to John after the five-month expedition on rolling seas. The crew had melted away as soon as the officers had gone; there was no sound but the creaking of hard-worked timbers. His cabin showed his neglect of it. These last few days he had spent all his time with Buckingham, and his pallet bed was damp. Even his plants had been forgotten; the earth in the little pots was dry. John fetched a jug of water and dribbled it in, feeling that he must have lost his senses completely that he should have carried his plants through so much and then forgotten to water them for the last three days of the voyage.

He thought that this was how a woman must feel when she has given her love and given her trust and found that her lover was lighthearted and fickle and negligent all along. She feels as if he has taken something precious, a rare seedling, and let it fall. She feels injured—Tradescant felt pain like a wound—but she also feels a fool. Tradescant felt humbled lower than ever in his life before. Being an apprentice gardener was a low station in life but you could be proud of your work and see where it might take you. But being a nobleman's lover was the work of a fool. Buckingham had used him, had taken him for consolation, to keep his fears at bay, to support his courage and confidence. Now he had his mother and Kate and the king and the court and all his wealth and joy. And all Tradescant had was a new gillyflower, wilting, a large wormwood plant in dry soil, a pain in his backside which was abuse, and a pain in his belly which was grief.

Grimly he picked up his pack, ducked his head to avoid the low beam of his cabin doorway and climbed the companionway to the waist of the ship. He trudged down the gangplank. No one was on board to bid him good-bye, no one was on the quayside waiting to greet him. The white-faced widow started up as she heard a footstep on the gangplank, but then dropped back. Tradescant went past her without a word of comfort. He had no comfort to give. He turned his face away from the sea and trudged, uncomfortable in his shoes on the cobbles, toward the city.

A man fell in beside him. "Did you speak to him about my promotion?"

It was Felton again. "I am sorry," said John. "I forgot."

But the man was not angry this time. "Then he must have seen sense himself," he said joyfully. "Those who call him a fool will have me to reckon with. He has promised me my captaincy. I shall retire a captain and that is worth something to a poor man, Mr. Tradescant."

"I am glad of it," John said heavily.

"I shall never fight again," Felton declared. "It was a bad campaign, badly planned, badly led, cruelly hard. There were times when I wept like a baby. I thought we would never get off that accursed island."

John nodded.

"He will never do it again, will he?" Felton asked. "The French can fight their own battles now. They don't need the pain of Englishmen. We should be as we were with the old queen—defenders of our own shores and our own counties. Safe behind our own sea. What are the French and their worries to me?"

"I feel that too," John said. They had reached the end of the quay. He turned and held out his hand to Felton. "God be with you, Felton."

"And with you, Mr. Tradescant. Now we are home, maybe the duke will think of the people at home. There's much poverty. It is pitiful to see the children in my village. They have neither school nor play, and the common land has been enclosed so they have neither milk nor meat nor honey. And bread itself is scarce."

"Maybe he will."

The two men shook hands, but still Felton lingered. "If I were the duke and could advise the king, I would tell him to stop the enclosing of land and free it for the people," he said. "So that every man can have his strip for vegetables or to keep a pig. Like it used to be. If I were advising the king, I would tell him that before he moves the communion table rightwise or sidewise or anywise in the church he should feed the people. We need bread before a mouthful of communion wine."

John nodded, but he knew, as Felton could not know, that the king never saw the beggars in the streets, never saw the hungry children. He went in his carriage from great country seat to hunting lodge. He went on his royal barge from one riverside palace to another. And besides, the permission granted to a landlord to enclose common land brought revenue into the royal coffers, while a refusal would benefit only the poor and leave the king as short of cash as ever.

"He is a merciful king?" Felton queried. "And Buckingham is a great duke, a good man, is he not?"

"Oh, yes," John said. The pain in his belly seemed to have stretched out to his fingers and his toes; he felt numb in his legs and shoulders. If he did not start to walk home soon, he thought he would lie down on the cobbles and die. "Excuse me, I must go; my wife will be waiting for me."

"I must go too!" Felton cried, remembering. "I have a wife waiting for me, thank God. I shall tell her to call me captain!"

He hefted his pack and strode off whistling. John looked down at his shoes and put one in front of the other, as if he had just learned to walk. At each step he thought he could hear Buckingham laugh and say: "I have given you leave. Don't be importunate, John. Go to New Hall. Don't offend me by asking for more."

He had not thought how he would get to New Hall. He had been on such a crest of desire and happiness that he had thought he and the duke would ride side by side, the two of them together. Or perhaps they would have used the duke's coach and horses and rocked along the badly made roads, and laughed when they had to stop for a loose wheel, or walked shoulder to shoulder up a hill to spare the horses.

But now he was trudging alone in stiff new walking boots. He had some money in his pocket; he could buy or hire a horse, or he could take a ride with any carter. But as the sun came slowly up—an English sun, he thought with a sudden pang of recognition—he found that he wanted to walk, walk like a poor man, walk slowly along the rutted road which led away from the port to London. He wanted to look at the changing blushing colors of the trees and the berries in the hedgerow and the grass seeds bobbing in the wind. He felt as if he had been in exile for a dozen years, he had dreamed of lanes like this, of a sun as warm and mild as this one, while they had been trapped on that island waiting for reinforcement, waiting for a decisive battle, waiting for victory, for glory.

At midday he knocked on the door of a small wayside farmhouse and asked if he could buy some dinner. The farmer's wife gave him a trencher of bread and cheese and a flagon of ale to drink. Her hands were ingrained with dirt and there was dirt under her fingernails and in the thorn scratches.

"You're a gardener," Tradescant guessed.

She rubbed her hand on her apron. "I struggle with it," she said in the broad accent of Hampshire. "But 'tis like a forest, like the forest of the Sleeping Beauty. When I rest it grows up to my very windows. I was clearing my strawberry bed and I find a plant growing thorns. A strawberry with thorns! The whole garden would grow weeds and thorns if it could."

"A thorny strawberry?" John demanded. He pushed aside the flask of ale. The pain was still deep in his body but he could not deny a small squirm of curiosity. "You have a thorny strawberry? May I see it?"

"Why, what use is it?" she asked. "It grows a green fruit; it is no good for eating nor bottling."

"It is a curiosity," he said, and found he was smiling, the muscles on his cheeks relaxing from their scowl. "I am a great one for curiosities; I would be glad if you would show it to me. Out of your kindness. And I would pay you . . ."

"You can have it for nothing," she said. "But you must fetch it yourself. I threw it with the other weeds on the midden. It'll take a deal of sorting through."

John laughed, and then checked himself at the strangeness of the noise. He had not laughed in months. His time with his lord had been a time of passion driving out grief in the darkness. But now he was home, on English soil again, under an English sun and here was this woman with her green thorny strawberry.

"I will find it," he promised her. "And I will see if I can grow it in my garden, and if it proves to be a curiosity, or to have some quality, then I will send you a shoot."

She shook her head at his folly. "Are you from London?"

"Yes," he said; he did not want to name New Hall. He did not want to be known as the Duke of Buckingham's man.

She nodded as if that would account for it. "Here we like our strawberries red and fit to eat," she said gently. "Do not send me a shoot; I do not want it. You can give me a penny for your dinner and for the thorny strawberry, and be on your way. In Hampshire we like our strawberries red."

Winter 1627

Elizabeth was in the garden before their cottage at New Hall when John came in at the gate. She was cutting herbs in the cool of the evening light, and the basket on the ground before her was bobbing with the seed-heavy heads of camomile flowers. When she heard his uneven step she looked up and started to run toward him but then she suddenly checked. Something in the slowness of his pace and his bowed shoulders warned her that this was not a happy homecoming.

Slowly she came toward him, noting the new lines of pain and disappointment in his face. His limp, which he thought she did not see, was more pronounced than ever.

She put her hand on his shoulder. "Husband?" she said softly. "You are welcome home."

He looked up from the ground before him and when she met his dark eyes she recoiled. "John?" she whispered. "Oh my John, what has he done to you?"

It was the worst thing she could have said. He reared up, his face hard. "Nothing. What d'you mean?"

"Nothing. Nothing. Come and sit down." She led him to the stone bench before the house, and felt his hand tremble in her own. "Sit," she said tenderly. "I will get you a cup of ale, or would you like something hot?"

"Anything," he said.

She hesitated. J was still at work, cutting back and weeding in the fruit garden, at the other side of the great house. She did not send for him yet, she feared a quarrel between father and son, and when she looked at John's weary face she feared that his son would be the victor. John had come home an old man. She whisked into the house and brought out a mug of ale and a slice of her home-made bread. She put them on the bench beside him and said nothing while he drank. He did not eat.

"We heard that it was a defeat," she said at last. "I was afraid that you were hurt." She shot a sideways look at him, wondering if there were some physical injury that he was keeping from her.

"I took not a scratch," he said simply.

The pain was in his soul, then. "And his lordship?"

There was a flash across his face, instantly hidden, like lightning on a dark night. "He is well, praise God. He is with the king who has rejoiced in his return, with his wife at his side, thank God."

She bowed her head briefly but found she could not say "Amen."

"And you . . ." she prompted him gently. "I can see that all is not well with you, John. I can see that there is no rejoicing for you."

He met her eyes and she thought that never before in their life together had she seen him look as if the light had gone out for him.

"I will not burden you with my sorrows, Elizabeth," he said gently. "I will mend. I am not a boy in springtime. I will mend."

Her grave look never wavered. "Perhaps you should tell me, John. Or tell your Saviour. A hidden secret is like a hidden pain; it can only grow worse."

He nodded as if he knew all about hidden pain now. "I shall try to pray. But I am afraid that my faith was never very strong, and I seem to have lost it."

She would have been shocked if she had believed him. "How can you lose your faith?" she asked simply.

He looked away, over his garden. Was it on the island? Did his faith fall sick like the soldiers who had to sleep on the wet ground? Or did it drown in the sea where the causeway was treacherous and they lost the last standard? Or did it bleed to death on the voyage home when the injured men cried out so loud that he heard them, even over the noise of the creaking ship? Was it always a chain that had linked John to his lord, the lord to the king and the king to God, and the loss of one meant the loss of all? Or had he forgotten his faith just as he had forgotten everything, even the gillyflower and the wormwood plants, because he had fallen deep into love and deep into joy and made a god of another man?

"I don't know," he said slowly. "Perhaps God has lost me."

Elizabeth bowed her head and made a quick silent prayer that she might have guidance as to how she might help him.

"You are right, and you have been right all along," he said at last. "We are ruled by a fool who is in the hands of a knave. I have seen men die for the folly of those two, for all my life: in the plague in London, in the villages up and down the land where people are driven out of their homes and out of their gardens for the landlords to make sheep runs, and on that cursed island where we set a siege with less food in our stores than the besieged, where we marched with ploughboys and criminals, where we had scaling ladders which were yards too short, and where the commander was playing at soldiers, and the king forgot to reinforce us."

His bitterness was like an explosion in that quiet garden, even worse than his blasphemy. She had thought she would never hear such words from him, who had been Cecil's man, who had served the old queen. This was a stranger to her—a bitter man carrying the scars of fatal betrayal, who finally spoke treason aloud.

"John—"

He bared his teeth in a hard smile at her surprise. "You should be pleased," he said cruelly. "You warned me enough. Now see: I have heeded your teachings and lost my faith in my lord, in my king and in my God. Wasn't that what you wanted?"

Dumbly she shook her head.

"Didn't you warn me and warn me that he was a sodomite and a puppet master? Didn't you beg me to leave his service on the very day we came here? Didn't you give me a long spoon to sup with the Devil when I started keeping his secrets safe?"

Her hands were over her mouth; her shocked eyes looked at him in silence.

John hawked and spat like a soldier, as if the taste of bile was too bitter for him.

Without thinking, Elizabeth scuffed dirt over the spittle. "John," she whispered. "I never meant that you should lose your faith. I meant only to caution you—"

"I am cautioned now," he said. "I am checked. I am stopped short."

There was a silence. Somewhere in the fine woods of the duke's estate the pigeons were cooing, warmly, easily. John looked up at the sky and saw a flock of rooks heading for home in the tall trees.

"What shall we do?" Elizabeth asked, as if she were in a wilderness with wreckage all around them.

He looked around, at the fine house and the garden, as if they gave him no pleasure at all. "I am his servant," he said slowly. "He has paid me all he is going to pay me; he told me that. He will use me as he wishes. When he needs me—I am to be there. I am the duke's man; I have sworn a solemn oath to be his man till death."

She took a sharp breath at that. "An oath?"

"He asked it of me and I gave it," John said grimly. "I gave him everything he asked and I swore a solemn oath that I am his man. I will have to learn to live with that. I am a servant; I am lower than a servant, for he has commanded me to be his dog and I have licked his foot."

"You think he is a fool and a betrayer and you have sworn to be his man?" she asked incredulously.

"Just so."

They were silent for long moments. She thought that some dark compact must have taken place between her husband and the master he now hated. She did not dare to think what one had done, what one had submitted to. Whatever had taken place it had sent John home as a broken man.

"Do you hate him?" she whispered.

The look he gave her was that of a man carrying a mortal

wound deep in his belly. "No," he said softly. "I love him still. But I know that he is no good. That's worse than hatred for me. To know that I have given my word and my love to a man who is no good."

She took his hands in hers and felt how cold they were, as if his heart were beating slowly, painfully. "Can't you escape him?"

He shook his head. "I am his, in every way that there is, until death."

They sat in silence for long moments, Elizabeth chafing his hands as if he were cold from sickness and she had to warm him. She thought that there was nothing that she could say which would take that dark painful look from his face. The sun was setting slowly in the deep red of autumn and a cool wind began to blow.

"The chestnut tree flowered this summer," she said inconsequently. "As you left, d'you remember you asked me to look to it, for you?"

He did not raise his gaze from his boots. "The sweet chestnuts?"

"No. Your sapling. The one you gave me. The chestnut from Turkey. It bore a strange beautiful blossom, like huge pine cones, a white blossom of many flowers with tiny scarlet freckles inside them, and smelling sweet."

"Eh? My sapling flowered? At last?"

"As you left. And it is setting seed," she said. "You will have nuts off it this year, John. You can see the seed cases already. They are very strange, I had forgotten how strange. They are fat and fleshy and with a few thick spikes. But they are holding to the tree and swelling with the ripeness of the nut inside."

He straightened up and looked at her. "Are you sure?"

"I think so," she said with loving cunning. "But you had better see for yourself; you know there is no one who has your skill with trees."

"Perhaps I should take a look." He got to his feet and winced as his boots rubbed his sore feet, but he stepped out down the garden path to where his tree was kept in its great carrying case at the bottom of the garden near the kitchen garden wall.

"I wish we had named it for you," she said, suddenly struck by how little they owned, now that he was a vassal and had lost everything. "I wish we had called them 'Tradescantia' when Lord Cecil first gave them to you to grow. You were the first to grow them; you had the right."

John shrugged his shoulders as if it did not matter what they were named as long as they grew tall and strong. "The name does not matter. Rights do not matter. But to grow a new tree, to put a new tree into the gardens of England—now that is to live forever."

J did not come home till dusk and he did not know his father was returned until he came in through the front door and saw the Portsmouth-bought walking boots side by side inside the doorway. He hesitated, but it was too late. John, sitting at the well-worn table, had already seen him.

J was dressed in a suit of gray broadcloth, white linen bands at his throat, plain without lace. On his head was a tall plain black hat, unadorned by feather or badge. Over his shoulder was his warm coat of black.

John, who had bathed and changed into his russet suit with a rich lace collar, rose slowly from the table.

"You're dressed very plain," he said cautiously.

Elizabeth heard the front door slam and came slowly from the kitchen, wiping her hands on her apron.

J measured his father and spoke steadily. "I believe that finery is a waste of a man's money and an abomination in the sight of the Lord."

John wheeled around and looked accusingly at Elizabeth. She met his gaze without flinching. "You've turned him into a Puritan at last," he said. "I suppose he preaches and bears witness and can fall down in a faint if required?"

"I can speak for myself," J said. "And it was not my mother's decision, but my own."

"Decision!" John scoffed. "What can a boy of eighteen decide?"

J flinched. "I am a man," he said. "I am nineteen now. I earn a man's wage, I do a man's work and I give a man's whole duty to my God."

For a moment they thought John would roar out his temper. J braced himself for the blast of anger, but to his surprise none came. The older man's shoulders dropped and he turned and fell heavily in his chair. "And how long will you draw a wage here, looking like that?" he asked. "When the king comes to visit? When Archbishop Laud comes to visit? Do you think they want to see a sectary in their garden?"

J's head went up. "I don't fear them."

"Yes, I daresay you are longing for martyrdom, to be burned at the stake for your beliefs, but this is not a burning king. He will merely turn away from you and Buckingham will dismiss you. And where will you work then?"

"For a nobleman who shares my faith," J said simply. "The country is full of men who believe in worshipping our God in simplicity and in truth, who have turned against the waste and sin of the court."

"Do I have to spell it out?" John shouted. "They will turn you off and no one will employ you!"

"Husband—"

"What?"

"You told me yourself that your faith in the king and the duke has been shaken," Elizabeth said gently. "J is trying to find his own way."

"What way?" John demanded. "There is no other way."

"There is going back to the Bible and seeking a way through prayer," J said earnestly. "There is the beauty of hard work, and turning away from show and masques and waste. There is sharing the land, every man to have his own piece of ground to grow his own food so that none go hungry. There is opening up the enclosed sheep runs and the enclosed parks so that everyone can share in the wealth which God has given."

"Opening parks?"

"Yes, even like this one," J said earnestly. "Why should my lord duke have the Great Park of five hundred acres and the Little Park of three hundred? Why should he own the common road, and the green before the gate? Why does he need an avenue of a mile of lime trees? Why should he enclose good fields, productive fields, and then plant a few pretty trees and grass and use it for walking and riding? What folly to take good farming land and plant it with shrubs and call it a wilderness when children are dying for lack of food in Chorley, and people are driven out of their cottages because their plots of land have been taken away from them?"

"Because he is the duke," John said steadily.

"He deserves to own half of the county?"

"It is his own, given to him by the king, who owns the whole country."

"And what did the duke do for the king to earn such wealth?"

John had a sudden vivid recollection of the rocking cabin and the swaying light and Buckingham rearing above him, and the wound like a swordthrust which was the extreme of pleasure and pain all at once.

J waited for a reply.

"Don't," John said shortly. "Don't torment me, J. It is bad enough that you should come into my house looking like a hedgerow lecturer. Don't torment me about the duke and the king and the rights and the wrongs of it. I have been close to death, my life hanging on whether the king would remember his friend on a barren island far away, or not. And then he did not. I have no stomach for an argument with you."

"Then I may wear what I choose, and pray as I choose?"

John nodded wearily. "Wear what you will."

There was a silence as J absorbed the extent of his victory. Tradescant turned his back on him and returned to his seat at the table. J stepped out of his mud-caked working boots and came into the room in his socks.

"I am thinking of taking a wife," he announced quietly. "And leaving the duke's service. I want to go to Virginia and start again, in a country where there are no lords and no kings, and no archbishops. I want to be there where they are planting an Eden."

He had thought his father defeated, and was pressing his advantage while he had it. But John raised his head and looked hard at his son. "Think again," he counseled him.

They ate dinner in awkward silence and then J put on his hat and went out into the darkness, carrying only a small lantern to light his way.

"Where's he going?" John asked Elizabeth.

"To evening prayers, at the big house," she said.

"They have prayer meetings on my lord's doorstep?"

"Why not?"

"Because the king has ruled how the church services are to be arranged," John said firmly. "And they are to be done by a certified vicar in church on Sunday."

"But Buckingham's own mother is a papist," Elizabeth pointed out. "And the queen herself. *They* do not obey the king and the archbishop. And they do far worse than simple men reading their Bible and praying in their own language to God."

"You cannot compare Her Majesty with simple men, with J!"

She turned her calm face to him. "I can, and I do," she said. "Except that my son is a godly young man who prays twice a day and lives soberly and cleanly while the queen . . ."

"Not another word!" Tradescant interrupted her.

She shook her head. "I was only going to say that the queen's conscience is her own concern. I know that my son takes nothing but what is his own, bows to no graven idols, avoids priests and their wickedness and says nothing against the king."

John said nothing. It was undeniable that the queen did all of these things. It was undeniable that the queen was a wilful papist who had sworn that she hated her husband and hated his country, and would neither speak the language nor smile at the people.

"Whatever his conscience, J has taken the duke's wage," John pointed out. "He is his man while he draws that wage. The duke, right or wrong."

Elizabeth got up from the table and stacked the dinner platters for washing. "No," she said gently. "He works for the duke until he can find himself another, better master. Then he can leave him, he can leave without a moment's regret. He has sworn no loyalty, he has given no promise. He does not belong to the duke until he is released by death. He does not follow the duke, right or wrong."

She looked across at John. The candle on the table showed the heaviness around his eyes, and the determination in her face. "It is only you who are so bound," she said. "By your own love for him. And by an oath of your own making. Not J. You have bound yourself, John; but my son, thank God, is free."

John heard in the kitchen of New Hall that the duke's homecoming had been sweeter than his own. The whole royal court had ridden out of London to meet him in a great cavalcade of riders with seventy coaches carrying the ladies to throw rose petals and rosewater and greet the returning hero. The queen alone had avoided his triumphal return, but only her immediate household had stayed away and sulked. The king had thrown a great dinner to celebrate the triumphal return, and after dinner he had drawn Buckingham away from the crowds and into his private bedchamber and the two men had spent the night together, alone.

"The evening together, you mean," John suggested. "The duke will have gone to his wife, the Duchess Kate, at night, when the dinner was over."

The messenger from London shook his head. "He lay that night with the king," he said firmly. "In the king's own bed in the king's own bedchamber."

John nodded briefly and turned away. He did not want to hear more.

"And he sent a letter for you," the man went on, digging into his pocket.

Tradescant wheeled around. "A letter! You damned fool, why did you not say so at once?"

"I did not think it was urgent—"

"Of course it's urgent. He may want me at a moment's notice;

you may have delayed me with your kitchen gossip and your nonsense about beds and nights and rose petals—"

John dragged the letter from the man's hand and took two stumbling strides to be away from him, so no one could see the words on the page. He glanced at the seal, the duke's own familiar seal, broke it and unfurled the page. He had written in his own hand. John tightened his grip on the paper. It was in his own idiosyncratic spiky handwriting, and it was headed "John—"

The relief was almost too much. He could hardly see the words as the paper shook in his hand. The duke had summoned him; the sharp word on the quayside meant nothing. Buckingham wanted him at his side and now their life would begin together as they had planned.

"Grave news?" the messenger enquired from behind John.

John flattened the letter to his body. "Private," he said shortly and took the letter out into the garden like a stolen sweetmeat to devour on his own. He found the knot garden deserted and he walked down one of his own neat paths and sat on a small stone seat at the end of a miniature avenue. Then, and only then, he opened the letter for his lord's commands.

John—

A ship, the Good Fortune, *is in the Pool of London with a dozen boxes of curiosities for my rarities room. They are goods from India, carved ivory and worked rugs and the like, some gold and some silver cabinets. Also there is a small box of seeds which will be of interest to you. Do fetch them to New Hall for me, or send someone you can trust. I shall be at Whitehall for Christmas with my king.—Villiers.*

That was all. There was no message bidding him to Whitehall, no summons. There was no word of love or even remembrance. He was not cast off, he was not a spurned lover. He did not stand high enough for rejection. Buckingham had simply forgotten the promises, forgotten the nights and moved on to other things.

John sat on the stone seat for a long time with the letter in his hand, the high skies of Essex arched cold and gray above his head. Only when the cold of the stone seat and the cold of the winter winds had chilled him to the very bone did he stir and realize that the coldness was from the world around him, and not seeping icily into his veins from his heart.

"I have to go to London," Tradescant remarked to J. They were working side by side in the duke's rose garden, pruning the year's growth down to sharp sticks cut carefully on the slant.

"Can I go for you?" J asked.

"What for?"

"I could help you."

"I'm not in my dotage," John said. "I think I can get to London and back with a wagon on my own."

"If you are carrying valuables . . ."

"Then I'll hire a man with a musket."

"You might like my company . . ."

"Or I might prefer to travel alone. What's the secret, J? You never liked London before?"

J straightened up and pushed his plain hat back on his head. "I would like to visit a young woman," he announced. "You could come and see her too. Her parents would make us both very welcome."

John stood up, one hand on his aching back. "A young woman? What young woman?"

"Her name is Jane. Jane Hurte. Her father has a mercer's shop near to the docks. While you were away, a package came for his lordship and they sent me down to London to fetch it. Mother wanted some buttons and I stepped into the Hurtes' shop. Jane Hurte took my money and we had a few words of conversation."

John waited, taking care not to smile. There was something deeply endearing about this stilted account of courtship.

"Then I took a lift with the sheep fleeces down to the market, and visited her again."

"In June?" John asked, thinking of shearing time.

"Yes. And then the duchess wanted something fetched from the London house, so I went down on the cart with her maid and spent the day with the Hurtes."

"How many times have you been there?"

"Six times," J said reverently.

"Is she a pretty lass?"

"She's not a lass, she's a young lady. She's twenty-three."

"I beg her pardon! Is she fair or dark?"

"Sort of dark; well, she's not golden-haired, but not altogether dark."

"Pretty?"

"She's not painted and curled and half-naked, like the women of the court. She's modest and . . ."

"Is she pretty?"

"*I* think so."

"If you are the only one that thinks so then she must be plain," John teased.

"She's not plain," J replied seriously. "She's . . . she's . . . she looks like herself."

John abandoned hope of getting much sense from his son about Jane Hurte's looks. "Does she share your beliefs?"

"Of course. Her father is a preacher."

"A traveling preacher?"

"No, he has his own chapel and a congregation. He's a most respected man."

"You are serious about her?"

"I wish to marry her," J said. He looked at his father as if measuring how far he could trust him with a confidence. "I wish to marry her soon. I have been disturbed recently."

"Disturbed?"

"Yes. Sometimes I find it hard to think of her only as a spiritual partner and companion."

John bit the inside of his cheeks to suppress a smile. "You can love her body as well as her soul, I suppose."

"Only if we are married."

"Does she want to marry?"

J flushed a deep brick red and bent over the roses. "I think she might," he said. "But I could not ask her while you were away. I needed you to meet her father and discuss her dowry and all the arrangements."

John nodded. "We'll stay overnight in London," he decided. J's apprentice lovemaking seemed very sweet and young compared to the complexity of his own pain. "Send them word that we can come at dinnertime and perhaps they will ask us to dine."

"I'm sure they will. Only, Father . . ."

"Yes?"

"They're very devout people, and they think badly of the king. We will have a better time if we do not talk about the king or the court, or the archbishop."

"Or Ireland, or the enclosures, or the Ile de Rhé, or my lord Buckingham, or my lord Stafford, or ship money, or the court of wards, or anything," John said impatiently. "I am not a fool, J. I will not embarrass you before your sweetheart."

"She's not my sweetheart," J said quickly. "She's my . . . my . . ."

"Intended helpmeet," John suggested, without a glimmer of a smile.

"Yes," J said, pleased. "Yes. She's my intended helpmeet."

John had expected an austere shop with an unsmiling proprietor and a whey-faced daughter, and was amazed by the well-stocked counter and the plump round-faced woman who sat outside the shop and invited customers to come in.

"I'm Mistress Hurte," she said. "My daughter's inside. My husband is visiting a sick friend and will be home in time for dinner. Step inside, Mr. Tradescant."

Jane Hurte was on her knees behind the counter, tidying the immaculate shelves. She rose up as they came in and John had to blink his eyes to prepare them for the dark interior of the shop. He saw at once that J had been baffled in his description of her because she had a complex intelligent face full of character, neither simply pretty nor plain. Her forehead was broad and smooth and her brown hair was swept back under a plain cap. Her gown was gray but well-cut and flowing, and her white collar was trimmed with lace. She looked at John with a keen intelligence, and a twinkle of humor.

"Good day, Mr. Tradescant," she said. "And welcome to our home. Will you step upstairs to wait? Father will be back in a moment."

"I'll wait down here with you if I may," John said. He looked around the shop, which was lined with small drawers, none of them marked. "It's like a treasure chest."

"John told me that the Duke of Buckingham has a room like this, but he stores curiosities," she said. With a shock John realized that she did not call his son J, but John.

"Yes," he said. "My lord has some very beautiful and curious things."

"And you arrange them and collect them for him?"

"Yes."

"You must have seen many marvels," she said seriously.

John smiled at her. "And many falsehoods. Foolish forgeries cobbled together to try to catch the unwary."

"All treasure is a trap for the unwary," she observed.

"Indeed," John said, disliking the tone of piety. "I shall buy something from you to take home to my wife. Do you have some pretty ribbons or lace for her to trim a collar?"

Jane bent below the counter and slid out a tray. She spread a little black velvet cloth so the lace was shown to its best advantage and laid out one piece, and then another, for him to see.

"And ribbons," she said. They came from a dozen little drawers, arranged by color. She spread them before him, the cheap scratchy thin ones, and the lustrous silkier lengths.

"Are they not a trap to catch the unwary?" John asked, watching her absorbed face as she smoothed the lengths of ribbon before him, and folded them so that he could admire their shine.

She met his smile without embarrassment. "They are the hard

work of good women," she said. "They work to put bread in their mouths and we pay them a fair price and sell at a good profit. It is not just what you earn, but how you spend your money, that is judged on the great day. In this house we buy and sell fairly and nothing is wasted."

"I'll take that lace," John decided. "Enough to make a collar."

She nodded and cut him the measure he needed. "A shilling," she said. "But you may have it for tenpence."

"I'll pay the full shilling," he said. "For the good women."

She gave a sudden, delicious gurgle of laughter, her whole face lighting up and her eyes dancing. "I'll see that they get it," she said.

She took his coin and put it away in a strongbox under the desk, entered the purchase in a ledger, and then wrapped the scrap of lace very carefully and tied it with a piece of wool. John stowed it in the deep pocket of his coat.

"Here's Father," Jane said.

John turned to greet the man. He looked incongruously more like a farmer than a seller of cloth and haberdashery. He was broad-shouldered and red-faced, well-dressed in sober black and gray and with a small lace collar. He held his hat in his hand and put out his other hand to John for a firm handshake.

"I am glad to meet you at last," he said. "We have heard nothing from John but about his father's travels since he first came here, and we prayed for you while you were in such peril off France."

"I thank you," John said, surprised.

"Daily, and by name," Josiah Hurte went on. "He is a mighty all-wise, all-powerful God; but there is no harm in reminding him."

John had to suppress a smile. "I suppose not."

Josiah Hurte looked at his daughter. "Any sales?"

"Just a piece of lace to Mr. Tradescant, here."

His tradesman's instinct warred with his desire to be generous to John's father. The desire for a small profit won. "Times are very hard for us," he said simply.

John looked around the well-stocked shop.

"It doesn't show yet," Josiah said, following his gaze, "but every month things are getting tighter. We have a constant stream of requisitions from the king, fines for this, new taxes for that. And goods which were free to buy and sell suddenly become farmed out to courtiers as monopolies and we have to pay a fee to the monopoly holder. The king demands a free gift from his subjects and the vicar or the churchwardens come round to my shop, look at the outside, decide on their own what I can afford, and I face prison if I refuse."

"The king has great expenses," John said pacifically.

"*My* wife and *my* friends would spend all my money too if I let them," the Puritan said shortly. "So I don't let them."

John said nothing.

"Forgive me," the man said suddenly. "My daughter swore me to silence on this matter and I broach it the moment I am in the door!"

John could not resist a laugh. "My son too!"

"They feared we would quarrel but I would never come to blows over politics."

"I have seen enough of warfare this year," John agreed.

"It is a criminal shame, though," Josiah continued, leading the way up the stairs from the shop. "My guild can no longer control the trade because the court favorites now run the market in thread and lace and silk, and so my apprentices are no longer guaranteed their work or their wages; other men come into the trade and force prices and wages down and up at their whim. I wish you would tell the duke that if the poor are to be fed and the widows and children safeguarded, we need a powerful guild and a steady trade. We cannot have changes every time a courtier needs a new place."

"He does not take my advice," John replied. "Indeed, I think he leaves the business of the city and trade to others."

"Then he should not have taken the monopoly for gold and silver thread into his keeping," the mercer said triumphantly. "If he cares nothing for trade then he should not engross it. He will ruin the trade and ruin himself, and ruin me."

John nodded, uncertain how to answer, but his host slapped the side of his head with a broad palm. "Again!" he cried. "And I promised Jane I would not. Not another word, Mr. Tradescant. So take a glass of wine with me?"

"Willingly."

Dinner was a respectable affair preceded by a lengthy grace, but Mrs. Hurte laid a good table and her husband was generous with small ale and had a good wine. J sat beside Jane and spent the meal regarding her with a steady admiring gaze. John watched his son with a wry amusement.

The Hurtes were a pleasant straightforward couple. Mrs. Hurte presided over the puddings at her end of the table and Josiah Hurte carved the beef at his end. Between them sat their guests and Jane, and two apprentices.

"We dine in the old way," Mr. Hurte confirmed, seeing John looking down the table. "I believe a man who takes an apprentice boy should bring him up as his own. He should feed his body as well as his mind."

John nodded. "I have only ever had my son work for me," he said. "My other gardeners are hired by my master."

"Is the duke at New Hall now?" Mrs. Hurte asked.

Even in this quiet parlor the mention of his name hurt John like a twinge of pain from an unhealed wound.

"No, he is at court," he said shortly. J directed a glance of unspoken appeal at him and Jane looked anxious.

"They are having great revelry this Christmas, now that the duke is safely returned," Mrs. Hurte observed.

"I daresay," said John.

"Shall you see him at Whitehall before you return to New Hall?"

"No," John said. He had a pain now, as sharp as indigestion, under his ribs. He pushed his plate away, sated with grief. "I may not go to him unless he sends for me."

He realized that the young woman, Jane Hurte, was looking at him and her face was full of sympathy, as if she understood a little of what he was feeling. "It must be a hard task to serve a great lord," she said gently. "He must come and go like a planet in the sky and all you can do is watch and wait for him to come again."

Her father bent his head and said softly: "I pray that we may all serve a greater master. Amen."

But Jane did not take her eyes from John and her smile was steady.

"It is hard." His voice was full of pain, even in his own ears. "But I have made my choice and I must serve him."

"Keep us all in service to the Lord our God," Josiah Hurte prayed again, and this time Jane Hurte, still watching John's strained face, said: "Amen."

The two young people were allowed out to walk together. Jane had some deliveries which had to be made, and J was to go with her to help with the basket. John thought that the sight of J carrying the basket as if it were made of glass and holding Jane by the arm as if she were a posy of flowers, mincing down the London street, was one he would never forget.

One of the apprentices walked behind them, bearing a stout stick.

"She has to be accompanied now," Mrs. Hurte said. "There are so many beggars and many of them sickly. She cannot go out alone anymore."

"J will take care of her," John said reassuringly. "See how he holds her arm! And see him with that basket!"

"He's a taking young man," Josiah Hurte remarked pleasantly. "We like him."

"He's very much in love with your daughter," John said. "Are you in favor of a match?"

The mercer hesitated. "Would he remain in the service of the duke?"

"I have some rented fields, and some land I bought on the advice of my old master, the earl. I have the fee for a Whitehall granary—"

"You are a garneter?" Josiah interrupted, surprised.

John had the grace to look embarrassed. "It is a sinecure. I don't do the work but I have the pay for doing it."

Josiah nodded. His daughter's future father-in-law was benefiting from the very system he condemned: places and work given to men who knew nothing about the trade, who had no intention of learning, who subcontracted the task and kept the inflated pay.

"But our main work is in the duke's gardens," John continued smoothly. "The planning and planting of his gardens and the collection in his cabinet of rarities. J has served his apprenticeship under me and will follow me into the place at my death."

"I would be unhappy at Jane joining the duke's household," the man said frankly. "His reputation is bad."

"With women?" Tradescant shook his head. "My lord duke can have the pick of every lady at court. He does not trouble his servants." He felt the pain beneath his ribs as he spoke. "He is a man very well loved. He does not need to buy his pleasure from his servants."

"Could she practice her religion in your house, as she wishes?"

"Providing that she gives no offense to others," John said. "My wife is of a Puritanical bent; her father was vicar at Meopham. And you know J shares your convictions."

"But you do not?"

"I worship on Sundays in the Church of England," John said. "Where the king himself prays. If it is good enough for the king it is good enough for me."

There was a discreet pause. "I think we might differ as to the king's judgment," Mr. Hurte volunteered. His wife, sitting lacemaking at the fireside, gave him a sharp look and clattered the bobbins together on the pillow.

"But enough of that," he said swiftly. "You're the duke's man and I've nothing to say against that. It is my daughter's happiness we must consider. Does J earn enough to keep a wife?"

"He draws a full wage," John said. "And they would live with us. I will see that she does not want for anything. Will she bring a dowry?"

"Fifty pounds now, and a third share of my shop at my death," Josiah answered. "They can have the wedding here and I will treat them."

"Shall I tell J he can propose, then?" John asked.

Josiah smiled. "If I know my daughter, he has already done so," he said as they shook hands.

Spring 1628

Jane Hurte and young John Tradescant were married in the city church of St. Gregory by St. Paul. The officiating priest neither wore a surplice nor did he turn his back on the congregation to prepare communion as Archbishop Laud had ordered. The communion table was placed where tradition said it should be: at the head of the aisle, close to the communicants. And the vicar stood behind it, facing them like a yeoman of the ewry laying the lord's table, doing his work in full sight of the congregation, and not like some secret papist priest hidden behind a screen, muttering over bread and wine and incense and water, with his back turned to the people he should be serving and his hands busy doing nobody knew what.

It was a good Baptist wedding and John, watching the priest about his business, serving his God and his congregation in the sight of them both, remembered the church at Meopham and his own wedding, which had been conducted the same way, and wished that Archbishop Laud had left things as they were, and not put honest men like him and Josiah Hurte on either side of a new divide.

Josiah Hurte gave them a good wedding dinner as he had promised and both sets of parents, the apprentice boys and half a dozen friends saw the young couple into their wedding chamber and put them to bed.

John, in the bed chamber overlooking the street with Elizabeth sitting in the four-poster bed behind him, was reminded of his own wedding night. "D'you remember, Lizzie?" he asked Elizabeth. "What a misery it was?"

She nodded. "I'm glad it has been quieter for our John. And I don't think anyone would dare make a game of Jane; she is a strong-minded young woman."

"You won't mind her coming into your house?"

Elizabeth shook her head. "She's a pleasant girl, and I will enjoy having someone to talk to during the day when you and J are both out." She turned back the cover on the bed. "Come to bed, husband; we have done a good day's work today."

Still he lingered at the window, looking down at the cobbled London street, empty except for a scavenging cat, silent except for the occasional call of the night watchman. "You have been a good wife to me, Elizabeth. I am sorry if I have ever grieved you."

"And you have been a good husband to me." She hesitated. The other love and the vow of love till death was still between them, even on this day. "Shall you call to see the duke to see if he needs any service before we go back to New Hall?"

"He's hunting at Richmond," John answered. "And I may not go to him until he sends for me."

"When will he send for you again?"

"I don't know."

She slipped from the bed and stood beside him, her hand on his shoulder. The draughts from the window were icy but John was not aware of them.

"Did you part on bad terms?" she asked. "Is that why he never sends for you now? And why you are waiting and waiting for him and why you look so pained when someone mentions his name?"

"We parted on no terms at all," John said heavily. "He dismissed me. There are no terms between us but those of a master and his man; it was I who forgot my place and he did right to remind me. You would have thought I would have known, wouldn't you, Elizabeth?" He shot her a brief unhappy smile. "Trained with Cecil. You would have thought that of all the men in England I would have known that you can be close to a great man, you can be in his confidence. But he is always the great man and you are always his servant."

"You forgot that?" she asked gently.

"I was reminded quick enough," John said quietly. The dismissal on the quayside when Buckingham had turned from him to his wife and the courtiers was still as sharply painful as when it had happened. "But he was in the right and I in the wrong. I thought I would stay with him but he did not need me. And still he does not need me now. He is busy with the king, with his wife, with his mistresses. He will not send for me until he needs an honest man, and he has no need of an honest man at court. Indeed, there is no room for an honest man at court."

"I am sure he will send for you soon," she said. It was the only comfort she could think of.

He nodded. "Soon he will need a dog," he said bitterly. "And then he will remember me."

John was wrong; the duke did not need a dog. Spring came to New Hall but not the duke. The earth warmed and John had the grass courts scythed and seedlings planted out from the nursery beds. He ordered that the roses have their spring pruning and that the buds be pinched off the fruit trees. He set charcoal burners in the hollow wall of the fruit garden to speed the fruit for his lordship to eat when he came . . . but still he did not come.

The tulips that John had bought with such joy when he and his lord had been adventurers together in Europe, gambling with the crown jewels of England, flowered in their pots and Buckingham did not even see them. As soon as the precious blooms were over John set the pots outside in the dappled shade of his own garden so that he could water them daily and watch the leaves flop and droop, and pray that deep inside the soil the bulbs were growing plump and strong.

"When will we lift them?" J asked him, eyeing the dispiriting sight of the limp leaves.

"In autumn," John said shortly. "And then we will know if we have made my lord a fortune, or if we have lost him one."

"But either way he missed seeing the bloom," J pointed out.

"He missed it," John agreed. "And I missed showing it to him."

Everyone in the town of Chelmsford, in the village of Chorley, in the kitchens at New Hall, and even the shepherds in the lambing pens spoke of nothing but the king and Parliament and the quarrel between them, the king and his wife and the quarrel between them, the quarrel between the king and the French, between the king and the Spanish, between the king and the Roman Catholics and between the king and the Puritans. Inside the enclosing walls of the duke's park they did not dare say it, but in the ale houses of Chelmsford they had a joke which went: "Who rules the kingdom? The king! Who rules the king? The duke! Who rules the duke? The Devil!"

It would have been bad enough if it had stopped there, but the joke spread from the ale-house men to the women, who were more apt to see the work of the Devil in the gross injustice of life and took the jest too literally. From them it spread to the preachers, who knew that the Devil did his work daily, and that the richest pickings for him were around the king who could not rule his wife, nor his court, nor Parliament, nor protect his country.

They said that the duke was the most hated man in England. One of the garden lads, employed to scare crows off Tradescant's new West Indian scarlet runner beans, boasted to another that they served a man worse-hated than the Pope. Everything was blamed on the duke: the plague which was again taking hundreds of men and women already weakened by a hungry winter, the wetness of the spring which would spoil the crops in the ground and, over and over again, the corruption of a king who surely would otherwise live in peace with his wife and strive to govern with Parliament.

The king was so desperate for money that he had called Parliament but the members, newly up from the country and determined to take a stand, had sworn that the king should have no money for any new wars without his signature on a Petition of

Right. He must accept that there would be no taxes without their consent—no more illegal demands, no more royal charges—and that men who refused the whim of the king should not be sent to prison without a judge hearing their case. The king, bankrupt on his throne, was driven to assent, a grudging assent which he resisted to the last moment and regretted as soon as he had put his hand to the new contract.

Jane, on the settle at John's fireside with her husband on a stool at her feet leaning his head against her knees, read the family her father's letter.

"The king's consent to the Petition of Right is seen as the start of a new era. It is hailed as a new Magna Carta which will defend the rights of innocent people against the wickedness of those who should be their betters and their guides. They are ringing the bells while I write this to celebrate the king's agreement with Parliament at last. I wish I could say that His Majesty welcomes it as does everyone else, but he insists that it is nothing new, that there are no new freedoms, and therefore, that he is not curbed. The older men of my congregation remember that when Parliament came against Queen Elizabeth she thanked them kindly, and when she was forced to do as they wanted, she smiled as if it was her heart's desire.

And the hot heads among my congregation are asking what will it take to teach this king to deal with his fellow men with respect?

At all events, he is to have the money he desires, and your husband's master, the duke, is to take another campaign to Rhé . . ."

"What?" John said suddenly, interrupting Jane's reading.

"He is to take another campaign to Rhé," she repeated.

Elizabeth glanced at her husband. "You will never go! Not again, John. Not again, to there! Not even if he summons you."

He jumped up from his chair and turned away from the circle of firelight and candlelight. She could see his hands, his whole body was trembling, but he spoke steadily. "If he summons me I will have to go."

"It will be the death of you!" Elizabeth exclaimed passionately. "You cannot be so lucky every time!"

"It will be the death of thousands," he said darkly. "Whether we take the island or lose it, it will be the death of thousands. I cannot face that place again. That tiny island is like a graveyard . . . I cannot bear it!"

Abruptly he turned back to Jane. "Does your father say why any man would want to go back there? What the duke is hoping for?"

She was pale, looking from John to Elizabeth. She thought she had never seen him in such distress before. It was as if he feared being press-ganged into Hell. "I will read you the rest of the letter," she replied, smoothing it on her lap.

" . . . *the duke is to take another campaign to Rhé to wipe out the disgrace of failure and to show the French that we mean to be masters. No men are volunteering, but the press-gangs are making the streets unsafe for everyone except for those actually dying of the plague. Everyone else is taken up and sent to Portsmouth and they are cursing the duke's name.*

These are hard times for us all. I pray that your husband and your father-in-law are spared the duke's demands. I have today lost my apprentice boy George, whom I loved like a son. He will never survive a campaign; he has a weak chest and coughs all the winter long. Why take a lad of sixteen who will be dead before they reach their destination? Why take a boy who only knows about cotton, linen and silk?

I am going to Portsmouth myself to see if I can find him and bring him back but your mother says, rightly, that we must tell his parents that he is as good as dead and pray for his immortal soul.

It is a bitter thing that a country which could be at peace is constantly at war, and that a country which could be prosperous is never well-fed.

I am sorry to send you such bad news, my blessings on you all, Josiah Hurte."

"I will go in your stead," J said steadily. "When he sends for you."

"He may not send . . . ," Elizabeth suggested.

"He always sends for my father when it is work that needs a trustworthy man," J said swiftly. "When it is dangerous or difficult, when he needs a man who loves him above everything else. A man to do work that no one else would do."

John shot him a look.

"It's true," J maintained. "And he will send for you again."

"You cannot go," Elizabeth breathed. "The mission is bound to fail again and you will risk your life for nothing."

"My John can't go," Jane said suddenly. She made a small betraying movement, her hand to her belly. "I need him here." She flushed. "We need him here. He is to be a father."

"Oh, my dear!" Elizabeth stretched across the fire and held Jane's hands in her own. "I am so glad! What a blessing."

The two women remained clasped for a moment, and Elizabeth closed her eyes in a swift silent prayer. John watched them with a weary sense of exclusion from the world of small joys. "I am glad for you," he said levelly. "And Jane is right, J cannot go with a baby on the way. If he sends for me, it will have to be me."

The little family was silent for a moment. "Perhaps he will not send for you?" Jane asked.

John shook his head. "I think he will. And I have promised to go whenever he calls me."

"To your death?" J demanded passionately.

John raised a weary face to his son. "Those were the very words of my oath," he said slowly.

Summer 1628

The message came in the middle of June, one of the best months of the year for a gardener. John had started his day's work in the rose garden, dead-heading the blowsy blooms and tossing the petals into a basket for the still room. They would be dried and used in pomanders, or for scattering in the linen cupboards to scent the duke's sheets. Or they might be claimed by the cooks and candied to decorate the duke's sweetmeats. Everything in the garden, from drowsily humming bees to falling rosy pale petals, was the duke's and grew for his pleasure. Except he was not here to see them.

At midday John went around to the front of the house to see the young limes, planted in the long, gently curving double avenue. He had a thought that they might grow better-shaped if their lower branches were pruned, and he had a small axe and a saw for the purpose, and a lad coming behind with a ladder. But before he had done more than whistle to the lad to set the ladder before the first tree, he heard hoofbeats.

John turned, raised his hand to shield his eyes and saw, like a dream, like a long-awaited vision, the single rider still a mile off, his lathered horse going from gray to black as it passed from brilliant sunlight into deep green shadow down the drive. John stepped out from the shade of the trees on to the broad sunny road, waiting in the hot light for the messenger, knowing that it would be his summons, knowing that he must obey. He felt for a moment that it was

Death himself, with his scythe over his shoulder, riding between the trees with the drunken bees buzzing wildly and the leaves dripping with nectar and pollen.

John felt a darkness within himself as if the shade of the limes had cast a deep green into his very blood, and a coldness which he thought must be fear. He had never known fear before in this bleak premonitory way. He understood now, for the first time, why the pressed men had whispered to him as he went through the ranks: "Ask him to send us home, Mr. Tradescant, ask him to turn back." Now he felt as slavish as they, as unmanned as they.

The rider came slowly toward him and Tradescant put up his hand for the letter as if he were warding off a blow from a knife.

"How did you know it was for you?" the messenger asked, sliding from his horse's back and loosening the girth.

"I have been waiting for it since I heard he was returning to Rhé," John said.

"Then you will be the only willing recruit," the man said cheerfully. "There were riots outside his house when the sailors heard he was taking them back there. His carriage is stoned every time he takes it out. They are saying that the expedition is cursed and that it will fall into a whirlpool which stretches down to Hell itself. They drink to his death in the ale houses; they pray for his downfall in the chapels."

"That's enough," John said roughly. "Go and take your horse to the stable. I won't hear the duke traduced on his own land by his own servant."

The man shrugged and twitched the reins over his horse's head. "I've left his service. I am on my way to my own home."

"You have work to go to?"

"No," he said. "But I'd rather beg from door to door than go with the duke to the Island of Rue. I'm not a fool. I know how it will be commanded, and how it will be paid, and what the risks will be."

John nodded, his face betraying nothing. Then he turned away and walked from the avenue, across the grass lawn to the lake. He made his way down the pretty little path to the landing stage opposite the boathouse where Buckingham used to row out on summer evenings, sometimes with his wife Kate in the stern, sometimes alone with a rod and line. John sat on the landing stage and looked across the water. The yellow flag irises were in flower as he had promised his master they would be; the fountain they had designed together played into the warm silent air of the afternoon. The water lilies he had planted bobbed gently as the wind breathed across the smooth surface of the lake, their buds just splitting to show cream and white petals. The ducks had had a second brood of ducklings and they came and quacked around him, hoping for corn. John held the letter in his hand, looking at the heavy seal on the fold of the thick cream notepaper. For a moment he did not break it, he did not shatter the impress of Buckingham's ring; for a moment he sat in the sunshine and thought what he would be feeling if this was a letter from a master who loved him, from a man who loved as an equal. How it would be for him now, if Buckingham was his lover as well as his lord.

John thought that if they were lovers still his heart would leap at the sight of the sealed note; he would be happy at being ordered to his lord's side; he would go glad-hearted, wherever he was ordered. If they were lovers he would go with his lord to the Isle of Rue, to that bleak island, to that certain death, with a sort of mad joy, that a love as encompassing and wild as theirs could only end in death and that there would be something erotic and powerful about it ending in a battle and the two of them side by side as comrades.

John rubbed his hand across his eyes. No point in dreaming like a lovesick maid and gazing out across the water. This would not be a love letter; these would be orders that must be obeyed whatever his private feelings. He tore the fold of the paper and opened the letter.

John,

I shall need my best traveling coach and some suits of clothes, my hats and the new diamonds. We will need a couple of cows and some hens—order everything as I would wish.

Bring it all to me and meet me at Portsmouth; we will sail at the beginning of July without fail.

You will sail with me and be at my side, as before.

Villiers.

John read the letter once, and then read it again. It was his death warrant.

The evening was very warm. John watched the midges dancing over the still water, his legs dangling above the glassy surface of the lake like an idle boy's. Even now he found it hard to believe that he must leave all this, and never see it again. The garden he had made, the trees he had planted, the vegetables and flowers he had introduced to New Hall—to England—all this would be taken from him, and he would die on an island half-rock and half-marsh for a cause he had never believed in, serving a master who was no good.

John's long unthinking uncritical loyalty to his masters had been destroyed. And when John lost his faith in his master, he lost his faith in the world. If his master was not a better man, closer to the angels than his servant, then the king was not set higher again, even closer to heaven. And if the king was not divine, then he was not infallible, as John had always believed. And if the king was not infallible then all the questions that thinking men were posing, about the king's new powers and the king's mismanagement of affairs, were questions that John should have been asking. He should have been asking them years ago.

He felt like a fool who had neglected the chance of a great education. Cecil had been his first master and had taught him not to think of principle but of practice. If he had watched Cecil he would have seen a man who always acted in public as if the king were divine, but always plotted in private to protect him like any fallible mortal. Cecil had not been fooled by the masque of royalty; he was a man like Inigo Jones whose work was to illustrate and support it. Jones had built the staircase and a marble bathroom at New Hall; Tradescant had watched him at work. This was not a priest before the mysteries; this was a man doing a skilled job. He made a stair, he made an illusion of majesty, all the same work, all in the same day. But Tradescant, even with the example of Cecil as chief stage manager before him, had been taken in by the show and the costumes and the ingenious machinery, and had thought that he had seen gods when all that had been before him was a cunning old woman, Elizabeth; her nephew James, a lecher; and his son, Charles, a fool.

John did not feel vengeful; the habit of loving and loyalty toward his masters and beyond them to the king went too deep for that. He felt that he would have to endure the loss of faith as if it were his own fault. To lose faith in the king and his lord was very like to losing faith in God. It was gone but a man still went through the rituals of attendance, and hat-doffing and minding his tongue, so as not to spread doubt among others. John might doubt his lord and his king but no one beyond his immediate family would ever know it. He might doubt that God had ordered him to obey the commandments or had recently included a commandment to obey the king, but he would not stand up in church and deny God when the preacher recited the new prayers for the king and queen which had been added as a collect for the day. John had been raised to be a man of loyalty and duty; he could not step out of his track just because his heart was broken and his faith gone.

For the duke his lover he thought he would never feel anything but a pain where his heart should be, and ice where his blood should be, and an ache where his belly should be. He did not blame his lord for turning away from his gardener to the court. The very suggestion was a foolish one. Of course Buckingham would cleave to the court, however well he was loved by his servants. It was Tradescant who blamed himself for forgetting that the man he loved was a great man, a man of the highest degree in the land, second only to the king. It was folly to think that he would need Tradescant in the days of his glory as he had needed him in the days of the voyage home when the ghosts of the men they had left behind cried every night in the rigging.

As John gave the orders in the stable and the big house to get the carriage ready, as he rode down to Manor Farm and requisitioned two cows in milk, he knew that Buckingham had forgotten him as a lover but trusted him completely as a servant, the most faithful servant of them all who would do everything, and overlook nothing.

Buckingham believed that John was his faithful servant; and Buckingham was right. As John ordered them to pack the duke's best clothes, and put the diamonds in a purse to wear around his own neck, he knew that he was acting the part of a faithful servant, and that he would act that part until he died. He would take the traveling coach and the clothes, the hats and the new diamonds, some cows and some hens, all the long way down the road to Portsmouth, see them loaded with the press-ganged soldiers on the *Triumph* and set sail with them to his death.

"We will go to our deaths like herded cattle," John said quietly to himself as he watched them pull the great traveling coach from the stables and start to polish the gilded ornaments on the corners of the roof. "Like the milch cows which low as they are pushed on board. I am bound by my oath that I will be his until death, and I see now that this was what he meant. He will never have finished with me, nor with any in his company, until we are all dead."

He turned away, his knee aching as he walked on the uneven cobbles of the stable yard, and went round to the pleasure gardens to find J, his son, who would now inherit all that he had, and would have to become head of the little family, for John was going to the war again and knew this time that he would not come back.

The pleasure garden had been laid out with fountains and waterworks designed by the engineer Cornelius van Drebbel. J had ordered the drying and cleaning of an enormous round marble bowl at the foot of a cascade, and was splashing round inside the bowl checking that it was perfectly clean before he let the water flow back in. In the heat of the day it was a pleasant job, and J was a man young enough to take pleasure in playing about with a cascade of water and calling it work. At the side of the fountain, in the shade, was a hogshead tub squirming with carp waiting to be returned to the water. J looked up when he heard his father's step on the white gravel and as soon as he saw his father's face he climbed out of the marble bowl and came toward him, shaking his thick black hair like a spaniel coming out of a river.

"Bad news, Father?"

John nodded. "I am to go to Rhé."

J held out his hand for the letter and John hesitated only for a moment before passing it to him. J read it swiftly and thrust it back.

"Carriage!" he cried scathingly. "Best diamonds! He has learned nothing."

"It is his way," John said. "He has the grand manner and he rides out the storms."

"Can we say you are sick?" J asked.

John shook his head.

"I will go in your place; I mean it."

"Your place is here," John said. "You have a child on the way, perhaps an heir for us, someone to grow the chestnut trees on." The two men smiled at each other, and then John was grave again. "You're well provided for, there's our own land, and the fee from the Whitehall granary. There's our own cabinet of curiosities; I know they are nothing much yet but you could raise a few pounds on them if you're ever in need, and with the training you have had under me at Lord Wootton's garden and here, you could work anywhere in Europe."

"I won't stay with the duke," J said. "I won't stay here. I shall go to Virginia where there is neither a duke nor a king."

"Yes," Tradescant said. "But, of course, he may not come back from Rhé, either."

"He came home last time without a scratch on him and was greeted in triumph," J said resentfully.

"Don't make an enemy of him."

"He has taken my father away from me for years," J said. "And now he wants to take you to your death. How do you think I feel?"

John shook his head. "Feel as you like. But don't make an enemy of him. If you go against him, you go against the king and that is treason and mortal danger."

"He is too great for me to challenge; I know that. He is too great altogether. There is not a man in England who does not hate and fear him, and now we are to go to war under him again when we know he does not know how to command, he cannot organize supplies, he cannot order an attack, he does not know how the business should be done. How should he know? He was a country squire's son and got his place by his skill in dancing and talking . . . and sodomy."

John flinched. "Enough, J. Enough."

"I wish to God we had never come here," the younger man said passionately.

John looked back down the years to the moment that he first saw Buckingham as green as a sapling in the dark allée at New Hall. "We wanted the best gardens in the country. We had to come here."

The two men were silent.

"Will you tell Mother?" J asked eventually.

"I'll tell her now," John said. "She'll be grieved. You will keep her to live with you and provide for her well when I am gone, J."

"Of course," J said.

Elizabeth packed John's clothes in silence, including his winter boots and warm cloaks and blankets.

"I probably won't need those; we will be back before autumn," John said, trying to be cheerful.

She was folding his clothes and putting them into a big leather sack. "He will never sail on time," she said. "He never does. Nothing will be ready on time and you will be sailing out into the autumn storms, and setting siege as winter comes. You will need your warm cloak, and Jane's father has sent me a bolt of oilskin to wrap your clothes in and try to keep them dry."

"Are you nearly ready? I have his wagons loaded and his coach is ready to go."

"All finished." She pulled the drawstring tight.

He held out his arms to her and she looked at him, her face very grave. "God bless you, my John," she said.

He wrapped his arms around her and felt the familiar warmth of the band of her cap and her smooth hair against his cheek. "I am sorry for the grief I have given you," he said, his voice choked. "Before God, Elizabeth, I have loved you dearly."

She did not reprove his swearing, but tightened her grip around his waist.

"Look after my grandchild," he said, and tried to make a joke: "And my chestnut trees!"

"Don't go!" she cried suddenly. "Please, John, don't go. You can get to London and on a ship to Virginia in a day and a night, before he even knows you have left him. Please!"

He put his hands behind his back and unfastened her fingers. "You know I cannot run away."

He picked up his bag and went down the stairs, his tread uneven as the arthritis in his knee made him limp. She stayed where she was for a moment, and then ran after him.

Buckingham's great carriage was drawn up outside their little cottage, but John could not ride in it without the lord's express permission, and Buckingham had forgotten to tell John he could travel in comfort. John slung his bag in the back of the carter's wagon and cast an experienced eye over the armed men who would ride before and after him, to guard the duke's treasures against violent beggars, highwaymen or a mob that might rise up against the sight of his crest in any of the towns on the way.

John pulled himself up beside the carter on the wagon's driving seat and turned to wave to Elizabeth. J and Jane stood beside her at the cottage doorway, looking out as John gave the signal for the carriage and the wagons to move.

He meant to call out, "Good-bye! God bless!," but he felt the words stick in his throat. He meant to smile and wave his hat so that the last sight they had of him was that of a cheery smile and a man going willingly. But Elizabeth's white face pierced him like a knife and he could only pull his hat from his head as a mark of respect for her and let the wagon pull out, and away from her.

He turned in his seat and watched them grow smaller and smaller, obscured by the dust of the luggage train, until the wagon turned the corner into the great avenue and he could see them no more. He could not even hear the bees above the rumble of wheels, and he had never smelled the heady perfume of the limes.

Buckingham was not at Portsmouth, as he had said he would be. The fleet was ready, the sailors on board; every day that he did not come the murmurings grew worse and the officers resorted to harsher and longer whippings to keep the men in order. The army melted away daily, the officers scouring the towns and the roads to the north of the city to arrest ploughboys and shepherd boys and apprentices who were running for their lives away from the ships that waited, bobbing at the harbor wall, for the commander who did not come.

John saw the duke's coach loaded aboard but kept the purse of diamonds on a string about his neck. The cows and the hens he penned up on Southsea Common and he took himself a lodging nearby. The landlord was surly and unhelpful; he had had soldiers billeted on him for months and his bills were never paid. John paid him directly from his own money, even though he knew that Buckingham would not remember to reimburse him, and then the man served him a little better.

On July nineteenth the king came riding down to inspect the fleet. The winds were blowing off shore; the ships were straining at their ropes as if they were willing to go, even if the men aboard had sulky faces. The king looked the ships over, but this time there was no handsome dinner on board the *Triumph.* All of them, even the king himself, waited for the Lord High Admiral.

He did not come.

John thought of his wife's prediction that they would not sail until autumn and went out to the hills beyond the city and bought a wagonload of hay for the cow.

The king left Southwick and went hunting in the New Forest. He had no objection to the fleet being delayed while Buckingham went about his business in London. Other men would have risked a charge of treason and imprisonment in the Tower as a punishment for keeping the king waiting for an hour, but it seemed that Buckingham could do nothing that would offend the king. His Majesty laughed and said that the duke was a laggard, and spent the night at Beaulieu and hunted deer. The sport was good and the weather stood fair. On board the ships the soldiers, cooped up in their quarters, sweated in the crowded heat, and many had to be carried out suffering from seasickness or worse. The crews and the soldiers ate up the provisions which had been laid aboard for the voyage, and the ships' stewards had to go out into Hampshire and Sussex to buy more food to restock the ships. Prices went up in the local markets and the little villages could not afford bread at the rate the fleet could pay. Buckingham was cursed at a hundred hungry firesides. And still he did not come.

John wrote to his wife that perhaps the whole thing would blow over. The fleet would not sail without the Lord High Admiral, and the Lord High Admiral did not come for the whole of July. Perhaps, John thought, he was bluffing, and had never meant to sail. Perhaps he was wiser and more skillful than anyone had allowed, as cunning as Cecil. Perhaps all this preparation, all this fear, all this grief, had been to give substance to the most tremendous trick of all time—frightening the French into withdrawing from La Rochelle without a shot being fired, without the expedition even leaving port. John remembered the trickery and mischief in Buckingham's smile, his cleverness and his wit, and thought that if any man could win a war without sending his fleet out, Buckingham was the man.

John paid his landlord for the month of August and began to wonder if he might be spared. On the hot summer mornings he awoke with such a desire to live that he could taste it on his tongue, like lust. He walked on the harbor walls and looked out to sea. He felt the light touch of linen on his sun-warmed skin and the warm air on his face and felt like a youth, faint with awareness of his own beauty, of his own health. He walked on the pebbles of the seashore, sending flocks of gray- and brown-backed dunlin scattering before him, and felt the life pulsing through his body from his boots to his fingertips. On a fine day he could see the Isle of Wight in its green loveliness, and John thought he might take a little ferryboat over to the island and hunt for new plants folded in the secret hollows of its chalk downs.

He walked inland north of the city, where there were great forests. John walked under the branches and remembered his hunt for Sir Robert Cecil's trees and the long journeys with the heavily laden carts. Sometimes he saw red deer and roe deer; always he watched his feet for a new fern, a new flower.

He did not walk to the east—there was a foul ill-drained marsh on that side of the city, lonely with the cry of wading birds and treacherous with tracks and deceptive paths. It stank of mud and decay under the hot summer sunshine, and when the heat haze shimmered above it he could not tell where the water began and the land melted unreliably away. In the drier fields the red poppies nodded their heads. It reminded John too much of their destination. He hated the flicker of sunlight on mud and water now; it was the light of death, he thought. After he had walked once to Farlington marshes he never went that way again.

Buckingham did not come until the end of August, just as the captains and officers were talking of having to disband for the winter rather than throw bad money after good on an expedition which was clearly not going to depart. Another month and the weather would break; it could take days to get out of harbor in the autumn, and no fleet could risk being separated running before a storm. It would be too late, it was too late, surely the Lord Admiral would be bound to see that it was too late—and then he came, sunny, smiling, delightful, in his best coach from London, and took breakfast at Captain Mason's house in the High Street, as blithe and merry as if that had not been the very house where he had washed his hands of the blood of his soldiers the last time he came back from Rhé.

The rumor that Buckingham had arrived in the city reached Tradescant as he fed the last of his hay to the cows. For a moment he shuddered as if someone had walked on his grave. It was both a premonition of death and a flicker of desire. John shook his head at his own folly, brushed down his suit of clothes, put on his hat and walked around to the High Street.

The house was crowded, the outer courtyard filled with officers waiting for news and the usual hangers-on and favor-seekers. One man put his hand on Tradescant's sleeve as he pushed through.

"He's come to cancel the sailing, hasn't he?"

"I don't know. I have not spoken with him."

"The captain of the *Triumph* says that they'll need to revictual and rewater before they sail. And there's no money to pay the chandlers. We'll have to delay until the spring."

"I don't know," Tradescant replied. "I don't know any more than you do."

The man slipped away in the crowd, and Tradescant pushed farther in. A man ahead of him turned at the tap on his shoulder and Tradescant recognized him.

"Mr. Tradescant!"

"It's Felton, isn't it? That was made captain?"

At once John saw that something was terribly wrong. The man's face was pale, and two deep lines grooved either side of his mouth. "What's the matter? Are you ill?"

He shook his head. "I prayed that I might take it, but I did not. She died in my arms."

John edged slightly back. "Who died?"

"My wife. Oh! you need not fear I carry it. They put us out of the village, both of us, and did not let me back into my house until I had buried her on the cold ground where she lay and stripped myself naked and burned my clothes. Then they let me into my home, walking as naked as a sinner. But when I got back into the house, d'you know what I found?"

John shook his head.

"My little daughter, dead of hunger, behind the locked door. No one had gone in to feed her, they were all afraid of catching the plague, and besides, there was no food in the whole village."

John was silent, facing the horror of the man's story.

"I was never paid, you see," Felton said, his voice a dull monotone. "Not the captain's pay that was promised me, not the lieutenant's pay that I had earned. Not my campaign money, not my discharge money. Not a penny. When I came home to my wife and daughter I had nothing but my Lord Admiral's promise, and we could not eat that. When she sickened, I could not buy physic for her; I could not even buy food. When she died I had to bury her in the ground where she lay."

He laughed shortly. "And they've enclosed it now. I cannot even get in to put up a cross at her head. It was common land. I thought I would plant a rosebush beside her grave, but now it is a sheep run, and my lord's beasts patter over her sleeping face."

John found he was scowling. "Before God I am sorry for you," he said.

"And now we are to sail again," Felton went on, his eyes burning in his white face. "Back to that damned island. It is all to be as it was before. More death, more pain, more folly. We will have to do it all again, and again and again until he has his fill of it."

"Are you serving?" John asked.

"Who would go willingly who had been there once before? Would you?"

John shook his head. "I am bound by a promise to go," he said.

"And I am bound by a promise too," Felton said. "A different promise from you, I should think. A sacred promise to God."

John nodded. "I will speak with him, when I can get near him," he said. "I will not forget you, Felton. You shall have your pay and perhaps you can start again somewhere . . ."

"He has forgotten me," Felton cried passionately. "But I will remind him. I will tell him what he has cost me; I will give him pain for pain."

"That's not the way. Be still, Felton; he is the duke, you cannot fight him any more than you can fight the king. He is untouchable."

Felton shook his head in brief disagreement and turned away. Tradescant looked after him, saw the hunched shoulders and the way his hand strayed to his pocket and saw the outline, through the ragged clothes, of a knife. He glanced around. The place was packed with the duke's retainers. When he saw one of the officers he could trust, he would warn him that Felton should be watched, and gently hustled out of the house. Then, when he had the duke's ear, he would tell him that the man must be paid, must be compensated. That men who had followed the duke to certain death, and who had seen their comrades die beside them, could not be cast off as lightly as a mistress forgets an old lover who has fallen from favor.

There was a roar of laughter from the inner room and then a bellowing of a toast. Tradescant knew that his lord must be inside, at the heart of the party. Now he was near to seeing him again he found that his palms were wet with sweat and his throat dry. He rubbed his hands on his breeches, swallowed, and then pushed through the crowd, through the open double door and into the room.

The duke was seated at a table, a map spread before him, his green jacket ablaze with diamonds, his dark hair tumbled about his perfect face, laughing like a boy.

John fell back at the sight and a man behind him swore as he bumped into him, but John heard nothing. He had thought that he knew every line, every plane, of that face, from the untroubled forehead to the smooth cheekbones, but when he saw Buckingham again, in his vitality, in the brilliance of his beauty, he realized he had remembered nothing, only a shadow.

John felt himself smiling, then beaming, at the very sight of the man, and felt a blaze through his body which was not fear or resentment or hatred, but was joy, a wild intractable joy, that there should be such beauty in the world, that there should be such grace. That such a man had once loved John and taken him into a place where pain and pleasure were one. And at the moment, the long intervening months seemed a small price to pay for having once, just once, been the lover of such a man. As in a dream he saw Buckingham laughing at the head of the table, his black curls thrown back from his face, his black eyes glinting and that exquisite face flushed with wine and laughter; and at the same time he saw him leaning close in the shadowy light of the gilded cabin where the horn lantern swung on its hook with the haunting rhythm of the waves as if it were dancing with their blended shadows.

"Ah, it's you," John said with a deep glad sense of recognition and felt that his world, which had been upside-down since he had lost his master, was suddenly powerfully restored to him. He knew it was love, besotted, impossible love, and could feel no shame, nor any sense that it was wasted love. Its very madness was part of the joy of tasting it. It was the taste of life at the very edge of life. It was love as few men ever know it. It was passion, rare passion. A desire that does not even look for return, but is worth all the pain for the few moments of joy, and for knowing that joy to the edge of madness is a possibility. Without this love Tradescant thought he would have lived a quieter life, a steady life. With it he had been ablaze, in the very heart of the furnace of feeling.

Buckingham had not seen him. He was laughing with the gentlemen around him. "I swear it," he shouted over the noise. "I will be avenged. We have been wronged by France and I will have satisfaction."

Another great shriek of approval drowned out his words. Tradescant watched, smiling, as the duke shook back his black curls and laughed again. "I have the ear of the king!" he said.

"Aye, and other parts!" came a bawdy yell.

Buckingham grinned but he did not disagree. "Does anyone doubt that if I wish it we will be at the doors of Paris this time next year?" he said. "I say we will return to France, and not stop at some pox-ridden island but we will march on Paris itself and I will have my revenge."

Tradescant pushed his way farther into the room. The men were a wedge of scented velvet and rich linen—the duke's aristocratic friends and courtiers, who had been waiting and waiting in Portsmouth to give him a hero's send-off. As they unwillingly stood aside Buckingham caught the movement and glanced down the room. His eyes met John's and for a moment, for one blissful moment, there was nothing and no one but the master and the man looking at each other with a deep connection.

"My John," Buckingham said softly, as sweet as a whisper after his bragging of a few moments earlier.

"My lord," Tradescant replied.

Buckingham put one hand on the table and vaulted over it to Tradescant's side. He put his hands on his shoulders.

"Did you bring everything?" he asked simply.

"I have everything you commanded," John said steadily. There was not a word that could have betrayed them. Only the two of them knew that the duke was asking if John was still his and his alone; and John was answering: yes, yes, yes.

"Where are you lodged?" Buckingham asked him.

"At a little house on Southsea Common."

"Get your things loaded and stowed in my cabin; we sail today." Buckingham turned toward his place at the table.

"My lord!" At the urgency in his tone Buckingham paused.

"What is it, John?"

"Stay a moment. Go down to the harbor and listen to your commanders," John said earnestly. "They are saying we may not be able to sail. Take some advice, my lord. Let's proceed cautiously."

"Cautiously! Cautiously!" Buckingham threw back his head and laughed and the room laughed with him. "I am going to free the Protestants of La Rochelle and give the French king such a trouncing that he will regret his impertinence to us. I shall have Queen Elizabeth back on her throne in Bohemia, and I shall take the war to the very doors of Paris."

There was a confused hurrah at the bragging. John scowled around at the gentlemen who had never been closer to a battle than a naval review. "Don't say such things. Not here. Don't speak like this in Portsmouth. There are families here still grieving for the men who went with you last time and will never come home again. Don't jest, my lord."

"I? Jest?" The duke's arched eyebrows flew upward. He turned to the room. "Tradescant thinks I jest!" he exclaimed. "But I tell him and I tell you all that this war with France is not finished; it will not be finished until we have won. And when we have beaten them we will take on the Spanish. No papist mob shall stand against us; I am for the true king and the true faith."

"And where will you get your army, Steenie?" someone cried from the back. "All the men who marched with you last time are dead or injured or sick or insane."

"I shall press-gang them," he cried. "I shall buy them. I shall take them out of the jails, and out of the hospitals for the mad. I shall order them to come on pain of treason. I shall take boys from their school desks, I shall take farmers from their ploughs. Does anyone doubt that I can force my will on this whole kingdom? And if I want to wager half of England to avenge this slight on my honor, I can do it!"

John felt as if he were clinging to a runaway horse that nothing could stop. He laid a rough hand on his lord's sleeve and pulled him close so that he could whisper in his ear. "My lord, I beg you, this is no way to plan a campaign. It's too late in the year; we will meet the autumn storms at sea; when we get there the weather will be bitter. You remember the island; there was no shelter, there were the stinking marshes and the constant storms. They will have reinforced the citadel, and it cost us four thousand lives last time and we still came home in defeat. My lord, don't take us there. Please, I beg you, think again. Think in silence, think when you're sober, not when you have a room of puppies barking at your every word. Think, Villiers. Before God I would die rather than see you there again."

Buckingham turned in John's grip but he did not throw off his hand, as he could have done. Just as he had done in the long-ago fruit garden beside the warmed peach trees, he put his own hand on top of John's and John could feel the warmth of the long soft fingers and the hardness of the rings.

"We have to go," he replied, his voice low. "A victory is the only thing which will pull me clear with the country. I would have to go if it took the life of every man in England."

John met his lord's dark determined gaze. "You would destroy this country for your own triumph?"

Buckingham put his mouth very close to John's ear. The silky curls tickled John's neck. "Yes," he whispered. "A thousand times over."

"Then you are mad, my lord," John said steadily. "And your country's enemy."

"Then cut me down like a mad dog," Buckingham dared him with a wolfish grin. "Behead me for treason. Because my madness will run its course. I have to win the Isle of Rue, John. I don't care what it costs."

It was John who drew his hand away first; it was John who broke their interlocked gaze. Buckingham let him go and snapped his fingers at one of his companions, and took his arm in John's place. "Come," he said. "I must get my hair curled and then I shall sail for France."

There was a roar of laughter and approval. Tradescant, sick and cold, turned away. The duke and his companions passed through the crowd and into the narrow corridor. One of the French officers bustled up.

"My lord duke! I bring news! The best news in the world!"

Buckingham stopped, the crowd behind him pressing forward in the corridor to hear.

"La Rochelle has broken out! The Protestants are free and the French army is defeated! The French are suing for terms."

Buckingham reeled, fighting for sobriety. "Never!"

"Indeed, yes!" the man declared, his English becoming less and less clear in his own excitement. "We have won! We have won!"

"Then we need not sail," John thought aloud. "My God, we need not sail."

Buckingham was suddenly powerful and decisive. "This alters everything," he said.

"It does," Tradescant agreed, pushing through to his side. "Thank God, yes. It does."

"I must speak with the king," Buckingham said. "Now is the time to strike against France; we need to go at once, we need to raise a greater army. We should go through the Netherlands, and then . . ."

"My lord," John said desperately. "There is no need. Now we are excused. La Rochelle is free, our wrongs are avenged."

Buckingham shook his head and laughed his wild boyish laugh. "John, after all the trouble I have taken to get here, d'you think I shall go peaceably home again without a cannon being fired! I am wild for a fight, and the men are wild for a fight! We will go to the very heart of France. Now is the time for an all-out attack, now they are failing. God knows how far we could go. We could take and keep French castles, French lands!"

He slapped the French officer on the back and stepped forward. Felton suddenly appeared at his side, pushing through the crowd. Tradescant recognized him with a gasp of fear, saw his eyes were wild and his hand was gripped on the knife in his pocket. He saw the officer who should protect the duke lounging in the doorway, his face buried in a cup of wine.

Buckingham turned to greet a new arrival and swept his graceful bow. There was a slice of time, which seemed to hold and wait, like a petal from a blossom lingering on its fall.

Tradescant saw Felton's determined face and knew that the great love of his life, his master, was not, after all, untouchable.

"Save us from him," Tradescant said softly. "Do it, Felton."

Late Summer 1628

He was dead within moments, and it was John who leaped forward to catch him, and lowered the long slim body to the ground. Even dying in pain he still had the face of the saint that King James had called him. His skin had flushed as scarlet as an embarrassed maid with the shock of the wound, and then drained white as Italian marble. John cradled his heavy lolling head and felt the smooth tumbling black curls against his cheek for the last time. There was a loud sound of hoarse dry sobbing and John realized it was his own voice; then someone pulled him away from his lord and pressed a glass of spirits into his hand and left him.

He heard the noise of Felton's capture, and the dreadful scream from Buckingham's wife, Kate. He heard the running to and fro of men who were suddenly leaderless. He sat quite still, the glass of Hollands in his hand, while the room brightened as men drifted away and the August sunshine poured uncaringly through the window. The little motes of dust danced in the sunshine as if everything was still the same, when everything was different.

When he thought he could stand, John walked to the door of the house. To his left at the end of the street, the gray wall of the harbor was still there, still crumbling and unfit. Before him the rambling skyline of ramshackle houses and beyond them the tops of the masts of the fleet, still flying Buckingham's flags. No one had ordered them to half-mast; people were still running around, denying the news, disbelieving their own denials. It was a beautiful day; the wind still blew steadily offshore. It would have been a good day to set sail. But Buckingham and John would never set sail together again.

John walked down the High Street like an old man, his boots unsteady on the cobbles, his limp pronounced. He felt that he was stepping into a new world, governed by new rules, and he could not honestly say that he was ready for it. He pulled his hat down over his eyes to shield him from the sun's hard dazzle, and when a lad ran up and skidded to a halt before him, he shrank back, as if he too feared a blow, a fatal blow, to the heart.

"Is it true?" the boy yelled.

"What?"

"That the duke is dead?"

"Yes," Tradescant said, his voice low.

"Praise God!" the boy sang out, and there was no doubting the relief and joy in his voice. "It's true!" he yelled to another boy, a few yards away. "He's dead! The Devil is dead!"

Tradescant put out his hand for the comfort of the sun-warmed wall and followed it, fingers trailing along the crumbling sandstone, like a blind man, to his lodging house. His landlord flung open the door.

"You'll know—I've heard nothing but wild rumors—is he dead?"

"Yes."

The man beamed as if he had been given a priceless gift. "Thank God," he said. "Now the king will see reason."

John felt his way to his room. "I am sick," he said. "I shall rest."

"You'll not get much rest, I'm afraid!" his landlord said cheerfully. From the town they could hear the crackle of fireworks and a roar of cheering which was growing louder. "The whole town is going mad to celebrate. I'm off!"

He let himself out of his front door and ran down the street to where people were embracing, and dancing on street corners. Soldiers at the quayside were blasting their muskets into the skies and women who had come to kiss their husbands good-bye, expecting never to see them again, were weeping with relief. In a dozen churches the bells tolled as if for a mighty victory.

In all the world it seemed that only Tradescant grieved; only Tradescant and his lord lay still and silent all the long sunny joyous day.

It was not until midnight, lying in his bed, still gripping his hat in his hand, that John realized that he was free from his promise. He had been the duke's man till death, and now death had come, and he was free.

Free and short of money, with no promise of wages and no job. Buckingham's widow was sick with grief and the king himself ordered her into hiding in case an assassin struck against her as well.

It was as if the world had gone suddenly mad and no one knew what might happen next. There was no Lord High Admiral to command the expedition, there was no Lord Treasurer to keep the treasures of the kingdom, there was no chief adviser to make policy, there was no Favorite to rule everything. There was no king either, for when they gave Charles the news that Buckingham was dead he finished his prayers and went in silence to his room and locked himself away for two days and nights in silence, in darkness and fasting.

Tradescant sometimes thought of that long royal vigil and wondered that he and the king had been together in a long night of mourning, both of them driven down into silence and grief at the loss of the most beautiful man that either of them had known; the most beautiful and the most daring and the most reckless, and the most dangerous. Tradescant knew that Buckingham would have led him to his death, and that he had only escaped through his lord's assassination. He sometimes wondered if the king felt the same, and if, during the two long days and nights of royal mourning, Charles too knew the same secret, shameful relief.

Tradescant could have left for his home at once, but he felt too frail even to start the journey. He had told Elizabeth that he was strong enough to voyage to France; but in this new life, this life without his master, he could not find the courage even to hire a wagon to go to Essex. He rested at his lodgings, and waited for his power to return. Every day he walked by the sea on the tumbled pebbles of Southsea beach and saw, on the horizon, the slow arc of Felton's knife and the cry of warning in his own throat which never came.

He regretted nothing. Somehow in his grief there was no room for regrets. Not for the way he had been loved and rejected. Nor for his oath of duty till death. Nor for the fact that a shout could have saved his lord from Felton's knife and that shout had never come. It was never a love which would linger and warm an old man. Buckingham was never a man who would age and diminish and decline. Those who loved him would always know passion and uncertainty and despair. He was not a comfortable man to love. Tradescant could think of no other end for Buckingham but one that cut him down like a rare flower in the very fullness of his beauty and which meant that those who loved him could hold him forever in their minds, like petals preserved in sand and sugar: in his perfection.

It was not until September that Tradescant could bring himself to load his wagon and start the long journey back to Essex, and by then his master's body had been taken to London and buried in Westminster Abbey followed by only a hundred mourners. Buckingham's family, his hangers-on, his courtiers, his placemen, all the hundreds and hundreds of men who had begged him for favors and counted on his support, all disappeared, melted away, denying him like a thousand false disciples at cock-crow. They sought new patrons, they tried to spot new rising stars, they tried to forget that they had promised loyalty and devotion to a man who was now everywhere despised.

The funeral was brief and unceremonious, and, like so much of his life, was a show. They buried an empty coffin and said the sacred words over a hollow box. The duke had been interred in secret, in darkness, the night before his funeral. The king's new advisers had warned him that there could be no guarantee that a mob would not rise up against the Favorite's funeral. The people of London were not satisfied with his death; they might tear the coffin open, disembowel his perfect body and hang it out at Traitors' Gate, slash off his dead face and spike it up on Tower Bridge. The king had shuddered at the thought of it, hidden his face in his hands and left them to make what arrangements they would.

There was no money to pay the duke's servants. John went back to Captain Mason's house to find the man in charge of the expedition accounts packing his bags in panic before he could be blamed for the empty coffers. Buckingham had been trading on credit and on the promise of a certain victory, for months. The ship's master for the *Triumph* had no money either. In the end John had to sell some of Buckingham's goods to raise the money to hire the wagon to take the remainder home again. But the diamonds he kept safe in a purse on a cord around his neck. He sold the milch cow to his landlord for the rent, and he exchanged the hens for a pair of muskets. He would have to be his own guard and his own driver; he could afford no other.

He hired an open wagon with two old stubborn carthorses which had to be whipped at every crossroads to make them go ahead, and even then never went faster than an ambling stroll. John did not care how slowly they went. He sat on the driver's bench, the reins slack in his hands, watching over the hedges the late summer landscape of browning wheat and barley and scrubby hayfields roll slowly past, and knew himself to be alive because the man he had loved more than anyone in the world was dead.

J was waiting for him on the south side of Westminster Bridge, where John always changed his horses. He stepped out of the doorway of the inn when he heard the rumble of the wagon and came to the driving box. He had expected to find a broken man, but was surprised. John Tradescant looked relieved, as if some burden had been lifted from him.

"J," John said with quiet pleasure.

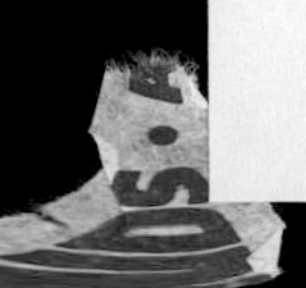

"Mother said to meet you and bring you to the Hurtes'."

"Is she well?"

"Worried about you, but well enough."

"And Jane?"

"Grown very stout around the middle." J flushed with embarrassment and pride. "When I put my hand on her belly the little lad kicks back at me."

John found that he was smiling at the thought of J's baby.

"And are you well, Father? We heard the news at New Hall. Were you with the duke?"

John nodded. "I am well," he said shortly.

"Did you see him?" J asked, curiosity overcoming him. "Were you there when he died?"

John nodded. He thought he would remember forever that timeless long moment when he could have cried out a warning, but instead he gave the word for the blow. "I was there."

"Was it very dreadful?"

John thought of the beauty of the duke, of the smooth slow arc of the knife, of the exclamation of surprise, of the duke's one word, "villain," and then his sinking down, his limp weight in Tradescant's arms.

"No," he said simply. "He fell in all his beauty and his pride."

J was silent for a moment, comparing his father's loss with the country's joy. "I'll never work for a master again," he vowed.

John looked down at him from the box, and J suddenly had a sense that there was more to the death of Buckingham than he would ever know, that there was more between the two men, master and vassal, than had ever been clear.

"Nor will I," said John.

J nodded and swung up onto the box seat beside his father. "There's another cart stored at the Hurtes'," he said. "Goods from India and from the west coast of Africa, sent for my lord Buckingham. He won't want them now."

John nodded and said nothing as J steered the cart carefully through the swarm of pedestrians, barrow boys, sellers, loiterers, idling militia men, to the Hurtes' door. At the rear of the house was a small yard for unloading and a couple of stables. The cart, loaded with treasures for Buckingham, was standing on the cobbles with a lad beside it to keep watch. J drew up alongside and helped his father down. John had to lean heavily on him when his feet touched the cobbles.

"I'm stiff from sitting too long," John said defensively.

"Oh, aye," J said skeptically. "But how ever would you have managed a long sea voyage and then sleeping on the ground with winter coming? It would have been the death of you! It's a blessing you didn't go."

John closed his eyes for a moment. "I know it," he said shortly.

J led the way through the storeroom at the back of the shop and up the stairs to the living quarters. As they came into the parlor Elizabeth started forward and flung herself into her husband's arms. "Praise God you are safe," she cried, her voice choked with tears. "I never thought to see you again, John."

He rested his cheek against the smoothness of her hair and the crisp laundered edge of her cap, and thought, but only for a moment, of a warm perfumed riot of dark curls and the erotic scratch of stubble. "Praise God," he said.

"It was a blessing," she said.

John met Josiah Hurte's gaze over the top of his wife's head. "No, it was an ill business," he said firmly.

Josiah Hurte shrugged. "There are many that are calling it a divine deliverance. They are saying that Felton was the saviour of his country."

"They are praising a murderer then." Inside John's head he could see Felton's pale determined face at the moment when John could have called out, and did not. "It was a sin, and any that stood by and failed to prevent it are sinners too."

Elizabeth, skilled with years of experience in reading John's moods, pulled back a little so that she could see his grim expression. "But you could not have stopped it," she suggested. "You were not the duke's bodyguard."

John did not want to lie to her. "I could have stopped it," he said slowly. "I should have been closer to him, I should have warned him about Felton. He should have been better guarded."

"No point in blaming yourself," Josiah Hurte said briskly. "Better thank God instead that this country is spared a war and that you are spared the danger."

Elizabeth said nothing; she looked into her husband's face. "Anyway, you are free now," she said quietly. "Free from your service to him, at last."

"I am free at last," John confirmed.

Mrs. Hurte gestured that he should take a place at the table. "We have dined because we did not know when to expect you, but if you will take a bowl of broth and a slice of pie, I can have it before you at once."

John sat at the table and the Hurtes' maid brought him small ale and food. Josiah Hurte sat opposite him and took a pint of ale to keep him company.

"No one knows what will happen to the duke's estate," Josiah said. "The family is still in hiding, and the London house is quite shut up. The servants have been turned away, and there's no money to pay the tradesmen."

"There never was any," John remarked wryly.

"It may be that the family decide to sell up to cover their debts," Josiah said. "If they decide to honor their debts at all."

Mrs. Hurte was shocked. "They'll never refuse to pay!" she exclaimed. "Good merchants will go bankrupt if they renege. His lordship had run bills for years; it would have been called treason to refuse him credit. What of the honest men who depend on his widow paying them?"

"They say that there is no money," J said simply. "I have had no wages. Have you?"

John shook his head.

"What will we do?" Jane asked. She had one hand resting on the curve of her belly, as if she would protect the baby from even hearing of such troubles.

"You can stay here," her father offered instantly. "If there's nowhere else you can always stay here."

"I promised to provide for her and I will," J said, stung. "I can get a place at any house in the land."

"But you swore you'd never work for a great lord again," Jane reminded him. "Such work leads us into vanity and no man in the king's service is to be trusted."

John raised his head at such radical thoughts but Jane met his gaze without shrinking. "I am only saying what everyone knows," she said steadily. "There are no good courtiers. There is none whom my John would happily call master."

"I have a little land," Tradescant said slowly. "Some woodland at Hatfield and some fields at New Hall. We could perhaps build a house near New Hall, near my fields, and set up on our own account . . ."

Elizabeth shook her head. "And do what, John? We have to find a business that will give us a living at once."

There was a brief silence. "I know a man who has a house for sale on the south side of the river; it has an established garden and some fruit trees already planted," Josiah said quietly. "There are fields around it that you could buy or rent as well. It was a little farm and now the farmer has died and his heirs are ready to sell. You might raise rare plants and trade as a plantsman and gardener."

"How would we afford it?" John asked them. The purse containing the diamonds was heavy around his neck.

Elizabeth shot a quick collusive glance at her son, and then moved from the chair at the window and sat opposite her husband at the table. Her face was pale and determined. "There is a cart full of goods in the yard below," she pointed out. "And another ship docked this morning with plants and curiosities for his lordship. If we sell the goods we can buy the house and the land. The rare plants and seeds you can nurse up and sell to gardeners. You've always said how difficult it is to get good stock for a garden. Remember how you traveled all around England for your trees? You could grow your stock and sell it."

There was a tense silence in the little room. John absorbed the evidence that this was a plan, formed among the Hurtes and his family and now presented to him for his consent. He looked from Elizabeth's determined face to J's stoical blankness.

"You mean that we should take my lord's goods," John said flatly.

Elizabeth drew in a breath and nodded.

"That I steal from him?"

She nodded again.

"I cannot believe that this is your wish," John said. "My lord has been dead and buried for a month and I am to steal from him like a dishonest pageboy?"

"There are the tulips," J said in a sudden rush. His face was scarlet with embarrassment, but he faced his father as one man to another. "What would you have had me do? The tulips were ready for lifting, they were in their bowls in our garden, the place was in uproar, men were running out of the house with wall-hangings and linen trailing behind them. I did not know what to do with the tulips. Nobody there would have nursed them up. Nobody there knew what to do with them. Nobody would advise me."

"So what did you do?" John asked.

"I brought them with me. And more than half of them have spawned. We have nigh on two thousand pounds' worth of tulip bulbs."

"Prices holding?" John's acumen flared briefly, penetrating his grief.

"Yes," J said simply. "Still rising. And we have the only Lack tulips in England."

"How much are you owed?" Elizabeth suddenly demanded. "In back wages? Did he pay you for the last expedition to Rhé? Did he advance you wages for this one? Did he give you money for the cost of the journey to Portsmouth? Or for your stay in Portsmouth, or this journey home? Because if he gave you nothing you will never have more from the duchess. She is in hiding and the king himself is refusing to tell anyone where she is. They say she is afraid of assassins, but we all know she is more terrified of creditors. How much are you owed, John?"

"I was not paid at midsummer," J reminded him. "They said they had no coin and gave me a note of promise, and I will not be paid this Michaelmas. That's twenty-five pounds I am owed. And while you were away I had to buy some plants and some saplings and they could not repay me."

Unconsciously John put his hand to his throat where the bag of diamonds nestled warm against his skin.

"*You* cannot agree to this?" He turned to Josiah. "It is theft."

The merchant shook his head. "I no longer know what is right and wrong in this country," he said. "The king takes money from the people without law or tradition, Parliament denies that he has the right, and so he closes Parliament and imposes the fines anyway. If the king himself can steal honest men's money then what are we to do? Your lord stole your service from you for years, and now he is dead and no one will repay you. They will not even acknowledge the debt."

"Stealing is still a sin," John said doggedly.

"These are times when a man's own conscience should be his guide," Josiah replied. "If you think that he treated you fairly then deliver the goods to his house, pile riches upon riches and let the king take them to pay for his masques and vanities, as you know he will. If you think that the duke died owing you for your service, owing J, if you think these are times when a man does well to buy himself a little house and be his own master, then I think you would be justified in taking what you are owed and leaving his service. You should take only what you are owed. But you have a right to that. A good servant is worthy of his hire."

"If you return the tulips to New Hall they will die of neglect," J said quietly. "There is no one there to care for them, and then we will have killed the only Lack tulips in England."

The thought of the waste of the tulips was as powerful as anything else for John. He shook his head like a bull does after a long baiting when it is so wearied that it longs for the dogs to close and make an end. "I am too tired to think," he said. He rose to his feet but Elizabeth's gaze held him.

"He hurt you," she said. "On that last voyage to Rhé. He did something to you then that broke your heart."

John made a gesture to stop her but she went on. "He sent you home with that pain in your heart, and then he recalled you, and he was going to take you to your death."

John nodded. "That's true," he said as if it did not much matter.

"Then let him pay," she said gently. "Let him repay us for the grief and terror he has caused us, and I will consider the matter settled, and I will remember him in my prayers."

John put his hand on the little purse of diamonds at his throat. "He was my lord," he said and they could all hear the deep pain in the back of his voice. "I was his man."

"Let him go in peace," she said. "All debts to us paid, all grievances finished. He is dead. Let him pay his debts and let us start a new life."

"You will pray for him? And mean it in your heart?"

Elizabeth nodded.

Silently John took the purse from his neck and handed it to his wife. "Go and see the farm," he said. "You decide. If you and J and Jane like it, then buy it and we will make our home there. And in return for that you must go and pray for his soul, Elizabeth. For he needs your prayers, and there are few enough praying for him, God knows."

"And the tulips?" J asked.

John met his son's questioning look. "Of course we keep the tulips," he said.

November 1628

They crossed the river at Lambeth with a waterman rowing them: Jane bulky and eight months pregnant in the stern of the boat, John, Elizabeth and J seated amidships. Elizabeth had the keys to their new home in her lap, bought outright with Buckingham's diamonds. When she turned the heavy key over and over the sun glinted on the cold metal.

On the south side of the river was the Swan Inn, where J had ordered a cart to meet them. He helped Jane up and then climbed up beside her. John smiled when he saw how his son held his wife as the cart lurched in the ruts of the South Lambeth road.

The journey was a short one and none of them spoke. They were waiting for John to break the silence but he said nothing. He had handed over the diamonds and the responsibility together. He sat in the wagon as if he were convalescent, weak from a long illness. His wife and his son could take the decisions for him.

"There it is," J said at last, pointing ahead. "I hope to God he likes it," he muttered in an undertone to Jane. "He let us buy it for him, but what if he refuses us now?"

Tradescant looked at his new home. It stood with its back to the road, an old half-timbered farmhouse with crisscross beams turning silvery gray from the weather of many seasons. The plaster between the beams had once been painted white but was mellowing to the color of pale mud. There was a little stream running between the road and the farm, crossed by a low bridge, broad enough for a cart. John got down and walked across it alone, the others waiting for him to speak.

The garden between the road and the house was a tiny patch, overgrown with briars and nettles. Tradescant walked around the house to the front. It faced southeast, placed to catch the morning and midday sun, and before it lay a good broad acre of meadow. Tradescant scuffed the heel of his boot in the soil and then bent down and inspected it. It was a dark soil, rich and easy to work. John took up a handful and rubbed it in his palm. He could grow things in this earth, he thought. Beyond the meadow was an orchard. He walked down to where the little wooden fence divided the meadow from the trees and measured it with his eyes. About two acres, he thought, and already stocked with apples, pears and plums; and along the south-facing wall a quince tree was growing in a ragged fan beside a pair of peach trees, roughly espaliered.

John had a momentary pang of homesickness for the kitchen garden he had left behind at New Hall with the tall heated wall built to his own innovative design, and the dozens of boys to carry dung and water for the trees. He shook his head. There was no point grieving. He had left beautiful gardens before now and started afresh. The worst had been leaving Theobalds Palace for the new house at Hatfield; and in the end Hatfield had been his great pride. He could make something of this garden, which would not be on the scale of Theobalds or Hatfield or New Hall, but would be his own. The fruit from these trees would be for his table. His grandson would sit in their shade. And no man could ever order him to leave them.

John turned back to look at the house, taking in for the first time the sloping roof of red clay tiles and the handsome tall clusters of chimney pots. Before the house there was a stone-flagged area overhung by the tiled roof and railed like the side of a ship, placed to overlook the meadow and the orchard. John walked back through the overgrown grass to the house and up the three creaking steps to the terrace. He turned, leaned on the rail and looked out over his property, the first good-sized garden he had ever owned.

He felt his face creasing in a smile of satisfaction. At last he had found a place where he could put down roots and see his son and his grandson secure in their future.

J, Elizabeth and Jane came around the corner of the house to see John leaning against the pillar of the terrace and surveying his acres.

"It's like the deck of a ship," Jane observed perceptively. "No wonder you look at home."

"I shall call it the Ark," John said. "Because we have come to it, two by two, to be safe from the deluge that is threatening the whole country, and because it will be an ark of rarities, which we will carry safe through the troubled times."

They moved in at once. John drew up plans for the garden, and sent to Lambeth for a couple of lads to dig and weed in the orchard, and to a nearby farm for the loan of a horse and a plough to turn over the earth before the house. They planned a garden that would grow fruit and herbs for selling in London, where good-quality provender could command high prices. But also they knew that every gardener in the kingdom would long for a chestnut tree, for a double plum, for the Russian larches. It was the launching of a trade which was in its infancy. Every good gardener had spare stock of ordinary plants; the excessive bounty of God saw that where there was one plant there were a hundred seeds in the autumn. Every successful gardener exchanged stock or sold it at a profit to other gardeners. But what they longed for was the rare, the exotic, the strange. When John had worked for a lord it was part of his task to ensure that the gardens were full of rarities and he had guarded his seeds and saplings, and given them away to only his dearest of friends like the herbalist John Gerard or the gardener John Parkinson. Now he could sell them to men who had begged him for a cutting only a few years earlier. Now he could sell them to any gardener who might write to him, and already there were letters from all over England, even from Europe, asking Tradescant for seeds and saplings and yearling plants.

John had plans also for the house. He commissioned a builder to construct a new wing which would nearly double the size of the house.

J took him to one side while the men were unloading a wagon of furniture, and spoke to him urgently while Jane and Elizabeth went to and fro watching the stowing of trunks.

"I know this is to be our family home, but we don't need to build it all at once," he said. "The windows you have planned for the downstairs room will go from ceiling to floor. How will we ever afford the glass? And what if it breaks?"

"You will be bringing up a young family here," John said to J. "It's time you had some room to yourselves. And we need a good-sized room, a handsome room, for the rarities."

"But Venetian windows . . . ," J expostulated.

John laid a finger to his nose. "This is to be my rarities room," he said. "We'll store them here in a beautiful room and show them to people who come to see them. We'll charge them sixpence each to enter, and they can stay as long as they like and look around at the things."

J was uncomprehending. "What things?"

"The two wagons of Buckingham's rarities," John explained precisely. "What did you think to do with them?"

"I thought we would sell them," J confessed, a little shamefaced. "And keep the money."

John shook his head. "We keep them," he said. "They will be the making of us. Rare plants in the garden, rare and beautiful things in the house. It is our ark with rare and lovely things. And every day the ships come in with more things ordered by my lord duke. We shall buy them on our own account and set them in our room."

"And we charge people for looking?"

"Why not?"

"It just seems so odd. I've never heard of such a thing before."

"My lord duke kept his cabinet of curiosities for his friends to look at and enjoy. And the Earl Cecil before him."

"He didn't charge them sixpence a time!"

"No, but we will open our doors to ordinary people. To anyone who wishes to come and see. Not friends of ours, or even people with letters of introduction. Just anyone who is curious about wonderful and peculiar things. We let them come!"

"But how would they know of it?"

"We will speak of it everywhere. We'll make a catalogue so people can read of all the things we have on show."

"D'you think people would come?"

John nodded. "In Leiden and Paris the universities have great collections and they show them to the students, and to anyone who applies to see them. Why not here?"

"Because we are not a university!"

John shrugged. "We have a collection which is equal to my lord Cecil's, and many men admired that. We make a beautiful room with the big things hanging from the ceiling and displayed on the walls and the small things bedded in little drawers in big cabinets. Seeds and shells, clothing and goods, toys and ingenious things. I'm sure we can do it, J. And it will mean that we are earning money in the autumn and winter when the garden work is less."

J nodded but then remembered the cost of the panes of glass. "But Venetian windows are not necessary . . ."

"We need good light if we are to show rarities," John said firmly. "This is not some little petty fusty cabinet. This is the first rarities show in the country; it will be one of the first things to see in London. A grand room with the things laid out handsomely. People will not come to see them at all if they are not housed in a proud and handsome manner. Venetian windows and waxed floors! And sixpence a head!"

J deferred to his father's judgment, and only muttered about grand schemes and a duke's tastes over his dinner that night, but the two men clashed again when J, trundling a sapling in a barrow around the wall of the new wing, glanced up and saw the stonemason fixing in place a handsome coat of arms.

"What are you doing?" he yelled upward.

The stonemason glanced down and pulled his cap to J. "Handsome, isn't it?"

J dumped the sapling and ran to the orchard, where John was at the top of a fruit-picker's ladder, pruning out the dead wood on an old pear tree. "D'you think this can be a Spanish pear?" John asked. "I brought one back for my Sir Robert from the Lowlands. Could they have gotten hold of one and planted it here?"

"Never mind that now," J said. "The stonemason is putting up a coat of arms on our house!"

John hung his saw on a protruding branch and turned his attention to his son. J, looking up at his father comfortably leaning against the trunk, thought that they had reversed their roles and that John was like a feckless laughing boy scrumping fruit up a tree and he was like the worried older man.

"I know," John said with a gleam. "Do us credit, I thought."

"You knew?" J demanded. "You knew he had some ridiculous coat of arms drawn up for us?"

"I don't think it's ridiculous," John said easily. "I drew them myself. I rather like it. Leaves as background, and then the shield laid across it with three fleurs-de-lys, and then a helmet on top with a little crown and fleur-de-lys on that."

"But what will the College of Heralds say?"

John shrugged. "Who cares what they say?"

"*We* will care when they fine us, and make us take it down, and humiliate us before our new neighbors."

John shook his head. "We'll get away with it," he said confidently.

"But we're not gentry! We're gardeners."

John came stiffly down his ladder and took J by the shoulder, turning him to see the house.

"What's that?"

"Our house."

"A good-sized house, new wing, Venetian windows, right?"

"Yes."

John turned his son southward again. "And what's that?"

"The orchard."

"How big?

"Only two acres."

"But beyond it?"

"All right, another twenty acres . . . but Father . . ."

"We're landowners," John said. "We're not gardeners any more. We're landowners with duties and obligations and a large family business to run . . . and a crest of arms."

"They'll make us take it down," J warned.

Tradescant waved a dismissive hand and climbed slowly back up his ladder. "Not they. Not when they see who's coming to the Ark."

J hesitated. "Why? Who is coming?"

"Everyone who is anyone," John said grandly. "And all their country cousins. When your baby is born he will grow up to be knighted, I don't doubt it. Sir John Tradescant . . . sounds very well, doesn't it? Sir John."

"I might call him Josiah, after his other grandfather, a respected city tradesman who knows his place and is proud of it," J said mutinously, and had the pleasure of seeing a flicker of doubt cross his father's face.

"Nonsense!" John said. "Sir John Tradescant of Lambeth."

December 1628

In the end, he was not Sir John Tradescant of Lambeth, nor plain John, nor even Josiah. She was Frances, and she came at four o'clock on a dark dreary December morning while J and his father drank brandy downstairs and the women and the women servants wailed and scolded and ran about upstairs until the men finally heard that tiny indignant cry.

J put down his glass with a crack and ran to the foot of the stairs. His mother was standing at the top, beaming. "A girl," she announced. "A lovely dark-headed girl."

J ran up the stairs and into Jane's bedroom.

"And Jane?" Tradescant asked, thinking of the birth of J and the dreadful pain Elizabeth had suffered, and then the news that there would be no more babies.

"She is well, thank God," Elizabeth said. "Resting now."

Husband and wife met each other's gaze with a steady faithful smile. "Our grandchild," John said wonderingly. "I thought I'd set my heart on a boy, but now it comes to it I am just glad that it is a girl and born sound and whole."

"Maybe a boy next time," Elizabeth said.

John nodded. "There will be a next time?"

She smiled. "I don't think this is the last time that you and J will be drinking brandy together while we women do all the work."

"Well, amen to that. I'll send the stable boy with a message to Josiah and Mrs. Hurte. They'll want to know at once."

"Tell them to come and stay for as long as they like," Elizabeth said. "I can make up a bed for them in the third bedroom."

John grinned at Elizabeth's casual use of the words "third bedroom" as if they had never had a house with fewer than a dozen rooms. "They could bring all their congregation as well," he said. "Now we live so grand."

Elizabeth flapped her apron at him. "Go and send your message. I have work to do."

"God be with you, wife," John said lovingly from the foot of the stairs. "And give Jane my blessing. Has she named the child?"

"She wants to call her Frances."

John went out of the front door to the veranda. The cold night air was crisp and sharp, and the stars were like pinheads against a deep blue silk sky. The moon was down and it was too dark to see more than the weathered boards of the veranda and the spiky stalks of the fruit trees. John had planted his chestnut sapling and its first rooted cutting as a pair before the house and, two by two, a dozen cuttings from them to make a little avenue of chestnut running the length of the orchard. Their bare branches were as thin as whips against the arching cold sky.

John exhaled and his breath was a brandy-tinged cloud before his face. He thought briefly of other nights when he had watched and waited. Nights on board ship when the only sound had been the creaking and shifting of the timbers, nights when he had been on watch for icebergs in the perilous cold seas around Russia or when he had swung dizzily to and fro in the crow's nest and looked for pirate ships in the darkness of the Mediterranean waters. He thought of keeping watch in the cold wet fogs of the Ile de Rhé, and of the one, two, three nights, when he had lain naked beside his lord and watched over his precious sleep.

"Sleep well now, my lord," he said into the silent darkness.

He thought he would carry with him always this inner life which was like grief, but which was not quite grief, which was like love, but which was not quite love, which was like homesickness, but which was not a longing for home. Now that Buckingham was dead and his goods had bought the Tradescants their ark, John felt as if all the struggle of his love for his lord was resolved. He could love him without sin, he could love him without shame. The death of his lord had been the only way out, for John, for Buckingham himself. He might grieve for it but he did not blame himself for failing to give that one word of warning. And Elizabeth was true to her promise and the duke's name was in her prayers every Sunday.

John sometimes wondered if the other man who had loved Buckingham, the King of England, felt like this; and if for him too, in the round of his court and daily pleasure and other loves and interests—birth like tonight, deaths and marriages—there was always a gap in the procession, always a face missing, that beautiful wilful angel face. And if he felt also that the world was a safer place, a calmer place, but a grayer place, without George Villiers.

John touched that face in his mind, as the king might lay his finger on the lips of a portrait as he passed it; and then he went round to the stable and rattled the door till the stable lad came tumbling down the stairs, and sent him to the Hurtes' house in London.

Frances set the house by the ears, as a new baby always does. She cried and would not settle at night, and J saw dawn after dawn from the big Venetian windows as he walked her round and round the big room which housed the rarities. Held in his arms, rocked by his continual steady pacing, was the only way she would settle, and the great rarities room was the only place in the house where Jane was not wakened by the distant sound of her cries.

"Sleep," J would say to his wife as the wail from the crib warned them of another restless night. "I will walk her," and he would wrap the tiny thing in a warm blanket, throw his father's soldiering cape over his nightshirt and take her downstairs to walk and walk her around the echoing moonlit room, sometimes for an hour, sometimes for three, until she quieted and slept and he could creep back into his bedroom and lay her, as tender as a seedling, back in her little crib.

Jane did not have enough milk and Elizabeth said there was nothing for it but for her to stay in bed, eat as much as she could bear, and rest, rest, rest. "You must think and worry no more than a milch cow," she insisted when her daughter-in-law protested. "Or else it will be a wet nurse for Frances."

In the face of such a threat Jane fell back against the pillows and closed her eyes. "I shall bring you some chicken broth at noon," Elizabeth said. "Sleep now."

"Where is Frances?" Jane asked. "With J?"

"J is sleeping like a dead man in the parlor," Elizabeth said with a smile. "He sat down at the table to bring the planting records up to date, and his head fell into the inkpot and he was gone. I've wrapped him with a rug and left him. Frances is with John."

"Does John know how to care for her? Will you watch him?"

"John has his own methods," Elizabeth said. "But I will watch him."

She glanced from the bedroom window and saw John and his granddaughter, but did not think she would point them out to Jane. John had strapped the baby to his back in an outlandish savage fashion that he must have seen on one of his voyages. She was wrapped in a fold of blanket against his back with two ends of the blanket knotted around his chest and two around his belly. With the baby held warm and snug against his homespun coat John was walking through the garden and down toward the orchard to see that his chestnut saplings were all surviving the frost.

Elizabeth watched for a moment, and curbed her desire to hurry out and take the child from him. The baby was not crying, John's rolling limp was soothing to her, and as he walked he was singing a low muttered song: "Tumelty tumelty tumelty pudding . . . ," a nonsense song. Frances, soothed by the gentle pressure of his warm back, lulled by the weak winter sunlight, and enjoying the irregular motion of his walk, slept and woke and slept again as

John went down to the end of his orchard to check his fruit trees, and came back again.

They could not yet afford a heated wall as he had built at New Hall. But John had curtained his trees with sacking and stuffed straw gently inside the bags, hoping to keep the frost from them and to warm them a little. He used the same technique on tender new saplings, especially those that came from the Mediterranean or from Africa and probably had never felt a frost. New plants from the Americas he thought might be a little more hardy, but anything small he planted in a new row of special beds near the house where the raised timber borders kept the soil a little warmer, and where he had great domes of glass, usually used for ripening melons, to keep the cold winds off them and to retain the weak heat of the winter sun.

Despite the duke's death the plants and the rarities still came in on the ships, and most days a sailor would make his way down the Lambeth Road to tap on John Tradescant's back door and offer him some little curiosity or treasure. The duke might be collecting no more, but now the ships' captains sent goods home addressed to John Tradescant, The Ark, Lambeth, certain that when they got home Mr. Tradescant or his son would offer them a fair price for whatever they had found, and that they might enjoy the pleasure of boasting that their find was the center of the Tradescants' increasingly famous exhibition. Sometimes the goods were enormous: the skeleton jaw of a whale, or a monstrous unnamed bone. Sometimes they were tiny: a carving of a house inside a walnut. They could be stone or hide, wood or ivory, fashioned by a craftsman or thrown up by nature; the Tradescant collection was gloriously eclectic. Who cared how a thing was made or what it was? If it was rare and exotic it was of interest, it had a place somewhere in the cabinets in the great room with the great windows.

John paused in his walk and looked back at his house with pleasure. He had thought he might attempt to glaze the terrace and keep his most delicate plants there during the winter, but his pleasure in the look of his house, and his joy at sitting out on the terrace and looking out over his orchard on sunny days, was too great. "It's a fine house," he said over his shoulder to the sleeping baby. "A fine home for a growing family, and when you have a brace of brothers and a sister, you shall all play on the grass court before the house and I shall buy a new field for you to keep a donkey."

Spring 1629

John's view of the house at Lambeth as an ark which would keep the family afloat during troubled times was proved before Frances was more than two months old. The king's steady resentment against the House of Commons, which had traduced Buckingham and tried to impeach him, flared up again to dangerous heights at their open delight at the duke's death. The king blamed Sir John Eliot, radical leader in the House, for the assassination of Buckingham and ordered the assassin, Felton, to be tortured till he revealed the conspiracy. Only the lawyers, standing against an angry king, preserved Felton from agony and he went to the gallows swearing that he had acted only for the love of his country, and alone.

Eliot, sensing that the mood of the country was with him, pressed his advantage in the newly called House of Commons in January, refusing to pay the king one penny of his dues until the House had debated the incendiary motion that the king on earth must give way to the king of heaven—a clear call for Puritans to withstand the earthly power of the increasingly papist Charles and his High Church bishops.

While the city seethed with rumors of the debate, there was a loud knocking at the back door of the Tradescant house, and then the cook ran into the rarities room where Jane was writing labels and rocking Frances's cradle with her foot. J was before the hearth, stretching a rare skin on a frame for hanging.

"A message for the master, from Whitehall!" the cook exclaimed.

Jane rose to her feet and went to the window. "He's by the seedling beds," she said, knocking on the glass and beckoning. "Here he comes."

John arrived, rubbing his hands on his leather breeches. "What's to do?"

"A message," the cook said. "And no reply waited for. From Whitehall."

John put out his hand and looked at the seal. "William Ward," he said briefly. "My lord's steward." He turned the page, broke the seal and read. J saw his father pale under the wind-worn tan of his skin.

"What is it?"

"It's the king. He has arrested Sir John Eliot and sent him to the Tower. He has closed down Parliament. He calls the members a nest of vipers and says he will rule forever without them." He read swiftly. "They locked the doors of the House against the king and voted tonnage and poundage illegal, and voted the king's theology illegal." He read a little, and then swore.

"What?" Jane asked impatiently.

"They held the Speaker down in his chair so that the resolutions could be passed before the king's guards burst in and arrested them."

Jane looked at once to the cradle and the sleeping baby. "What will he do?" she asked.

John shook his head. "God knows."

J waited. "What does it mean for us?"

John shook his head again. "For us and the country? Stormy weather."

1630

It was not stormy weather, but a sort of peace which caught the country by surprise. The MPs dispersed in obedience to the king's order and though they took their complaints to their homes in every corner of the kingdom, there was no popular groundswell to sweep them back to confrontation in the city. The king set to work to rule without Parliament—as he had threatened to do—and that turned out to be almost no rule at all. The silence in the Houses of Parliament meant there was no forum for debate. The vacuum of power meant that things rubbed along as they had always done. The towns and cities were run, as they had always been, by a loose alliance of magistrates, gentry and vicars, and by the powerful weight of custom and practice.

In Lambeth, Frances's promised brother did not come, though she outgrew her baby complaints, learned to walk, learned to talk and was even given a small corner of the garden and a dozen cuttings of pinks and twenty sweet pea seeds for her to try her hand at gardening. She was indulged—as the only baby in a house of four adults is bound to be indulged; but nothing spoiled her. As she grew older she still loved the echoey airiness of the rarities room, and would still go piggyback with her grandfather down to the end of the orchard. As she grew stronger and heavier John's limp became more and more pronounced under the extra burden of her weight and he would roll in his walk like the old sailor he sometimes claimed to be.

He had a special voice for her, a meditative nonsense-telling voice which he used for no one else. Only his seedlings in the frame and Frances were treated to his "tumelty tumelty tumelty pudding." Elizabeth would watch him and the little girl from the window as they went hand in hand down the garden and feel at last a sense of relief that she and John, J and Jane were settled at last.

"We've put down some roots," John said to her one night as he saw her smile across the dinner table. The girl laid their dinner before them—they had a girl now, and a woman cook in the kitchen and a lad in the house, as well as three gardeners. "I think we should have a motto."

"Not a motto," J said under his breath. "Please, no."

"A motto," John said firmly. "To go under the crest. You shall write it, J. You have Latin."

"I can't think of anything that would fit a man who was born and bred a gardener and made up his own crest, and had some fool of a mason carve it in stone for anyone to see," J said scathingly.

John smiled, unperturbed. "Why, the king himself is the grandson of a mere Mister," he said. "These are times for men to rise."

"And the Duke of Buckingham was called an upstart to the end of his days," Jane observed.

John dropped his eyes to his plate so that no one could see his sharp pang of grief.

"Even so," J said. "I can't think of a motto which would suit."

They were a family which did not fit the usual tags handed out by the College of Heralds. They were on the way to being gentry, with their own house and land, and rents coming in from the fields at Hatfield, and a couple of houses newly bought at a bargain price in the city. But John and J still worked with their hands deep in the dark earth of their fields and gardens, and could tell to the nearest farthing how much a seedling had cost them in terms of labor and the price of the seed.

Tradescant plants went all over the country, all over Europe. John Gerard the herbalist borrowed from their garden and gave new cuttings back to them. John Parkinson quoted them by name in his book on gardening and acknowledged his debt to them, even though he was the king's own botanist. Every gardener at every great house in the land knew that for something strange and lovely the Tradescants at the Ark were the only men to ask. The Ark was the only place to buy rare tulips outside the Low Countries and their prices were as reasonable as they could be in a market which was still growing and growing every season.

The orders came in almost every day. Once the MPs were forced home to their estates there was little for the gentlemen to do but to look to their fields and their gardens.

"His Majesty did us a great favor," John remarked to Elizabeth as she sat at the dining table and sorted seeds into packets for Jane to label and dispatch. "If the squires were still at Westminster they would not be planting their gardens."

"We're the only ones likely to be grateful for it then," she said with something of her old sharpness. "Mrs. Hurte was telling me that in the city they are saying that we might as well never have had a parliament if the king is going to run the country like a tyrant and never hear the will of the people. There are new taxes every day. We had a demand for a salt tax only yesterday."

"Peace," John said quietly, and Elizabeth bent her head to her work.

They were both right. The country was enjoying a sort of peace bought at the price of never addressing the difficulties between Parliament and king. King Charles was ruling as he fondly imagined his great aunt Elizabeth had ruled, with little regard for Parliament, with little advice and on the smooth oil of his subjects' love. He and the queen went from great house to great house, hunting, dancing, playing in masques, watching theater, assured everywhere that they went, in a dozen pageants of loyal verse, that the people loved them next only to their God.

Henrietta Maria had learned a little wisdom in her hard years as an apprentice queen. When she heard that Buckingham, her worst enemy, was dead, she did not allow one word of delight to escape her. She went straight to the king and when he emerged from his lonely vigil of mourning she was there, dressed in black and looking as grief-stricken as she could manage. In a moment he transferred to her the passionate need which he carried with him always, like a sickness in his blood: the sickness of the less favored son, the sickness of the plain son of a man who liked handsome men. Henrietta Maria staggered under the weight of his embrace but kept her footing. There was nothing in the world she wanted more than his adoration. It made her complete as a woman; it made her complete as a queen.

Nothing contradicted his newfound happiness; nothing was ever allowed to distress or trouble His Majesty. The plague in London meant merely that they moved early to Oatlands Palace near Weybridge, or Windsor, or Beaulieu in Hampshire. Poverty in Cornwall, Presbyterianism in Scotland, the papers from local lords or JPs warning the king that all was not completely well in his kingdom, pursued him from hunting lodge to palace, and waited for a rainy day for him to give them his fleeting attention. His early appetite for work had deserted him once he had found how little rewarded he was for duty. Parliament had never thanked him for the memoranda in his tiny handwriting, and in any case there was no Parliament now. The holders of the great offices of state, incompetent and corrupt, worked as well without supervision as they did under the king's erratic gaze. It was easier, and pleasanter, for him to turn the business of kingship into a country-wide masque with people demonstrating their devotion in dances and songs, and the king play-acting at ruling with a crown of gold wire on his head.

The king's first son and heir was born in May 1630, and three months later a messenger from the court, currently at Windsor, knocked peremptorily on the door of the Lambeth house and glanced upward, but did not comment, at the coat of arms fixed proudly on the wall.

"A message for John Tradescant," he announced as Jane opened the door.

She stepped back to show him into the parlor and he went ahead of her as he would have preceded a Quaker serving woman. Jane, who knew that she should despise the vanity of worldly show, gestured rather grandly to the chair at the fireside. "You may be seated," she said with the dignity of a duchess. "*Mr.* Tradescant, my father-in-law, will join you shortly." She turned on her heel and stalked from the room, and then fled to the garden where John was transplanting seedlings.

"Get up! and get washed! There is a royal herald for you in the parlor!" she exclaimed.

John got slowly to his feet. "A royal herald?"

"Trouble?" J asked. "Not the coat of arms?"

"Surely not," John said comfortably. "Give him a glass of wine, Jane, and tell him I am coming at once."

"You will change your coat," she reminded him. "He is in full livery and with a powdered wig."

"It's only a herald," John said mildly. "Not Queen Henrietta Maria herself."

Jane picked up her skirts and fled back to the house to order the kitchenmaid to pour a cool glass of wine and put it on the best silver tray.

She found the herald looking out from the window to the garden. "How many men does Mr. Tradescant employ here?" he asked, trying to engage her in conversation to make amends for his earlier mistake.

She glanced out. To her embarrassment it was not the garden lads but her husband and her father-in-law, strolling up from the orchard with a hoe and a bucket apiece. "Half a dozen in midsummer," she said. "Fewer in winter."

"And do you have many visitors?"

"Yes," she said. "Both to the garden and to the cabinet of rarities. The garden is rich with both rare fruit and flowers; you are welcome to walk in it, if you wish."

"Later perhaps," the herald said loftily. "I must speak with Mr. Tradescant now."

"He will come shortly," Jane said. "I could show you some of the rarities in the cabinets while you wait."

To her relief, the door behind her opened. "Here I am," John said. "I am sorry to have kept you waiting."

At least he had washed his hands, but he still wore his old gardening coat. The herald, whose face revealed nothing, realized that the workingman he had seen from the window was in fact the gentleman he had come to visit.

"Mr. Tradescant," he began. "I am carrying a letter from the king, and I am to await your reply."

He held out a scroll of paper with a thick red seal at the bottom. John took it and went to the window, where the August sunshine poured in.

Jane had to prevent herself from moving behind him and reading over his shoulder.

"Hmmm hmmm hmmm," John said, skimming the customary compliments and addresses at the start of the letter. "Why! His Majesty is commanding me to be his gardener at Oatlands Palace! I am honored."

"His Majesty has just given the palace to Her Majesty the Queen," the herald informed them. "And she wants a garden like Hatfield or New Hall."

John raised his head. "It's a long time since I planted a garden for a palace. And I am sixty years old this year. There are other gardeners Their Majesties could employ, and I would have thought the queen would have preferred a garden in the French style."

The herald raised his neat plucked eyebrows. "Perhaps. But I am not in a position to advise His Majesty or Her Majesty as to their course of action. *I* merely obey their royal decree." The inference was clear.

"Oh," John said, corrected. "I see."

"His Majesty ordered me to take back a reply to him," the herald continued loftily. "Is it your wish that I tell him you are sixty years of age and that it is your opinion that he didn't want you in the first place?"

John grimaced. An invitation from the king was tantamount to a royal command. He was not able to refuse. "Tell His Majesty that I am honored for the invitation and that I accept, I gratefully accept, and that it will always be my pleasure to serve Their Majesties in any way I can."

The herald unbent slightly. "I will deliver your message. His Majesty will expect you at Oatlands Palace within the week."

John nodded. "I shall be delighted to attend."

The herald bowed. "An honor to meet you, Mr. Tradescant."

"The honor is all mine," John said grandly.

The herald bowed himself from the room and left John and his daughter-in-law alone.

"Royal service," she said grimly. "J won't like it."

John grimaced. "He will have to bear it. You can't refuse the king. You heard him. My acceptance was just a matter of form; he knew what day I had to start work."

"We said we would never work for another master," Jane reminded him.

John nodded. "We never thought of this. But perhaps it won't be so bad." He turned and looked out of the window at his little farm. "I've heard they have a great orangery," he said. "But they've never had much luck with getting the trees to flower. There's a garden just for the king's use and another for the queen. There's a massive fountain in the great garden. The whole place is like a village set about with gardens, built all ramshackle with one court running into another, overlooking the Thames. The trick of it will be to make sure that every corner has a pretty plant, that the gardens pull the whole site together so that every corner has a view."

Jane heard her father-in-law casting aside the principle of independence for the offer of a fine garden to make. She stalked to the door. "Shall I tell J or will you?" she asked coldly. "For he will not care for making pretty views for such a king."

"I'll tell him," John said absently. "I wonder if we have enough chestnut saplings to use one at the center of each court?"

* * *

John told J the news at dinner but he knew from the moment his son entered the dining room that Jane had forewarned him, and that J was forearmed.

"I swore I'd never work for another master," he said.

"This would be for me," John corrected him, mildly. "Working for us all. For the good of us all."

J glanced at his wife.

"It would be for the queen," she said bluntly. "A woman of vanity and a heretic."

"She may be both of those," John agreed without hesitation. "But she's only the paymaster. She will not supervise us at all. J need never speak to her."

"There's something about them, though, that sticks in my throat like dry bread," J said thoughtfully. "There's something about a man calling himself nearer to God than me. Something about a man thinking himself a better man than me—almost an angel. Even if I never saw him and never served him, there's something about it which goes against the grain for me."

"Because it's heresy," Jane said flatly.

J shook his head. "Not just because of that," he said. "Because it denies me—it denies that I think, just as he thinks. That I have ideals, just as he has ideals. That I too want, think and pray for better days, for the coming of the Great Day, the Last Day. If he is as far above me as an angel then I need not think and hope and pray, for God would hardly listen to me when the king is on his knees. It's as if his importance makes me more little." He glanced around at their surprised faces. "I daresay I'm not making any sense," he said defensively. "I'm not good at arguing these things. It's just what I've been thinking."

"But what you're saying would deny any king," John said. "This one or any other. A good one or a bad one."

J nodded reluctantly. "I just can't see that any man should set himself up to be above another. I can't see that any man needs more than one house. I can't see that any man needs dozens of houses and hundreds of servants. I can't see that he can be closer to God with these things—I would have thought he would be farther and farther away."

John shifted uncomfortably on his wooden seat. "This is Leveller talk, my son. Next thing you will be denying any king but King Jesus and taking off for the common and waste lands."

"I don't care what it's called," J said steadily. "I wouldn't be frightened from speaking my mind because others think the same thoughts but express them wildly. I know that I must think that England would be better without a man at its head who claims to speak for us, and know us, and yet clearly knows nothing at all of what it is like to be a man such as me."

"He has advisers."

J shrugged. "He is surrounded by courtiers and flatterers. He hears what they tell him and they only tell him what he wants to hear. He can have no judgment, he can have no wisdom. He is trapped in his vanity and ignorance like a fish in a fishpond and since it knows nothing else it thinks it is something divinely special. If it could breathe air and see the sky it would know it is nothing more than a large fish."

John snorted with laughter at the thought of the long mournful face of his monarch and the juxtaposition of the face of a carp.

"But who will you employ if J will not go?" Elizabeth asked practically.

"I'll have to find someone," John said. "There are dozens of men who would be glad of the place. But I would rather work with you, J. And it seems to me you are bound to work for me if I ask it."

J shifted on his seat. "You would not drive me to rebellion," he said. "You would respect my conscience, Father. I am a full-grown man."

"You're twenty-two," John said bluntly. "Barely into your majority. You make your own choices; you are a man with a wife and child of your own. But I am still your father and it will be my work which will put the bread on your table, if you refuse to work."

"I work here!" J exclaimed, stung. "I work hard enough!"

"In winter we earn almost no money," John pointed out. "We live off our savings. There is no stock to sell, and the visitors tail off in the bad weather. Last year we were down to the bottom of our savings by the spring. The work at the palace would be money paid to us all the year round."

"Papist gold," Jane muttered to her plate.

"Honestly earned by us," John countered. "I am an old man. I did not think to go out to work to keep you, J. I did not think your conscience would be more precious than your duty to me."

J shot a furious look at his father. "It's always the same!" he burst out. "You are always the one who is free to come and go. I am always the one who has to obey. And now that we have a home where I *want* to stay, and now you are free to stay yourself, you are still going away. And now I have to go too!"

"I am not free," John said sternly. "The king commands me."

"Defy the king!" J shouted. "For once in your life don't go at some great man's bidding. For once in your life speak for yourself! Think for yourself! Defy the king!"

There was a long shocked silence.

John rose from the table and walked to the window and looked out over the garden rinsed of color and lovely in the gray light of dusk. A star was shining over the chestnut tree and somewhere in the orchard a nightingale started to sing.

"I will never defy the king," he said. "I will not even hear such talk in my house."

The pause stretched till breaking point and then J spoke low and earnestly. "Father, this is not Queen Elizabeth and you are not still working for Robert Cecil. This is not a king as she was a queen. This is not a country as it was then. This is a country that has been run into debt and torn apart by heresy. It is ruled by a vain fool who is ruled in turn by a papist wife, in the pay of her brother, the King of France. I cannot bear to go and work for such a king nor for her. I cannot bear to be under their command. If you force me to this I would rather leave the country altogether."

John nodded, taking in J's words. The two women, Elizabeth

and Jane, sat silent, hardly breathing, waiting to hear what John would reply.

"Do you mean this?"

J, breathing heavily, merely nodded.

John sighed. "Then you must follow your conscience and go," he said simply. "For the king is my master before God, and he has ordered me. And I am your father and should command your duty and I have ordered you. If you choose to defy me then you should go, J. Just as Adam and Eve had to leave *their* garden. There are laws in heaven and earth. I cannot pretend to you that it is otherwise. I have tolerated loose thoughts and wild talk from you all your life, even in my lord's garden. But if you will not serve the king then you should not garden in his garden. You should not garden in his country."

J rose from the table. His hands were trembling and he swiftly snatched them out of sight, behind his back.

"Wait—" Elizabeth said softly. Neither man paid any attention to her.

"I shall go, then," J said as if he were testing his father's resolve. John turned his back on the room and looked out to his garden.

"If you do not accept your obedience to me, and to the king above me, and to God above him, then you are no longer my son," John said simply. "I would to God that you do not take this path, J."

J turned and walked jerkily to the door. Jane rose too, hesitant, looking from her husband to her father-in-law. J went out without another word.

"Go to him," Elizabeth said swiftly to Jane. "Soothe him. He can't mean it. Keep him here tonight at least—we'll talk more in the morning." A swift nod toward John at the window showed Jane that meanwhile Elizabeth would work on her husband.

Jane hesitated. "But I think he is right," she whispered, too low for John to hear.

"What does it matter?" Elizabeth hissed. "What do the words matter? Nothing matters more than Frances and you and J living here now, and living here when we are gone. The gardens and the Tradescant name. Go quick and stop him packing at least."

Jane prevented J from leaving home that night by presenting the folly of taking a sleeping baby out of her cradle into the night air, into a city filled with plague. The two men, father and son, met at breakfast and went out to the garden together in stiff silence.

"What can we do?" Jane asked her mother-in-law.

Elizabeth shook her head. "Pray that the two of them will see that the interests of this family are more important than whose gold pays the bills."

"Father should not force J to work for the king against his conscience," Jane said.

Elizabeth shook her head. "Ah, my dear, it was so different for us when we were your age. There was no other way to work but for a lord. There were no other gardens but those belonging to great lords. At J's age his father would never have dreamed of owning a house, or fields. At J's age he was an under-gardener in the Cecil household and living in hall; he didn't even choose his own meat for breakfast—everything came from the lord's kitchen. Things have changed so fast, you two must understand. The world is so different now. And J is still a very young man. Things could change again."

"Things are changing," Jane agreed. "But not in favor of lords and the court. Perhaps this family should not be linked with the king. Perhaps we would do better to be like my family, independent traders who do not fear the king's favor. Who are not dependent on any master."

"Yes, if we were mercers," Elizabeth answered gently. "And could trade from a little shop, and every man and woman in the country would need our goods and could afford them. But we are gardeners and keepers of a rarities collection. Only the wealthy men will buy what we have to sell and show. And we cannot get our stock without owning land to grow it in. It is not a trade that can be done on a small scale. This is a business that puts us in the hands of the great men of the country. We sell to the great houses, we sell to the courtiers. Of course, sooner or later, we would come to the mind of the king."

"And he wants us, as he wants everything that is beautiful and rare," Jane said bitterly. "And he thinks he can buy us too."

Elizabeth nodded. "Just so."

The men came into dinner in silence. Jane and Elizabeth exchanged a few remarks about the weather and the progress of the work in the garden but gave up when neither man responded with more than a word or a nod.

As soon as they had eaten the men went back outside and Jane, looking from the window of the rarities room, saw J heading down for the orchard, as far away from the house as he could go, while John was weeding the seed beds in the cool shadow of the house. The day was hot. Even the wood pigeons that usually cooed in the Tradescant trees were silent. Jane took Frances to feed the ducks in the pond at the side of the orchard and saw her husband scything nettles in a distant corner. When he saw her he carefully sheathed the blade and came over.

"Wife."

She looked into his unhappy face. "Oh, John!"

"You don't want to leave here," he said flatly.

"Of course not. Where could we go?"

"We could go to your father's while we looked about and found some position."

"You swore you would garden for no master."

"The Devil himself would be better than the king."

She shook her head. "You said no master."

Frances leaned longingly toward the deeper water. Jane took the little hand in a firm grip. "Not too near," she said.

"There are two places I would choose to live, if you would consent," J said tentatively.

Jane waited.

"There is a community, of good men and women, who are trying to make a life of their own, to worship as they wish, to live as they wish."

"Quakers?" Jane asked.

"Not Quakers. But they believe in freedom for men and even for women. They have a farm in Devon near the sea."

"How have you heard of them?"

"A traveling preacher spoke of them, a few months ago."

Jane thought for a moment. "So we don't know them directly."

"No."

He saw her grip on Frances's hand tighten. "I can't go among strangers and so far from my family," she said firmly. "What would become of us if one of us were ill? Or if they are no longer there? I can't go so far from my mother. What if we have another baby? How would we manage without my mother or your mother?"

"Other women manage," J said. "Leave home, manage among strangers. They will become your friends."

"Why should we?" Jane asked simply. "We, who have two families who love us? We, who have a house to live in which is the most beautiful house in Lambeth and famed throughout the world for the rarities and the gardens?"

"Because it comes with too high a price!" J exclaimed. "Because I rent this beautiful house with my obedience, by putting my conscience in the keeping of my father who himself has never thought a thought which was not licensed by his lord. He is an obedient dutiful man, Jane, and I am not."

She thought for a moment. Frances pulled at her hand. "Frances feed ducks," she said. "Frances feed ducks."

"Down there," Jane said, hardly looking. "Where the bank is not so steep. Don't get your feet wet." She let the little girl go and watched her progress to the water's edge. The ducks gathered hopefully around; Frances plunged her hands into the pockets of her little gown and came out with fistfuls of breadcrumbs.

"What is your other wish?" Jane asked.

J took a deep breath. "Virginia," he said.

Jane looked into his face and then came into his arms as simply as she had done the day they were married. "Oh, my love," she said. "I know you have such dreams. But we cannot go to Virginia; it would break my mother's heart. And I could not bear to leave her. And besides—we don't *need* to go. We are not adventurers, we are not desperate for a fortune or to run away from here. We have a place here, we have work here, we have a home here. I would not leave here for choice."

J would not look at her. "You are my wife," he said flatly. "You are duty-bound to go where I go. To obey me."

She shook her head. "I am bound in duty to you as you are to your father, as he is to the king. If you break one link they all go, J. If you do not acknowledge him as your father then I need not acknowledge you as my husband."

"Then what do we become?" he demanded in impatience. "All whirling, unconnected, unloving, atoms; like thistledown finding its own way on the wind?"

She said nothing. Behind them, Frances put one tentative foot in the water.

"If you are guided by your conscience and only by your conscience then that is what we must become," she said thoughtfully. "All of us, guided by our own consciences, coming together only when it suits us."

"A society cannot live like that," J replied.

"A family cannot," Jane said. "As soon as you love someone, as soon as you have a child, you acknowledge your duty to put another's needs first."

J hesitated.

"The other way is the king's way," Jane continued. "The very thing you despise. A man who puts his own desires and needs before everyone else. Who thinks his needs and desires are of superior merit."

"But I am guided by my conscience!" J protested.

"He could say the same," she said gently. "If you are Charles the king, then your wishes could very well seem to be conscience and there would be no one to tell you your duty."

"So where is my course?" J asked. "If you are my adviser this day?"

"Somewhere between duty and your own wishes," Jane said. "Surely we can find a way for you to keep your soul clear of heresy and yet still live here."

J's face was bleak. "You would put your comfort before my conscience," he said flatly. "All it is with you, is living here."

She did not turn away from him but tightened her grip around his waist. "Think," she urged him. "Do you really want to walk away from the garden that is your inheritance? The chestnut tree which your father gave to your mother the year you were conceived? The black-heart cherry? His geraniums? The tulips that you saved from New Hall? The larches from Archangel?"

J turned his head away from her pleading face but Jane did not let go. "If we never have another child," she said bravely. "We both come from small families, we might only ever have Frances. If God is not kind to us and we never have a son to carry your name, then all that will be left of the Tradescants is their name on their trees. These are your posterity, John—will you leave them to be named for another man, or grown by him? Or worse, neglected and felled by him?"

He looked down at her. "You are my conscience and my heart," he said softly. "Are you telling me that we should garden for the king—even such a king as this—because if we do not then I lose my bond to my father and my rights to his name, and my claim to history?"

She nodded. "I wish it were an easier road to see," she said. "But surely you can plant the king's garden and take the king's gold without compromising your soul or your conscience. You don't need to be his man, as your father was wedded to Cecil and then to Buckingham. You can just take his wage and do his work. You can be an independent man working for pay."

J hesitated for one more moment. "I wanted to be free of all this."

"I know," she said lovingly. "But we have to wait for the right time. Who knows, there may come a time when the whole country wants to be free of him? Then you will see your course. But until then, J, you have to live. We have to eat. We have to live with your father and mother and keep the Ark afloat."

Finally he nodded. "I'll tell him."

J did not speak to his father till dinnertime the following day when the family was gathered together again, Frances beside her mother, John at one end of the big dark wood table and J at the other, Elizabeth seated between her husband and son.

"I have been considering. I will work with you at Oatlands Palace," J announced abruptly.

John looked up, swiftly concealing his surprise. "I'm glad to hear it," he said, keeping the joy from his voice. "I shall need your skills."

Elizabeth and Jane exchanged one swift, relieved glance. "Who will run the business here while we are away?" J asked, matter-of-fact.

"We will," Elizabeth said, smiling. "Jane and I."

"Frances too," Frances said firmly.

"And Frances, of course. Peter will show people round the rarities, he does it beautifully now, like a barker in a fairground; and you will be home often, one of you would be home for a day or two, surely?"

"When the court moves on from Oatlands we will be able to do as we please," John said. "They will want beauty when they visit; we can do half of that with plants grown here in the seed beds and set in at the right time. When they are not at Oatlands we can go about our business here."

"I will not hear heresy," J warned.

"I myself shall guard your tender conscience," his father assured him.

Reluctantly J chuckled. "Aye, you can laugh, but I mean this, Father. I will not hear heresy, and I will not bow down low to her."

"You will have to uncover your head and bow," John told him firmly. "That's common politeness."

"The Quakers don't," Jane volunteered.

John gave her a swift sideways look under his brows. "I thank you, Mistress Jane. I know the Quakers don't. But J is not a Quaker—" he glared at his son as if to dare him to confess yet another step down the road to a more and more radical faith "—and the Quakers do not work for me in the king's garden."

"They are still his subjects," she said staunchly.

"And I honor their faith. Just as J is the king's subject and has a right to his conscience, inside the law. But he will be obedient and he will be courteous."

"And what shall we do if the law changes?" Elizabeth asked. "This is a king who is changing the shape of the church itself, whose father changed the Bible itself. What if he changes yet more and makes us outlaws in our own church?"

J glanced at his mother. "That's the very question," he said. "I can bend for the moment, but what if matters get worse?"

"Practice before principle," John said with Cecil's old remembered wisdom. "We'll worry about that if it happens. In the meantime we have a road we can all take together. We can obey the king and dig his wife's garden, and keep our consciences to ourselves."

"I will not listen to heresy and I will not bow down low to the papist queen," J stated. "But I can be courteous to her and I can work for my father. Two wages coming in is better than one. And besides—" He glanced up at his father with a silent appeal. "I want to do my duty by you, Father. I want there always to be a Tradescant at Lambeth. I want things working right in their right places. It's because the king does not work right in his right place that everything is so disturbed. I want order—just as you do."

John smiled his warm loving smile at his son. "I shall make a Cecil of you yet," he said gently. "Let us put some order in the queen's garden and keep the steady order of our own lives, and pray that the king does his duty as we do ours."

The queen had commanded that John should have lodgings in the park at Oatlands and that everything should be done as he wished.

His house adjoined the silkworm house and was warmed by the sun all day and by the charcoal burners which were set about the walls of the silkworm house all night. John at first found the thought of his neighbors the maggots, silently munching their way through mulberry leaves night and day, immensely distasteful; but the house itself was a miracle of prettiness, a little turreted play-castle of wood, south-facing with mullioned windows and furnished by the order of the queen with pretty light tables, chairs and a bed.

He was to eat in the great hall with the other members of the household. The king demanded that dinner be served in the great hall in full state whether he was there or not. The ritual demanded that a cover be set on the table before his chair, that dishes be put before the empty throne and that every man should bow to the throne before entering the hall and on leaving it.

"This is superstition," John exclaimed unwarily when he saw the men bowing low to the empty chair.

"It is how the king orders it," one of the grooms of the bedchamber replied. "To maintain the dignity of the throne. It's how it was done in Queen Elizabeth's time."

John shook his head. "Well, I remember Elizabeth's time, which is more than most do," he said. "Men bowed to her chair when she was going to sit on it, and bowed to her dinner when she was going to eat it. She was too parsimonious to have dinner served in ten palaces when she was only going to eat in one."

The man shook his head, warning John to be silent. "Well, this is how it's done now," he said. "The king himself ordered it."

"And when does he come?"

"Next week," the groom said. "And then you will see a change. The place is only half-alive when Their Majesties are not here."

He was right. Oatlands Palace was like a village with the plague when the court was elsewhere, the passages between one building and another empty and silent, half the kitchens cold, their fires unlit. But early in September a trail of carts and wagons came down the road from Weybridge, and a hundred barges rowed upstream from London bringing the king's goods as the court moved to Oatlands for the month.

The palace was under siege from an army of shouting, arguing, ordering, singing cooks, maids, horsemen, grooms, servers and minor gentry of the household. Everyone had an urgent task and an important responsibility, and everyone got in everyone else's way. There were tapestries to hang and pictures to place and floors to sweep and carpets to lay. All the king's most beautiful furniture traveled with him; and his bedroom and the queen's bedroom had to be prepared and perfect. The chimneys had to be swept before fires could be lit, but fires had to be lit to air the damp linen at once. The whole village, spread over nine acres, was in a state of complete madness. Even the deerhounds in the kennels caught the excitement and bayed all night long under the yellow September moon.

Tradescant broke the rule of dining in the great hall and went to Weybridge village to buy bread, cheese and small ale, which he took home to his little house in the gardens. He and the silkworms munched their way through their dinners in their adjoining houses. "Goodnight, maggots," Tradescant called cheerfully as he blew his candle out and the deep country darkness enveloped his bedroom.

John had given no thought to meeting the king. When he had last seen His Majesty, they had both been waiting for Buckingham to come to Portsmouth. The time before that had been at the sailing of the first expedition to Rhé. When John was led into the king's state bedchamber he found, with the familiar pang of sorrow, that he was looking around for his master. He could not believe that his duke was not there.

At once, like a ghost summoned by desire, he saw him. It was a life-size portrait of Buckingham painted in dark rich oils. One hand was outstretched as if to show the length and grace of the fingers and the wealth of the single diamond ring, the other hand rested on the rich pommel of his sword. His beard was neatly trimmed, his clothes were bright and richly embroidered and encrusted, but it was his face that drew Tradescant's look. It was his lord, it was his lost lord. The thick dark hair, the arrogant laughing half-raised brows set over dark eyes, the irresistible smile, the sparkle, and that hint of spirituality, of saintliness, which King James had seen even as he had loved the sensual beauty of the face.

John thought how he still touched his lord in his mind, almost every morning and every night, and how he had thought that perhaps the king too reached out over death to his friend. But now he saw that the king had a greater comfort, for every night and every morning he could glance at that assured smiling face and feel the warmth of those eyes, and if he wished he could touch the frame of the picture, or even brush a kiss upon the painted cheek.

The portrait was new in the chamber, along with the rich curtains and the thick Turkey rugs on the floor. The king's most precious goods traveled with him everywhere he went. And the king's most precious thing was the portrait which hung, wherever he slept, at his bedside where he could see it before closing his eyes at night and on waking in the morning.

Charles came silently into his bedchamber from his private adjoining room and hesitated when he saw John looking up at the portrait. Something in the tilt of the man's head and the steadiness of his look reminded the king that John too had lost a man who had been at the very center of his world.

"Y . . . you are looking at my p . . . portrait of the . . . duke."

John turned, saw the king and dropped to his knees, flinching a little as his bad knee hit the floor.

The king did not command him to rise. "Your l . . . late master." His voice still held traces of the paralyzing stammer he had suffered from as a child. Only with his intimates could he speak without hesitation; only with two people, the duke and now his wife, had he ever been fluent.

"You m . . . must miss him," the king went on. It sounded more like an order than an offer of sympathy.

John looked up and saw the king's face. Grief had changed him; he looked older and more tired, and his brown hair was thinning.

His eyes were heavily lidded, as if he were weary of what he saw, as if he no longer expected to see what he wanted.

"I grieve for him still," John said honestly. "Every day."

"You l . . . loved him?"

"With all my heart," John replied.

"And he l . . . loved you?"

John looked up at his king. There was passion behind the question. Even after his death Buckingham could still inspire jealousy. John, the older man, smiled wryly. "He loved me a little," he said. "When I served him especially well. But one smile from him was worth a piece of gold from another."

There was a silence. Charles nodded as if the statement was of little consequence and turned away to the window and looked out into the king's court below.

"H . . . Her Majesty will tell you wh . . . what she wants done," he said. "But I sh . . . should like one court planted with r . . . roses. Rose petals for throwing in masques."

John nodded. A man who could turn from the death of his friend to the need of rose petals for masques would be a difficult master to love.

The king looked round, his eyebrow raised.

"Yes, Your Majesty," John said from his place on the floor. He wondered what his master Sir Robert Cecil, who had scolded a greater monarch than this one, would have thought of a king who confided his grief in a gardener but left him kneeling on an arthritic leg.

There was a rustle of silk and high heels tapping.

"Ah! My gardener!" said the voice of the queen.

John, already low, tried to bow from a kneeling position and felt himself to be ridiculous. He glanced up. She was a short plump woman, beringed, curled, painted and patched with a low-cut gown which would have incurred Elizabeth's censure, and a powerful scent of incense around her skirts which would have inspired outrage in the Ark at Lambeth. She gave him a bright dark-eyed smile and extended her small hand. John kissed it.

"Get up! Get up!" she commanded. "I want you to walk me all around the garden so that I can see what we must do!"

The flood of words came so quickly after her husband's halting speech, and her accent was so strong, that John could not immediately understand what she said.

"Your Majesty?" He glanced toward the king for help. Charles made a brief dismissive gesture with his hand, which clearly indicated that John should go, so he bowed low once again, and backed from the room. To his surprise, the queen came with him. John pressed himself back against the wall as a footman flung open the door.

"This way! Come on!" the queen said, and ran prettily down the stairs and out into the summer sunshine of the king's privy garden.

"I want this garden full of scented flowers," she told him. "The king's windows look out over it; I want the scents to blow up to him."

John nodded, taking in the grand sweep of the walls around the court. The south-facing walls would provide extra warmth; the walls to the east would provide shelter. "I could grow almost anything here," he said.

"It was the king's mother's garden," the queen said. It was evident from the slight movement of her head that she did not think much of her predecessor's taste for low-growing herbs and knot gardens made of colored gravel. "I want roses against the walls and lilies everywhere. Those are my flowers, in my crest. I want this garden filled with roses and lilies to remind the king of me whenever he looks from his window."

John bowed slightly. "Any preference as to colors?" he asked. "I can get some very handsome red and white roses, Rosamund roses. I have them growing at my garden in Lambeth."

"Yes, yes," she said, falling over the words in her haste. Even after five years in the country she still spoke English as if it was a strange and ugly foreign language. "And in the center bed I want a knot with our initials entwined. C and H M. Can you do that?"

John nodded. "Of course . . ."

She suddenly stiffened. "Of course, Your Highness," she corrected him abruptly.

"I beg your pardon," John said smoothly. "I was so interested in what Your Highness was saying that I forgot my manners. Of course, Your Highness."

At once she smiled at him and gave him her hand to kiss. John bowed low and pressed his lips gently to the little fingers. His sense that he had served steadier, more intelligent and more noble masters did not show on his face.

"It is to be a garden which expresses Love," she said. "The highest love there can be below the heavens. The love that there is between a man and his wife, and higher than that: between a king and a queen."

"Of course, Your Majesty," John said. "I could plant you some symbolic flowers around the roses. White violets for innocence, and periwinkle for constancy, and daisies."

She nodded enthusiastically. "And one corner in blue as a tribute to Our Lady." She turned her dark eyes on him. "Are you of the true faith, Tradescant?"

John thought briefly of Elizabeth in her gray Quaker-like gown, the staunch Baptist faith of his daughter-in-law and his promise to J that his conscience would not be offended by this work. He kept his face perfectly steady. "I attend the church of my fathers, Your Majesty," he said. "I'm a simple gardener; I don't think much of things other than plants and rarities."

"You should think of your immortal soul," she commanded. "And the church of your fathers is the church of Rome. I am always telling the king this!"

Tradescant bowed, thinking that she had just said enough to get both of them hanged if the king applied the laws of the land—which he manifestly only did when it suited him.

"And I shall want flowers for my chapel, for my private chapel," she said. "Blue and white for Our Lady."

"Of course, Your Majesty."

"And for my private rooms, and strewing herbs, and the king

wishes you to maintain and replant the physic garden and look at the herb garden."

Tradescant bowed again.

"I want the house to be like a palace in a fairy tale," she said, changing at once from the evangelical Roman Catholic into the flirtatious queen. "Like a bower for a fairy-tale Princess. I want people all over the country, all over Europe, to hear of it as a fairy-tale garden, a perfect garden. Have you heard of the Platonic ideal?"

John felt a sense of weariness he had never before known while talking about a garden. He had a sudden sympathy for the king, who had lost the easy male companionship of Buckingham and had no one to turn to but this vain woman.

The queen was laughing. "I suppose not!" she cried. "It does not matter, Gardener Tradescant. It is an idea which we make much of at court, in our masques and poetry and plays. I will just tell you that it is an idea that there is a perfect form of everything—of a woman, of a man, of a marriage, of a garden, of a rose, and the king and I want to attain that ideal."

John glanced at her to see if she was speaking seriously. He thought of how the duke would have roared with laughter at the pedantry, at the pretentiousness. He would have slapped John on the back and called him Gardener Tradescant forever after.

"Think of it," she said, her voice as sweet as syrup. "A perfect garden as a shell for a perfect palace for a perfect king and queen."

"In a perfect country?" John asked incautiously.

She smiled. She had no sense that there might be anything behind his question but spellbound admiration. "Oh, yes," she said. "How could it be otherwise when it is ruled by my husband, and by me?"

Summer 1631

John had thought he would enjoy some time away from his home—never in his life before had he been so settled and he feared that the domestic life of Lambeth would be too narrow for him. But he found that he missed the daily changing business of the Ark, the midsummer flowering of the garden and, more than anything else, the rapid changing of Frances, who grew, in the summer of 1631, from a rosebud-mouthed, lisping toddler to a little girl of rare determination.

He went home to Lambeth at every opportunity he could, to choose his stock from his own garden, and so that he could see his granddaughter. Each time he set off back to the palace, J would loiter in the stable yard, helping to pack the wagon with the heavy earthenware pots of plants.

"D'you need me at the palace?" he would ask, and John would drop his hand on his son's shoulder.

"I can manage without you another week," he would say. "I'll tell you when I need you there."

"I'll come then," J would promise. "As I agreed to."

He would watch his father swing into the seat and go, and John would chuckle to himself at the seriousness of his beloved son who had bound himself in so many contradictory ways: to his conscience, to his promise, to his father, to his wife.

By the end of the summer John had completed the designs for the work in the king's court, had shown them to the queen and was ready to start the labor of digging over the garden and replanting it. He had a team of men ready to start but he needed J to supervise the work while he went on to the queen's court, so that it should be designed in time for autumn planting.

"Will you come back to the palace with me this time, J?" he asked as the family were seated on the terrace one evening. J was drinking a glass of small ale; John had a small tot of rum. "There's the physic garden which needs replanting, and now the queen has asked for a flowery mead."

Jane looked up from her sewing, affronted. "A what?"

John smiled. "A flowery mead," he said. "Modeled on an old tapestry, those you see with the unicorn surrounded by hunters. It's supposed to be like a meadow, a perfect meadow, with all the flowers of the field but no stinging nettles. You plant it with wild and garden flowers and then you cut a little path around it for the pleasure of walking with wildflowers."

"Why not walk by a meadow, then?" Jane asked.

John took another sip of rum. "This is not a woman of sense, this is the queen. She would rather that everything was fashioned to perfection. Even a wildflower meadow. It's an old fashion in gardening; I did not think to plant one again. And although it is supposed to look wild and untouched, it takes unending work to keep it in flower and keep the weeds checked."

"I can do it," J said. "I've never worked on one before. I'd like to do it."

John raised his glass to his son. "And you'll have little or nothing to do with Her Majesty," he said. "Since she first showed me the garden and told me what she wanted I have hardly seen her. She is with the king most of the day or with the courtiers. She wants the garden as the backcloth to her theater of being queen. She has no interest in planting."

"Well enough," J said. "For I have no interest in her."

John had intended that J would miss the king and queen altogether, and timed the arrival of his son to the date when the court was due to have moved on. But there was the usual delay and confusion, and they were a week late in going. J, cutting the full-blown roses in the rose court and carefully shaking the petals into a broad flat basket for drying, looked up and saw that a short dark-haired woman was watching him.

He took in the wealth of jewels, the rich silk and lace of her gown and the straggle of courtiers behind her, and pulled off his hat and bowed, as low as he should go for courtesy, but no lower.

"Who are you?" she asked abruptly.

"I am John Tradescant, the younger John Tradescant, Your Highness," J said.

"I want the white petals separated from the pink," she told him.

"I am keeping them apart, Your Majesty," J said.

"You may take them to the still room when they are dry," she said.

J bowed. They were to be dried in the silk house and the woman who ran the still room did not need them. These were for the masquing, and the Master of Revels and the Wardrobe Mistress would receive them, but there was little point in arguing when a queen wished to pretend that she understood the running of her palace.

"I want a tree planted in the middle of this court," she announced suddenly. "A large tree, and roses growing up to the roots. It is to symbolize my husband's care of his people. An oak tree, to symbolize his power and strength, and white roses to symbolize the innocent good people, clustered all around him."

"Roses don't like shade, Your Majesty," J ventured cautiously. "Unfortunately I don't think they will thrive under an oak tree."

"Surely you can plant some!"

"They need the sunshine, and they like the air through their branches," J said. "They will wither and die if they are planted beneath an oak tree."

She pouted at him, as if he were being deliberately obtuse. "But it is symbolic!"

"I see that," J said. "But the roses won't thrive."

"Then you must plant and replant every time they die."

J nodded. "I could do that, Your Majesty, if it is your wish. But it would be very wasteful."

"I don't care what it costs," she said simply.

"And you would never have a large rosebush, because it would never have the time to be established, Your Majesty."

She nodded, and paused in thought, tapping her little foot on the perfectly raked gravel. J thought that it must be rare that anyone refused to do her bidding. The courtiers, who had been lagging behind, had caught her up and were staring at him, and eyeing the queen as if they feared that his intransigence might cause them all to suffer the explosion of royal temper.

Instead she smiled. "The oak tree is to symbolize the benevolence of my husband's rule," she said, speaking slowly and clearly as if J were an idiot. "Underneath the protection of the oak you must plant something which symbolizes the people of his kingdoms, sheltering beneath his power. And around the outside, a border of roses and lilies which symbolize me."

J had a sweet sense of the power of symbolism which his years at grammar school had quite failed to teach him. "I understand, Your Majesty," he said courteously, "but unfortunately the shade of an oak tree is very injurious to all plants. Nothing grows beneath it except perhaps moss and grasses. The oak tree smothers and strangles the plants which try to grow beneath it. Strong and handsome plants need their own space and sunshine."

Her brows snapped together and she turned away from him. "I hope you are not trying to be clever beyond your position in life!" she said sharply.

J kept his face perfectly straight. "I'm just a humble gardener, Your Majesty. I only know what will grow in your gardens. I know of nothing more than planting and weeding."

She hesitated for a moment and then she decided to smile. "Well, plant something pretty in the center of the court," she said, avoiding the discomfort of having her plans defeated. "I don't care what."

J bowed low and saw the courtiers exchange one swift glance of relief. The queen moved on; a man went forward and took her hand and whispered in her ear and she laughed and tossed her little head. One courtier delayed and watched J as he bent once more to snipping the rose-heads and shaking the petals.

"What were you saying, gardener? That the power of a king who is forever extending his power strangles growth and health in the kingdom?"

J turned an innocent gaze on the man. "I, sir? No. I was talking of oak trees."

The man met his gaze. "There are many who would think that it is as true of royal power as it is of plants," he said. "There are many who would think that the power of the monarch needs to be pruned and snipped to fit well in the garden and to look well alongside the other grand plants of Parliament and church."

J was about to agree, his face relaxing from the mask of discretion which he had worn since his arrival; but he remembered his father's warnings. "I don't know about that," he said stolidly. "I'm just cutting the roses."

The courtier nodded and moved away. J did not straighten up until the man was gone. Then he looked after him. "The Levellers are in good company then," he said thoughtfully. "If they're in the very palace itself."

J was right. Not everyone who danced in the masques and admired the growing collection of portraits which showed Charles as the fount of wisdom and Henrietta Maria as the greatest beauty believed the images they saw or the words they repeated. To some of them it was a game, to while away the leisure of a kingdom where governing was now done by default; local landlords enforced local laws, and national issues were only intermittently remembered. The young sons of nobility came to court and pretended to be in love with Henrietta Maria, writing sonnets to her dark curls, praising the whiteness of her skin. They hunted with Charles; they entertained him with singing, with dramas, with tableaux. It was an easy life, if inconsequential. Only the more intelligent or the more ambitious wanted more. Only the very few patriots thought that it was no way to run a kingdom which had once been thought of as a world power.

Henrietta Maria would have no talk of change. To assert English power abroad would need an effective army or navy and neither of these could be created without money. There was never any money in the royal coffers, and the only way to raise money was the invention of new and ingenious taxes which could create new revenue without recalling Parliament. The last thing either king or queen wanted was to recall Parliament and suffer the critical commentary of the House of Commons on their plans, on their expenditure, on their religious practices, on their household.

"Or we could borrow," Henrietta Maria suggested at a meeting of the king's council.

The men bowed. No one liked to tell the king and queen that England's credit was at rock bottom.

"Yes, that's it," Charles said, pleased. "See to it, my lord," and he smiled and went from the council meeting with the air of a man who has completed his work.

No one had the authority to call him back. Charles only listened to the queen and she listened to her confessor, to the French ambassador, to the favorites of her little court, to her servants and to anyone who took her fancy. She was beyond bribery and beyond corruption because her tastes were so fickle. Not even the French ambassador—representing her own country—could be sure of her full attention. She would look out of the window while he was speaking to her, or wander about the room, turning over pretty ornaments with her fingers, always distracted, always seeking distraction. Only in the king's presence were her thoughts focused. Her one genuine interest was ensuring that he attended to her, and to her alone.

"Well, she shared him for so long with your lord Buckingham," Elizabeth said to John as they got into bed one night. "She must always be wary that he might find another favorite."

John shook his head. "He's faithful," he said. "She's a plain ordinary little woman but she holds his heart now. You see no passion between them, and no liveliness, but he cleaves to her as if he were a little dog."

Elizabeth smiled. "The king a dog? You sound like J!"

"His eyes follow her around the room." John pulled on his nightcap. "And when he is watching her she is never still. She is always acting the part of a delightful woman." He pulled the blankets higher up the bed with a grunt of pleasure. "She would drive me mad," he said frankly.

Elizabeth sat up in bed and folded the sheet back over the blankets around his shoulders. "Nights are drawing in. Are you warm enough in your house at Oatlands?"

"Of course," John said. "The maggots and I live like lords. They have eight charcoal burners set around their house and I have all the benefit. You're a chilly companion compared to my maggots."

Elizabeth chuckled, not taking offense.

"He was a sad little boy," John continued, returning to the king. "I used to see him at Hatfield sometimes. King James had no time for him, and his mother never saw him. Nobody thought he'd ever be king with such a stronger older brother before him, so no one bothered with him. Some of them said he'd never survive. He doted on his older brother and sister, and the one died and the other was sent far away. It was only when my lord duke befriended him that he found someone to love."

"And then he died too," Elizabeth said.

John bowed his head. "God rest his soul. Now, all he has left is the queen, and the only real friend in the world she can be sure of is the king. Everyone else wants something from her or hopes to gain something from him through her. They must be lonely."

"Then why not live less rich?" Elizabeth suggested, practical as ever. "If they are surrounded by hangers-on and flatterers who do them no good, why not be rid of them? Why not spend time with their children? Why not seek out the men who care for their own consciences and would not hang on them and flatter them? God knows there were enough men of principle in the last Parliament; the king must have seen them often enough."

"The price a king must pay is the loss of his common sense," John said dryly. "I've seen it over and over, with kings and great men. They are lied to so sweetly and so often that they lose the taste of truth. They have sugar and honey dripped on their tongue until they are sick of the taste of it, but they still cannot call for bread and cheese."

"Poor them," Elizabeth said with cheerful irony.

"Poor them indeed," said John, thinking for a moment of his duke who died friendless at the end, and was buried at night and in secret.

Winter 1632–3

Jane was not well. She was tired all the time and disliked her food. Christmas came and went and she was no better. When Frances came running in to her parents on the morning of the twelfth day after Christmas for her presents she found her mother pale and sickly.

"Should she see a doctor?" Elizabeth asked J.

"She wants to go to her mother to stay for a few days," J said. "I'll take her tomorrow in the wagon."

"Leave Frances here," John said across the breakfast table. "You'll stay with your grandfather, won't you, Frances?"

He could see little of her but a head of golden brown curls and two interrogative curves of eyebrows. She bobbed upward. "Yes," she said firmly. "And we'll make things."

"What sort of things?" John asked cautiously.

"Big things," she said ominously.

"I'll stay overnight with the Hurtes and come back the next day," J said. "I'll call in at the docks in case there's anything of interest to be had on my way home."

"I'll put up a hamper for you to take," Elizabeth said, rising from the table. "Come and help me, Frances, you can go into the storeroom and choose a jar of plums for Grandma Hurte."

John did not go down to his orchard before Jane left. He waited by the wagon in the yard until he had seen her safely on the seat with her bags stowed. "You will come back soon," he said, in sudden anxiety.

She was pale but she still managed her familiar smile. "No, I shall stay with my mother and tell her you beat me and overwork me."

"You're very dear to me," John said gruffly. "I don't like to see you so pale."

She leaned forward to whisper in his ear. "I think I may be sick for a good reason," she said. "A very good reason. I've not told John yet, so mind you hush."

It took him a moment to realize what she meant and then he stepped back and beamed up at her. "Sir John Tradescant of Lambeth?"

"Sir John Tradescant himself," she said.

Summer 1633

It was an easy pregnancy for Jane this time, and the work at the palace was easy for her husband since in May the king left England on a grand progress north.

"He has sucked all the praise he can from the English," J said sourly to his wife. "He has to go to the poor Scots to see them dance to his tune."

She nodded but did not reply. She was sewing baby clothes on the terrace in the warm June night and John was within earshot.

"Have you heard how the king's progress is going?" she asked.

J nodded. "He went riding and hunting as he traveled up the north road. And everywhere he goes there are feasts and knighthoods and processions. He sees the country turn out to greet him and he thinks that all is well."

"And is it not?" Jane asked. Her hand went gently to the soft curve of her belly. "With Parliament dissolved and the country at peace? Is it perhaps only a few men like you, J, who are not content with this king?"

J shrugged. "How can I say? When I meet a lecturer or a traveling preacher they tell me of men arrested for talking out of turn and for complaining about unjust taxes. I know that there are more papists in the city than I have ever seen before and that they are allowed to hear Mass in the very heart of the kingdom. I know that the king's best friends are papists and his wife is a papist and the godparents of his child are papists. And I know that our own vicar at Lambeth is at odds with the new Archbishop of Canterbury, William Laud, who is bishop of everywhere it seems, and now archbishop overall. But you are right—there are no voices raised against it—maybe it is just me."

Jane leaned forward and touched his brown cheek. "And me," she said. "I don't thank the archbishop for ordering how I should pray. And Father is furious about the taxes. But there is nothing anyone can do. There's no Parliament—who can tell the king that he is doing wrong?"

"Especially not when the fools troop out and throw roses down in the road before his horse," J growled crossly. "And when he touches a bunch of poxed fools for the king's evil and convinces them they are cured by his hand."

Jane was silent for a moment. "I want to believe that better times are coming," she said.

The wistfulness in her voice caught J's attention. He took her hand and put his other hand gently on her belly. "They are for us," he said reassuringly. "Whatever is happening for the king and his foolish court. A new baby on the way and the garden growing well. These are good times for us, Jane, and better times coming."

John's prediction of a grandson was accurate. Jane gave birth to a large-boned brown-haired baby in the middle of the afternoon of a warm September day. J was picking apples at the farthest end of the orchard, finding the cries of Jane's labor quite unbearable. John and Frances were keeping each other company looking for the early fallen chestnuts down John's little avenue.

"We'll roast them," Frances teased her grandfather with the cleverness of the bright three-year-old.

"They're not sweet chestnuts." John fell into the trap. "They're no good for eating."

"It's no good as a tree then," she said innocently. "I don't like it."

"Oh, Frances . . . ," John started and then he saw the bright twinkle in her eyes. "You are a wicked girl!" he pronounced. "And I think I will beat you." He started to run toward her and she picked up her little gown and ran out of his reach, down the avenue of trees toward her father.

"John! J!" It was Elizabeth's voice, calling from the terrace. John saw his son's white face turn toward the house, then his slithering fall down the ladder, and then his run, past his daughter and his father, up the avenue toward the house.

"Is she all right?"

His mother's face alone was reassurance enough. "She's fine," she said. "Very tired. And you have a son."

J gave a little yelp of delight. "A son!" he yelled down the avenue where Tradescant was limping up with Frances bobbing in his wake. "A son! A boy!"

John checked and a broad smile spread across his face. He turned to Frances. "You have a brother," he told her. "Your mother has given birth to a little boy."

She was on her dignity, the powerful dignity of the three-year-old, and determined to be unimpressed. "Is that very good?" she asked.

John scooped her up and swung her to her usual place on his back. "It's very good," he said. "It means our name will last forever, with a son to continue the line. Sir John Tradescant of the Ark, Lambeth. It sounds very well indeed."

"I shall be a Sir too," Frances said, rather muffled with her face pressed into his back.

"Yes, you will," John said agreeably. "I shall make sure that the king knows that you need a knighthood, when we next speak."

Winter 1633–4

The queen took a fancy to J. It was as if she had to find some way of encompassing his refusal to do exactly as she wished about the oak tree. She could not leave his rejection of her plans alone; it rubbed the tender spot of her vanity. When she was walking in the gardens with her ladies, wrapped up in the richest of furs, or watching her courtiers practicing archery at the butts, she would stop if she saw J and call him over. "Here is my gardener who will only plant what he pleases!" she would exclaim in her strong French accent. "The young Tradescant."

J would take his hat off his head in the chill wind, in obedience to his father's instructions, and bow, but not very low, in obedience to his wife, and assume an expression of dogged patience as the queen was once more charming to him.

"I want you to plough up the allée of yews. It is so very dark and dreary now it is winter."

"Of course," J replied. "Only . . ."

"There you go!" she cried. "I can never do what I wish in my own garden; Tradescant will always have his own way. Why may I not have those trees grubbed out?"

J glanced down the court to the beautiful allée of trees. They were so old that they had bowed together and interlinked at the top so that they made a perfectly round tunnel. A bare brown earth path ran beneath them, marked with perfectly round white stepping stones. Nothing grew beneath them in the deep greeny light; not even in midsummer did the sunshine filter through. In the heat of the day it was as cool as a cave. To touch such trees other than to prune and shape them would be an act of wanton destruction.

"They are useful to Your Majesty for bows for your archers," he said politely. "The yew is specially grown for it; it is very strong, Your Majesty."

"We can get yew anywhere," she said lightly.

"Not as good as this."

She threw back her head and laughed like a little girl. J, who knew the ring of real laughter from a mischievous girl, was not impressed by the queen's coquetry.

"You see how it is? You see?" she demanded, turning to one of her courtiers. The young man smiled responsively. "I am allowed to do nothing with my own land. Tradescant, I am glad I am not your wife. Do you have a wife?"

"Yes, Your Majesty." J disliked it most when the queen became intimate with him.

"At your home? At—what do you call it?—the Ark?"

"Yes, Your Majesty."

"And children?"

"A boy, and an older girl."

"But this is very good," she exclaimed. "And do you adore your wife, Tradescant? Do you do her every wish?"

J hesitated.

"Not all wives are as fortunate as you, Your Majesty," the courtier swiftly interposed. "There can be few wives who have a husband who adores them as the king adores you. You are a goddess to His Majesty. You are a goddess to us all."

Henrietta Maria blushed a little and smiled. "Ah, that is true; but all the same, you must be kind to your little wife, Tradescant. I would have every woman in the kingdom as blessed as me."

J bowed to avoid answering.

"And she must be obedient to you," the queen went on. "And you must bring up your children to obey you both, just as the king and I are like kind parents to the country. Then both the country and your household will be at peace."

J pressed his tongue to his teeth to stop himself arguing and bowed again.

"And everyone will be happy," the queen said. She turned to the courtier. "Isn't that right?"

"Of course," he said simply. "As long as people remember that they must love and obey you and the king as if you were their parents, everyone will be happy."

J bore the brunt of the queen's interest because he was more often at Oatlands than his father in the autumn days. Elizabeth was sick in October with pains in her chest and a nagging cough which would not be eased, and John did not want to leave her.

She got up from her bed to see Baby John baptized at their church in November, but she left the baptismal feast early and John found her lying on their bed shivering, though the maid had lit a fire in the bedroom.

"My dear," he said. "I did not know you were so ill."

"I'm cold," she said. "Cold in my bones."

John heaped more logs on the fire and took another quilt from the press at the foot of the bed. Still her face was white and her fingertips were icy.

"You'll mend in the spring," he said cheerfully. "When the ground warms up and the daffodils come out."

"I'm not a plant, shedding my leaves," she protested through her pale lips. "I won't bloom like a tree."

"But you will bloom," John said, suddenly anxious. "You will get better, Lizzie."

She shook her head so slightly that he could hardly see the movement on the pillow.

"Don't say so!" he cried. "I had always thought I would go first. You're years younger than me; this is just a chill!"

Again she made that small movement. "It is more than a chill," she said. "There is a bone growing in me, pressing on me. I can feel it pressing against my breath."

"Have you seen a physician?" John demanded.

She nodded. "He could not find anything wrong, but I can feel it inside, John. I don't think I will see your daffodils next spring."

He could feel his throat tightening and his eyes burning. "Don't say such a thing!"

She smiled and turned her head to look at him. "Of all the men who could do without their wives you would be the first," she said. "Half of our married life you have been away with your gardens or on your travels, and the other half you were with your lord."

The usual complaint struck him very painfully now she said it for the last time. "Did I neglect you? I thought—you had J and your house—and it was my life before I married you . . . I thought . . ."

Elizabeth gave him her gentle, forgiving smile. "Your work came first," she said simply, "and your lord before everything. But I had third place in your life. You never loved a woman more than you loved me, did you, John?"

Tradescant had a brief memory of a dimpled serving girl at Theobalds, decades, it seemed like centuries, ago, and a dozen half-remembered women between then and now.

"No," he said, and he spoke the truth. "None that came anywhere near my love for you. I did put the gardens first, and my lord before all else, but there was always you, Elizabeth. You were the only woman for me."

"And what a long way we have come," she said wonderingly. Through the wooden floorboards of their bedroom came the muffled sounds of the baptismal party. They could hear Josiah Hurte's voice above all the others, and then, in a sudden silence, Frances's delighted giggle as someone swung her up in the air.

John nodded. "A grand house, a collection of rarities, a nursery garden and an orchard, and a post at the king's palace."

"And grandchildren," Elizabeth said with satisfaction. "I feared when there was only J—and then when they had only Frances . . ."

"That there would be no one to carry our name?"

She nodded. "I know it is a vanity . . ."

"There are the trees," John said. "The flowers, the fruits, and my chestnut trees. We nursed them up just as we nursed J. And now there is one in all the greatest gardens of the country. That is our legacy. The chestnut trees we nursed up together."

She turned her head and closed her eyes. "You *would* say that," she said, but it was not a complaint.

"You lie quiet," John said, rising stiffly from the bed. "I will send up the maid with a posset for you. Lie quiet and get well. You will see my daffodils this spring, Elizabeth, and even the pink and white candle blossoms on our chestnut trees."

In January, as the new baby thrived, and Elizabeth grew weaker and never left her bed, J found his father supervising the lad digging up a small chestnut sapling and transplanting it, roots and all, into a large carrying tub. J and the boy slid their carrying poles into the rings of the tub and moved it, as John directed them, right into the house, into the rarities room, and set it down beside the huge window where it would catch the winter light.

"What are you doing?"

"Forcing it," John said abruptly.

Beside the tub was a big half-barrel of daffodils that had been lifted from the orchard, their green shoots only just showing above the damp earth.

"We need an orangery," John said. "We should have built one years ago."

"We do," J agreed. "But for delicate plants from abroad; not for daffodils and chestnut saplings. What are you doing with them?"

"I want to get them in flower," John said. "As soon as I can force them."

"Why?"

"To please your mother," John said, telling only half the story.

* * *

Every night John banked in the fire so the plants were warm all night, every day he sprinkled them—three, four times a day—with warm water. In the evening he set candles around them to give them extra light and warmth. J would have laughed but there was something about his father's intensity which puzzled him.

"Why d'you want them to bloom early?"

"I have my reasons," John said.

Spring 1634

John achieved his goal. When Elizabeth died in March, her room was filled with the golden light of dozens of daffodils, and the sweet scent of them perfumed her room. The very last thing she saw as her eyes wearily closed was John coming in the door, his face warm with a smile, and his hands filled with the exquisite pink and white pyramid blossoms of his chestnut trees.

"For you," he said and bent and kissed her.

Elizabeth tried to say, "Thank you. I love you, John," but the darkness was creeping in; and in any case, he knew.

After the funeral John moved back to the silk house at Oatlands for the rest of the season. He did not feel that he wanted to be at his home, without Elizabeth. At night he could not sleep; but he liked the warmth of the pretty wooden house, and there was something strangely comforting about the thought of the thousands of silkworms, sleeping in their little cocoons, next door, dreaming whatever dreams silkworms spin.

The queen had authorized the building of a coalhouse and a new and beautiful orangery, and John supervised the building in the short hours of springtime daylight. It was another light-timbered fanciful building like a little wooden palace. It went up quickly and John wrote to J, telling him to bring some citrus whips when he next came.

Apart from the building, there was little to do in the gardens in the cold spring days, but John liked to walk around and see that the streams and fountains were clear of leaves, and that the little green snouts of bulbs were pushing their way defiantly through the cold earth. When it was warmer he would plant a new bowling green for Their Majesties, and he watched the men digging, rolling and harrowing the earth until every smallest stone was gone and the ground was ready for the seed. They grumbled when he made them dig in the old rotted dung from the stables and then water it till it froze and melted and froze again, but John insisted that the ground be rich and smooth before the seed was scattered.

When the snowdrops were thick as ice under the trees, snow-white and green, John thought of his lord Buckingham, who had loved to see the first snowdrops at New Hall. But when the daffodils came through he thought of Elizabeth, who had died with their golden color all around her. There could be no doubt that Elizabeth had gone straight to heaven, he thought. She had lived a life which was as blameless as any woman's, and she had died surrounded by that golden blaze of glory. At least he had been able to give her that.

As for the duke, it was impossible that there could be a God who loved beauty who could resist him. The king himself loved him and prayed for his soul every day. John felt that the two people in the world that he had truly loved were at peace, and he found he could bear the short cold days and the long cold nights.

He was thinking of the two loves of his life—his passion for the duke and his steady reliable affection for Elizabeth—and watching the water in the fountain of the great court when a shadow fell on the basin of the fountain and he looked around. It was the king. John pulled his hat from his head and dropped to his knee on the cold stone.

"How many years is it now, since your master died?" the king asked abruptly. He did not look at John, but kept his gaze on the cold water in the marble basin.

"Five years and seven months," John said instantly. "He died toward the end of summer."

"You can get up," the king said. He turned from the fountain and started to walk down the path, a small gesture that commanded John to follow him.

"I don't think a man like that can ever be r . . . r . . . replaced," the king said, half to himself. "Not in a king's council, not in the heart."

John felt the usual dull ache at the thought of Buckingham.

"And a woman's love is not the same," the king remarked. "To please a woman you have to try and keep trying, and women are changeable: first one thing pleases them, then another. But a man's love is easier, s . . . steadier. When George and I were young men we spent whole days thinking of nothing but hunting and play. The king used to call us his dear l . . . l . . . lads."

John nodded. The king paused and abruptly turned to him. "Did you ever see my brother Henry?"

"Yes," John said. "I was gardener at Theobalds, and then for my lord Cecil at Hatfield. I saw Prince Henry and King James often; I remember you too, Your Majesty."

"Do you think he was like the D . . . Duke of Buckingham? My brother? In his ways?"

John thought. They had the same arrogance, the same easy smile. They had the same sense that the world was half in love with them and that all they had to do was to accept homage.

"Yes," he said slowly. "The prince was like the duke in many ways. But the duke had . . ." He broke off.

"What?"

"The duke had that shining beauty," John said. "The prince was a handsome boy, as handsome as any. But the duke was as beautiful as an angel."

Charles suddenly smiled, his grave face warming. "He was, wasn't he?" he said. "It's so easy to f . . . forget. All the portraits I have of him show his beauty, but all p . . . portraits are beautiful even when the sitters are plain. It's good to know that you keep a picture of him in your heart, Tradescant."

"I do," John said simply. "I see him night and day. And sometimes I dream of him."

"As if he w . . . w . . . were alive?"

John nodded. "I can never remember in my dreams that he is dead," he confessed. "And sometimes I wake and think he is calling for me, and I jump from my bed as if I were a young man and in a hurry to go to him."

"The queen didn't l . . . like him," the king said thoughtfully.

Tradescant tactfully said nothing.

"She was jealous."

Tradescant gave a little nod. The king glanced at him. "Was your wife jealous of your love for your lord?"

Tradescant thought of Elizabeth and her long enmity for the duke and all he stood for: luxury, popery, waste and carnal sin.

"Oh, yes," he said with a smile. "But women were always besotted with him or his worst enemy, or both."

The king laughed shortly. "It's true. He was a l . . . lamentable man with women."

The gardener and the king smiled at one another, the king looking into Tradescant's face for the first time.

"D'you have any of his things at your Ark?" the king asked.

"Some plants from the garden at New Hall, and a couple of rarities from the Ile de Rhé," Tradescant replied carefully, conscious of the danger of this conversation. "He gave me some things from his own collection of rarities. Anything he did not need, anything he already had. I was collecting for him for many years."

"I'll come and see it," the king said. "I'll bring the queen. I have some things you might l . . . like, some gloves and things."

Tradescant bowed low. "I should be honored."

When he rose up the king was looking at him as if they shared a secret. "He was a very very great man, wasn't he?"

"Yes," Tradescant agreed, looking at the king's melancholy face and sparing him the truth, as everyone always did. "He was the greatest lord in England and the most fit for his high office."

The king nodded and turned away without another word. Tradescant, unseen, knelt again as the king strolled off. When the king had gone he got awkwardly to his feet; his bad knee was painful in the cold weather.

* * *

While John was at Oatlands, J stayed at Lambeth. Jane was now complete mistress of the house and the place was run with godly care. The day started with prayers for the household which J read aloud and then any one of them, from the youngest kitchen maid to the senior gardener, would pray extempore, saying what that person wished to the congregation and to his or her own personal God. The household went about their work all day and then came together again in the evening, before bedtime, for another brief session of praying together. Imperceptibly, the dress of the household altered, the servants naturally copying Jane's modest muted style.

J rather thought that his father would complain when he finally returned home, but there was no explosion of disapproval.

"You must run the house as you wish," he said equably to Jane. "You are the mistress here now. You must order what you wish."

"I think it is what everyone wishes," Jane said eagerly.

John gave her a little knowing smile. "But what if it were not?" he asked. "What if the cook and the kitchen maid, Peter and the two gardeners and their lad all agreed that they would rather have some dancing and some singing and a cup of ale instead? That they wanted to wear green and scarlet and ribbons in their hair? Would you provide it?"

"I would reason with them," Jane said stiffly. "And wrestle with their souls."

"So people are free to do as they wish as long as they choose right?"

"Yes," she said; and then, "No, not exactly."

John smiled at her. "When you have power over people, it is very easy to forget that they are doing as you order because you order it," he said. "You can mistake obedience for consent. I say that my household shall be obedient to you. I don't think that they prefer it that way. But they will be obedient to you because I order it. However, I shall come to prayers only now and then—when I really want to."

"I am sure you would find it a comfort . . ." Jane began.

John patted her cheek. "I think you are wrestling with my soul," he said. "I want my soul left in peace."

Jane smiled at him. "All right," she conceded. "D'you want to see Baby John?"

"Yes," John said.

Frances brought the baby and placed him carefully in his grandfather's lap. Baby John put his fists against his grandfather's chest, reared back and inspected his face.

"He still doesn't eat properly," Frances said disapprovingly.

"Why not?" John asked.

"He still sucks," Frances said. "He's like a little goat."

John smiled. "Don't you love your little brother?" he asked.

Frances drew closer to him. "He's all right," she said. "But I don't like how everyone makes such a fuss of him. I'm still your favorite, aren't I, Granddad?"

John kept one hand firmly on Baby John, and with the other drew his granddaughter to him and kissed her smooth warm head, just before the plain white cap which Jane insisted that she wear.

"It's not always the best thing to be, the Favorite," he said, thinking of his lord and the parliament that impeached him, and the king who mourned for him.

"Yes it is," she said instantly. "I was always your favorite and I still am."

He settled her into the crook of his arm. "Yes, you are," he said. "You are my precious girl."

"And when I am grown I shall be gardener to the king," she said firmly. "And run the Ark."

"Girls cannot be gardeners," John said gently.

"Cook says that girls can be gardeners because women are equal to men at the Day of Judgment," Frances volunteered. "And that prophesying and preaching comes natural to women who es . . . es . . . eschew carnival knowledge."

"I think you mean carnal knowledge," John said unsteadily.

"Carnival," Frances corrected him. "It means you can't go maypole dancing or buy fairings, or play in the churchyard on feast days."

"I suppose it does," John said. He was very near to laughter but he managed to turn it into a gruff cough.

"And I am going to eschew carnival knowledge and be free of sin," Frances went on. "And then I can be the king's gardener."

"We'll see," John said pacifically.

"Is Baby John going to be the king's gardener?" she demanded.

John nestled the baby back into his arm and took up the plump dimpled hand. "I think he's too small to work yet," he said tactfully. "Whereas you're a great big girl. By the time he's ready for work you'll have been prophesying and gardening for years."

It was exactly the right answer. Frances beamed at him and went to the door. "I have to go now," she said seriously. "I've got some seedlings that want watering."

John nodded. "You see? You're a gardener already and all Baby John can do is sit inside with his grandfather."

Frances nodded and slipped through the door. John looked out of the window and saw her heaving the heavy watering bottle down toward the seed beds set against the warm south wall. Her little thumb was too small to fit the hole at the top of the bottle and she was sprinkling a shiny trail of water behind her like a determined snail.

January 1635

The letter that arrived for the Tradescants at Lambeth bore the royal stamp on the bottom. It was a demand for a tax, a new tax, another new tax. John opened it in the rarities room, standing beside the Venetian windows to catch the light, J beside him.

"It's a tax to support the Navy," he said. "Ship money."

"We don't pay that," J said at once. "That's only for the ports and the seaside towns who need the protection of the Navy against pirates and smugglers."

"Looks like we *do* pay it," John said grimly. "I imagine that everyone is going to have to pay it."

J swore and took a brief step down the room and back again. "How much?"

"Enough," John said. "Do we have savings?"

"We have my last quarter's wages untouched, but that was to buy cuttings and seeds this spring."

"We'll have to dip into that," John told him.

"Can we refuse to pay?"

John shook his head.

"We should refuse," J declared passionately. "The king has no right to levy taxes. Parliament levies the taxes and passes the money raised on to the king. He has no right to demand on his own account. It is Parliament that should consent to the tax, and any complaint the people have is heard in Parliament. The king cannot just charge what he pleases. Where is it to end?"

John shook his head again. "The king has closed down Parliament, and I doubt he'll invite them back. The world has changed, J, and the king is uppermost. If he sets a tax then we have to pay. We have no choice."

J glared at his father. "You always say we have no choice!" he exclaimed.

John looked wearily at his son. "And you always bellow like a Ranter. I know you think me an old fool, J. So tell me your way. You refuse to pay the tax; the king's men or the parish officers come and arrest you for treason. You are thrown into prison. Your wife and children go hungry. The business collapses; the Tradescants are ruined. This is a master plan, J. I applaud you."

J looked as if he were about to burst out but then he laughed a short bitter laugh. "Aye," he said. "Very well. You're in the right. But it sticks in my throat."

"It'll stick in many throats," John predicted. "But they'll pay."

"There will come a time when they will refuse," J warned his father. "You cannot choke a country year after year and not have to face the people at the end of it. There will come a time when good men will refuse in such numbers that the king has to listen."

"Maybe," John said thoughtfully. "But who can say when?"

"If the king knew that his subjects object, that they don't like being ordered to church and the prayers ordered for them, that they don't like being ordered to play like children in the churchyard after the service, that there are men in the country who want to use the Lord's Day for thought and reflection and who don't want to practice archery and sports—if the king knew all that—"

"Yes, but he doesn't know that," John pointed out. "He dismissed the men who might have told him, and those left at court would never bring him bad news."

"You could tell him," J observed.

"I'm no better than the rest of them," John replied. "I've learned to be a courtier. Maybe it's late in life, but I've learned it now. I told the truth as I saw it to all the lords I ever served and I never flattered one of them with lies. But this king is a man who doesn't invite the truth. I tell you, J, I *cannot* speak the truth to him. He is surrounded by fancy. I would not dare to be the one to tell him that he and the queen are not adored everywhere they go; I couldn't tell him that the men he has thrown into prison are not wild men, madmen, hotheads, but men more sane and careful and honorable than the rest of us. I cannot be the one to tell him that he is in the wrong and the country is slowly coming to know it. He has made sure that the world appears as best pleases him. It would take more than me to turn it upside down."

The king kept his promise to visit the Ark, though Tradescant had thought it was a royal promise—one thrown off in the moment with no thought other than to please by the graciousness of the intention. But early in January a Gentleman Usher of the court came to the Ark and was shown into the rarities room.

He looked around, concealing his surprise. "It's an imposing room," he remarked to J, who had shown him in. "I had not thought you had built such a grand room."

J inwardly congratulated his father for overweening ambition. "We need a lot of accommodation," he said modestly. "Every day we get something new for the collection, and the things need to be shown in the best light."

The usher nodded. "The king and queen will visit you tomorrow at noon," he said. "They want to see this famous collection."

J bowed. "We will be honored."

"They will not dine here, but you may offer them biscuits and wine and fruit," the usher said. "I assume you will have no difficulty with that?"

J nodded. "Of course."

"And there is no need for any loyal address, or anything of that sort," the usher said. "No poem of greeting or anything like that. This is just an informal visit."

J thought that the king and queen were very unlikely to get a poem of greeting from his staunchly independent wife but he merely nodded his assent. "I understand."

"And if there are any in your household who suffer from strong and misguided views—" the usher paused to make sure that J was following him "—it is your responsibility to make sure that they do not appear before Their Majesties. The king and queen do not want to see long Puritanical faces on their visit; they do not want anyone reflecting on them. Make sure that only your well-dressed and joyful neighbors are on the road."

"I can make sure that they enjoy their visit to my house, but I cannot clear Lambeth of beggars and paupers," J replied sharply. "Are they coming by boat?"

"Yes; their carriage will meet them at Lambeth."

"Then they should drive swiftly through Lambeth," J remarked unhelpfully. "Or they may see some of their subjects who are not happy and smiling."

The usher looked at him sharply. "If anyone fails to uncover his head and shout 'God save the king,' he will be sorry for it," he warned. "There are men in prison for treason for less. There are men with cropped ears and slit tongues who did nothing more than refuse to take their hats off when the royal carriage went by."

J nodded. "They will meet with nothing but courtesy and respect in my house," he said. "But I am not responsible for the crowd on the quayside by the horse-ferry."

"I am responsible for them," the gentleman usher replied. "And I think you will find that every one of them shouts for the king."

He swung back his coat and J saw the bag of pennies at his belt.

"Good," J said. "Then I am sure Their Majesties will have a merry visit."

He had feared that Jane would be rebellious, but the challenge to her housekeeping was such that, for the moment, she put aside her principles. She sent a message to her mother in the city and Mrs. Hurte arrived at dawn on the day of the royal visit with her own store of damask tablecloths, and her own box of ginger biscuits and sugared plums. Josiah Hurte had disapproved; but the women were on their mettle and were determined that there should be no critical comments at the court about the chief gardener's house.

The rarities room and the parlor had been swept and polished ever since the gentleman usher had left the house. Jane laid the table in the parlor and set the fire against the cold of the January day, while J and his father prowled around the rarities room for the hundredth time, ensuring that every case stood open and that every rarity—even the smallest carved hazelnut shell—was laid out to its best advantage.

When everything was polished and prepared, there was nothing to do but wait.

Frances went to sit on the front garden wall at half past ten. At eleven, John sent the garden lad down the road to keep watch and give them warning when he saw the royal carriage roof rocking down the bumpy road toward them. At midday Frances came in, her fingertips blue with cold, saying that there was no sign of them, and that the king was a liar and a fool.

Jane shushed her and rushed her to the kitchen to get warm before the fire.

At two o'clock John said that he was too starved to wait, and went to the kitchen for a bowl of soup. Frances, perched on her stool and with her face inside a large bowl of broth, emerged only to say that the king shouldn't say he was coming if he did not mean it, as it caused a lot of people, especially those who had to wait in the cold, a great deal of discomfort.

"If he's the king, he should do what he promises."

"You're not the first to think that," John remarked.

At three o'clock, after tempers had frayed and the fires in the parlor and the rarities room had burned down and been renewed, there was a thunderous knocking at the garden door and the lad poked his frozen face into the room, his nose blue with cold, and said, "They're coming at last!"

Frances screamed and ran for her cloak, all complaints forgotten, and rushed to her station on the front wall. J leaped from his seat at the kitchen table, wiped his mouth and rubbed his hands on the cloth.

John pulled on his best coat, which he had laid aside in the heat of the kitchen, and rolled, with his limping gait, to the front door to hold it open as the king and queen visited the Ark.

Their Majesties did not see Frances as the coach drew up, though she stood up on the wall and did her best curtsey, perched on top. When they walked past her without even a glance in her direction, Frances, who had hoped to be appointed as the king's gardener on that very day, scrambled down from the wall, tore round to the back door and stationed herself by the door of the rarities room, where they could not possibly miss her as they entered.

"Your Majesties." John bowed low as the queen stepped over the threshold. J, behind him, matched his bow.

"Ah, Tradescant!" the queen said. "Here we are to see your rarities, and the king has brought you some things for your collection."

The king waved at an usher, who unfolded a bolt of cloth. Inside was a handsome pair of light suede gloves.

"King Henry's hunting gloves," the king said. "And some other goods you can see at your leisure. Now show me your treasures."

John led the way around the room. The king wanted to see everything: the carved ivories, the monstrous egg, the beautifully carved cup of rhinoceros horn, the Benin drum, the worked Senego leather, the letter case a woman on the Ile de Rhé had tried to smuggle out of the fort by swallowing it, the curious crystals and stones, the body of the mermaid from Hull, the skull of the unicorn and the animal and bird skins, including that of a strange and ugly flightless bird.

"This is remarkable," the king said. "And what is in these drawers?"

"Small and large eggs, Your Majesty," John said. "I had the drawers especially made to house them."

The king drew open one drawer and then another. John had arranged the eggs in size from the smallest in shallow drawers at the top to the largest in deep wide drawers at the bottom. The eggs, all colors from speckled black to purest shining white, sat on their little beds of sheep's wool like precious jewels.

"What a flock of birds you would have if they hatched!" the king exclaimed.

"They are all blown, and light as air, Your Majesty," Tradescant explained, giving him a tiny blue eggshell, no larger than his fingertip.

"And what is this?" the king said, returning the egg and moving on.

"These are dried flower blossoms of many rarities from my garden," John said, pulling out tray after tray of flower heads. "My wife used to dry them in sugar for me, so that men might come and see the blossoms at any time of year. Often an artist will come and draw them."

"Pretty," the queen said approvingly, looking at the tray with the flowers laid out.

"This is from the Lack tulip, which I bought for my lord Buckingham in the Low Countries," John said, touching one perfect petal with the tip of his finger.

"Does it grow still?" the king asked, looking at the petal as if it might hold some memory of its lord.

"Yes," John said gently. "It grows still."

"I should like to have it," the king said. "In memory of him."

John bowed as he gave away a tulip worth a year's income. "Of course, Your Majesty."

"And many mechanical things? Do you have mechanical toys?" the king asked. "When I was a boy I had a small army made of lead with cannons which actually fired shot. I planned my campaigns with them; I had part of Richmond laid out as a battlefield and drew my men up in the proper way for an attack."

"I have a little model windmill, as they use in the Low Countries for pumping out their ditches," John said, crossing to the other side of the room. He moved the sails with his hand and the king could see the pump inside going up and down.

"And I have a miniature clock, and a model cannon." John directed the king to another corner. "And a miniature spinning wheel carved in amber."

"And what do you have from my lord Buckingham's collection?" the king asked.

J, suddenly wary, glanced at his father.

"Something very dear to me and worth all the rest put together," John said. He drew the king to a cabinet under the window and opened one of the drawers.

"What's this?" the king asked.

"The last letter he ever wrote to me," John said. "Ordering me to Portsmouth, to meet him for the expedition to Rhé."

The queen glanced over at them with impatience; even now she did not like to hear Buckingham's name on the king's lips. "What's the largest rarity you have?" she asked J loudly.

"We have the whole head of an elephant, with its great double teeth," J said, pointing up to where they had hung the skull from the roof beams. "And a rhinoceros horn and jawbone."

The king did not even turn his head, but unfolded the letter. "His own hand!" he cried as soon as he saw the dashed careless style. He read it. "And he commands you to go at once," he said. "Oh, Tradescant, if only everything had been ready at once!"

"I was there," John said. "Just as he wished."

"But he was late, weeks late," the king said, smiling ruefully. "Wasn't that just like him?"

"And what is *your* favorite?" the queen demanded loudly.

"I think I like the Chinese fan the best," J said. "It is so delicate and so fine-painted."

He opened a drawer, took it out and laid it in her hand. "Oh! I must have one just like it!" she exclaimed. "Charles! Look!"

Reluctantly he looked up from the letter. "Very pretty," he said.

"Come and see," she commanded. "You can't see the painting from there!"

He handed back the page of paper to John and went toward her. With a sense of relief, J saw that the question of how many of the exhibits had been the property of Lord Buckingham had completely slipped away.

"I must have one just like this!" she cried. "I shall borrow this and have it copied."

J was not courtier enough to assent. John stepped quickly forward. "Your Majesty, we would be honored if you would have it as a gift," he said.

"Do you not need it in your collection, to show to people?" she asked, opening her eyes wide.

John bowed. "The collection, the Ark itself, is all yours, Your Majesty, as everything lovely and rare must be yours. You shall decide what you leave here, and what you take."

She laughed delightedly and for a moment J was afraid that her greed would outrun her desire to seem charming. "I shall leave everything here, of course!" she said. "But whenever you have something new and rare and pretty I shall come and see it."

"We will be honored," J said, with a sense of a danger narrowly avoided. "Will Your Majesty take a glass of wine?"

The queen turned for the door. "But who is this?" she asked as Frances leaped forward and opened the door for her. "A little footman?"

"I'm Frances," the little girl said. She had forgotten all about the curtsey which Jane had reluctantly taught her. "I was waiting for you for ages."

For a moment J thought that the queen would take offense. But then she laughed her girlish laugh. "I am sorry to keep you waiting!" she exclaimed. "But am I what you thought a queen would be?"

Both John and J moved forward, J smoothly standing beside Frances and giving her thin shoulder blade a swift admonitory pinch, while John filled the pause. "She was expecting Queen Elizabeth," he said. "We have a miniature of Her Majesty, painted on ivory. She did not know that a queen could be so young and beautiful."

Henrietta Maria laughed. "And a wife, and the mother of a son and heir," she reminded him. "Unlike the poor heretic queen." Frances gasped in horror and was about to argue but to J's enormous relief the queen went past the little girl without another glance. Jane threw open the parlor door and curtseyed.

"I wasn't expecting Queen Elizabeth, and anyway she wasn't a heret—" Frances started to argue. J leaned heavily on her shoulder as the king went past.

"She is my first granddaughter and has been much indulged," John explained.

The king looked down at her. "You must repay favor with duty," he said firmly.

"I will," Frances said easily. "But may I come and work for you and be your gardener, as my grandfather and father do? I am very good with seeds and I can take cuttings and some of them do grow."

It would have cost the king nothing to smile and say yes; but he was always a man who could be ambushed by shyness, and by his own desire to be seen to do the right thing. With only one person had he been free of his need to set an example, to be kingly and wise in all things; and that man was long dead.

"M . . . maids and wives must stay at home," he decreed, ignoring Frances's shocked little face. "Everyone in their r . . . right place is what I wish for my kingdom now. You must obey your father and then your husband." Then he passed on toward the parlor.

J threw a quick harassed glance at Frances's appalled face, and followed him.

Frances looked up at her grandfather, and saw that his face was warm with sympathy. She turned and pitched into his arms.

"I think the king is a pig," she wailed passionately into his coat. John, a lifelong royalist, could not disagree.

Mrs. Hurte went home that evening, pleasantly shocked and appalled by the queen's jewels, the richness of her perfume, the king's lustrous hair, his cane, his lace. As the wife of a mercer, she had taken particular note of their cloth and she was anxious to hurry home with news of French silk and Spanish lace, while English weavers and spinners went hungry. The king had a diamond on his finger the size of Frances's fist, and the queen had pearls in her ears the size of pigeon's eggs, and she had worn a cross, a crucifix, a most ungodly and unrighteous symbol. She had worn it like a piece of jewelry—heresy and vanity in one. She had worn it on her throat, an invitation to carnal thoughts as well. She was a heretical wicked woman and Mrs. Hurte could not wait to get home to her husband and confirm his worst fears.

"Come and see me next month," she said, pressing Jane to her heart before she left. "Your father wants to see you, and bring Baby John."

"I have to be here to guard the rarities when Father Tradescant and John are away," Jane reminded her.

"When they are both here then," her mother said. "Do come. Your father will want to know about Oatlands too. Did you see the quality of the lace she wore on her head? It would buy you a house inside the city walls, I swear it."

Jane packed her mother into the wagon and handed her the basket with the empty jars and the crumpled tablecloths.

"No wonder the country is in the state it is," Mrs. Hurte said, deliciously shocked.

Jane nodded, and stood back from the wagon as the man flipped the reins on the horses' backs.

"God bless you," Mrs. Hurte called lovingly. "Wasn't she a scandal!"

"A scandal," Jane agreed and stood at the back gate and waved until the wagon was out of sight.

Spring 1635

Jane did not visit her mother all through the spring. Both John and J were either at Oatlands Palace or busy in the orchards and garden of Lambeth. There was always someone knocking at the garden door with a little plant in a pot, or some precious thing in a knotted handkerchief, and Jane would judge its value and buy it with the authority of a good housewife and a partner in the business. Then, there were the tulips to be watched into leaf and into flower. John had ordered an orangery to be built for them to raise up the tender plants and the builders needed to be watched as they knocked a doorway through into the main house. It was not until May that Jane felt she had enough leisure to leave the Ark and go to see her mother in the city. But then she went and stayed for a week.

The house was oddly empty without her. Frances did not miss her much; she was always her grandfather's shadow, and when he was away she was always out in the garden with her father. But Baby John, nearly two, toddled round the house and demanded all day, "Where's Mama? Where's Mama?"

They expected her to come home rested and happy after a week's cosseting in her old home, but when she finally returned she was tired and pale. The city had been unbearably hot, she said. There were more beggars on the streets than ever; she had seen a man dying in the gutter and had feared to touch him in case he was carrying the plague.

"What sort of country is this, that the act of a good Samaritan is too dangerous to do?" she demanded, genuinely grieved at the struggle between her conscience and her safety.

Her father and all the merchants were complaining that they were taxed for trading, and then taxed for selling, and then taxed for storing goods. They too were ordered to pay ship money, which was set by an assessor who would come around and guess how much you were worth by the appearance of your house and business, and there was no appeal against him.

Josiah Hurte had to stand the charge of paying for his own lecturer in his own chapel, and also had to pay his parish dues to a church he never entered, and tithes to a vicar he despised for Roman practices. Meanwhile the price of goods soared; there were pirates openly operating up and down the English Channel; there were rumors of a rebellion in Ireland; and the king was said to spend more on his collection of pictures than he did on the Navy.

Jane, as the wife and daughter-in-law of a man in the employ of the court, had been pestered for scandalous details and had suffered from association. "Nothing good will come from this king," her father had said. "You may think your husband is high in his favor but nothing good can come from him because he is a king halfway to damnation already. And if you do not beware, he will drag you all down with him. Now that your father-in-law and husband have a fair house in Lambeth, why can they not bide there?"

Useless to try to explain to Josiah that if this king issued a command you could be hanged for treason if you said "no." "The king himself ordered it," Jane said. "How could we refuse?"

"By simply refusing," her father said stoutly.

"And do you refuse to pay your taxes? Do you refuse to pay ship money? Other men do."

"And they lie in prison," Josiah said. "And shame the rest of us who are less staunch. No, I do as I am ordered."

"And so does my husband," Jane insisted, defending the Tradescants despite herself. "The king and court take our skills and service just as they take your money. This king takes whatever he desires and nothing can stop him."

"You must be glad to be home," J said in bed that night. He put his arm around her and she rested her head against his shoulder.

"I'm so tired," she said fretfully.

"Then rest," he said. He turned her face toward him and kissed her lips but she moved away.

"The room stinks of honeysuckle," she cried suddenly. "You've brought cuttings into the bedroom again, John! I won't have it."

"No," he said. He could feel a small niggle of fear, as small as a seedling, in his heart. "There's nothing in the room. Does the air smell sweet to you, Jane?"

She suddenly realized what she had said, and what he was thinking, and she clapped her hand over her mouth as if she would hide her words and stop her breath from reaching him. "Oh God, no," she said. "Not that."

"Was it in the city?" John asked urgently.

"It's always in the city," she said bitterly. "But I spoke to no one knowingly."

"Not the servants, not the apprentice boys?"

"Would I take the risk? Would I have come home if I had thought I was carrying it?"

She was half out of bed, throwing back the covers and throwing open the window, her hand still cupped over her mouth as if she did not want the smallest breath to escape. John reached out for her but did not pull her to him. His fear of the illness was as great as his love for her. "Jane! Where are you going?"

"I'll get them to make me up a bed in the new orangery," she said. "And you must put my food and water at the door, and not come near me. The children are to be kept away. And my bedding is to be burned when it is dirty. And burn candles around the door."

He would have held her but she turned on him with a face of such fury that he recoiled. "Get away from me!" she screamed at him. "D'you think I want to give it to you? D'you think I want to tear down this house which has been the joy of my life to build up?"

"No . . . ," John stammered. "But Jane, I love you, I want to hold you . . ."

"If I survive," she promised, her face softening, "then we will spend weeks in each other's arms. I swear it, John. I love you. But if I die you are not even to touch me. You are to order them to bolt down the coffin and not even to look at me."

"I can't bear it!" he cried suddenly. "This can't happen to us!"

Jane opened the door and called down the stairs. "Sally! Make up a bed for me in the orangery, and put all my clothes in there."

"If I take it, I will join you," John said. "And we will be together then."

She turned her determined face to him. "You will not take it," she said passionately. "You will live to care for Baby John, and for Frances, and for the trees and the gardens. Even if I die there is still Baby John to carry your name, and the trees and the gardens."

"Jane—" It was a low cry, like a hurt animal's.

She did not soften for a moment. "Keep my children from me," she ordered harshly. "If you love me at all. Keep them from me."

And she turned, gathered up all the clothes she had brought from the city, went down the stairs into the new-built orangery, lay down on the pallet bed which the maid had thrown on the floor and looked up to where the warm summer moonlight poured in the little window in the wooden wall, and wondered if she would die.

On the fourth day Jane found swollen lumps under her arms, and she could not remember where she was. She had a lucid interval at midday and when John came to speak to her from the doorway, behind the wall of candle flame, she told him to put a lock on the door so that she could not come out looking for Baby John, when she was out of her mind with the fever.

On the fifth day a message came from her mother to say that one of the apprentices had taken the plague and that Jane should burn everything she had worn or brought from her visit. They sent back the messenger with the news that the warning came too late, that already there was a white cross on the front door, and a warden standing outside to make sure that no one left the house to spread the plague in Lambeth. All the goods and groceries, and even the new rarities, were left on the little bridge which led from the road to the house, and all the money was left in a bowl of vinegar, to wash the coins clean. No one would go near the Tradescants' door until they were all recovered or dead. The parish wardens were legally bound to make sure that any plague victims were isolated in their houses until they were proven to be dead or proven to be clean, and no one—not even the Tradescants with their fine business and their royal connections—could escape the ruling.

On the sixth day of her illness Jane did not tap on the door to have it unlocked in the morning. When John opened it and looked in, she was lying on the bed, her hair tumbled all over her pillow, her face thin and ghastly. When she saw him peering in she tried to smile, but her lips were too cracked and sore from fever.

"Pray for me," she said. "And don't take the plague, John. Keep Baby John safe. Is he still well?"

"He's well," John said. He did not tell her that her little son was crying and crying for her.

"And Frances?"

"No signs of it."

"And you, and Father?"

"No one in the house seems to have it. But they have it in Lambeth. We're not the only house with a white cross on the door. It's going to be a bad year, this year."

"Did I bring it?" she asked painfully. "Did I bring the plague to Lambeth? Did it follow me over the river?"

"It was here before you came home," he reassured her. "Don't blame yourself for it. Someone had it and tried to conceal it. It has been here for weeks and no one knew."

"God help them," she whispered. "God help me. Bury me deep, John. And pray for my soul."

Impulsively, he stepped over the candles and came into the room. At once she reared up in her bed. "Do you want me to die in despair?" she demanded.

He checked and walked backward, as if she were the queen herself. "I want to hold you," he said pitifully. "I want to hold you, Jane, I want to hold you to my heart."

For a moment her gaunt strained face, lit by the dozen golden candle flames, was suddenly soft and young, as it had been when she had sold him inch after inch of ribbons in the mercer's shop and he had called again and again on one pretext after another.

"Hold me in your heart," she whispered. "And care for my children."

She lay back on the pillows as John stepped over the wall of candle flames and hunkered down on the threshold.

"I shall stay here," he said determinedly.

"All right," she agreed. "Have you a pomander?"

"A pomander, and I am sitting in a sea of strewing herbs," John said.

"Stay then," she said. "I don't want to die alone. But if I am feverish and wandering and start to come to you, you must slam the door in my face and lock it."

He looked at her through the haze of the heat of the candles, and his face was nearly as haggard as her own. "I can't do that," he said. "I won't be able to do that."

"Promise me," she demanded. "It's the last thing I will ever ask of you."

He closed his eyes for a moment, to find his resolution. "I promise," he said eventually. "I will not touch you, I will come no closer. But I will be here for you. Just outside the door."

"That's what I want," she said.

At midnight Jane grew feverish and tossed on the pillow and cried out against heretics and popery and the Devil and the queen. At three in the morning she grew quiet and he could see her shivering, and yet he could not go in and put a shawl around her shoulders. At four she grew quiet and at peace, and at five she suddenly said, as simply as a child: "Good night, my dear," and fell asleep.

When dawn came and the sun rose warm on the apple blossoms at six, she did not wake.

Summer 1635

There was a brief unhappy argument about how Jane was to be buried. The parish authorities, responsible for the impossible task of trying to contain the plague, sent an order that the cart would come for her at midnight and her body was to be loaded on it by her family, who must then lock themselves indoors for another week until they were proved to be free of the disease.

"I won't do it," J said briefly to his father. "I won't send her into the plague pit in a sack of hessian. They can order all they like. They're not going to come in the house to fetch her; they're too afraid for their own skins."

John hesitated, thinking to argue.

"I won't," J said fiercely. "She's to be buried with honor."

John spoke to the church warden, who kept a careful distance on the other side of the little bridge that spanned the roadside ditch. The man was reluctant, but John was persuasive. A small heavy purse was tossed from one side to the other and the next day a lead-lined coffin was delivered to the bridge. A week later, when the Tradescant family and servants were thought to be safe to go out again, the funeral was planned. Jane's cause of death would not be entered as plague but as the more neutral word "fever," and she would be buried, as J insisted, in the family plot.

The Hurtes came to Lambeth from the city, with their own midwife to lay her out. She was an ancient woman, her face pocked with the scars of old plague sores. She said that she had taken the disease when she was a girl and had survived it, that the Lord of Hosts had saved her for the godly work of laying out the wealthy dead and nursing the few survivors.

"But why should He save you and not Jane?" J asked simply, and left her to the task of putting Jane in her special lead-lined coffin.

The Hurtes had wanted to take her to be buried in the graveyard near their chapel in the city but J forced himself to argue with them, and see that his wish was carried out. Jane should be buried at St. Mary's, Lambeth, where her children would go past her grave twice every Sunday. J felt as though he were wading through a thick sea of distress and that if he paused for a moment the waves of grief would wash into his face and drown him completely.

In the end the funeral was an ornate affair with half of Lambeth turning out to honor the young Mrs. Tradescant's passing. J, deep in unhappiness, begrudged everyone else's grief as if only he could know what it was to love Jane Tradescant and then to lose her; but it comforted John. "She was very well-loved," he said. "She lived so quietly that I never knew she was so well-loved."

Mrs. Hurte took J to one side when the funeral was over and offered to take the two children back with them to the city.

"No," he replied.

"You cannot care for them here," she argued.

"I can," J replied. Even his voice was different: taut and colorless. "My father and I can care for them here; I will find a good woman to be a housekeeper for us all."

"But I should be like a mother to them," Mrs. Hurte said.

John shook his head. "Baby John will stay here with me," he said. "And Frances could not bear to live anywhere but here. She loves her grandfather; she is never out of his sight. And she loves the garden and orchard. She would pine to death in the city."

Mrs. Hurte would have argued but J's pale tight face prohibited any further talk. "I will expect you for her memorial service in our chapel. We can pray for guidance, then."

He helped her onto the box seat beside the driver. "I won't come," he said. "She made me swear not to go into the city in the plague months. She was desperate that we would not bring it to the children. I promised her I would care for them here and if the plague comes any closer I would take them to Oatlands."

"You won't come to see her father preach her memorial sermon?" Mrs. Hurte exclaimed, scandalized. "But surely it would be such a comfort for you!"

John looked up at her on the wagon seat above him and his face was a white mask of pain. It was useless to tell this woman that his belief in God had gone in an instant, gone the moment he saw Jane throwing open the bedroom window, breathing the air and trying to rid the room of the imaginary smell of honeysuckle. "Nothing will comfort me," he said blankly. "Nothing will ever comfort me again."

Instead, he sent flowers. He sent a great boatload of flowers down the river to the city; and the chapel was a garden of the striped white and red Rosamund roses that she had loved so much. On the day of the memorial service J worked in the garden at Lambeth, pricking out seedlings and watering them with a quiet determination, as if he would deny that his wife's soul was being prayed for that day; as if he would deny his grief itself. At midday the bell of St. Mary's Lambeth tolled thirty-one times—one for each year of her short life—and J uncovered his head to the hot sun and listened to the slow clear sound of the bell, then he went back to his work separating the long silky stems of the seedlings and bedding them soft in the soil, as if only in the seed bed could he escape the memory of her dying, just out of his reach, and forbidding him to come any closer.

They dined as usual that night and John waited for his son to speak, but J said nothing. It was left to John to lead the prayers of the household. He did not have Jane's easy gift for addressing the Almighty as if He were a benevolent friend of the family. Instead he read the service for Evening Prayer from the King James Bible, and when the kitchen maid was disposed to speak out and give witness he shot her a sharp discouraging look from under his gray eyebrows and she fell silent.

"Perhaps you should lead the prayers," John remarked to J after a week of this. "I have not the knack for it."

"I've nothing to say to such a God," J said shortly, and left the room.

1636

In January, during the most difficult time for a gardener who lives off his plants, and the most frustrating time for a man who is only happy with his hands in the loam, the Tradescant luck turned. They were offered the work of the Oxford physic garden, a wonderful compact garden lying alongside the Isis, to grow herbs for the faculty of medicine at the university.

"You go and see what is needed," John said, watching his son's face, which had grown leaner and harder in the long cold months of winter. "They're paying us fifty pounds a year and we have made next to nothing on the Ark this season. Go and see what work needs doing and take it in hand, J. I cannot go to Oxford in midwinter; the cold will get into my bones."

John had hoped that the notorious rich hospitality of the town would divert J from the deep silence of his grief. But he came back within a month saying that there was only careful planting and thorough weeding needed. Lord Danby, who had gifted the garden to Magdalen College, had ordered a wall and a gatehouse built, and protection from the winter-flooding river.

"Nothing needs doing," J said when he was home again. "I'll grow some extra herbs to stock it in the spring, and I've appointed a couple of weeding girls."

"Pretty ones?" John asked carelessly.

J looked grim. "I didn't notice," he said.

* * *

In February a man came to the door bearing an earthenware pot with the tips of green bulbs showing.

"What's this?" J asked, hiding his weariness.

"I need to see John Tradescant," the man said eagerly. "Himself and no other."

"I am John Tradescant the younger," J told him, only too well aware that that would not be enough.

"Yes," the man said. "So it's your father I want."

"Wait here," J said shortly and went to find his father. John was in the rarities room, enjoying the warmth from the fire, moving from cabinet to cabinet, admiring the precious things.

"There's a man at the door with a bulb in a pot," J reported. "Will only speak to you. I s'pose it's a tulip."

John turned at the word "tulip." "I'll come at once."

The man was waiting in the hall. John drew him into the front room, J following, and they closed the door.

"What d'you have for me?"

"A Semper Augustus," the man said softly. From the depths of his pocket he produced a letter. "This attests to it."

"D'you think we're fools?" J demanded. "Where would you get a Semper Augustus from? How would they ever let it out of the country?"

The man looked shifty. "This attests to it," he repeated. "A letter for you alone, signed Van Meer."

John broke the seal and read. He nodded at J. "It does," he said. "He swears to me that there is a bulb in that pot from the original Semper Augustus. How did it come to your hands?"

"I'm merely the courier, master," the man said uncomfortably. "There was a bankruptcy in a house. Whose house need not concern you. The bailiffs took goods, but there was a man who did not know his job and did not spot the bulbs." He gave a sly smile. "I heard the mistress bundled them into a crock with a string of onions. So here they are, available for sale. The bankrupt gentleman, whose name we don't mention, wanted them offered out of Holland. He thought of you and commissioned me to bring them to you. Cash," he added.

"We'll pay when we see the blooms and not before," J said.

"The letter certifies them," the man said. "And I have orders to give you only a day to decide and then take them elsewhere. There are other great gardeners in England, gentlemen."

"They are all friends of ours," J growled. "And if I think this is an onion, they will think so too."

The man smiled. He was completely confident. "It is no onion. But if you spread it on your bread it will be the most expensive dinner you have ever eaten."

"May I take it from the pot?" John asked.

The man flinched a little, and it was that which convinced J as much as anything that the bulb was indeed the priceless Semper.

"Very well," he said. "But have a care . . . I'd let no other man disturb it."

John upturned the pot and tapped it hard. Earth, wiry tangled white roots and bulb slid out into his hand, scattering the soft soil on the floor. It was unquestionably a tulip bulb. John's rough hand caressed the smooth nut-brown papery skin, admired the perfect roundness of the bulb. The shoots at the top were strong and green, the bulb was growing away. There would be good leaves and no reason not to hope for good blooms. Of course he could not tell the color of the flower from the skin of the bulb, but the letter attested the bulb as a Semper Augustus, Van Meer was a trustworthy trader and the story of the bankruptcy and the bailiffs coming in was a not uncommon one in Holland now, where bulbs were changing hands a dozen times in a day, and where prices were soaring again.

Best of all, there was a little bump on the side of the bulb. It could be a little misshape, or it could be the start of a bulblet which would grow through the summer and by autumn would be a new bulb of its own—a profit of one hundred percent from the labor of leaving a bulb in the earth.

John showed it to J, his finger smoothing over the lump, and then carefully repotted it.

J drew him to the window bay, out of earshot of the waiting man.

"It could be anything," he warned. "It could be one of a dozen we already grow."

"Yes. But the letter looks genuine, that is Van Meer's seal, and the story is likely. If it is indeed a Semper then there is a fortune sitting in that pot, J. Did you see the lump on the side? We could double our money on the mother bulb in a year and then quadruple it with two where we once had one."

"Or we could grow a red tulip and we have fifty already."

"I think we should risk it," John said. "There's a fortune to be gained here, J."

John turned toward the man. "How much do you want for it?"

The man did not hesitate. "I have orders to take a thousand English pounds."

J choked but John nodded. "Do your orders permit you to take some now and some when the bulb has bloomed? Any buyer would want to see the flower."

"I can take eight hundred now and a note of hand to be redeemed in May."

J drew close to his father. "We cannot. We cannot lay our hands on such a sum."

"We'll borrow," John said softly. "It's half the price we'd have to pay in Amsterdam."

"But we're not in Amsterdam," J argued urgently. "We don't speculate in bulbs."

But John was glowing with excitement, his eyes alight. "Think what the king will pay for a Semper!" he said. "If it makes two bulbs instead of the one, think what profit we will make. We'll take it back to Amsterdam and sell it, and we'll make a fortune and our name as bulb growers. To sell a Semper grown in England on the Bourse itself!"

"I don't believe this," J muttered to himself. "We've been scraping the bottom of the barrel to meet the new tax, we missed two months of visitors in the summer because of the plague, and now we are staking eight years' wages on one bulb?"

John turned to the man. "Here's my hand on it," he said

grandly. "I shall have the money for you tomorrow. Come back at noon."

For the rest of the day the Tradescants, father and son, called in their debts all around the city, then moved on to favors owed them, and went frankly to the great men in the trading houses and borrowed money, offering the bulb as security and finally selling shares in it outright. Their name was so good and the desire to cash in on the Dutch speculation was so strong that they could have borrowed money against the bulb's profits twice over. The hysteria in Holland had spread to the whole of Europe. Everyone wanted shares in tulips, the market for which had been rising for years and was rising in great leaps every day. John did not have to struggle to find shareholders in his bulb; he could have sold it outright by midday. By the time they met back at the Ark at dusk they had covered the loan.

John was triumphant. "I could have sold it over and over!" he crowed. "This will make our fortune. I shall buy us a knighthood with this profit, J. Your son will be Sir Johnny on the wealth that we have made today!"

He broke off, seeing J's solemn face and the heaviness of his eyelids. "Is it just that you have no zest for anything?" John asked his son tenderly.

The young man's face was bleak. "She has not been in her grave a year and we are speculating and gambling."

"We are trading," John said. "Jane had no objection to honest trade. She was a merchant's daughter. She knew the value of profit. Her own father has taken a share in this venture."

"I think she would have called it gambling," J said. "But you are right—I have no zest for anything. It is the heaviness of my heart which makes me think this too great a risk for us, I suppose. Nothing more than that."

"Nothing more than that!" John clapped his son on the back. "The profit from it will make your heart light," he promised.

* * *

They kept the bulb in the orangery, warm in the pale spring sunshine as it poured through the windows, but shaded from the midday sun so the leaves should not scorch. Every morning John watered it himself with tepid water spiced with his own mixture of stewed nettles and horse dung. The bulb put out fresh green leaves and then finally, from its secret heart, the pointed precious snout of a flower.

The whole household held its breath. Frances was in and out of the orangery every day watching for the green of the flower to blush into color. John never passed the door without glancing in. Only J remained wrapped in his own darkness. He could not see the orangery as a place where their fortune was slowly blooming; he could not forget that Jane had lain there, and it seemed to him that nothing good could come out of that room, in the wake of her small lead-heavy coffin.

"It's white! It's red and white!" Frances exploded into her grandfather's bedroom one morning while he was dressing.

"The tulip?"

"Yes! Yes! It's red and white!"

"A Semper Augustus!" he crowed and, still half-dressed, grabbed her hand and ran down the stairs with her. At the door to the orangery they stopped, afraid to run toward the plant as if the very pounding of their feet on the bare boards could shake the color from the petals.

The exquisite rounded perfect petals had blushed into color in the dawn light, though they were still tightly closed together. They were clearly a deep blood-colored crimson slashed like a silk doublet with white.

"I have made my fortune," John said simply, looking at the miracle-flower on its slender wax-green stem. "This day I have made my fortune, Baby John will be a baronet and none of us will ever work for another man again."

They showed it in the rarities room, of course, as the most valuable tulip in the world. When the courier came for the rest of his money they had borrowed only two-thirds of it. The rest they had taken from visitors, flocking to see the priceless tulip.

When the queen at Oatlands heard of it she said she would buy it as it stood, in the pot, and J was about to name a figure which would cover their purchase price and give them a Christian profit of two percent. But John was there to forestall him.

"When the bulb is lifted, Your Majesty, we will be honored to give it to you," he said grandly.

She beamed; she loved presents. John pulled J away before he could argue. "Trust me, J. We will plant up one of the bulblets for her and still have the mother bulb. And she will reward us later for our generosity. Don't fear. She knows as well as I how these matters are gracefully done."

They watched the flower open in its glorious blaze of color and then become full-blown. "Can't we keep the petals?" Frances asked.

"You can have the petals," John said. "Perhaps they will keep in sugar and sand in one of the rarities cases."

Then in November, leaving it as late as possible to give the bulb the greatest chance to grow well, John, watched by J and Frances, tipped the pot and waited for their new wealth to spill out into his hands.

The priceless bulb had not one, not two, but three bulblets growing around the mother plant. "Praise God," John said devoutly.

With infinite care he took a sharp knife and cut them gently away from the mother bulb and placed them in their own little pots. "Four where there was one before," he said to J. "How can you call it usury when it is the richness of God himself who doubles and quadruples our wealth for us?"

One pot was assigned to the queen. John would keep one. And the remaining two he would send back to Holland in triumph, to Amsterdam in February in bulb-buying time, to make them the richest gardeners the world had ever known, to make them as rich as nabobs.

December 1636

They had a quiet Christmastide at the Ark that year. Jane had always been the one to decorate the house with holly and ivy and hang a kissing bunch of mistletoe over the front door. Neither J nor his father had the heart for it. They bought the children their presents for the twelve days of Christmas, gingerbread, candied fruit, a new gown for Frances and a book, beautifully engraved, for Johnny, but there was a terrible sense of going through the motions of present-giving and celebration. There was a dreadful hollowness at the heart of it where before there had been the unthinking spontaneity of joy.

On Christmas night the two men sat either side of the fire drinking mulled wine and cracking nuts. Frances, allowed to sit up late for the occasion, was between them, seated on a footstool, gazing unblinkingly into the flames, sipping hot milk as slowly as she dared to prolong the moment.

"D'you think Mama wishes she was here?" she asked her grandfather. John looked quickly over to J in time to catch his grimace of pain.

"I am sure she does. But she is happy with the angels in heaven," he said.

"D'you think she looks down on us and sees that I am being a good girl?"

"Yes," John said gruffly.

"D'you think she would do a miracle, a little miracle, if I asked her?"

"What miracle d'you want, Frances?" John asked.

"I want the king to understand that he should make me Father's apprentice," Frances said, putting her hand on John's knee and looking earnestly up at him. "I thought Mama could do a small miracle and open the king's eyes to me. To my solid worth."

John patted her hand. "You can always do your apprenticeship here," he said. "You don't have to serve a master to be a great gardener. You don't need the king's recognition. I shall teach you the skills you need here, myself. I am aware of your solid worth, Frances."

"And I can garden here after you are gone? So that there is always a Tradescant's Ark at Lambeth?"

John dropped his hand on her warm head and held it there, like a blessing. "A hundred years from now there will be a little bit of a Tradescant in every garden in England," he predicted. "The plants we have grown are already in bloom in every garden in the country. I've never sought for greater fame than that and I have been blessed with seeing it. But I should like to think of you gardening here after I am gone. Frances Tradescant, the gardener."

1637

The courier did not even enter the house at Lambeth. He stood in the hall on a February morning with the dirt of the roads still thick on his boots, and he brought the two precious tulip pots out from under his cloak.

"What's this?" John asked, astounded.

J, coming in from the garden, his fingers blue with cold, heard the fear in his father's voice and ran quickly up the hall, tracking mud on the polished wooden floor.

"Your bulbs, returned," the man said shortly.

There was a stunned silence.

"Returned?"

"The market has crashed," the man said. "The Bourse has closed down the trade in tulips. Men are hanging themselves in their rich houses and throwing their children into the canals to drown. The mania for tulips is over and everyone in Holland is ruined."

John went white and staggered back. He fell into a chair. "Henrik Van Meer?"

"Dead. By his own hand. His wife gone to relatives in France as a pauper with an apron full of tulip bulbs."

J put his hand on his father's shoulder. He had a sickly sense of his own fault for never speaking strongly against this passion for mingling plants and money. Now plants and money had split apart.

"You warned me," John said softly to his son, his face shocked.

"Not well enough," J replied bitterly. "I spoke as quiet as a child when I should have shouted like a man."

"Could you get *nothing* for them?" John asked. "My Semper Augustus? I would take five hundred for each. I would take four."

"Nothing," the man said precisely. "People are cursing their very name. They are worthless. They are less than worthless because people do not even want to see them. They blame them for everything. They are saying that they will never grow tulips again in Holland. That they hate the very sight of them."

"This is madness," John said, struggling to smile. "These are the finest flowers that were ever grown. They cannot turn against them, just because the market has gone sour. There is nothing like a tulip—"

"They never saw them as flowers," the courier explained patiently. "They saw them as wealth. And while everyone ran mad for them they were wealth itself. But the moment that people don't want them, they are nothing more than bulbs which grow pretty flowers. I felt a fool carrying these around with me. I felt as foolish as if I were a madman carrying turnips and saying they were treasure."

He dumped the two pots on the floor. "I'm sorry to bring you such bad news. But you should think yourself lucky that you have only two. The men who bought a dozen at the height of their fame are lying in the canals singing to the fish."

He turned and went out, closing the door behind him. J and his father did not move. The beautiful tulip pots gleamed mockingly, reflected in the shine of the waxed floorboards.

"Are we ruined?" J demanded.

"Please God, no."

"Will we lose the house?"

"We have things we can sell. We can part with some of the rarities. We can trade and stay afloat."

"We are at the very edge of bankruptcy."

John nodded. "At the edge. At the edge. But only at the edge, J."

He rose from his chair and hobbled to the door that led to the terrace and the garden. He opened the door and looked out, careless of the blast of cold air which billowed down the hall and might chill the tulips in their pots.

The saplings of the chestnut trees were as gawky and awkward as colts. Their buds were thick on the slender branches. There would be the tiny palmate leaves and then the magnificent white blossoms, and then the glossy brown nuts hidden soft in their thick casing. John gazed on them as if they were a lifeline.

"We'll never be ruined. Not while we have the trees," he said.

But they were hard-pressed to make ends meet. All spring and summer they juggled debts, took payments on plants and sent the money out straightaway to satisfy the creditors.

"What we need," J said one evening in autumn, as they were lifting bulbs from the bed, brushing them gently with a soft rabbit's-tail brush and laying them in long flat crates, "is a batch of new rare garden plants that everyone will be desperate to own. A new collection that everyone will want."

John nodded. "There are plants coming in all the time. I had a nice little flower from the West Indies this very week."

"We need a sudden rush," J said. "So that everyone comes and buys from us. So that everyone remembers our name. We need to make our own mania, a mania for the Tradescant plants."

John was on his hands and knees beside his son, but he leaned back to rest for a moment. "You have an idea," he said, looking at J.

"I thought I should go to Virginia," J said. "Go and collect rarities by the boxful, bring them back in time for the planting season, spring next year. Hope to bring back some flowers that people will pay good money to own."

"We'd have to find the price of your passage," John said cautiously. "It's a good plan. But it's thirty pounds or so to send you out in the first place. And things are tight, J. Very tight."

J said nothing and John looked again at his son's bleak face. "It's not just business, is it? It's because you have lost Jane."

"Yes," J admitted honestly. "I find I cannot bear this place without her."

"But if you went to Virginia, you would come back? You are thinking only of a visit? There are your children, and the Ark, and our gardening for the queen. And I am getting old."

"I will come back. But I have to get away now. You don't understand what it is like for me to sleep in her bed at night, and for her not to be there. And I can't bear to go into that damned orangery. Every time I walk in there to see to a plant or water a tray of seedlings I think she is still lying in the corner and forbidding me to come in and hold her. She died alone like a beggar on a street corner without nursing—and there was so much that I wanted to say to her and ask her—" He broke off. "You don't understand," he repeated.

"I do," John said slowly.

"No. You can't possibly understand. When Mother died you had months of warning, and you were even able to give her some flowers at the end. You had time to say farewell. You could hold her—"

"Once I lost a love, a great love, without warning," John said with difficulty. "And with much left unsaid. I do know what it is to dream and long for someone, and to think of their death over and over, and of the thousands of ways you could have prevented it, and the thousands of ways you should have prevented it, until you are sick of your own life, since it was not given in exchange."

J looked into his father's face. "I didn't know."

John realized that his son thought he was speaking of a woman, perhaps a lover from long ago. He did not correct him. "So I do understand," he said.

"You will let me go?"

John rested his hand on J's shoulder and hauled himself to his feet. He recognized again, to his continual surprise, that the stripling had grown to be a man with a shoulder as broad and strong as his own. "It's not for me to order you," he said. "You are a man grown and an equal partner with me. If you need to go, you must go, and my blessing will go with you. I'll care for Frances and Baby John, and for the Ark and for Oatlands while you are away.

And I will trust you to come back as soon as you can. I'm getting old, J; I need you here and your children will need you."

J rose too but his shoulders were slumped. "I shan't forget my duty."

"And they will need a mother," John ventured.

J flung his head up. "I can't marry again," he said flatly.

"Not for love," John said gently. "No one is asking for that. But the children need a mother. They cannot be raised by me and by a couple of maidservants. Baby John is only just walking; he will need a mother to bring him up and teach him his manners and play with him. And you will need a wife. You're a young man, J. There are long years ahead of you. You will need a companion and a friend for those years."

J turned away and put his hand on the rough bark of the apple tree to steady himself. "If you knew how it hurts me even to think of another woman, you would not say that," he said. "It is the cruelest, most unkind thing you could say. There will never be a woman in her place. Never."

John put his hand out once more, and then let it drop back. "I will not say it again," he said gently. "I miss her too." He paused. "I don't believe there is another woman who could take her place," he acknowledged. "She was a rarity. I have only ever seen one of her." It was his greatest praise.

They could not find the passage money; the Ark was a sinking ship. Then J thought that he could put the idea of sending him into the queen's mind. He briefly mentioned it when she stopped beside him in the queen's court one day as he was tying back the creepers against the wall.

"You would think of leaving my garden? Of leaving my service?" she asked.

J dropped to his knee. "Never," he said. "I was thinking of the wealth that Raleigh and Drake brought back for Queen Elizabeth. I was thinking that I would like to bring back treasures for you."

Her ready vanity was stimulated at once. "Why, you would be

my knight errant!" she exclaimed. "Gardener Tradescant on a quest for his queen."

"Yes," J agreed, hating himself for the play-acting even as he let the masque sweep on.

"And there must be gold and silver somewhere there," she said. "The Spanish got enough from it, as our Sweet Lord knows. If you could bring back some precious stones it would help His Majesty. It is a wonder to me how much it costs to buy a few pictures and to keep the court."

"Indeed, Your Majesty," J said to the earth beneath his knee.

"You will bring me back pearls!" she exclaimed. "Won't you? Or emeralds?"

"I will do all that I can," he said cautiously. "But I will certainly bring you back rare and beautiful plants and flowers."

"I shall ask the king to give you a letter patent," she promised. "He will do it at once."

Such was the erratic detail of the Stuart court management that there could be riots and rebellions about the collection of ship money up and down the country, and proud men accused of treason and flung into jail alongside criminals and beggars, and the king scarcely aware of it. But the queen was excited about Tradescant the young gardener visiting Virginia, and she told the king, and that became the business of the day.

"You must bring back some fine p . . . plants," the king said pleasantly to J. "Flowers and trees and shells, I hear they have precious sh . . . shells. I shall give you a letter of authority. Anything you see that would profit me, or the k . . . kingdom, you must have, free of charge, and bring it back. I shall give you a patent to collect. My loyal subjects in the new world will help you."

J knew that a good proportion of the king's loyal subjects had fled to the Americas determined never again to live directly under such a ruler, and paid their dues to England only with the most irritated reluctance.

"You must come back with r . . . rarities too," the king said. "And see if you can bring Indian corn to grow here."

"I will, Your Majesty."

The king gestured and one of his yeomen stepped forward. "A p . . . patent to collect in Virginia," the king said, his lips hardly moving. The yeoman, new at his work, had not yet learned that the king hated giving orders. Half of his servants' work was guessing what he required. "Have it written up. To Mr. T . . . Tradescant."

J bowed. "I am obliged to Your Majesty."

Charles extended his hand for J to kiss. "You are indeed," he said.

December 1637

J took ship in the *Brave Heart,* sailing out of Greenwich, and John came down to the quay to see him off. They ate a last meal together in the Three Choughs while J's bags were taken on board the ship bobbing at the quayside below the window.

"Make sure you carry enough water to keep any plants in the earth damp all the way home," John reminded him. "At sea in a storm, even the rain is salty."

J smiled. "I've unpacked enough dying plants to know how to care for them."

"Get seeds if you can. They travel much better than young plants. Seeds and roots are the best. Make sure you crate them up so they stay dark and dry."

J nodded and gave his father a glance which warned him that there was nothing more that he could teach his son.

"I want it to go well for you," John explained. "And there are treasures to be gathered there, I know it."

J looked out of the little window at the ship at the quayside. "All my childhood I seemed to be watching you sail; it's odd that it's my turn now."

"It's right that it is your turn now," John said generously. "I don't even envy you. My back aches and my knees are stiff; my voyaging days are over. This winter was hard on me, cold weather, sorrow, ill-health and worry altogether. I shall limp from my fireside to my gardens until you return."

"Write me news of the children," J said. "That they keep their health."

"The plague must be less this year," John said. "It took so many last year. There must be better times coming. I shall keep the children away from the city."

"They still grieve for their mother."

"They will learn to feel it less," John predicted. "Frances is already caring for Baby John, and sometimes he forgets and calls her Mama."

"I know," J said. "I should be pleased that he has stopped crying for her; but I can't bear to hear it."

John drained his tankard and put it down on the table. "Come on. Let's get you aboard, and you shall leave this country and your grief together."

The two men went down the narrow stairs and out to the quayside. "That house is riddled with passages like a rabbit warren," John remarked. "When the press-gang comes in the front, there are men scattering out of houses up and down the street through a thousand doorways. I saw it when my duke was pressing men for the war against the French."

J looked toward his ship. The tide was on the turn and she was pulling at the ropes as if testing their strength. He turned and his father took him awkwardly into his arms.

"God bless you," John said gently.

J had a sudden superstitious dread that he would not see his father again. The loss of his mother and then his wife had shaken his confidence. "Don't work too hard," he urged him. "Leave it to me to repair our fortunes. I shall bring back barrels full of plants in time for the spring. I swear it." He gazed into his father's face. The old man looked as he had always, dark-eyed, weather-beaten, hardy as a clump of heather.

"God bless," J whispered and then went up the gangplank of the ship.

John sat on a barrel on the quayside, stretching his tired legs before him, and waited for the ship to sail. He watched them run the gangplank aboard and then throw the mooring ropes. The little barges came out and took her in tow out to the middle of the river, and then John heard the faint shouted order and saw the lovely sight of the sails being flung open to the wind.

John raised his hand to his son as the ship caught the wind, slewed a little in the current, corrected her course, and then slipped away downriver, ploughing through the busy traffic of outbound boats and cross-river wherries, fishermen and rowing boats.

From his place at the railing, J saw the figure of his father grow smaller and smaller as the quay itself shrank and became part of a larger view, an outcrop of stone against the green of the Kent hills behind it; then as they were farther and farther out, the dock was nothing but a darker line on the blur of the shadowy land.

"Good-bye," he said quietly. "God bless." It seemed to him that he was leaving not just his father and his children and the memories of his wife and mother, but that he was leaving his own childhood and his long apprenticeship, and going to a new life which he could make his own.

Spring 1638

John did not neglect the garden at Oatlands while J was away. He had planted a new consignment of daffodils in the autumn and that spring he was in the king's court every day, watching the green spears break through the soil. For the queen he had planted tulips in great china bowls, and forced them to bloom early. They might be worth a fraction of their original value but John would not throw good bulbs on the midden because they had once been worth a fortune and were now sold for shillings. He had bought them for love of their color and shape and he loved them still. He put them in the orangery by the windows for the light and kept them warm. Their Majesties were due at the palace in late February and John wanted the bulbs in flower for their private apartments.

He was lucky; the royal party were delayed at Richmond and did not come to Oatlands until early March, and the tulip buds were fat and green and striped with the promise of color when they arrived.

They were accompanied by a troop of new designers and decorators. It was the queen's desire that her apartments should be remodeled and repainted. "What colors shall I have on the walls?" she asked John. "Here is Monsieur de Critz, who will paint me cherubs or angels or saints, or whatever I will."

John looked at the tulips on her table, which were slowly going a deep glossy red. "Scarlet," he said.

She rounded on him, spitting with anger. "D'you think to insult me?" she demanded.

He realized at once that she was smarting from the bawdy songs they were shouting in the streets of London about the two scarlet whores—the Pope and the Queen of England, who was shamefully in his toils.

"No!" John stammered. "No! I was looking at your flowers!"

She turned and caught sight of the tulips. "Oh." Her charm had quite deserted her. "Well, anyway. Cream and pink and blue, the ascension of Mary," she said shortly to the painter, and left the room.

The painter raised a cautious eyebrow at John.

"I'd best have a care," John said.

"Both she and the king are quick-tempered these days," the man said in a quiet undertone. "The news from the country gets worse every day. It is not always easy, serving at court."

John nodded and extended his hand. "Good to see you again, Monsieur de Critz."

"It's been a long time," the man said. "I last saw you years ago, when I was commissioned by my lord Cecil."

"I remember," John said. "You did the portrait of my lord which was made into a mosaic for the fireplace at Hatfield."

They heard the queen's voice raised in temper in the inner room.

"I'm off to my garden," John said hastily.

"Will you show me around before you go? I am halfway to being lost here."

John nodded and led the way from the rooms. "These are the queen's apartments; the king's rooms match them but lie the opposite side. Down below is the king's court. On the other side, the queen's."

The painter looked down from the window to where John's intricate knot garden was green and white and yellow. The outside border was the bright green of fresh growing bay, clipped tight and neat, and inside the square, as the queen had first commissioned, was a love-knot made of bay with H M and C monograms at each corner made with the brilliant iridescent blue of violets and the bright white-gold of the new daffodils.

"If they had been a month later, it would all have had to be redug with pansies," John said.

"Did you design it?" John de Critz asked, impressed.

"My son designed it," John told him. "But we both worked on the planting scheme. It is harder with Their Majesties than with a lord who is at home most of the time. When they come on a visit they expect it to be perfect, but you never know when the visit will be. We have to grow everything in pots or nursery beds, and only put the plants in when we know they are coming. We can't wait to let the plants grow fine and strong in the beds and succeed each other. Their Majesties need it perfect at each visit."

"You are a painter yourself," the man remarked. "What patterns and color! This is even better than Hatfield."

"I have no sense of smell," John explained. "My son prizes flowers for their scent, and loves working with herbs for their perfume. But, since I can smell nothing, I love bright colors and shapes."

The two men turned from the window and John led the way down to the great hall where the king and the household would dine, and then out into the court before the hall.

"Do you sleep in the hall?" John asked.

"My niece is with me; we have rooms in the old wing," the man replied.

"Does she always accompany you?" John asked, surprised. The aristocratic members of the court might confine themselves to platonic love or to delicate trysts, but the rest of the royal household could be a rough place for a young woman when the fanciful romantic behavior of the royal parade had passed by.

"Her father died of the plague and her mother cannot support her," the man said. "And, to tell you the truth, she has a fine eye and can work as well as any draftsman. I often let her draw for me and block the designs out on paper, and then I transfer them to the walls."

"I will see you both at dinner then," John said. The spring sunshine was warm on his face and he could hear the birds singing. "I must get out and see how they are digging in the kitchen garden."

De Critz raised his hand and went back into the palace to start his drawings for the queen.

John joined de Critz at the dinner table at midday in the great hall. At the top table were the king and queen and the favored courtiers of the day, with hundreds of rich and elaborate dishes laid before them. The queen held out her white hands for her lady-in-waiting to pull off, one at a time, each of the priceless rings, and pour a stream of warm clean water over her fingertips and then dab them with a napkin of the finest damask.

John noted, with no sign of disapproval showing in his face, that seated on one side of the queen was her confessor, and beside the king was the French ambassador. Grace was said in a quiet mutter in Latin by the queen's confessor and it was undoubtedly a Roman Catholic grace. There was no sign at all that this was a Protestant court in a Protestant country.

There was no sign, either, of the royal family. Their portrait was there, right enough, all five children as lovely as angels under the painter's tactful depiction. But the real children were never at their parents' dinner table. The queen prided herself on the passion of her maternal feelings, but tended to exercise them on her real children only occasionally, and mainly when she was being watched in public.

A young woman in her mid-twenties, dressed simply but elegantly in subdued colors, walked briskly into the hall, bowed low to the top table and dropped a slight curtsey to her uncle.

"This is my niece, Hester Pooks," John de Critz said. "John Tradescant, the king's gardener."

She did not bob a curtsey to John but looked him straight in the face with a smile and held out her hand for a brief firm handshake. "I am glad to meet you," she said. "I have been walking round and round the gardens and I think I have never seen anything more lovely."

It was the quickest route to John's heart. He pulled out a chair for her and helped her to a piece of bread from the platter, and meat from the serving bowl which was before them. He told her about the making and improving of the Oatlands gardens, about the new breeds of tulips just blushing into colors, about the deep digging in the kitchen garden and the enormous asparagus bed.

"I made some sketches of the fruit trees in bud and those little daffodils beneath them," she said. "I've never seen an orchard so pretty."

"I should like to see your sketches," John said.

"The grass is like a tapestry or a painting," she remarked. "The true flowery mead. You can hardly see the green for flowers."

"Now that's just what I intended," John said, his enthusiasm growing. "It has to be balanced all the time, and mown at the right time so that you don't cut the flowers before they are seeded, and you have to pull the plants which are running away and drowning the rest . . . but I am so glad you saw it. It is supposed to look artless, and that is the hardest thing to get right!"

"So now I have a drawing based on a garden, which is based on a tapestry, which will have been based on a drawing."

"And perhaps at the very back of it all, there was a garden."

She looked at him with quick comprehension in her dark eyes. "The first garden? Of Eden? Do you see that as a flowery mead? I have always thought of it as a French garden, with beautiful walks."

"Certainly there must have been an orchard." John had an enjoyable sense of intellectual freedom, being allowed to speculate about the Bible, which, at home, had to be accepted as a revealed truth and read with uncritical devotion. "There must have been at least two apple trees."

"Two?"

"To pollinate. Otherwise the Devil himself would have had no fruit for tempting poor Adam!"

"But I thought the scholars were now saying that Adam did not eat an apple but an apricot."

"Really?" John had an alarming sense of the world shifting

beyond the limits of his lighthearted skepticism. "But it says apple in the Bible."

"Our Bible in English is translated from the Greek, which was translated from the Hebrew. There are bound to be errors in the translations."

"My son would say—" He broke off. He was no longer sure what J would say. "A man of faith would say that there cannot be errors. That since it is the revealed word of God it *must* be perfect."

She nodded as if it did not matter very much. "A man of faith would have to have faith," she said simply. "But a man who questions would be bound to question."

John looked at her doubtfully. "And are you a woman who questions?"

She smiled at him, a sudden smile illuminating her face and making her suddenly a pretty young woman. "I have a brain in my head to think for myself—but no elevated principles."

Her uncle was shocked. "Hester!" He turned to John. "Indeed, she does herself an injustice. She is a very principled young woman."

"I don't doubt it . . ."

Hester shook her head. "I am completely respectable, which is what my uncle means; but I am talking about convictions and political principles."

"You sound as if you are a doubter," John commented.

"I think for myself but I never neglect the conventions," she explained. "This is a hard world for all of us, and especially for women. My study has been to avoid giving offense and to advance my own career."

"As a painter?" John asked.

She gave him her open, honest smile. "As a painter and a maid for now. But I shall want to marry well and care for my family and further my husband's prosperity."

John, accustomed to Jane's high morality, was torn between shock at her frankness and a sense of freedom at her honesty. "Nothing more than that?"

She shrugged. "I don't think there *is* anything more than that."

"And she can certainly draw." Her uncle moved the conversation into safer areas. "I thought I would use her sketches of your flowery mead as a background in some of the pictures for the queen's walls."

The young woman flushed with pleasure. "I will block them out for you," she promised.

"Can you draw and color tulips?" John asked. "There are some in the queen's apartment which are just coming into flower and I should like to have a picture to show my son. He chose them, bought them and planted them. He will want to know how they have done. We have had our disappointments with tulips—"

"Money?" she guessed acutely. "Were you caught in the tulip crash?"

John nodded. "But I should like him to know that they are still beautiful, even if they are not profitable."

"I would be pleased to try," she said. "I have not had the chance of seeing many tulips in flower. I know the Dutch tulip paintings, of course."

"Come to my house this evening," John suggested. "I live adjoining the silkworm house. I'll bring a little bowl of them."

Hester did not curtsey as she left them but dipped her head, like a boy, and went away. Her stride was like a boy's as well, firm and matter-of-fact.

"It is all right that she comes?" John asked, suddenly remembering his manners. "I had thought I was speaking to a young draftsman. I forgot she was a young woman."

"If she were a boy I would have had her as my apprentice," her uncle said, watching her go. "She can come to your house, Mr. Tradescant, but I have to guard her around the court. It is a nuisance. Some of these gentlemen write sonnets to the queen all day and then go wenching like lechers at night."

"I have a lass like her at home," John said, thinking of Frances and her desire to be gardener to the king. "She's been told that she will have to marry a gardener, that is the closest she can get to the work; but she wants to be one herself."

"What does her mother say?"

"She has none now. Plague."

The man nodded in sympathy. "It's hard for a maid to grow up without a mother. Who cares for her?"

"We have a cook who has been with us for many years," John said. "And housemaids. But when my son comes home from Virginia he will have to remarry. There's my grandson as well. They cannot be left in the care of servants."

De Critz slid a thoughtful sideways glance at him. "Hester has a good dowry," he said casually. "Her parents left her with two hundred pounds."

"Oh," said John, thinking of that straightforward nod of the head and the confident walk. "Did they, indeed?"

Hester Pooks sat at the table in John's little sitting room and drew the queen's bowl of tulips, squinting against the candlelight and the last rays of the evening sunshine.

"I've seen the tulip books," she said. "My uncle borrowed one to copy once. They show the bulb, don't they? And the roots?"

"You can't show these bulbs," John said hastily. "They must be left undisturbed. Please God they are spawning underneath the soil and I will soon have two or three tulips everywhere I once had one."

"And what do you do with the extra tulips?" she asked, never taking her eyes from the flower except to look down at her page. John watched her; he liked her direct, searching gaze.

"Some I replant in new pots here and keep them for the king and queen next year, and some I take home and plant in my own garden and keep them as stock for my nursery."

"So who owns them?" she persisted.

"The king and queen own the parent plants," John said. "For they commissioned my son to buy them, and paid for them. And the little bulblets we share. My son and I take half and the king and queen take half."

She nodded. "You double your stock every year? That's a good business," she observed.

John thought that she was surprisingly astute for the niece of an artist. "But it does not show the profits anymore," he said ruefully. "The market smashed in February. The best of the tulip bulbs were going for prices that would buy you a house. Passed from trader to trader as a paper bond, getting more expensive each time."

"So what happened? What stopped the market?"

John spread his hands. "I don't know," he said. "I saw it happen; but I still don't understand it. It was like magic. One moment they were bulbs, rare and rather precious, but priced within the reach of a gardener who might grow them. Next moment they were priced like pearls and everyone wanted them. All of a sudden it's as if the Bourse woke up to the fact that they were going mad over flowers, and they were priced like bulbs again. In truth, less than bulbs, because nobody wanted to be a tulip trader anymore; to be a tulip gardener was like standing up in public and saying you were a greedy fool."

"Did you lose much money?"

"Enough." John was not going to tell her that all of their savings had been in tulip bulbs. That their wealth had crashed as the bulb market had crashed and that he and J had sworn a solemn oath, a peasant's oath, never to trust anything but the value of land ever again.

Hester nodded and drew a smooth swift line on the page, the tulip's curving veil-like leaf. "It is an awful thing to lose your money. My father used to have a shop of artists' supplies; he lost his money when he fell sick. When he died there was nothing left for us at all. The only money we had was on a ship coming from the West Indies. It did not arrive for a year. In that year, as I sold first the carpet and the curtains, and then every stick of furniture we had, and then my dresses too, I swore that I would never be poor again."

She gave him a quick sideways glance. "I learned that nothing matters as much as holding on to what you have."

"There is God's guidance and your faith," John suggested.

She nodded. "I don't deny it. But when you have sold your chair and are sitting on a small chest which holds every single thing you own, you gain a good deal of interest in the life here, and less in the life hereafter."

Jane would have been appalled at such free speech, but John was not. "A hard lesson for a young woman," he commented.

"It's a hard world for a young woman, for anyone without a secure place," she said. Her eyes followed the tulip's neck and her charcoal drew a swift line on the page. John watched her at work. She made it look absurdly easy. She was a plain girl, he thought, plain-featured and plain-spoken, and he thought that his wife Elizabeth would have liked her enormously. A straightforward girl who could be relied on to run a small business, a sensible girl who would look for reliability and dependability in a husband and not necessarily expect more. A girl who knew the value of money, not a spendthrift woman from court. A good girl who would care for children who needed a mother.

"D'you like children?" he asked abruptly.

She drew another smooth line for the tulip's sensuous wavy stem. "Yes," she said. "I hope to have children of my own one day."

"You might marry a man who has children already," John said.

She shot him an acute glance over the top of her drawing block. "I'd have no objection."

"Even if they were up and running around?" John asked incautiously, thinking of Frances and her determined nature. "Another woman's children, brought up in her ways and not yours?"

"You are thinking of your grandchildren," she said, cutting through his hedging with one swift slice. "My uncle has told you that I have a good dowry and you are wondering if I would care for your grandchildren."

John choked slightly on his pipe. "You are a frank speaker," he exclaimed.

She turned her attention to her drawing. "Something has to happen," she said quietly. "I cannot travel around with my uncle forever, and I want a home of my own and a husband to settle down with. I should like children, and a good little business to run."

"My son is grieving for his wife," John warned her. "There may be no room in his heart for another woman at all. You might marry him and live with him all your life and never hear a word of love from him."

Hester nodded, her hand steady and skillful as she turned the charcoal on its side and rubbed it gently against the grain of the paper to show the delicate veining on the tulip leaf. "It is an understanding. An agreement; not a love affair."

"Will that be enough for you?" John asked curiously. "A young woman of your age?"

"I'm not a young maid," she said steadily. "I am a spinster of the parish of St. Bride's. A maid is a girl with a life of promise before her. I am a spinster of twenty-five in need of a husband. If your son will have me, and treat me kindly, I will have him. I don't care that he has loved another woman, even if he loves her still. What I care about is getting a home of my own and children to care for. Somewhere I can hold up my head. And you and he are well-known; he works for the king direct and he has the ear of the queen. With Parliament dissolved and London trade doing badly, there is no other route of advancement other than the court. This would be a very good match for me. It's nothing more than adequate for him, but I will make it worth his while. I will guard his business and his children."

John had the delightful sensation that he should not be having this conversation at all, that J was not a lad to have these things arranged for him, he was a man who should make his own choices. But it was a great pleasure to organize things as he wished, and he was afraid for his grandchildren.

"Frances is nine and her brother is four years old. A girl needs a mother, and Johnny is not out of his short coats. You would care for them and give them the love they need?"

Still Hester did not take her eyes from the tulip. "I would. And I would give you more grandchildren, if God is merciful."

"I won't be with you for long," John predicted. "I'm an old man. That's why I'm in a hurry to see my grandchildren safe and my son married. I want to know that I leave it all in safe hands."

She put down her paper and for the first time her eyes met his. "Trust me. I will care for all three of them, and for your rarities, for the Ark and for the gardens."

She thought that a look of immense relief passed over his face as if he now saw the way out of some complex thick-leaved maze.

"Very well, then," he said. "When Their Majesties leave here, I'll go home and you can come with me. You should see the children and they see you before we go further. And then J will come home from Virginia and the two of you can see if you like each other enough."

"What if he doesn't like me?" Hester asked bluntly. "I'm not a beauty. He might think he could do better."

"Then I'll bring you back to your uncle and you're no worse off," John said. He thought he had never met a woman so frank. The lack of vanity and the plain speaking suited him; he wondered if J would like her for it, or if she would embarrass him. "Of course, you might not like him."

She shook her head. "I'm not a princess in a romance pining for love," she said. "If he can give me a house and business and a couple of children, that's all I want. I could shake on the deal today."

John reminded himself that to put out his hand and shake on the deal now would be to trap her as well as to trap his son. He heard Cecil's wise cynicism in his head urging him to do it and turned away. "I won't let you be too hasty," he said, resisting the temptation. "Come with me to the Ark at Lambeth, meet the children, see the house and see if it suits you before we say more."

Hester nodded, her eyes back on the tulips again. "Good," she said.

John was weary to the very marrow of his bones on the journey home from Oatlands to Lambeth. The road seemed longer than usual and the river crossing was cold, with a bitter wind that swept down the river and cut through his leather waistcoat and his woolen cloak. The ague that he had brought home from Rhé, which descended on him whenever he was tired, made him ache in every bone of his body. He was glad that Hester was there to pay the ferryman and to commandeer a wagon for them to ride down the South Lambeth Road. She had an eye to his comfort all the way but not even her care could stop the wind blowing chill or the wagon jolting down the road in the winter ruts.

When they halted outside the house she had to help him over the little bridge and into the house, and as soon as she was in the door she was giving orders for his comfort as if she were mistress already.

The servants obeyed her willingly—lighting a fire in John's room, bringing a chair for him to sit in, bringing him a glass of hot wine. She knelt before him, her cloak still tied around her neck, her muff pushed to one side, and rubbed his cold hands until they lost their blueness and tingled.

"Thank you," John said. "I feel a fool, bringing you here and then needing your help."

Hester rose to her feet with a slight smile which made little of her care of him, and set him at his ease. "It's nothing," she said easily.

She was a woman who could set a house to rights in moments. In a very short time she had clean sheets on John's bed, and a bowl of hot soup and a loaf of white wheaten bread sent up to him so that he could dine in his bedroom. Then she turned her attention to the children and sat with them in the kitchen while they ate their supper.

She heard them say grace after the meal, both heads bowed obediently over their hands. Baby John still had the golden silky curls of infancy falling over his white lace collar. Frances's brown sleek hair was hidden under her white cap. Hester had to stop herself from reaching out and gathering the two of them onto her lap.

"The mistress used to say prayers every morning and evening," the cook volunteered from the fireside. "D'you remember, Frances?"

The girl nodded and looked away.

"Would you like us to pray, as your mother used to pray?" Hester asked her gently.

Again Frances nodded wordlessly, turning her head away so that no one could see the pain in her face. Hester put her hands together and closed her eyes and prayed, from the prayer book issued by Cranmer, as if there were no other way to address your maker. Hester had never been inside a church where prayers were spoken from the heart; she would have thought such behavior unsettling, perhaps illegal. She said the words the archbishop had ruled, and prayed by rote.

And Frances, slowly, without turning her head or indicating in any way that she wanted an embrace, stepped backward, toward Hester, closer and closer and then finally leaned back against her, still not looking around. Gently, carefully, Hester dropped her hands from where they were clasped in prayer and rested one hand on Frances's thin shoulder, and then the other on Johnny's silky curls. Johnny was comfortable under the caress and leaned at once toward her, but she felt the little girl's shoulder tense for a moment, and then relax as if the child were relinquishing a burden which she had been carrying alone. While the others said "Amen" out loud to the familiar prayer, Hester added a private silent wish that she might take these children who belonged to another woman, and bring them up as their mother would have wanted, and that in time they would come to love her.

She did not move away when the prayers ceased but stood still, her hand on each child. Johnny turned his little round face up to her and lifted up his arms, mutely asking to be picked up. She stooped and lifted him and settled him on her hip, and felt the deep satisfaction of a child's weight at her side and his arms around her neck. Still without looking, and with no word of appeal, the girl Frances turned toward Hester and Hester folded her into the crook of her arm and pressed the sad little face into her apron.

John recovered after a few days at home, and was soon setting seeds in pots and sending Frances out in the frosty garden to gather up, without fail, every single one of the last chestnuts as they fell from the trees down the avenue.

The nuts were so precious that the household linen was spread beneath the wide branches of the trees from autumn to springtime to ensure that not a single prickly casing or warm brown nut was lost in the grass. Hester mentioned the risk of staining or tearing the sheets, but John said firmly that one nut was worth a dozen sheets and that the garden must always come before the house.

He took Hester on long cold walks down to the bottom of the orchard, showed her every single tree and named it for her. In the blustery wet days of March he stayed in the orangery before a potting table with a barrel of sieved earth at his side and taught Hester how to set seeds. He showed her the tender plants which lived in the orangery from autumn to spring to protect them from winter frosts, and he showed her the winter jobs: the cleaning of the big tub planters, the washing of the pots and airing them, ready for the fever of spring planting. One lad spent all the winter sieving earth for the seed beds and for the pots. Another brewed up a fearful barrel of water fortified with horse and cow manure and a nettle soup of John's own devising, which would be sprinkled on every precious seedling.

They passed a quiet few weeks. A sailor, fresh into port, had a sealed parcel of seeds for John and a letter from Virginia.

"He says he will be home by April," John read. "He says he is writing this before going out into the woods for a week. He has an Indian guide who leads him around and shows him plants and brings him safe in." He paused and looked into the embers of the fire. "I wish he would come home," he said fretfully. "I am impatient for him to be here and everything settled."

"He will come in good time," Hester said soothingly. There was a single disloyal thought in her head that they were managing very well without him, John busy and contented, the museum taking a small but steady flow of money and the children taught by her every morning and kissed good night by her every night.

"He should be already on his way," John said. "This letter is eight weeks old. He may be at sea now."

"God keep him safe," Hester said, glancing out of the window at the dark March skies.

"Amen," John said.

Toward the end of the month John fell ill again. He ached in every bone and complained of the cold. But he was adamant that nothing ailed him, he was well enough. "Just tired," he said, smiling at Hester. "Just old bones." She did not press him to rise from his bed, nor to eat. She thought he looked as if he had reached the end of a long and arduous road.

"I think I should write a letter for J," he announced quietly one morning as she sat at the foot of his bed, sewing an apron for Frances.

At once she put her sewing to one side. "He will not get it if he left the colony as he planned. He should be at sea now."

"Not a letter to send. A letter for him to read here. If I am not here to speak to him."

She nodded gravely; she did not rush to reassure him. "Are you feeling worse?"

"I am feeling old," he said gently. "I don't imagine that I will live forever, and I want to make sure that it is all settled here. Will you write it for me?"

She hesitated. "If you wish. Or I could send for a clerk to write it. It might be better if it were not written by me."

He nodded. "You are a sensible woman, Hester. That's sound advice. Get a clerk for me from Lambeth and I will dictate my letter to J and finish my will."

"Of course," she said and went quietly from the room. At the doorway she paused. "I hope you will make it clear to your son that he is not bound to have me. Your son will have to make his own decision when he comes home. I am not part of his inheritance."

There was a small gleam of mischief in John's pale face. "It never occurred to me," he said unconvincingly. He took a difficult breath. "But it shall be as you wish. Send for a clerk from Lambeth, and also send for the executors of my will. I want to leave everything straight."

The clerk came and the executors with him—Elizabeth's brother, Alexander Norman, and William Ward, Buckingham's steward, who had served with John all those years ago.

"I shall be your executor with the greatest of pleasure," Alexander assured him, taking a seat at the bedside. "But I expect that you shall be mine. This is just a winter rheum. We'll see you in the garden again this spring."

John managed a weary smile, leaning back against his pillows. "Maybe," he said. "But I'm a good age now."

Alexander Norman glanced over the will and set his name to it. He reached toward John and shook his hand. "God keep you, John Tradescant," he said quietly.

The Duke of Buckingham's old steward, William Ward, stepped forward, and signed the will which the clerk showed him. He took John's hand. "I shall pray for you," he said quietly. "You shall be in my prayers every day, along with our lord."

John turned his head at that. "D'you pray for him still?"

The steward nodded. "Of course," he said gently. "They can say what they like about him but we who were in his service remember a master to worship, don't we, John? He wasn't a tyrant to us. He paid us freely, he gave us gifts, he laughed at mistakes and he would flare into a rage and then it was all forgotten. They spoke ill of him then and they speak worse of him now; but those of us who knew him have never served a better master."

John nodded. "I loved him," he whispered.

The steward nodded. "When you get to heaven you will see him there," he said with simple faith. "Outshining the angels."

The will was signed and sealed and posted with the clerk, the executors in agreement, but Hester thought that John would not go until he could see his tulips one last time. There is no gardener in the world who does not worship spring like a pagan. Every day John would take a seat at the window of his bedroom and peer outward and down to try to see the tiny spears of green springtime bulbs piercing the cold earth.

Every day Frances came to his room with her hands filled with new buds. "Look, Grandfather, the lenten lilies are out, and the little white daffodils."

She would spread them on the coverlet wrapped around his knees, both of them careless of the sticky juice from the cut stems. "A feast," John said, his eyes on them. "And they smell?"

"Like heaven," Frances replied ecstatically. "Yellow, they smell like sunshine and lemons and honey."

John chuckled. "Tulips coming?"

"You'll have to wait," she said. "They're still in bud."

The old man smiled at her. "I should have learned patience by now, my Frances," he said gently, his breath coming short. "But don't forget to look tomorrow."

Hester thought that John's stubborn will would not let him die in early spring. He wanted to see his tulips before he died; he wanted to see the blossom on his cherry trees. She thought his soul could not leave his weary body until he had some warm summer flowers in his arms once more. As the cold winds died down and the light at the window of his bedroom grew brighter and warmer, his breath slowly slipped away, but still he hung on—waiting for the summer, waiting for the return of his son.

At the end of March he turned his head to her as she sat at his bedside. "Tell the gardener to send me in some flowers," he said softly. He was breathless. "Everything we have. I may not be able to wait for them to bloom. Tell him to pot me up some tulips. I want to see them. They must be nearly showing by now."

Hester nodded and went out to find the gardener. He was weeding in the seed beds, preparing them for the great rush of planting out which would come when the danger of night frosts was over.

"He wants his tulips," she told him. "You're to pot them up and take them in. And cut some daffodils, armfuls of them. But I want us to do more for him. What are the best plants he has made? The rarest, most special plants? Can we not put them all in a pot and take them in so that he can see them from his bed?"

The gardener smiled at her ignorance. "It'd be a big pot."

"Several pots then," Hester persisted. "What are his other plants?"

The gardener's gesture took in the whole garden, and the orchards beyond. "This is not a man who gardens in pots," he said grandly. "There's his orchard: d'you know how many cherry trees alone? Forty! And some of his fruit trees were never grown before, like the diapered plum he got from Malta.

"And he found wonderful trees for the park or garden. See those beauties so fresh and green with those pale needles? He grew them from seed. They are Archangel larches, from Russia itself. He brought the pine cones back and managed to make them grow."

"They're dead," Hester objected, looking at the spiky yellowing needles clinging to the brown twigs.

The gardener smiled at her and took one of the swooping bare branches. There was a tiny rosette of green needles at the tip of the rusty brown branches.

"In the autumn they turn as golden as a beech tree and shed their needles like yellow rain. Come the spring they burst out, all fresh and green like grass. He reared them from seed and now look at the height of them!

"In the orchards he grows the service tree, and his favorites are the great horse chestnuts. Look at that avenue down the garden! And every one of them flowers like a rose and makes leaves like a fan. It's the greatest tree that has ever been seen, and he grew the first from a nut. On the lawn before the house? That's an Asian plane. And nobody can say how big it will grow because nobody has ever seen one before."

Hester looked down the avenue at the arching swooping branches. "I didn't know," she said. "He showed me all around the garden and the orchard but he never told me they were all his own, discovered by him and grown here in Lambeth for the very first time. He only told me they were rare and beautiful."

"And there's the herbs and vegetables," the gardener reminded her. "He's got seven sorts of garlic alone, a red lettuce which can make seventeen ounces of good leaves, allspick lavender, Jamaican pepper. His flowers come from all over the world, and we send them all over the country. Spiderwort—he gave his name to it. Tradescant's spiderwort, a three-petaled flower the color of the sky. On a wet day it closes up so you think it's dead; on a sunny day it is as blue as your gown. A flower to lift your heart, grow for you anywhere. Mountain valerian, lady's smock, large-flowered gentians, silver knapweed, dozens of geraniums, ranunculus—a flower like a springtime rose, anemones from Paris, five different types of rock rose, dozens of different clematis, the moon trefoil, the shrubby germander, erigeron—as pretty as daisies but as light and airy as snowdrops, his great rose daffodil with hundreds of petals. In the tulip beds alone we have a fortune. D'you know how many varieties? Fifty! And a Semper Augustus among them. The finest tulip ever grown!"

"I didn't know," Hester said. "I just thought he was a gardener . . ."

The gardener smiled at her. "He is a gardener, and an adventurer, and a man who was always there when history was being made," he said simply. "He's the greatest man of this age for all that he's always been someone's servant. Fifty tulip varieties alone!"

Hester was gazing along the avenue of the horse chestnut saplings. Their buds were green, breaking out of the bud casings which were fat and shiny, wet and brown like molasses.

"When will they bloom?"

The gardener followed her glance. "Not for another few weeks."

She thought for a moment. "If we cut some branches and took them indoors and kept them warm?"

He nodded. "They might dry up and die. But they might open early."

"Pot up the tulips then," she decided, "all of them, every one of his fifty varieties. And anything that is ready to bloom in the rarities room or the orangery. Let's make his bedroom a little forest; let's make it a flowery mead, with branches and flowers and plants, everything he loves."

"To help him get better?" the gardener asked.

Hester turned away. "So that he can say good-bye."

Tradescant lay propped high on thick pillows to help him to breathe, his nightcap on his head, his hair combed. The fire was burning in the grate and the window was slightly opened. The room was filled with the perfume of a thousand flowers. Over his bed arched boughs of chestnuts, the leaves broken out of the sticky buds. Higher again were beech branches, the buds like dried icicles on the thin twigs, but every plumper bud was splitting and showing the startling sweetmeat-pink and white lining, where the leaves were pushing to come through. In great banks around the side of the room were the tulips, fat and round, showing every color that had ever come out of the Low Countries: the blaze of scarlet, the magnificent stripes and broken colors in red and white and yellow, the shining purity of the Lack tulip, the wonderful spiky profile of the bizarre tulip and the flower that was still John's joy, the white and scarlet Semper Augustus. There were boughs of roses, their tight buds promising the beauty of their flower if John could stay just another month, or another month after that. There were clumps of bluebells like spilled ink on the carpet, and white and navy violets in pots. There were late daffodils, their little heads nodding, and everywhere threaded through the riot of color and shape was Tradescant's own lavender, springing fresh green shoots from the pale spines and putting out violet blue spikes.

He lay back on his pillows and looked from one perfect shape to another. The colors were so bright and joyous that he closed his eyes to rest them, and still saw, on the inside of his eyelids, the blazing red of his tulips, the shining yellow of his daffodils, the sky-blue of his lavender.

Hester had left a little pathway from his bed to the door so that she could come and go to him, but the rest of the room was banked with his flowers. He lay like a miser in a gold vault, half-drowned in treasure.

"I have left a letter for you to give to John when he returns," he said quietly.

She nodded. "You need not worry for me. If he will have me then I will stay, but whatever happens I will be a friend to the children. You can trust me to stand their friend."

He nodded and closed his eyes for a moment.

"Why did you not name the plants for yourself?" she asked softly. "There are so many. You could have had your name remembered with thanks a dozen times a day in every garden in the country."

Tradescant smiled. "Because they are not mine to name. I did not make them, like a carpenter makes a newel post. God made them. All I did was find them and bring them into the gardens. They belong to everyone. To everyone who loves to grow them."

He dozed for a few moments.

In the silence Hester could hear the household going about its business, the noise of the lad sweeping the yard and the continual murmur from the rarities room where visitors came and stayed to study and to marvel. The bright yellow spring sun poured into the room.

"Shall I close the shutters?" Hester asked. "Is it too bright?"

John was looking at the Semper Augustus, with its radiant white petals and the glossy red dappled stripe. "It's never too bright," he said.

He lay very still for a while and Hester thought he had gone to sleep. Quietly, she rose from her chair and tiptoed to the door. She looked back at the bed embedded in flowers. Above Tradescant's sleeping head his chestnut tree was bursting into leaf.

The creak of the wooden door disturbed his sleep. He was awake, looking toward the door; but he did not see Hester. His gaze went a little higher than her head, and his entranced look of delight was that of a man who has seen the love of his life coming, smiling, toward him. He raised himself up, as if he would move lightly forward, like a young man greeting his love. His smile of recognition was unmistakable, his face was filled with joy.

"Ah! You at last!" he said softly.

Hester went quickly to the bed, her skirts brushing the banks of flowers, pollen and perfume swirling like ground mist as she ran to him, but by the time she touched his hand the pulse had stopped and John Tradescant had died in a bed of his flowers, greeting the person he loved most in all the world.

A TOUCHSTONE READING GROUP GUIDE

Earthly Joys

1. Authors often challenge themselves by writing from the point of view of characters of the opposite sex. Do you think Gregory does a convincing job of creating her main male character, John Tradescant? Do you think he is more or less realistic than the women in this novel, such as his wife, Elizabeth, or his daughter-in-law, Jane?
2. Sir Robert Cecil teaches John that "practice, not principles" is the surest path to success and, in dangerous times, the wisest path all around. Do you agree with him? Why or why not?
3. John seeks a higher purpose and seems to find it when he realizes that to collect and display an array of rare plants is to honor the glory of God. Yet, his conventional and religious wife resents his traveling to achieve this goal. What is it that bothers Elizabeth so much? Do you think John's motivations for traveling change as the novel progresses? Do you think he is being honest with himself about these motivations?
4. There is much talk in *Earthly Joys,* particularly between John and his family, about the "Divine order" that keeps every man, woman, and child in a prescribed place of servitude and responsibility. How do you feel about this philosophy? How does John argue against Elizabeth, who says, "You are a gardener—so stay at home and garden"?
5. Gregory sprinkles her historical fiction with colorful and delightful scandal. How does reading about the lives of famous men like Sir Robert Cecil, George Villiers, and Prince Charles in this context make you feel about history? If you were familiar with this time period before reading *Earthly Joys,* did the novel affect your understanding at all?
6. John describes his love for the Duke after they have sex as being wholly different from the love between a man and a woman (and, ostensibly, between John and his wife). Is their

brief affair a continuance of John's belief that his master always comes first and must be served in all ways, or something more? Do you think he is being unfaithful to Elizabeth? Given his explanation of the event, does your opinion of John change after he becomes sexually intimate with the duke? If so, how?

7. John has spent his whole life in willing servitude to great men, a fact that he is proud of. However, when King Charles comes to power, John's feeling about men being destined to serve their "natural" masters begins to change. Why?
8. Throughout the novel, John and J clash often over their ideals and desires. Do you think John treats his son fairly? How might you deal with your own child if your fundamental beliefs and loyalties rested on opposing sides?
9. John Tradescant has three loves over the course of this novel: his first master, Sir Robert Cecil; his wife, Elizabeth; and his greatest love, George Villiers. What do you think each of these people represents to John, and why does each retain his love and loyalty?